Torin Reed

Paula Reed has been an English teacher for twenty-five years and for the last twenty-three years has taught at Columbine High School in Littleton, Colorado. After surviving the tragic shooting there, she, not unlike many students and teachers who were there that day, decided the time to pursue all of one's true passions is now. Paula's passions are teaching and writing. Long a favorite teaching text in her English courses, *The Scarlet Letter* inspired Paula to combine her two passions by reimagining this beloved classic in *Hester*.

Hester

Hester

The Missing Years of
The Scarlet Letter

A Novel

———◆———

PAULA REED

———◆———

St. Martin's Griffin
New York

HESTER. Copyright © 2010 by Paula Reed. All rights reserved. Printed in the United States of America. For information, address St. Martin's Press, 175 Fifth Avenue, New York, N.Y. 10010.

www.stmartins.com

Design by Rich Arnold

The Library of Congress has cataloged the hardcover edition as follows:

Reed, Paula, 1962–
    Hester / Paula Reed.—1st ed.
        p. cm.
    ISBN 978-0-312-58392-7
    1. Prynne, Hester (Fictitious character)—Fiction. 2. Puritans—England—Fiction. 3. Cromwell, Oliver, 1599–1658—Fiction. 4. Great Britain—History—Commonwealth and Protectorate, 1649–1660—Fiction. I. Hawthorne, Nathaniel, 1804–1864, Scarlet letter. II. Title.
    PS3618.E43567H47 2010
    813'.6—dc22

                                                                    2009039227

ISBN 978-0-312-67307-9 (trade paperback)

First St. Martin's Griffin Edition: January 2011

10 9 8 7 6 5 4 3 2 1

To all my students over the years who have read *The Scarlet Letter* with me and loved it . . . or pretended to love it . . . or at least resisted the lure of SparkNotes and read every word Hawthorne wrote. I love you.

Hester

Prologue

If it is a lonely life to be the embodiment of sin, lonelier still it is to be a legend. Day to day, little enough changes. I need never jostle my way through a crowd, for it parts where I walk, my neighbors never quite certain what might become of them should they brush against me. Once they feared I might taint them. Then they feared that I might come to know them too deeply, and through me, they might come to know themselves better than they would have wished.

That was long ago. Now, women come to my little cottage to seek my words of advice and comfort, for they see in me a woman not unlike themselves: One who has sinned, suffered, and survived. My touch, however, is not a thing to be borne until, like the minister I loved, one reaches the end of the journey and must lay open the soul and confess all that it was, good and bad, to be human. Fearful of hell, those at the brink hold my hand—a fellow sinner to walk them to the gates. I do not take them past the threshold, but I have felt the heat of eternal fire and showed no fear, so they trust me to give them courage, too. Such is the nature of my legend.

As with all legend, there is some truth and much fiction. The fiction was embellished in the decade that passed between my departure from Boston and my return. The stories people told of *me became as elaborate as the letter I wear upon my breast, its gold thread still glittering against the faded red cloth, and the fact that I have been back much longer than ever I was gone has done nothing to diminish those accounts.*

In truth, the tale of the letter I wear was but the beginning of my journey. That story may fade as it will, until it is little more than a footnote in some public record house. Herein lie the events of my years away—the middle of my story. For myself, it is my favorite part.

One

———✥———

Even the most domestic, mundane tasks present us with moral choices, and for better or for worse, we make them. For example, should I err to the side of maternal modesty and say that when my daughter, Pearl, was eight, she was competent with a needle, or should I speak with upright honesty and say that her talent exceeded my own at that tender age? As a girl, I, too, sat beside my mother in the lamplight and stitched samplers to hone my skills. It took me weeks to fashion "A good name is to be chosen rather than riches" in silk letters even enough to suit my mother's exacting standards. All around this wisdom from Proverbs, I nursed a thread garden of daisies and other simple blooms. It was a fair effort, but I had much to learn.

My Pearl, her dark, glossy head bent over her frame, had been working on her new sampler all week. In time, it would read, "And be not conformed to this world: but be ye transformed by the renewing of your mind." It was to be my birthday gift, she said, which, to be fair, did give her some months to complete it. Still, when she told me what she wished to stitch, I advised her that it was too much and recommended she choose a briefer text. She was resolute. She spent the first three nights on the "A" alone, illuminating it with scrolls and flourishes. Though the colors she selected included neither scarlet nor gold, I thought perhaps it was some of her previous mischief, mocking my own design. Heaven knew, in her earliest years she had been utterly fixated upon my scarlet letter. If her current labors were some new manifestation of this, she hid it well, concentrating on every stitch without a glance or comment to me. On the night our fortunes changed, she had nearly completed the word "transformed," subtly embellishing on her own each of the letters I had blocked out for her in lead.

I found it so hard to converse with her that night. For the first seven years of her life, I had never once wondered what we should speak of. She was the empress of all our dialogue. "What does the scarlet letter mean, Mother, and why does the minister keep his hand over his heart?" And I would engage my mind in how best to answer, telling her neither the truth nor a lie. If Arthur had chosen to hide his part in our lives, who was I to reveal him?

It was in that seventh year, 1649, that he ascended the scaffold and claimed her as his own, disclosing to all the sin that had destroyed him. He kissed Pearl before the whole village and died, taking with him the only child I knew how to raise.

That is imprecise. I never knew how to raise that girl of mine. Arthur altered the child with whom I was familiar. Another Pearl descended the scaffold with me that day. After that, she had no excruciating questions to ask, so we often sat in silence.

Nearly a year had passed since then, and Pearl was carefully drawing her floss through the linen, composing wisdom I had yet to fully understand, while I adorned a christening gown with pale pink roses for the babe of a wealthy family. It was nearly finished, and the compensation I received would help pay our month's meager expenses. I made little for my work (a relic of days when I was held in absolute contempt) and spent even less. Much of my earnings I set aside for charity. By my purchase of cloth and labor of needle, the poor of our village were clothed, and I strove as much as the wealthiest of citizens to ease the hunger of the destitute. I must, however, confess one indulgence—the lavish garments I wrought for my daughter. Once the christening gown was finished, there would be time to work on the lovely azure dress I had begun for Pearl. She was beautiful in red, but we'd both had enough of that. I had set aside my scarlet badge the day Arthur Dimmesdale died, and for reasons I could not fathom, she never asked where it went. In return, I ceased my previous involuntary yet inevitable inclination to create gowns for Pearl that echoed that mark of infamy.

"Those are fine letters," I praised her, and though she was a much more agreeable child than she had once been, she could still unnerve me with her precocity. She looked at me with my own dark eyes and said, "Yes, they are, aren't they? When I am finished, I will stitch roses like yours around them."

She did, eventually, and though her petals were not as fine as the ones that unfurled under my needle that night, they showed much promise.

So I have made my choice: honesty above modesty. I am untransformed.

In any event, we had exhausted the conversation. It had been so many years since I had engaged in idle chatter that I'd lost whatever aptitude I once possessed, and it was an unexpected relief when someone chose that moment to knock at the door. Pearl started and pricked herself with her needle, then stuck her finger into her mouth and cast an anxious look at the door. Even though it was long past dark, and we were far from the company of others, I felt no alarm. Many times over the years, people from town had ventured to our little cottage to ask my help in calamity, and I was ever inclined to lend it, for I knew what it was to want for human kindness. All that had passed between my neighbors and me became obscured at night, and we tried to pretend that the strain between us was not there, but our ambivalence returned again with every sunrise.

The pretense was never easy, even in the dark, so when I opened the door, there was nothing strange about the rigid, discomfited stance of the aged man waiting on the wooden steps, lantern in hand. "Mistress Prynne?" he inquired, though he was well acquainted with me.

He was the Reverend John Wilson, a good and decent man, and the first to implore me to name my baby's father so that I might not bear the burden of shame alone. When Pearl was very small, there were times that he'd shown greater patience than I with her passionate, wild temperament. In his kindness, he even spoke to the governor and urged that I be allowed to remove the letter, having borne its weight long enough in his view. In the end, it was I who chose when to remove it and I who would decide when to take it up again, but I appreciated his efforts.

It was a late-summer night, and the air outside was cool, so I invited him in and offered him the wooden chair I had been sitting in. I was about to chase Pearl from the only other seat in the room, but he preferred to stand, so in the end I let her stay and stood with him. He searched markedly for the words to express his purpose in coming, and I wished things were easier between us. As I said, he was a good man.

In the market, I still covered my hair—no sense in raising new ire while everyone foundered for the old. At home, however, I left it uncovered, and I knew that he was looking at me and remembering the young woman he had helped to sentence—the one who, before her release from jail, had been made to stand for three hours upon a scaffold, facing the scorn of the entire village. Outwardly, I had rebelled against their judgment. Instead of appearing with my head bowed and my person soberly clad, I held my head high. My long hair fell shamelessly loose down my back, and I wore a fanciful and reckless gown with the letter boldly emblazoned upon the bodice. It was a farce. Inside, I had never before known such shame. After that day, I wore only gray and kept every strand of hair hidden.

At last, he fixed his eyes on Pearl, who looked just as she always had, despite her changed nature. This appeared to reassure him, and he said, "I come on behalf of the late Roger Chillingworth."

Roger Chillingworth! There was not a soul in the village who did not endeavor, at any inconvenience, to avoid crossing that dark physician's path, I most of all. And then I realized what he'd said. The *late* Roger Chillingworth. I spoke, but I hardly dared to hope, and my voice was a mere whisper. "Roger Chillingworth is dead?"

The Reverend Mister Wilson nodded. "He is, mistress."

"How?"

"Of that no one is certain. He was found in his laboratory, his body wasted and dry, but no cause was apparent. There is much conjecture about the matter. Age and a life ill-spent, the hand of his Dark Master—who can know?"

"A fitting end," I murmured. That Roger had served the devil himself I had no doubt.

The minister seemed disinclined to reply. Instead, he said, "He had become a most eccentric old man. For some reason, though surely reason had no piece in it, he listed your child as his next of kin. You were to be informed immediately upon his death, and all his wealth, here and in England, is to go to young Pearl. I assure you, Mistress Prynne, that wealth is considerable."

For a moment, I was speechless, but Pearl looked at me, and there was no surprise in her keen gaze. She had kept that preternatural perceptiveness with which she was born, and suddenly she was again the Pearl I knew best. "First the minister stood with us upon the scaffold," she said, "and now the old man . . . ?"

I could not keep the wonder, even relief, from my speech when I answered her. "And now the man who was my husband and once kept me from my happiness has given you the means to find yours."

"He was often nice to me, though he was old and ugly," Pearl observed, and I went to her, taking her fair, artless face between my hands.

"Roger never blamed you; I credit him for that. He soothed you as a troubled babe, and again he eases your way in the world." I pulled her close to me and closed my eyes against tears—eight years of shame for myself mingled with loathing for Roger that I had kept tightly locked away. "Yet even this act of generosity cannot buy my forgiveness of him."

"Excuse me. Your *husband*?" the Reverend Mister Wilson asked.

In my mind, I suppose, I had dismissed him, so I was a little taken aback that he was still there. "My husband is dead," I told him. If only I could have spoken those words a decade ago. How differently my life would have turned out.

The minister stood before me, mouth agape, dignity forgotten. "Am I to understand that old Roger Chillingworth was your husband?"

I looked past his shoulder, through the still-open door, and into the dark night beyond. I had thought myself free of Roger before and been wrong. Could it be that this time he was truly gone?

If some malicious bit of him still drifts in the damp sea air,

I thought, *let it stop my mouth from speaking the truth at last.* I took a deep breath and said, "My husband was a scholar by the name of Roger Prynne. He was lost at sea ere my Pearl was conceived. Somehow, he denied the sea her due and, two years after, found his way back to me, a dark shadow of the man to whom I'd given my maidenhood. I once exchanged the secret of his identity for the protection of the man I loved, but it was a false deal, and I am no longer bound by it. Yes, you knew that dark shadow of my husband as Roger Chillingworth."

The words were out, and there was no misshapen demon to silence me.

The minister said nothing; he merely closed his mouth. I knew there had been much speculation about Roger's role in Arthur's death, but no one had ever come close to the truth: Roger had learned the identity of the man with whom I had betrayed him, and he had exacted unpardonable revenge. Afterward, there was no point in revealing our true relationship, and we had a tacit agreement to keep it to ourselves while Roger lived and I remained in my cottage by the sea.

The silence between us stretched on, and though I was much accustomed to silence, he seemed embarrassed by it, his cheeks flushing. At last he found his tongue. "Well, Mr. Chill—— rather Pry—— the physician has left your daughter the wealthiest girl in New England." He looked at my Pearl with some concern. "It is a sorry truth that even the most virtuous-seeming men may hide demons of desire and greed in their hearts. Pearl is an unusual girl, beautiful and now rich, but notorious as well, child though she may be. She will be on the edge of womanhood in but a few years . . ."

No one ever knew; it was not the shame of the scarlet letter that punished me daily. It was the knowledge it imparted—the ability to look into a man's eyes and see what was in his heart. The Reverend Mister Wilson, I saw, still regarded Pearl as a danger. He could not forget the demon-child of those first seven years, and though it disheartened me to know this, it was a reality that I had to face.

No one in that village would ever forget the speculation that Pearl was the devil's child. My own steadfast refusal to name a mortal father and her wildly tempestuous behavior prior to

Arthur's death had led them to draw their own fantastic conclusions. Never mind that they had finally learned that her father was simply a man—and a good man, too. They remembered only that she had once refused to bend to any will save her own dark and unnatural one: the stones and invectives she hurled at other children, even when she was very tiny, her insistence that she had not been made by God, but rather plucked by me from the rosebush that grows by the prison door. This was the Pearl they knew best.

"Others cannot comprehend her transformation, and so they do not trust it," I said to him, wondering if he might not feel chastened knowing that he was no better, but he did not seem at all abashed. He simply shook his head, and I shrugged, admitting, "I hardly trust it myself. No man in New England could love the scandalous offshoot of Hester Prynne without reserve, but for her fortune alone, many would be willing to wed her anyway."

"Precisely my concern," he agreed.

"Roger left her wealth enough to buy a fresh start, I presume, far away from the woe we have known here?" At his nod, I added, "If I may, I beseech you to speak of this to no one until we are gone."

He flushed again, and I knew that he was embarrassed by his relief that I would be quitting his province. "You are indeed a wise woman, Hester Prynne." Mumbling a hasty good-night, he made his way back out into the darkness, lantern aloft.

"Where are we going, Mother?" Pearl asked.

I tried not to feel bitter, but I had learned only to mask my emotions, not to master them. I said, "Where your father and I should have taken you long ago, child. England."

Two

Pearl sat next to me at the deck rail, looking out over the ocean. Her face was still wan from seasickness, but it would have taken rather more than a few days of tossing nearly everything she ate over the side of the ship and into the sea to weaken her too much for questions, and now she was on the mend.

"Which do you think I will like better, Mother, London or your old village?"

"Best you should like the village, child. We'll only stay in London long enough to settle the estate."

"What if the people there do not believe that I am the old man's heir?"

"You bear his name."

"I bear yours."

"It is the same, Pearl. Now, hush. The deck is no place for this conversation."

"They are inquisitive creatures, aren't they?" a man's voice asked me. I twisted my neck to look up at him, wondering how much he had overheard. Though the air was cold, the sky and sea were clear, and his face was indistinct against the brilliant blue behind him.

"Yes," I said. "Full of questions."

"My boy is that one." He pointed halfway across the deck to a lad of six or seven years, dogging the steps of a sailor.

"Have you been all the way up there?" the boy asked the sailor, his head tilted back as far as it would go so that he could look up at the top of the main mast.

"Aye," the sailor grumbled. "Care to go up with me, lad?"

Without another word, the boy scampered toward us and the safety of his father.

"Will you take me up there?" Pearl called out, and the sailor grinned at her, beckoning with one hand.

I scowled at him and held Pearl back. "He only said that to frighten the boy away. He doesn't think you really mean to go, either."

"But I want to."

"Come, little one," the sailor invited again, and I did not like the way he looked at her, so I kept her tight to my side and said, "No." Time enough for Pearl to learn that beauty is not always an advantage.

"Bold girl you have," the man next to me said. "She must run you ragged."

I turned back to him and nodded to his son. "Have you any besides him?"

He leaned against the rail, and I saw that he was a plain-faced man, perhaps in his forties. "I have five in all—three more be-lowdecks with my oldest girl."

"And your wife?"

"I left her and two other children behind in the churchyard. It was sad to leave them buried so far from home, but I've received word that my older brother is dead, too, so I am on my way back to my family's farm or we will lose it. England will be kinder to us, I'm hoping, now Cromwell's in charge."

"I imagine it will be," I replied, trying to imagine an England without a king. It was like trying to imagine it without hills.

He examined me, trying to decide what to make of me. He was not from my village, so it was unlikely that he knew the signifi-cance of the slightly less faded square on my bodice. But like my daughter, I had left my hair uncovered so that I could relish the sensation of the wind blowing through it, and this concerned him.

He had, after all, noticed that Pearl and I were alone, and he had a wife to replace.

The means by which I knew all this is hard to explain, precisely. I suppose it was easily surmised from what he had said and the appraising look in his eyes, but my thoughts did not have the feel of mere speculation. I understood such things the same way that I divined who had committed my sin or worse. I could take the letter off, but I could not seem to rid myself of that insight. When I gazed straight back at him, he looked away and blushed.

Once he was back in his proper place, I returned to my previous occupation—looking at the horizon. The air was fine, and the sea was dazzling; the sunlight glinted over the surface. I did not mind if the man stood with us and shared the moment, and he seemed content to be silent. The children chattered. The boy's name was Michael, and Pearl explained we were on our way to her grandfather, who was a baron and would be surprised and thrilled to see us. Their presence was a relief, for I had found over the years that children lacked the tincture of corruption ever present in adults.

Michael's father spoke again. "A baron's daughter all the way in New England?"

"A penniless baron's daughter, widowed and returning home," I replied, lest he see even greater opportunity here than he had before.

"But I am not penniless," Pearl said.

"Hush!" I commanded before she could say more. "It is unseemly to discuss money with strangers."

Pearl scowled. "You spoke of it first."

"I am sorry to hear of your husband," the man said, and his voice was sincere.

"And I of your wife," I said.

"It is hard to raise children alone." Brave man, venturing here again, or merely persistent.

I did not look at him again. "I have only this one. She and I will fare just fine in my father's house."

"Of course. Well, I suppose Michael and I should return to the others."

He was long gone when I realized that I should have said good-bye. I wanted to discourage him, not to be uncivil. I was simply unused to conversation. Long before Arthur's death, people had begun to forgive me—or at least to be truthful enough to realize they were no less sinners than I—but that did not mean they sought me out for pleasant banter. In the end, the letter was ever between us—a reminder that, while all knew the worst of me, they themselves still had much to hide.

Pearl interrupted my thoughts. "Will you marry, Mother?" The child listened closely to adult discourse, and overheard too much of what was unsaid.

"No," I told her.

"Why not?"

"Because in my heart I have a husband."

I expected the answer to raise another question, but with a child's quixotic curiosity, the one she asked was not the one I expected. "Who is Cromwell, and will he be kind to us?"

"Cromwell?"

"Michael's father said England will be kind to us because Cromwell's in charge."

"King Charles is dead, and Cromwell has taken his place. He is a very important man, and we are two very unimportant people. We will never meet Oliver Cromwell."

Pearl glanced over at me, a skeptical look on her young face. "If he is important, then he will have need of your needle. Every ceremony or parade I have been to, all the most important people wore things you embellished."

I smiled and tousled her hair, then ran my fingers through the silk-soft curls. She ducked away, and I let her have her freedom. "When you see London, you will see the difference. Besides, my father's house is in a tiny village that Cromwell will care nothing for."

Pearl leaned forward with her elbows on the rail, and her round eyes sparkled. "He will find us. Someone is sure to tell him about you."

I tried to assure myself that Pearl was like any child, fancying her mother, the center of her world, to be of equal consequence to everyone else. Likewise, surely I was like any mother, merely imagining that my child was more keenly perceptive than she ought to be. That was what I told myself on the ship's deck that day.

Three

Pearl tugged at my hand as our carriage rumbled down the narrow lane. She gazed first out the window closest to her, then leaned across me to the other in the small enclosure, plying me with questions that came so fast there was no time to answer. "Who lived there, Mother, in that big house? Did you know them? Did you play there, in that garden? It is cold now, but surely there are a thousand flowers there in spring. What flowers are there? Have I ever seen their like, or are English flowers nothing like ours? Is that the town hall? Where is the jail? Is that not a grand church for such a tiny village? Not so grand as the ones we saw in London, but . . ."

And though I was exhausted from weeks on the ship and in rented carriages, I had to laugh at her undiminished exuberance. The sound of my own laughter had become an unaccustomed thing. For a moment I fancied it made by the ghost of my girlish self, caught forever here, in the village of my maiden years. I felt that ghost in the close confines. She leaned across me with Pearl, and the three of us looked out the windows at the familiar streets and buildings, my ghost whispering memories in my ear.

"Indeed, Pearl, I did know the family in the big house, and can well recall the flowers that once bloomed in its garden," I told my daughter. "I and the girl who lived there, Miss Mary Starke, gathered them by the armfuls. Mary's mother always insisted that I take as many home as I wished." I remembered the blooms brightened the dark house I shared, first with both parents, then with Father only. "I went to that very church you spy. When I was four years older than you are, Father and I laid my mother to rest in its yard."

Pearl contemplated that a moment. "You must have been very sad."

I nodded. "I was."

So was my father. He aged before my eyes as we stood beside the casket, retreated into some deep inner darkness, left me to endure my grief alone. As though it were not enough to have lost my mother there, on the cusp of womanhood, he had abandoned me as well. I do not think I ever fully forgave him for that.

Now it seemed it was England that had retreated into a kind of inward-facing gloom. In some regards, it looked less like the home of my childhood than like the village we had left across the ocean. Scarce were the merry faces and colorful clothes of the countrymen I remembered. Instead, severe visages and plain, practical apparel prevailed. Even in the towns where we had lodged, no ne'er-do-wells tossed dice in alleys, and very few theaters offered an afternoon's diversion anymore. Changes had been wrought so effectively by Oliver Cromwell and his New Model Army that had we not currently been so far from the sea, I might have been tempted to seek my little cottage rather than the ancestral home I was raised in.

"Oh, Mother!" Pearl cried. "Look there! Does that house not look like a home for ghosts and goblins? Might the old man have lived there before he sought us out across the sea?"

Gently I nudged aside the girl leaning over my lap. The ancient gray stone had crumbled still further than when last I'd seen it, and all the windows were broken. Above the door an indistinct lump of stone endured where an ancient shield had once been carved. "Stop," I commanded the driver, knocking hard upon the ceiling. "This is the place we seek."

Pearl laughed. "Do not tease, Mother." Then her laughter faded as she peered into my face and realized that I spoke the truth.

She must have seen something deeper in me, for I was moved by the look of genuine sympathy in her dark eyes. To think I had once despaired that Pearl would ever be capable of human sympathy. I had lost so much in New England, but this child was more than recompense for it all.

"How cruel of someone to destroy your old home!" Pearl declared, her voice quivering with indignation.

I stroked her hair to comfort her. "Time has done this damage. It was not much better when I lived here."

We climbed from the carriage, and I told the driver not to take our trunks from the top yet. Outside the house, a splintered garden gate dangled from a single rusted hinge, and Pearl's questions began anew, though with less enthusiasm. "How did you live with no windows, only those big holes that let in the cold?"

"We had windows then, and the door was not broken. No one has lived in this house in many years." Which meant my father was dead. He would not have left otherwise. I wanted to cry but could not fathom it. I had not loved my father any more than I had loved my husband when I married him. I didn't hate Roger then, either. Both men were merely necessities in my life—neither really of my choosing.

If Roger had been there, I was certain that he would have shrugged his good shoulder, and we would have been on our way. Had Arthur been there, and had we been entirely alone, I liked to think that he would have held me without a word, and I would not have felt like crying anymore. He was so weak, in the end, but once he had been my pillar.

But it was Pearl who was with me, so she asked another question. "Then Grandfather will not be here to take us in?"

"I fear that he will not," I told her.

What now? She was a child. I had planned to raise her quietly here, cultivate the connections a baron's granddaughter was due— connections that my mother would have thought to make for me had she lived. In due time, Pearl's money was to produce opportunities for her that my family's poverty had once denied me. Of course, the money was still there, and in truth it carried more weight than my father's title would have anyway.

Pearl interrupted my thoughts again. "Where is he?"

"I cannot say."

Down the lane, a woman called to me. "Miss Hester? Miss

Hester Lathrop, is it?" She stood in the yard of a modest house, and even at a distance I knew her at once—Mistress Foster. When last I saw her, her hair was still somewhat dark, but it was now entirely gray. My friend Mary and I had adored her, for she always had sweets in her kitchen, and her children were great playmates, never shy of trouble. At the sight of her, my urge to cry evaporated.

"I am Hester Lathrop!" I answered. The name tasted familiar on my tongue, like a recollection of my mother's plum pudding.

"Good heavens, you are," she said, then nodded to Pearl. "And who have we here?"

Pearl bobbed a curtsy. "I am Pearl *Prynne*, even as my mother is called. She is not Hester Lathrop at all."

Mistress Foster laughed out loud. "Prynne! Of course—the scholar who took your pretty mama away from us, back when she was Hester Lathrop, indeed." She looked again to me. "The baron said you had gone to America."

"And so I did, but I have returned a widow."

Mistress Foster shook her head. "How sad."

"I have come to find my father. Do you know where he may have gone?"

Her mouth opened into a small "O" before she answered. "Oh my! Did no one write you? Oh, how could they? No one here knew how to send word to you, and who else would have? Oh my dear, I am so sorry . . ."

I looked back toward the ruin of my family's house—the house we Lathrops had lived in for generations. "Then he is gone, too? I thought he must be. And he had no child but me, so the old title died with him." He had known that it would, but he hadn't cared much. Otherwise, I supposed, he would have taken another wife after Mother and tried for an heir. But the title had no money, no land attached anymore. The family wealth had dwindled away over the course of two or three generations' mismanagement. It was just as well my father left no sons behind.

Pearl wrapped her small hand around my wrist. "If Grandfather is dead, then where are we to go? Are we to stay in that scary old house with no windows?"

"Of course not, child."

"But—"

"Please, Miss Hester," Mistress Foster said, "won't you and your daughter come to my home? I cannot leave you here in the street."

I shook my head. "I had hoped to stay here for a while, but now we must seek lodging elsewhere."

"Nonsense. You'll stay in my Lucy's room. She married last summer, and she was my last. It will be good to have a little one in the house again—if only for a while."

"May we, Mother? The carriage is so small and it bounces so much." She turned to Mistress Foster. "I have told you my name, but you have not told me yours. Have you known my mother her whole life? Were you friends with my grandparents? Was my grandmother pretty?"

While Mistress Foster answered Pearl's many queries, I asked the coachman to drive a little down the lane and deposit our trunks in the Fosters' extra room. Outside the window, chickens scratched in the yard, heedless of the two goats meandering among them. Our things settled, we followed our benefactress to the kitchen for tea and cake. Supper, she explained, would be late, as Mister Foster had been gone for several days and was expected back near nightfall. Mistress Foster entertained Pearl with tales of my youth, and though I, too, remembered the stories of childish mischief and tears, it seemed she was speaking of my dreams, not things that ever really happened. Was I truly that Hester?

When I left England some ten years ago, Lucy Foster had been very nearly the same age as Pearl. It was hard to imagine her a woman grown. Then again, what constituted a woman grown? I myself had been but ten and seven when I married my father's friend. Roger was planning to move to Amsterdam, and his proposal offered me a life of comfort and some adventure.

I had a love of art and beauty that had been deeply offended by the sale of all our ancestral paintings and fine furnishings to pay for such dreary things as taxes and food. For many years after, my only artistic indulgence became my needle, with which I embellished my old, worn gowns with flowers, vines, and illuminated monograms. As for adventure, the greatest in our village was when a goat escaped down the lane or boys got into fisticuffs in someone's yard—not nearly enough for a restless maiden. I imagined that life in a foreign city would satisfy all my heart desired, so when my father told me that he had secured my future with Roger Prynne, I made no protest. My mother's death had taught me how fleeting was the security of love. The auctioning of my family's heritage had taught me to be pragmatic. What young man of means would want a penniless girl like me, I thought, when there were plenty of merchants' daughters as pretty as I, with dowries besides? My destiny was to take what I could get, and Roger's wealth and intelligence seemed fair compensation for his age.

I had given too little thought to what it would mean for a girl as passionate as I to share the bed of a man in his waning years, and less thought still to how such a man—aged, misshapen, and withdrawn—had amassed the small fortune he possessed. The latter I learned far too late.

"What of you and your mother, dear?" Mistress Foster asked Pearl. "I would very much like to hear of America."

"I did not like our village," Pearl said in her usual forthright manner, "but we lived right upon the sea, which was always a sight to behold. It never seemed the same way twice. And on the other side of the village there were dark woods with so many animals and a beautiful little brook that always spoke to me of the whole village's troubles. She wasn't a gossip, mind you. That is just the way of brooks."

Mistress Foster chuckled, commenting on children's imaginations. Then her tone shifted, and she spoke more carefully. "I imagine that the stern folk in Massachusetts offered poor fun for a child Pearl's age."

"Very poor indeed," I replied, and my shared censure of the Pilgrims' descendants emboldened her.

"It's glad I am not to be raising little ones now. Seems every giggle and every skip is a sin. It's likely that you and young Mary Starke would have been put in the stocks for all the flowers you girls used to pick. Do you still hear from Mary?"

"Not in many years."

She warmed to the subject, and I was relieved to have moved swiftly and safely past my life in New England. Leaning forward, Mistress Foster said, "Mary lives in London now, and her name is Wright. Her husband is Colonel Robert Wright of the New Model Army, and a more solemn man you've never met."

And my heart sank at the thought of happy, spirited Mary

trapped with a staunch Puritan. Error though it may be, I hoped that she, too, might have found a lover, and that she enjoyed him without discovery. While I would not have her lonely, nor would I wish upon her the suffering imposed on a woman convicted of love.

"Oh, yes," Mistress Foster continued, "her husband is a regular stick-in-the-mud, but now that Cromwell controls more than the Rump Parliament, Colonel Wright is a man of great means. Greater than we can imagine. If money can buy happiness, Mary is well off."

"And if it cannot?" Too late, I realized that I had spoken aloud. Again it occurred to me how very much time I had spent alone, save Pearl, with little need to guard my tongue.

Mistress Foster snorted. "Have you not heard, Miss Hester? Happiness is illegal now. Why, they've outlawed Christmas!"

Which was a shame, but I had not celebrated Christmas in ten years, so it was of less consequence to me. I reached out and placed my hand on hers. I was no longer Hester Prynne of the scarlet letter, sent to soothe the ills of the wretched. I was just one woman comforting another, so it was easy to give her a conspiratorial smile and say, "But naught will prevent *you* from roasting a duck and baking a pudding come the twenty-fifth of December."

She laughed, and I felt a piece of the ice so long inside me begin to thaw. "Right you are, Miss Hester," she said. "Right you are."

Four

=━━━━>■●■<━━━━=

Changes in environment are most conspicuous at night. In my cottage by the sea, waves washed against rocks, crashing in rough weather while my roof groaned. On the ship, incessant creaking kept me up the first few nights, then lulled me to sleep the rest, so that I could not bear its absence when we arrived and spent the first night at an inn in London. There, I tossed and turned to the sound of laughter late into the night, the clip-clopping of horses' hooves, the footsteps and voices of people in rooms next to mine. At last, my mind shrugged these sounds off as unimportant, only to have to adapt to falling asleep in smaller villages amid a comparative silence that drove me mad.

The sounds I heard lying in Lucy Foster's bed, with Pearl snuggled against me, were at once strange and familiar, like everything else about the village. The occasional bleat or whinny of an animal in the stable, the insistent gusts of winter winds whipping about the house, the low crackle of a fire that was dying and should be fed (though I was loath to rise in the cold and do it)—all were the sounds of my youth. When I was a girl, an ice-cold nose and persistent shivers drove me from my bed in the dark morning long enough to feed the fire. Then I would run back across the cold floor and plunge under the bedclothes, seeking the meager warmth I'd left behind.

In Lucy's room, I had Pearl's warmth to keep me abed, and I realized that the sound of her breathing had been my one constant on this voyage—from New England to the ship to London to the inns in tiny villages, and now here, my Pearl breathed.

Lying there, listening to her, I thought of the first night I could ever remember sharing my bed. An only child, I'd had my room to myself my whole life. Mary and I had shared a bed in her home, but she never visited mine. After our wedding, Roger and I returned to my father's house until we were ready to leave for Amsterdam. I changed into a shift while Roger and my father conversed downstairs, and then I climbed into bed and fell asleep.

I wasn't nervous. I was naive. Roger was as old as my father. It honestly never occurred to me that I would be a wife to him, not entirely. I thought we would travel, and I would learn great things from him about science and philosophy. In the evenings, he would study and I would sew, and he would impart to me all the wisdom his books contained. Then we would go to bed and sleep.

I started awake that night, having never had anyone slide into my bed next to me before. I nearly screamed, then suddenly remembered I was married. My body became stiff, and I tried to resolve myself to a new way of sleeping. When he touched me, I stopped breathing. I don't know when I started again, though obviously I must have at some point.

His breathing. Now *that* was an unaccustomed sound. It was labored, and all the more so when he took me. The pain was nothing to the violation. He took me, and his breathing quickened, became strident. He took *from* me and gave nothing back—not so much as a loving gaze. In the dim moonlight, his face tilted up toward the headboard, all I could see was the flaccid skin under his chin stretching to his throat like a turkey's wattle as he strained. Then it was over, and he slept while I lay awake in the certain knowledge that I could not endure this nightly.

That, too, was naive. For one thing, his own endurance was limited by his age and reclusive sensibilities, so his intimate demands were altogether infrequent. For another, one can endure anything one must—violation, disappointment, shame, hate. There is a certain triumph in endurance.

When we arrived in Amsterdam, Roger seldom ventured out, preferring instead to stay in our house, silently poring over his

books and penning notes I never read. We sat together in the firelight, I at my needle, he at his studies. It was not a bad life, mostly
what I had expected, but I was utterly discontent. I was young
and full of the same boundless energy then as Pearl was now. It
seemed to me that one day all that unspent vitality would consume me and that I would dissolve before my ascetic husband in
a sudden burst of effervescence, like a geyser whose water is at
once soaked into the parched earth.

After a while, though, I came to feel that I was stronger somehow, precisely *because* I could contain that force, feel it bubbling
away inside me without ever showing on the surface. It was like a
game. Inside I was a sparkling, ebullient Hester whom Roger could
not pierce, could not know. I was too inexperienced, too arrogant
to recognize that one day she would break free—must break free.

It was freedom that made her so hard to contain. The freedom
of being a woman alone on the vast open sea when Roger stayed
behind in Amsterdam and I sailed ahead to America. He had business associates among the Puritans in Holland, though what
business they had was neither known nor of any interest to me.
When they came to our home, he asked that I adopt their somber
clothes and keep my hair tucked away. I was married, after all,
and my unbound hair unseemly even to those less severe than my
husband's business partners. At sea, with no husband to command
me, I did as I pleased and wore what I liked.

It was agonizing to go back under the thumbs of men, but
when I arrived in New England, I learned about sumptuary regu-
lations regarding lace, embroidery, and certainly hair. Of necessity, I submitted to the oppressive weight of that new land's laws,
but without Roger to thwart, containing my nature ceased to be a
game. It became unbearable torment, and so I went to the Reverend Arthur Dimmesdale for counsel.

He understood so entirely; it was as if we were two halves of
the same soul, two halves drawn inexorably together toward com-
pletion. Once released, the passion was far from spent. It intensi-
fied and seemed to distill into an elixir, infusing itself into the blood
of the child it had produced.

Pearl sighed and murmured softly in her sleep, and I buried my
nose in her hair, breathing in the scent uniquely hers. It was little
wonder that she was born such an impetuous child. The marvel

was the fact that she seemed to have mastered herself. I wondered if perhaps she was playing my old game, patiently allowing her sensibilities to simmer in secret.

One moment, she was deeply asleep. The next, she opened her eyes and looked straight into mine. "Good morning, Mother."

I smiled at her. "Good morning."

It seemed to me a simple enough matter to escape the mistake my father made when he married me to Roger. Surely in all of London there would be a man who was a match for my Pearl.

My match lay under the earth in New England. I could not imagine another.

Five

We stayed with Mistress Foster and her husband for two days, and then Mister Foster took us to town, where I hired a carriage back to London. There I sought Mary Starke Wright.

Wright House, it turned out, was a brick parlor house facing a square—a fairly new configuration for building houses, and I must say that I heartily approved of it. The park in the center was filled with bare trees and snow, but it took little imagination to see those trees bedecked in leaves and stretching across grass rich and green. Pearl's eyes lit with pleasure, and she exclaimed over the "little woods in the middle of such a big city."

A manservant welcomed us into the spacious parlor just inside the front door. An indigo-and-ocher carpet covered most of the floor, and in the middle stood a long trestle table with ten tall carved chairs spaced evenly around it. When I was a girl, my father had sold a great deal of the family belongings, but what remained had been ornate and rich. I found that my nervousness at coming to Mary as a supplicant from childhood was somewhat assuaged by the sparseness of her furnishings. It was a bit of assurance that our new lives had some similarities after all, both marked by Puritan influences.

A painting hung over the hearth, and I immediately recognized Mary, looking appropriately stern as the mate of the tall, thin man beside her, his hair cropped short in the "Roundhead" fashion. The Mary who had once been my playmate had had long yellow hair and bright cheeks, and she was almost always laughing. She favored gowns of pink and lavender, and while I lived in New England, I thought of her most in May, when the lilacs bloomed. This woman's pale face seemed lost between the white cap that entirely covered her hair and the wide lace collar that dominated the bodice of her gown. Her blue eyes gazed earnestly at me, and there was no hint of a curve on her lips.

There were paintings on the flanking walls, but the subjects were strangers to me. They seemed mainly to be faint echoes of the man next to Mary, and their chins rested on old-fashioned starched ruffs. Closer scrutiny of a group portrait revealed Mary's husband surrounded by a group of men, their collars and utilitarian clothing too familiar to me.

"Do you suppose Mistress Wright has any children now?" Pearl asked. "Might they run races from one end of this room to the other? Is that why it is so big but has so little in it? Do you think her children might be faster than I am? If we run in the little woods in front, I am sure that I could win, but here—"

"They do not run races in here, Pearl," I snapped, then regretted at once my impatience.

My agitation proved to be wasted energy when Mary arrived, her face aglow, two young girls behind her. Unlike the one in the painting, her head covering left much of her blond hair exposed around her face, and her smile, youthful and bright, was unchanged.

"Hester! Hester Lathrop, it is you! You cannot imagine my joy when I received your letter last night! You should have come yourself. There was no need to send word ahead or spend the night at an inn." First she took up my hands, and then we embraced before she pulled away and led me in a sort of twirl at arm's length, as young girls are wont to do. "Look at you! Still a dark beauty!" She straightened her face and said, "I am so sorry about Mister Prynne."

"Do not be," I answered. Ah—too bitter! Truly, I needed to learn again the art of polite conversation. "I mean—"

"I know. He was so much older, and . . ." She let the sentence drift, then shook her head and shrugged. "Oh, to be fifteen forever!"

She embraced me a second time, and while I had been able to

return the first such gesture, transported to that tender age with her, now that we had acknowledged we were women in the world, I remembered that we hardly knew each other. It felt awkward to stand thus in the vast, empty room with so many strangers watching from the picture frames.

Mary released me again and looked at Pearl. "This is your Pearl? She must be or you have brought yourself of twenty years past back from our village. She looks just like you!" She paused long enough to beckon to her own daughters. "This is Jane, who is nine." The girl curtsied, and the pale brown curls that escaped her braid waved softly where they brushed her cheeks. I wondered if I should have bound Pearl's hair, but it was too late. At least Mary's Jane wore saffron, so Pearl's robin's-egg dress did not seem out of place.

"Mother says that you are eight," Jane said to Pearl, who nodded. I expected the usual barrage of questions, but for once my child seemed shy and tongue-tied. If she and Jane got on well, this would be Pearl's very first friend in life, and I think that she was acutely aware of the magnitude of this meeting.

"And this," Mary continued, "is Annie. She is nearly five."

Annie sidled up to her mother, grabbed a fistful of deep brown skirt, and popped the thumb of her free hand into her mouth. Like her sister, she had light brown hair that curled about her cherubic face.

"How do you do, Miss Annie?" I said, and she turned away, wrapping her mother's skirt around her as she went.

"Take Pearl up to the nursery and play," Mary instructed, and Jane took my daughter's hand to lead her from the room. Annie lingered a moment, then let go of Mary and ran after. "The nursemaid is up there. Baby Georgie is sleeping, so you'll have to see him later. He's almost three."

"Will the girls not wake him?"

"Nothing wakes that boy. I lost two in their sleep, so he worried me to death at first. Thank heaven for Miss Walton. She has an evenness I envy and prevents me from smothering the children with my fears. Come." She gestured to the chair closest to the hearth, then took her seat next to me at the table's end.

I twisted around to the portrait of Mary and the man beside her. "That is your Robert? Mistress Foster told me about him."

Mary laughed softly. "I remember Mistress Foster, and Meg, and Nell, and Percy, and Lucy. How are they?"

"Grown and gone, the children. Mistress Foster is still merry and kind. She sends you her warmest regards."

"I shall always remember her fondly." Mary looked over her shoulder and contemplated the painting a moment. "That is Robert. He is in Ireland now, where English hold is tenuous at best. He is there more than here, but he hopes to be home for a few weeks in the spring."

"It must be lonely without him," I said.

Mary's face betrayed nothing, and I sensed little else in her than grim resolve. "When a woman marries a man in the army, she expects long absences." Then she brightened. "But now you and Pearl are here! Jane will love having a girl so close in age, and the nursery is large. There is a trundle under Jane's bed, and a room above that where I know you'll be quite comfortable."

It was the invitation I had hoped for, but out of courtesy I protested. "I have no wish to trouble you."

"Trouble? Hester, how can you say such a thing? You have no idea—" Mary stopped, and I waited. At last she said, "In a country without a king, loyalties are ambiguous. A man may count only upon his wife, since his friends may be swayed by ideology. Therefore his wife dares not hold close the wives of her husband's colleagues. Political winds shift quickly between men, and if we women have become friends, then we are left to choose between each other or our husbands, which leaves us little choice indeed."

I had no answer for this. It was far beyond my experience, I whom no one cared or dared to befriend. Surely there are inanities that one is expected to murmur in polite response, but I could conceive of none. I did not even think to look away, and it seemed my watchfulness rattled her, for her cheeks turned pinker still.

"I—I do not mean that I would choose my friends before my husband. I only mean that men's loyalties are different—these men's are—and it is so hard to take a friend to your bosom and lose her for her husband's politics."

I shook my head. "I know nothing of politics. I only wish to raise my daughter and settle her happily."

"Then you must stay here," Mary insisted.

"Until we can find a house," I conceded, but now Mary shook her head.

"You cannot live alone."

"We will be fine."

"A woman alone is suspect, Hester."

This much I knew. "I will be careful."

"Especially a woman of means. Hester, you do not know England as it is now. Zealotry and intolerance reign in absence of a king." Mary's face had gone as pale as in her portrait. "Truly, you are welcome here. My girls and I will enjoy your company, and you will find your goals much more easily met under my husband's protection."

"And if he does not wish to extend that protection?"

Mary lifted her chin. "He will. You need only know that he is a devoutly religious man who values character in men, silence in women, and obedience in children." Then a little smile played about her lips. "Of course, these things only matter when he is at home, and that is seldom. When he is here, I keep the girls upstairs or accompany them outside as much as possible."

Silence was easy. Obedience in Pearl? It would test the extent of her transformation.

Six

<figure>◆━━━━━◆◎◆━━━━━◆</figure>

The months from January until April passed pleasantly. Mary and I sewed and told each other of our lives in the years we had been apart, and it was not lost on me that she spoke more of our country and its metamorphosis under Cromwell than of herself. Her husband had attended the execution of Charles I and was bitterly disappointed by the complete inability of the Rump Parliament to gain any sort of efficacy since then. England was in need of a leader, and there was much dissension among the people as to whether it should be Charles II or Oliver Cromwell. Cromwell, of course, was adamantly opposed to reestablishing any sort of monarchy. In the meantime, Scotland had embraced Charles II, Ireland was proving unexpectedly contumacious, and the Dutch were inducing much trouble at sea, all of which kept Mary's husband abroad or preoccupied, neither of which seemed to perturb Mary in the least.

Since none of these events had had much effect upon my village in New England, I could speak of little but my own life, and I was as careful in stitching my tales as I was in the designs of my needle, fashioning both to my own purposes.

"Roger," I explained as we sat at our frames, "was the village physician for many years. I suppose it was not unlike you and your Robert, for he spent so much time in his laboratory that, for all intents and purposes, we kept separate houses." It was strictly true, the deception indirect. He'd kept to his laboratory and I to my cottage, and no one even knew we were married.

"He had a soothing hand with Pearl when she was born," I said, which was also factual, though he demonstrated this but once, as a physician, nothing more. "As she grew, she would have naught to do with her father." This I said remembering Pearl's aversion to Arthur on the two occasions in her whole life when we three had met in private. Recalling the kiss she had given Arthur upon the scaffold, I added, "She made amends with him, though, just before he died."

I told myself that if Mary mistook all this to mean that Pearl's father and Roger were one and the same man, the failing was hers, not mine.

Mary took all I told her at face value, my life appearing in many ways parallel to her own, and this seemed to ease whatever caused her often somber demeanor when she spoke of such things. Whether it was her husband's long absences that troubled her or his infrequent returns I could not fully determine, but I respected her silence on the current state of her marriage. Either way, I used the comfort my commiseration gave her to justify the fine line I walked between truth and falsehood, between all that the scarlet letter had taught me and the chicanery I felt compelled to engage in for the sake of my daughter. Despite Mary's insistence to the contrary, I was well acquainted with the temperament of men such as those now in control of England. After all, I had sailed back across the ocean to save Pearl from men much like them in New England. A bastard daughter, no matter her wealth, would pay dearly for her mother's sin.

Occasionally, Mary's inquiries were too personal to easily evade.

"Who was your dearest friend," Mary asked once, "and did it break your heart to leave her? Why not stay and find a husband for Pearl in New England?"

I was sewing an apron for Mary and had planned to create a border of forget-me-nots, but I changed my mind. I set down the skein of blue thread and picked up red, choosing poppies instead. "You know how Puritan women can be. They are a hard company to join in with. There was one I might have befriended, but life in the Colonies is harsh. I sewed her funeral gown."

Mary reached out to comfort me, and I felt the sting of my affronted conscience. I was not friends with the woman I spoke of; I only thought she was kinder than the rest. Perhaps I sighed more over her loss than any other, but I could not genuinely say it grieved me.

Seeking to change the subject to one that required no lies, I said, "As for Pearl, I had thought to marry her to a happier sort of man. Perhaps I was mistaken to search here."

Mary shrugged. "There are many who chafe under the new laws, and we have some years before we must marry off our girls. Much may change."

Let us hope hung unspoken between us. Though I had yet to meet him, there was ever a sense that Wright House belonged to the colonel and that the walls might have ears, eavesdropping upon sentiments of which he would not approve.

Still, we found a thousand ways to spend happy hours together. The days lengthened and the weather warmed. The branches of trees in the square were tipped in tender green that deepened over the weeks as it spread throughout the limbs. The children begged to play there, even on days when the damp cold cut right through our cloaks. Annie and Baby Georgie were a constant wonder to me with their curiosity about the world and their bright, beaming faces. If they fell and scraped their knees, they wept, but they were seldom angry. Perhaps what I loved best about them was the fact that, like all children, they were unshadowed by sin. I felt no sympathetic pain in their presence.

Mary noticed my fascination and said, "Does it not seem only yesterday that Jane and Pearl were thus? 'Why is the grass green, Mama, and the sky blue? How do the plants know that it is time to wake?'"

My silent thoughts recalled Pearl's inquisitive refrain at Annie's age. *"What does the scarlet letter mean, Mother, and why does the minister keep his hand over his heart?"*

That was behind us now. These were new times, new circumstances.

I found that I did not care for London. The houses were so close together that only the rats could scuttle between. The air smelled of waste and soot, and it was never quiet. The street around the square was lightly traveled, but not the roads that passed behind

6

the strings of parlor houses. Horses and people created a mélange of hoofbeats, footsteps, whickering, and voices. On Sundays, officials patrolled to ensure that no child made merry under the trees, and on the last Wednesday of each month, when fasting was mandatory, they called unannounced to ascertain whether the house smelled of forbidden meat or bread.

With the warm weather came a restlessness of spirit among all the people who had stayed inside during the bitter months of winter, and visitors began to come and go through Wright House. I met the wives of soldiers and statesmen, began the occupation of becoming a "well-connected woman," and wondered whether my own mother might not have been better off in dying before she had been forced to do this for me.

"Mistress Prynne, have you ever seen a Red Indian?" Mistress Joyce asked.

"Yes."

She looked at me, her gray eyes wide.

I looked back. That sensitive region in my breast throbbed, as it always did when I looked upon a fellow sinner, though her sin was not my own. Her full face was completely framed by her cap, and her plump body was snugly encased in a gown of ocher linen that had probably fit properly last spring. She had eaten three currant buns while the rest of us were still nibbling our first. Here was a woman who strove to be virtuous in all things and could not understand why she was unhappy—and she battled constant hunger. On the one hand, she hoped that the abundance of food on her table was a sign of God's grace; on the other, gluttony was a deadly sin. Every bite she ate consumed her, and yet she could not stop.

It was nearly impossible to hold a frivolous conversation with this woman when all her secrets revealed themselves to my unwilling mind, but I was unable to obstruct those revelations. This ability had plagued me from the moment I donned the letter, and as I have said, removing it had proved no remedy.

Mistress Joyce's face turned red, and she looked nervously over to Mary.

"Hester?" Mary prodded.

"Yes?"

"I think Mistress Joyce would be very interested to hear about them."

Her doubts? She knew them well enough. "What shall I say?"

A slight frown marked Mary's brow. "You told me once they dressed in a manner most peculiar."

Ah, the Indians! "Yes, they did."

Mary and Mistress Joyce looked at me. I looked back. It was perhaps another minute before I realized that I was to detail the Red Indians' peculiar clothes. With great effort, I forced myself to hear her spoken words, willing them to drown out the other.

Thank God for the Red Indians. I could speak of them quite openly, revealing nothing about myself, and they were an endless source of fascination for the women I came to know. In truth, it was their *lack* of clothing that intrigued these women rather more than my accounts of feather and bone embellishments. A part of my mind would put descriptions in my mouth, while a separate part noted that one woman coveted a secret love and another's affectation of honeyed sweetness masked a bitter heart. They tut-tutted over the heathen savages, and it diverted them for an afternoon from thoughts of their own shortcomings.

At times, I would have no choice but to answer questions about myself, and I would explain that my husband, an elderly scholar and physician, had died in his laboratory. Pearl's father, I assured them, was a man of passion and great learning, a man devoted to his God, well known and respected for that devotion. I had returned to England because I so grieved his passing, and I sought the comfort of my mother country.

All of these were highly satisfying answers to the women's questions, but their visits tapered off as they came to know me better. I could see hesitation on their faces when Mary and I called upon them in their homes. Who could fault them? For eight years I had lived with people who knew my greatest sin the moment they looked upon me. No one understood better than I the distress they must have felt in my presence, for I looked upon these new women with the very same knowledge. That they could not know of my perception mattered not. Surely they felt it. Doubtless their discomfort did not bode well in my quest for the right associations.

One afternoon, Mary and I took our children to the square, as did many of the neighbor women. Across the green, the others seemed drawn toward one another by an invisible force, but we remained apart, as though that same force repelled them from me.

Some yards away, Jane and Pearl sat in the grass beneath a tree, taking imaginary tea, and three girls scampered toward them to join the party. The girls giggled and poured invisible tea for one another. Annie had grown weary of the game earlier and was now digging in the dirt with Georgie.

"I am glad to see that Jane has helped Pearl to make friends," I commented.

"Hester . . ." Mary began, then stopped.

It was a gray day, and the park was bathed in soft light. I turned to Mary, and though she stood close enough to touch, the dim light seemed to blur the features of her face. Maybe the trick was in my mind rather than the light. In my months of living at Wright House, I had steadfastly refused to acknowledge the frailties her eyes would have betrayed about her, just as I had hidden my own sins from her. Now it occurred to me that I was tired of deception. Sooner or later, we would have to see each other clearly.

"Yes?" I said.

"I would have you make friends, too."

"You said that it was dangerous, that if your husband fell out with theirs—"

"A kind of friends, then. Not close, but . . ."

"Have we not done that? I know Mistress Higgins, there, and Mistress Tobin, whose daughter is taking tea with ours, and—"

"And none of those women has so much as nodded in our direction," Mary interrupted.

"I have tried to be cordial."

"Cordial you are, but you unsettle them."

"I do not mean to."

"I believe that to be true, but you—you often look so intensely at people without speaking. At times even I feel uneasy with you."

"Too often," I offered, "I can think of nothing to say."

Mary looked down and traced her fingers over the embroidered cuffs I had made for her. "We have grown quite close again, have we not?" she asked. "I truly delight in having you here, and sometimes it is just as if we were girls again."

She did not wish to hurt me, but she must. I needed no strange powers of perception to sense this. It was woven among her words within her voice. "Somewhat," I said. "Though there was a time when we spoke all that was in our young hearts to each other."

"It is harder now," she murmured.

"It should not be. If ever I might wish to hear hard advice, Mary, I would rather hear it from you than anyone."

She sighed, then looked at me. "No one wishes to be scrutinized too closely, Hester. Who among us can bear it? And you are at an unfair advantage."

"An advantage?" I asked.

"Yes, for no one can gaze so long at you." As if prompted by her own words, she turned to face the girls as she continued. "You are like a mirror." I nodded my understanding, and she cried, "Do you not see? The words I just spoke make no sense! No one is like a mirror to *everyone* she meets, and yet *you* are, and you *know* that you are, for you act as though it were a perfectly reasonable thing to say."

"I am what I am, Mary."

She wrapped her arms across her chest as though she were suddenly cold. "And what *is* that?"

"A woman like you. One who felt no love for her husband, who did not respect him, care for him, or know him."

Mary, sweet Mary's sunny face twisted into something bitter. "I suppose that there is nothing uncommon in that. And yet you speak of Pearl's father as if he were a saint on earth."

"As far as I know, his only sin was in loving another man's wife."

Surprise at first, then sympathy washed across her face, and she took my hand. "Hester—" she began, then her gaze shifted and her eyes widened. She drew a sharp breath and said, "Robert!"

Seven

———⊰⊙⊱———

The likeness in the parlor was excellent. I would have known Colonel Wright in a moment. His slender frame was clothed in the highest quality, though the style was subdued and practical. His hair was close-cropped around his narrow head, and his features were sharp as a raptor's.

His most striking attribute, however, I knew was visible only to me. Vitreous and ghostly, an illusory mantle floated about his shoulders—gossamer scarlet elaborately embellished in gold thread, and when he looked at me, he knew that I saw.

"R-Robert," Mary stuttered, "this is Hester Prynne, my dear friend of whom I wrote." Her blue eyes were wide, a little fearful. At first, I thought perhaps she had only told him that I had returned from America, failing to mention that I was living at Wright House. Then I realized; though she did not see the cloak when she looked at him directly, when she saw him reflected in my eyes, the garment was as evident as if it were material.

The girls' voices drifted to us. They had not yet noticed the colonel's return. Mary and her husband exchanged stricken glances, and for once it was I who first remembered conventional civilities. "How do you do, Colonel Wright? I am pleased to make your acquaintance."

He cleared his throat and nodded. "Mistress Prynne." I doubt he knew that his hand stole slowly up to his heart.

Jane looked up and paused, her hands poised as though she were pouring a cup of tea from a pot. She said something to Pearl, whose own head lifted so that she could follow her friend's gaze. Georgie, without prompting, looked toward us as well and tugged at Annie's sleeve.

"The children will be so glad to see you," Mary murmured, but her voice was strained. "Come children," she called. "Your father has arrived!"

Georgie ran, tripped over his childish robes, allowed Annie to right him, then ran again. The girls came forward somewhat more slowly, Jane holding her sister's hand, my child behind them. The colonel picked his son up and the two males inspected each other solemnly for a moment, until the colonel smiled and Georgie laughed. Jane curtsied and Pearl followed suit. Then Jane tapped Annie on the shoulder, and the little girl sank unsteadily, her skirt held wide.

"Welcome home, Father," Jane said.

"My daughter, Pearl," I said, gesturing to her.

"How do you do, sir?" Pearl asked.

"I am told you and my daughter have become fast friends," he replied.

"Yes, sir," Pearl said.

"I trust you keep one another on a path of virtue and obedience."

"Sometimes," Pearl answered. She looked directly into his face, in innocence rather than defiance, but I wondered if he saw that. "More often it is our mothers who keep after us."

He handed Georgie to Mary. "And what will you do when you are women grown with no mothers to guide you?"

"I suspect we will wander a bit from time to time, sir, but from our wanderings we will gain much wisdom. My mother says we learn more from our mistakes than our accomplishments."

"Is that what your mother has taught you?" Colonel Wright scowled at her, but Pearl only cocked her head curiously. I had schooled her in this philosophy so well that I have no doubt it did not occur to her that he might disagree.

"One hopes it to be true," I said, drawing his frown to me.

"We all make mistakes, do we not?" His face reddened slightly, and his hand rubbed against his heart.

"Surely you have things to unpack," Mary interjected. "Hester, if you will watch after the children?"

"Stay with them, Mary," Colonel Wright insisted. "The housekeeper and I shall manage." He bowed to me without meeting my eyes. "Until dinner." I nodded in response, and he strode toward the house.

Turning to my friend, I said, "Mary—"

"Don't!" she commanded, her hand held up between us. "Do not say it. I do not wish to know."

That night, the children dined in the nursery, rather than at the table with us as they had since I arrived at Wright House nearly a half year before. Afterward, Georgie and Annie stayed upstairs to play with the nurse, for they were too young to understand that their accustomed habit of playing chase around the parlor table with the older girls would have to change while the colonel was in residence. Jane and Pearl came down to the parlor, and we all sat together at the table while the girls took turns reading aloud from Exodus.

"'And all the firstborn in the land of Egypt shall die,'" Pearl recited, "'from the firstborn of the Pharaoh that sitteth upon his throne, even unto the firstborn of the maidservant that is behind the mill.'" Pearl paused and said, "Mother, do you never wonder if God—"

"Do not stop the story, Pearl." Too late, it occurred to me that we should have told the girls that we would not be having the sorts of discussions that had previously been encouraged between them, Mary, and me.

"I am interested in what the child has to say," the colonel said.

"She is young," I told him. "Some of this is hard for her to understand."

"Then her questions should be answered," he insisted. "What clarification do you need, Pearl?"

"Do you suppose God took the Egyptians' children into heaven when the angel of death killed them?"

Colonel Wright scoffed. "Certainly not! What would He want of His enemy's children?"

"Were they not innocent? What could the maidservant have

done to make God angry? She might feel better if she knew her baby would go to heaven," Pearl replied.

"Innocent? They were born in sin, just like you. Furthermore, if the Egyptians suffered, it was also for their Pharaoh's sins."

I wished that I might dare to say, "If that is so, why do I never see sin in children?"

"But look here," Pearl protested, pointing to the page before her. "It says right here that 'the LORD hardened the Pharaoh's heart, so that he would not let the children of Israel go out of his land.' Does that not make God responsible—"

"Pearl," I said, "I think it is time for bed."

"But—"

Colonel Wright stood. "In this house, children honor their parents. If your mother decrees that you should retire, then you will do so without question."

Pearl gave him a mutinous glare, but to her credit she stood, calmly closed the Bible from which she had been reading, and walked from the room, though I had fully expected her to stomp.

"Good night, Father," Jane said, her voice barely above a whisper.

"You are a good girl, Janie," he said.

"Thank you, sir." She sank into a curtsy and received a pat on the head as her reward.

As soon as she had left, Colonel Wright turned to me. "I am very much interested to know how you would have answered your child."

How to answer with neither the truth nor a lie . . . ? "I would have told her that God is always just."

"That is an ambiguous answer."

Well, yes. Perhaps diversion would be better. "God's justice, ambiguous?" I asked.

He glared at me. "No. Your responses are ambiguous. Do you think religion an ambiguous thing, Mistress Prynne?"

In truth, I found nearly everything ambiguous. I still do. In an attempt to end the dubious conversation entirely, I laid my hand upon my heart and replied, "I mean that, in the end, we must all have faith in God's perfect justice."

The colonel fell silent, the movement of his hand mirroring mine, creeping to his own heart.

Mary broke the quiet. "Hester, will you see that the children are all tucked in?"

"Of course," I replied. It was a relief to leave. It had been foolish to contradict the man whose roof sheltered my daughter and me, to risk angering a man who could stand between me and my only friend. Still, I had swallowed an inordinate amount of such nonsense in New England; I had little stomach left for more in my homeland. Thus, I am afraid it was that *other* Hester, the passionate, rebellious one, who spoke next.

I rose, bowing my head. "You are right, of course. A more direct answer would have been best. I should have told her that God is just, and those who, like the Egyptians, will not heed God's word must bear full responsibility for the harm their sins do to those they love."

And then I left for the nursery, before I dug the hole any deeper.

Eight

———⊱•⊰———

A single candle burned in my bedchamber, though the rest of the household had gone to bed hours ago. I could not sleep. For too many years had I wandered in my own mind, unimpeded by conventional wisdom or theology. Too long had I seen into the darkest places of my fellow man's heart. It chafed me sorely to know that, like it or not, I again had a master upon whom I depended, though it was now for rank rather than money. There was little difference. With the colonel, I must assume a submissive demeanor, regardless of his faults. His family offered me the social connections I desperately needed, whereas he could easily do without the monies I gave them from Pearl's inheritance to pay for our place in the house.

Tomorrow I would make amends. I would defer to his wisdom and demands in all things. I would be silent and teach my daughter obedience. She must learn it sooner or later anyway. God's perfect justice, indeed.

Man's justice, that was what it was. I opened a drawer in the wardrobe and dug to the farthest corner. Without looking, I knew that I had found it. My fingers had touched it a thousand and a thousand times. I pulled the badge out and fingered the letter in the shadows. The one woman in all of New England that I might have befriended once said that there was not a stitch in that letter that I had not felt in my heart, and she was utterly correct. I could never take it off, not really. Its specter hovered always over my bosom.

I had only picked at dinner, so at length I decided to go to the kitchen to see what I could find to eat, slipping the letter into the pocket of my dressing gown. The way was dark, but I carried the candle and found my way by its meager light.

With a slice of mince pie and a mug of milk, I slipped from the kitchen into the parlor, where I was surprised to find Mary in the light of a dying fire.

"I could not sleep either," I told her as I slid into a chair beside her.

She did not look at me. Instead, she stared into the faint, flickering flames. "Why do you do that?" she asked.

"What?"

"You know very well what. I did not want to know, Hester. What good does it do me? What made you think that I cared?"

"I did not—"

"Yes, you did! You looked at him, and he knew that you knew. As soon as you left, he made a full confession. He would never have said anything to me at all had it not been for you!"

I wished that she would look at me. "I—I am sorry."

"You have estranged my every acquaintance, upset the balance with my husband—"

"I should think the scales tipped to your favor."

Her countenance was stiff, her nostrils flared. "Would you? My husband will have no weakness in the eyes of those who serve him. He may have had no love for me before, but he was satisfied with me as a wife. Now he detests me because I know he has been weak. Why, Hester? Why do you peer into places where you are uninvited?"

"Do you think I want this?" I asked. "Do you think I gain any joy from it? I have no more desire to know these things than you. Your husband detests you? Well, *everyone* is repelled by me."

Now she turned to look into my face. "Then stop!"

"I cannot! If I brought to you a woman mourning the loss of her child, though her eyes might be dry, would you tell me that you could not see her weeping? What if I told you to unsee her grief? I see sin. I cannot unsee it."

"Are you so stainless then, Hester? You whose child is not her late husband's?"

"If you had never mourned, would you know grief when you see it, Mary? I do not claim to be stainless."

We sat in silence, Mary with her back rigid, I toying with my food—my appetite having fled again. In time, Mary broke the silence. "Did Roger know?"

"He did." ·

"And yet he claimed her?"

"In the end, he made her his heir, but no, he never claimed her."

She looked at me again, her face more curious than hostile. "What do you mean?"

"He willed her his fortune, but while he lived, he claimed neither of us."

"He cast you aside?" She gave a disgusted little huff. "Robert would do the same to me if I were untrue, though he clearly assumes that I will forgive him. How can I forgive what I cannot fathom? He is a man obsessed with religion, and yet . . ." She hesitated, then said, "But you can fathom it, can you not, Hester?"

"There are forces stronger than mere religion," I told her.

"Love? He swears that was not the case."

"Then perhaps I cannot help you understand after all." I sighed at the pang in my heart. *Be true, Hester, to Mary if no one else.* "No, I will not lie to you. If I had only loved Arthur, if my body had not craved his, do you not suppose we would have resisted?"

Mary shrugged her shoulders. "I have met no man who tempts my heart or body." We were quiet again for a moment, accentuating the fire's occasional pop and crackle. "Will you—will you tell me about him?" Mary asked. "Pearl's father?"

I drew a deep breath and slipped my hand into my pocket to reassure myself that my one connection to Arthur was still there. "Do you remember when we were girls, and we spoke of our dreams of the men we would marry?"

Mary closed her eyes. "I dreamed of a knight, virtuous and bold, one who would prize me for my virtue and beauty." She opened them again and glared into the fire. "Well, I found him, didn't I?"

"I dreamed of a man gentle and sweet, with a face soft, like an angel, and a voice like music."

"I remember. A far cry from Roger," she said.

"I went to America ahead of Roger and took lodgings in a widow's house. New England has always been as England is now, and church attendance was mandatory. I went with the widow on the very first Sunday, and when the minister took the pulpit, I saw him."

"The minister? Of course you saw him, if he was in the pulpit."

"No. I saw *him*. The man I had dreamed of. His name was the Reverend Mister Arthur Dimmesdale, and he was everything I had imagined—the saintly face, the dulcet voice. That voice. It was filled with every yearning, every longing I had ever known. It spoke of my craving for freedom and beauty, my desire to be known—fully known—and loved with all that knowledge."

"Oh, my," Mary breathed.

"I knew at once that he would understand me. I was certain that I could tell him how much I loathed Roger, how I hated America, how I wanted to go back to sea and feel the wind in my hair, and he would judge me not."

"And he did—understand?"

I nodded. "He said that it was tortuously hard to walk the path he had chosen. He wanted so much to be perfect, but perfection eluded him. He said that he had never known perfection until one Sunday morning he looked out upon his flock and spied a face he had not seen before, a face that gazed up at him and saw in him his perfect self—the man he always strove to be. My face.

"For over a year, we met frequently at the church. He was a much-loved pastor and seen by all as above reproach, so no one thought twice about my seeking his counsel, especially so openly. In time, the nature of our discourse became so intimate that we moved to his office. He began to fear that the regularity of my visits would raise curiosity, so often we met in the forest, where he would read to me from Psalms. His voice caressed me, stole my breath, played sweet music to my heart.

"One day, under the dark canopy of the trees, I told him that I felt he was the only soul on earth to know all there ever was to know of me and that it filled my heart to bursting. He said, 'Ah Hester, would that I could know all there ever was to know of you.' "

"Sweet Jesus," Mary whispered.

"I took his hand and kissed it, not once, but many times, and then I pressed it to my bosom and said, 'Then know me, Arthur, and let me know you.' "

" 'I am not this strong, Hester,' he said. 'Tempt me not, for I cannot resist this any longer.' Roger had yet to arrive, and I was beginning to suspect he was lost at sea. I said as much to Arthur. 'The laws of men keep us apart,' I told him, 'not the will of God. In my heart, I am no man's wife save yours.'

"He touched my face, kissed my lips, and said, 'What we give to each other shall have a consecration of its own,' and I cried, 'Yes! A sacred marriage in God's cathedral will we make here in these consecrated woods.' "

Her animosity forgotten, Mary leaned toward me and put her hand on mine. "Oh, how I envy you, Hester."

"Envy me not, Mary. That day in the wood we gave life to Pearl and sentenced Arthur to death."

She gasped. "He was executed?"

"Worse. Those moments, those few precious moments were sublime, beyond perfection. His eyes never left mine, and our souls were poured one into the other, but when it was over—when our clothes were restored and we braced ourselves to return to the world beyond the woods, he wept and said that he had betrayed his office, betrayed my soul entrusted into his care. He begged me to forgive him." As I spoke of his tears, my own eyes burned. "Nothing else he could have said could have wounded me so deeply. Would that he had called me a whore rather than suggest that he had betrayed me by loving me.

"We did not speak in private again. He said that he could not be trusted near me. He took it all upon himself, as though I had not begged him to take me." I closed my eyes, but a tear slipped through my lashes. "Oh, God, Mary, I loved him so."

She made soft shushing sounds such as she might for little Georgie when he was hurt.

"By the time I was six months along with Pearl, I could hide it no longer. I spent the next six months in jail, where I gave birth and made this." I pulled out the letter and laid it upon the table, and a choked sound of sympathy slipped through Mary's lips. "For seven years I wore it."

"And Arthur?"

"He had work to do, Mary, work that could not be done by a

fallen minister. If the open wearing of my sin gave me the power
to see the sin in others, Arthur's hidden guilt gave him a sympathy
few pastors possess. That which was his burden was also his gift.
He saved so many souls, achieved such greatness. I would have
died rather than take that from him."

"What of Roger?"

"The first day that I wore my badge of shame in public, I was
released from jail long enough to stand upon a scaffold as an example of the punishment that would be meted out to sinners such
as I. It was on that very day that Roger arrived. The first time I had
set eyes upon him in over two years, Pearl and the letter were at
my breast, and I was just beginning my life of shame and ignominy. Before the sun set, he had taken the new name of Roger
Chillingworth and came to the prison to swear me to secrecy. He
did not wish the shame of a husband cuckolded, he said."

"Coward," Mary spat.

"Demon," I corrected. "He used my oath to torture Arthur in
secret."

"No! How could he have known Arthur was the father? You
said you would have died—"

"Foolish girl that I was, I never wondered how Roger had
come by his wealth."

"Did it matter?"

"Alchemy. Necromancy. My husband's studies had gone far
beyond those of traditional scholars'. I cannot say for certain that
he used black magic to ascertain Arthur's identity, but I have no
doubt that he used it to draw out and exacerbate the remorse that
slowly killed that good and decent man."

I tucked the letter back into my pocket. "Roger did but infect
the wound I myself inflicted upon my love. Since I left New England, I have come to realize that my penance lies not in the public humiliation of the scarlet letter, but in my unwanted knowledge
of my fellow man. If only I *could* unsee what invades my sight,
unhear what assaults my ears—illuminated sin upon every breast,
dark confessions whispered between innocuous words."

Mary pondered my tale. At last she said, "Might Roger have
thrust that upon you? Might he have used magic to curse you with
this sight?"

"I cannot say. He told me that the scarlet letter had avenged him fully for my part in the crime committed against him, but he was a dark man."

Reaching over, Mary took my hand, lacing her fingers with mine. "I forgive you," she told me, "but not Robert."

"Did he say that he loved her?" I asked.

"No. There was not one woman; there were many. I should be comforted, he said, for the number was an assurance that his betrayal was corporal, not spiritual, and was therefore of less consequence."

"No!" I cried. "He did not say that!"

Mary snorted. "He did. He went on to say that he did not expect me to fully understand because in women, bearers of lives and carriers of human souls, the body and soul are one. For us, corporal and physical betrayal are one and the same."

"How convenient for men. Did you ask him to cite the Scripture that says such a thing?"

"Do you think it may be true, Hester? Sometimes with Robert, I do not even feel anything corporal. I feel nothing at all."

"With Roger I felt revulsion. With Arthur—I touched the edge of heaven."

She rested her head upon my shoulder, and I laid mine against her hair, and there we sat until the small hours of the morning.

Nine

Pearl stood on a chair in my bedchamber while I pinned her dress up for hemming. It was a pretty frock the color of a ripe peach, and when I finished it, the collar and cuffs would be adorned with tiny leaves and buds. The light slanted in through the window, illuminating Pearl's face, but it did not reach beyond her, so I sat in shadow and tended to the task.

"How much longer will the colonel be home?" she asked me. "Twelve days more?"

"Given that when you asked yesterday, the answer was thirteen, and when you asked the day before that it was fourteen, I would say that twelve days more is a reasonable guess." I slipped another pin into place.

"Jane is no fun since he's come. She won't run with me in the park or whisper with me late at night. And don't you think Auntie Mary is rather dreary, too?"

"The colonel has that effect on people, but mind you don't say that I told you that—not even to Jane. She has enough worrying that she will displease her father without worrying that he displeases her friends."

"I know. I do not say anything, even though he picks the absolute worst parts of the Bible for evening reading. First Corinthians, Chapter Eleven?" She rolled her eyes and paraphrased. "A woman must cover her head, or shave it, or both, or not shave it if so shaving shames her but then cover it. But *men* needn't shave their heads for *they* are God's glory, and women merely the glory of men. Pah! I should think God has better things to do than worry about our heads."

"He does, but the colonel doesn't. He gets restless in London."

"If God wishes men to have long hair, why does the colonel cut his so short?"

"I'm sure I don't know."

"Well, it was a boring chapter. I prefer Thirteen, about love and charity and such."

"As do I," I agreed. "I am finished. Jump down." Pearl did so with enthusiasm, and I winced at the loud thud of her feet upon the floorboards. "Ssh!" I admonished.

Pearl sighed. "Twelve days more?"

I helped her out of the dress and regarded her thin form through her shift. Nearly half her maidenhood was past, and it seemed I might have done her an injustice to have spoken my own thoughts so openly to her of late. After all, my own moral wanderings had not brought me any happiness, only misery. Perhaps Colonel Wright was correct, and it was better to teach children only one way of thinking. Of course, that hadn't kept him from straying.

"Well, tonight will be better. Mister and Mistress Tobin will be coming to dinner, and Susan will come with them."

"I like Susan. Can you make something for her someday? A collar or an apron? She always says such kind things about my gowns, and hers are so plain."

"I will ask her mother if she approves. You could make something for her."

"I gave her the ribbon I embroidered—the blue one, you remember?"

"I do. The one with the violets. It was very pretty."

"She was very happy for it, but she likes the fancier things you make. Can you make an 'S' for Susan and illuminate it?"

"I told you that I would ask her mother. The Chaphams are coming, as well."

Pearl pulled a face at me. "Ugh! They have the most dreadful children! That boy Christopher is so lordly. He even pushed little Georgie down when all Georgie was trying to do was get

Christopher to play. And Elizabeth! Just because she is twelve, she thinks she is superior. 'Do not slouch, Janie. Do not fidget, Pearl. Lower your voice, Annie.'" Her mimicry of Elizabeth's imperious tone was so exact that I had to hide my smile in my sleeve. It wouldn't do to encourage her.

Tugging Pearl's old dress over her head, I said, "Mary says she consorts with the Chaphams very little when her husband is away, so you need only tolerate them this one night."

Once she was laced up, Pearl raced out the door of my room and back down one flight of stairs to the nursery, where she and Jane would doubtless complain about their unwanted playmates in hushed tones.

I would have liked someone to complain to, as well, but there was no sense adding to Mary's burdens any more than Pearl adding to her friend's, so I went downstairs to help Mary with the roast beef and pudding.

For our gathering, I changed into my Sunday gown, a deep leaden gray, entirely unadorned. Mary often chided me for my lack of decoration, given my passion for needlework, but it seemed to me that I attracted enough attention with my oddness. I need not draw more with flowers and scrolls.

The Wrights' neighbors, Mister and Mistress Tobin, arrived first with their daughter, which allowed the girls to set up their play without Elizabeth directing it from the start. Susan took both Pearl's and Jane's hands, and the trio tripped upstairs amid giggles.

Mistress Tobin was carrying their fifth child, a prominent swelling on her thin frame, and I needed no special sight to see her gnawing worry. It was there in her tight mouth and the circles under her eyes. Of all her children, only Susan had lived past three. The men settled at once at the far end of the table to discuss politics, while Mary and I exclaimed, perhaps too enthusiastically, about the way that Mistress Tobin's cheeks glowed (which they assuredly did not) and how her own good health must surely be an excellent sign for the baby.

But poor Mistress Tobin's faith was flagging. If this child did not live, neither would her belief in God. These desolate, unspoken thoughts surrounded me in her presence. Every time I looked into her eyes, her sorrow and fear pierced me through.

Mister Tobin, a clerk for Parliament, was as good and simple a soul as one could ever hope to meet. His face was round, his smile genuine, and he was untroubled. This was probably why he actually seemed to like me. There was nothing disconcerting about him that I might reflect back. I often wondered how he could have lost so much and still held such optimism, but hold it he did.

Perhaps a quarter of an hour later, Captain Chapham knocked on the door, and Mary welcomed him, his wife, and their two offspring. The utter failure of my sight when it came to children affirmed my general belief that children are without sin, and yet it was a wonder to me that some shadow of the young Chaphams' excessive pride did not obscure everyone else in the room. I was no more pleased to spend the evening with their parents than Pearl was with them, so I simply bowed my head politely to Mistress Chapham and allowed her to do that at which she excelled.

"Mistress Wright, Mistress Tobin, Mistress Prynne!" She pronounced my name "Prine." I had corrected her on two previous occasions, then given up. "How lovely to see you all." She leaned over the table toward us women and whispered, "I see the rumors are true. Congratulations, Mistress Tobin. I do hope this child fares as well as your Susan. She seems hale and healthy enough. When are you due?"

"In the autumn," Mistress Tobin murmured, her voice soft and anxious.

"Autumn." Mistress Chapham sighed. "Spring babies are best, for they have time to gain strength against the winter maladies, and yours have been so susceptible to lung fevers. Well, I have several good remedies for such things, so you must come see me before the baby is born so that I can give them to you."

Despite the stricken expression on her face, Mistress Tobin managed a barely audible "Thank you for your concern."

"Not at all, dear. Have you all heard about young Mister Darnley? He was in the stocks earlier this week . . ."

I could study Mistress Chapham as openly as I pleased, for she seldom glanced my way. She had seated herself next to me, which placed her directly across from a window, where she watched her own prattling reflection in rapt fascination. Though her face was beautiful by any measure, it was hard and cold, like flesh-colored marble—Galatea in love with herself.

Turning my attention to the other end of the table, I looked at her husband, a captain in the army. He, too, was a handsome man, but shrouded in something dark, something I could not quite identify. Though I was trying harder of late not to stare at people and to concentrate upon their words rather than their secrets, he was too intriguing to resist.

Like anyone else, I have been guilty in my life of most sins to some degree or other. I have never murdered anyone, but more than once I had wished Roger dead. I have never stolen anything, but in the eyes of most I gave to Arthur that which was not mine to give. It seemed to me that the captain was guilty of something I was innocent of, and it was hard to resist the urge to solve the mystery.

Throughout dinner, conversation passed around and through me.

"Those worthless Scots Presbyterians ought to side with us, not Charles the Second! When those who claim to be upright Christians side with debauchery . . ."

"Mark my words, that girl will be nothing but trouble if they do not rein her in soon . . ."

"Corruption is rife. I am telling you that Parliament cannot be saved . . ."

"Have you seen Mistress Hall at church? No? I asked the Reverend Mister Bartlett, and he said that he would look into it . . ."

"No king? No Parliament? We must have order . . ."

"If Cromwell's health continues to flag . . ."

No one seemed to mind or notice that I wasn't fully listening. I simply made sure that I didn't stare at anyone too long. I looked at my plate or just past everyone at paintings and the flickering flames of candles.

After dinner, Mary and I brought down our latest projects. She had been sewing a new coat for her husband to keep him warm in Ireland when he returned, and she was especially pleased with the rich wool she had purchased for it. I showed the others Pearl's new gown and explained my plans for the collar. It seemed a good time to ask whether I might do the same for Susan, which pleased Mistress Tobin. Mistress Chapham lamented that we could not see the wondrous gown she had nearly finished for Elizabeth. This one thing I held in common with the shrew—that which we could not indulge ourselves in we lavished upon our daughters. Soon, even they would reach an age where such finery would be discouraged, as it would draw too much attention from young men.

The husbands had settled with pipes when an unexpected visitor showed up at the parlor house. "John Manning!" Colonel Wright exclaimed when he opened the door. "Good to see you. I thought you were in Scotland."

Mister Manning smiled, and his blue eyes twinkled. He doffed his black hat and raked a hand through thick, dark hair. "I was; I returned just yesterday. Good evening to you, Joseph," he said to Captain Chapham. Then he looked at the remaining man. "Teller, is it?"

Mister Tobin smiled, unoffended. "Tobin."

"Tobin! Yes. Good to see you. Ah, Mistress Wright—"

And there it was, that flash of lust in his eyes, so subtle and so fast that no one could have seen it but me, not even Mary.

"Mister Manning, how good of you to call. You remember Captain Chapham's wife—?"

Interesting that I had not seen it before, perhaps because Mistress Chapham's vanity and arrogance had overshadowed it, but the moment those two looked at each other, faces carefully aloof and polite, I knew that they had known each other as I had known Arthur.

"And my dear childhood friend, who has returned to England from America, Mistress Hester Prynne."

"Mistress Prynne." He bowed, and when he straightened we looked directly into each other's eyes. A shocking jolt of recognition struck me, though I knew beyond doubt that I had never before seen this man. It was oddly like looking into a mirror, and for once I knew exactly how others felt when they met me.

"Do I know you?" he asked.

"I do not think so," I replied.

"Are you quite certain?"

"Quite," I told him.

"Come, come, John, we were just talking about Scotland."

"They adore Charles," John replied. "I hear we're losing Ireland as well."

"Hardly a lost cause," Robert replied, and the men retreated to their end of the table.

"I do wish I had brought the shawl I just finished," Mistress Chapham said to Mary, Mistress Tobin, and me. "I hear that Mistress Prynne is gaining quite a name with her needle, but truly, if you could see what I have done . . ."

John Manning had bedded this harpy, I thought to myself. Not a man of exacting taste. Since I had listened to her grating voice quite long enough, I tuned my ear to the men.

"I'm telling you, Robert," Captain Chapham insisted, "you must crush them utterly. You must strike the fear of God into them!"

"What do you think we did at Drogheda? We executed every last rebel we could find."

"And what of those who aided them?" Chapham pressed.

"Those who would give aid to the rebels should have learned a thing or two at Wexford. It was a bloodbath, though not by our command."

"Never lose control over your troops," Chapham chided.

"So I'm not to keep the killing to the soldiers, but I am to keep complete discipline? Would you have me *order* my men to kill civilians?"

"You might just as well. The Irish think you ordered it anyway."

"Which is what's given the Catholics the advantage," Wright fumed. "Shall I add fuel to the fire?"

"Gentlemen," Mister Tobin chided, "we are all friends here. No need to argue. Right will prevail."

Captain Chapham glared at Mister Tobin. "What did you say that you do for a living?"

Mister Tobin smiled. "I am a clerk for the Parliament, a very interesting business, that." He took a deep breath, clearly happy to move the conversation in a direction in which he had some knowledge, but Chapham interrupted.

"A clerk? To a Parliament that has been nothing short of a disaster, and you wish to enthrall us with the manner in which you administer their chaos? Blood has been spilled in great buckets, and you would speak of resolutions broken before the ink is dry?"

At Mister Tobin's crushed face, I could not hold my tongue. "Good Mister Tobin never pretended to be the shaper of a nation.

He but registers the acts of this new kingless order so that history may know your glory, or would you rather history never speak of your efficacy thus far?"

The room fell silent. Even Captain Chapham's dreadful wife, whose mouth was still open from spewing gossip, could not produce so much as a squeak.

Captain Chapham's dark shroud roiled and undulated all around him, and I felt myself go cold. "Who was your late husband again?" he asked.

"No one of consequence," I replied. If he hoped to conjoin me with some traitor, he would be disappointed. "My thoughts are none but my own."

Colonel Wright, back on the same side with his friend, asked, "Do you not find the religious freedom we have achieved worthy of glory? Can you not see the sense in choosing a leader for his skills rather than his family? Would you really see England back under the rule of depraved and tyrannical monarchs?"

John Manning fixed me with a look that was intense, but entirely without animosity. It was a warning, not a threat. "You tread on dangerous ground, here, Mistress Prynne," he said.

"Perhaps I overstepped my bounds," I conceded. "I have no interest in politics, as Mary can tell you. I simply could not bear to hear Mister Tobin, whom I know to be a man of the very best intentions, so maligned."

"A woman with a tender heart," Mister Manning said. "Who can fault such a one?"

"I—I appreciate your concern," Mister Tobin stammered. "But really, there is no need. These worthy men are justified in their frustration. Please, do not let our men's discourse upset you."

Prudently I returned to talk of stitches and children and tried to ignore the men, but every now and again John Manning caught my eye, and I wondered what, besides adultery, we had in common.

Ten

―――――∗◦∗―――――

The next morning, Mary informed me that she had mitigated the aftermath of my previous night's folly. When her husband would have insisted that I find habitation elsewhere, she reminded him that the danger he faced in Ireland had given her cause enough for worry, but that his most recent return had given her yet other misgivings. Would he truly ask her to endure her distress with no intimate companion? Must she seek another woman in whom to confide?

"He says that he is willing to forgive you, Hester."

"Thank God," I replied.

She shook her head and placed a hand upon my shoulder. "He is *willing* to. That does not mean that he has. You would do well to win his kind regard before he leaves."

So I kept my silence and embellished a pair of gloves for the colonel as a peace offering, as well as a scarf for the captain. When next Mistress Chapham called, through a clench-jawed smile, I declared her pitiful needlework superior to my own.

Come May, the colonel was called to Ireland for a council of war, and life at Wright House resumed as though he had never been there. Mistress Chapham was no longer included on our guest lists, nor we on hers, and none took offense. The girls sought their own understanding of Scripture, and footraces resumed around the parlor table.

Summer waned, but before the true chill of autumn set in, the children were determined to spend as much time in the park as possible. Susan spent her days with us as her mother had taken to bed in hopes of strengthening the child she carried. It was a delight to watch the girls share secrets and poppets. They played chase with little Georgie and often allowed him to catch one or another. Annie, they insisted, must work harder at catching her friends, for she was of an age to learn that little is just handed to one in life.

Upon this day, they had concluded their games and lay or sat on the grass catching their breath when it seemed that every neighbor came to play, too. The Perkins children were led by twelve-year-old Samuel, the eldest. Behind him came his sisters, Sarah and Bess, and his brothers, Thomas and Walter. The entire clan put me in mind of the children we had known in New England who had once so vexed Pearl that she had screamed at them and thrown dirt clods. It was fortunate for the Perkinses that she was now beyond such antics. The Durham children arrived at a run, all holding hands and smiling. Rose Durham was Jane's age, with an older brother, Robin, and younger one, Francis. I seemed to recall a somewhat more recent addition to the family but could not recall whether it was a boy or a girl, and I did not immediately see their mother.

The newly arrived girls sat delicately on the grass with ours while Georgie abandoned his sisters (among whom he now counted Pearl) to play with the boys.

"You've a new sash, I see," Sarah, the elder Perkins sister, said to Susan.

Susan's face lit up. "Pearl stitched it! Look closely—amid the design it says 'truest friend.'"

"Hmmm. So I see. Another new frock?" Sarah asked Pearl, her eyes slightly narrowed in scrutiny.

Envy. It was not my strange sight that revealed the weakness; it was plain upon her face. Still, I could hardly fault her. Mistress Perkins (who even now advanced toward us from across the park) dressed her children in plain, strictly serviceable clothes.

"Mistress Prynne," she acknowledged with a nod then turned to Mary. "Mistress Wright, is there any news of Mistress Tobin?"

"None yet," Mary said.

I stepped back and allowed Mary and Mistress Perkins to converse without me. In my pale gray dress, my hair fully covered, I strove to become invisible. I had discovered this to be the best way to get along with Mary's associates. Watching the children, I listened more to their conversation than the one between my own peers. Several of the boys approached Pearl and her friends. They stood among the seated girls, arms crossed, confident in their masculine superiority, except for Georgie and little Walter, who ran past the group to show their mamas pretty stones gleaned from under a tree.

"Annie claims you've seen pirates," said Samuel Perkins to Pearl. The phrase rang out like a challenge.

Pearl stood. At nine, she was tall for her age, but her head only came to the older boy's chin. "I have. They came often to Boston Harbor."

"And Red Indians?" asked Thomas, his brown eyes wide with awe. "Have you really seen Red Indians? With bows and arrows and all dressed in deer hide? Are they truly red?"

"I have seen them," Pearl assured him. "And they do wear deer hide, but they are more brown than red."

"What did the pirates look like?" Samuel demanded to know.

"Dirty," Pearl replied, "and hairy, but mostly like ordinary men. They would come to town drunk and play music and sing, which made the governor and ministers very angry, but the pirates only laughed at them. They asked me to dance with them once."

For the moment, even Sarah had to set aside her ill will for the richness of the tale. "They didn't! Did you? Dance with them?"

I started to intervene in the conversation, but my Pearl was no fool. "Of course not! They were terrible men. They called me witch baby!"

"Why?" asked Robin Durham, a gentle boy two years older than Pearl. "Witches are ugly old hags, and you are a beautiful girl."

His comment seemed to startle both him and Pearl, and the two children looked away from each other, blushing. I smiled at their innocent affection.

The exchange clearly annoyed Sarah, however. "A witch may look like anything. Why, when you think on it, would a witch not make herself beautiful so that none would suspect her?"

Robin's sister, Rose, responded. "I have never heard of a pretty witch, and Pearl *is* very pretty."

Ordinarily, Bess let Sarah speak for them both, but all this praise for Pearl was too much. "Any of us would be as pretty as she is if our mothers dressed us like princesses."

Sarah put her hand on her sister's shoulder. "Beauty is only skin-deep, or in some cases, thread-deep."

Jane stood up now, fire in her eyes. "You are just jealous!"

"My, my!" Mistress Durham chided, calling her presence to my attention for the first time. I wondered if she had greeted me upon her arrival, for if she had, I had surely ignored her. Her youngest child on her hip, she waded into the knot of children. "Why these harsh words?"

Annie, her eyes wide and brimming with tears, said, "Sarah said Pearl was a witch!"

"I did not!" Sarah snapped. "Pearl said the pirates called her a witch."

"Pirates?" Mistress Durham asked.

I could hide behind my veil of invisibility no more. Walking quickly to Mistress Durham, I explained that Pearl was relating a strange incident in America, that a group of pirates had found her enchanting. "Clearly the incident frightened her and has left its mark," I concluded.

It was a patent lie—the occurrence had been before Arthur's death, and it would have taken far more than mere pirates to intimidate my wild little Pearl. Still, the talk of witches worried me. I had come many miles to rid Pearl of the stigma of her early years. To have the same sentiments arise anew was alarming.

"You know very well what you meant—all that about how witches can be pretty," Jane hissed at Sarah.

"That is enough," Mistress Durham chided. "Witches are nothing to make light of. And we'll have no more talk of pirates, either. Surely you can all make more wholesome conversation."

"Yes, madam," they chorused.

"My uncle has a new horse," Thomas offered.

"Has he?" Robin asked obligingly. "Tell us about him."

The youngsters watched us closely, keeping their talk centered around the animal until Mistress Durham was again engaged in conversation with Mary and Mistress Perkins; they took no more notice of me than their mothers did. Satisfied that they were no longer being observed, Samuel lowered his voice.

"Robin a-and Pe-arl," he sang softly. "Robin a-and Pe-arl."

"Stop that!" Robin snapped.

"Pearl is a beauuutiful girl!" Samuel cackled. "Tell us, Robin, do you looove her?"

"Of course not!" Poor Robin was bright red, even his prominent ears. "I don't love her. She's only a child!"

Pearl cast a look over her shoulder, but once she saw that I was the only mother watching, she said, "Stop that right now, Samuel!"

Samuel cackled again. "No wonder you love her, Robin. She even fights your battles for you."

"I said I don't!" Robin cried. Then, just to prove his point, he snatched an embroidered ribbon from Pearl's dark hair and took off running across the park with the prize held, fluttering over his head. The girls screamed and gave chase (excepting Sarah and Bess, who stayed primly in place, smiling smugly). The boys shouted encouragement to Robin as they raced along the sides.

This prompted us mothers to call out reprimands, marching across the lawn; the children quickly settled down and returned to us. There was much scolding and general agreement that the children had taken quite enough fresh air for the day. Mistress Durham commanded Robin to return the ribbon, though she was distracted by the baby as Robin handed the strip toward Pearl. Thus she did not see him snatch it back at the last second, earning him a sneer of approval from Samuel before the older boy turned to go. Only Pearl and I were still looking at Robin when he gently wound the ribbon around his hand and tucked it carefully into his pocket. She blushed again and made no attempt to retrieve it.

God help me, I thought. *She's only nine.*

Eleven

‒‒‒⇒»•◦•«⇐‒‒‒

A year later, Mary's and my quiet freedom came to an abrupt end. With the signing of the Act of Settlement, the Catholics were routed at last from six counties in Ireland. Colonel Wright was promoted and returned to England, where he moved more deeply into Oliver Cromwell's inner circle.

This meant a new cluster of wives to welcome to Wright House, although it did not often mean new children. This new tier of politics was not a family affair. While Mary was called away to dinners and teas in important households, I stayed at home. Susan still spent many hours in the Wright House nursery, while at her home, her mother fretted over Susan's baby brother, who was plump and healthy and seemed in no need of worry.

I also came to know Miss Nell Walton, the nursemaid, better. She was a sensible girl of twenty-three, the oldest of fourteen children at home. Her hair was carrot-colored and her plain face freckled, and I wondered whether her looks were what kept her unwed, caring for another's children. In time, I learned that her mother was a nervous, unhealthy woman, a condition that Nell had come to associate with too many children, an uncontrollable consequence of marriage. This had led her to resolve to stay single as long as possible.

"Now, Mistress Prynne," she said to me one day as she finished bathing Georgie, "if you'll pardon my saying, I wouldn't mind a life like yours. I'd marry in a trice if I could know my 'usband would give me a pretty girl to dress like a poppet and then leave me a wealthy widow whilst I was young enough to enjoy it."

"Then choose yourself an old man," I advised her.

She shuddered. "I'll just keep watching after these three and whatever else Mistress Wright brings into the world."

"And if there are eleven more?" I asked.

"I'll find me another post elsewhere," Nell assured me.

Within months of her husband's arrival, Mary did indeed conceive another child, and though the first stages of pregnancy exhausted her, she refused to rest. Brigadier General Wright's career was on the rise, his presence even requested as a representative of the army at certain state affairs. Mary may have cared little for him or his politics, but she had her children's futures to consider, so for as long as she was able, she was determined to accompany him and further his ambitions.

I would not have objected to remaining upstairs when Mary fulfilled her obligations to play the hostess to Robert's associates, but she correctly insisted that I, too, had a responsibility to participate. After all, these were the very connections that offered Pearl the most promising future, as well.

"How can any mother consider Pearl for her son if she has never met you or seen your daughter?" Mary asked when I tried to demur joining her latest gathering.

"Pearl accompanies your children when they go downstairs to be presented," I asserted.

"And as a member of our household, she gains some acknowledgment, but people want to know the character of her blood."

There was no arguing that, I admitted.

"And Hester—about your clothes . . ."

I glanced down in confusion. "They are modest and unassuming."

"Yes. Too much so. There is modest and then there is ghastly."

"I thought them utterly inoffensive."

"You could be a nun."

"People think I am a Catholic?"

Mary huffed in frustration. "No! You are a handsome woman, Hester, testament that Pearl will retain her beauty. You must take greater part in drawing the right interest to her."

"She is only ten."

"And a young man of fifteen or sixteen is too young to be a husband now, but his parents will have begun to consider his prospects. When the time comes, they will already have formed a good idea of which young ladies he may choose from. And if not that son, then a younger brother. At eleven, Jane has already impressed several of Robert's colleagues with boys whose futures are even now in the shaping."

I sighed, resigning myself to my duty. "What would you have me do?"

We left our lovely square and ventured into the heart of London, seeking fabrics of indigo, myrtle, and russet for stomachers that would relieve gowns made of rich black linen or wool. Even the most devout Puritans kept some appreciation for beauty, though their religion declared such a worldly matter temporal and unimportant. It was a subtle art, creating a look that was charming without appearing self-indulgent. For the first time since I had stitched my infamous letter, I plied my needle in artistic endeavors for myself, using silken threads to nurse muted floral borders upon those stomachers. My caps and collars I adorned with modest trimmings of lace upon the edges. Since wide, uncuffed sleeves had become the fashion, displaying the sleeves of the shift underneath, I embellished my shifts in white on white. The results were elegant but unostentatious.

For all the joy of dressing my daughter, I had nearly forgotten the joy of dressing myself. I had forgotten how different a beautiful gown could make a woman feel, even if these gowns were not as colorful as the ones I had worn before I wed, when Charles I had reigned.

Through the days and weeks, Mary and I kept to our needles and our offspring, and I was able to avoid discussions of religion or politics with Robert entirely. He spent his days at Whitehall or Parliament, and we seldom saw each other until evening, when I took dinner with the family and sat with them afterward, working on gowns at the fire.

At the table, I lent myself mainly to the task of ensuring proper behavior from the children, though Robert's potent presence did much to quash childish antics on its own. Between bites he spoke of affairs of state as they affected Mary: who must be received at Wright House, who must be discouraged for the time being, and who was to be spurned outright. After the meal, the girls read from the Bible while Georgie did his best to sit still and listen, though the boy had taken to picking apart the hems of his skirts and committing other small acts of mayhem in his boredom. Robert quizzed the children after the night's reading, and they kept strictly to the text in their answers, replying only at the most literal level.

Mary and I would excuse ourselves to tuck them in, and it was as we helped Nell ready the children for bed that the best discussions took place.

"If God placed a sword at the tree of eternal life," Pearl wondered one night, "to keep Adam and Eve from it after the fall, why did He not place such a one at the tree of knowledge *before* Eve ate from it?"

"I thought the same thing," Jane said. "They were as innocent as children. Mama does not merely tell Georgie not to run into the street when we go to the market. She holds his hand."

Mary answered. "Suppose Georgie had a little playmate beckoning to him from across the road, vowing that there was far more fun to be had there? If he were to slip from my hand and dart into the street, the results would be disastrous. Naught I could do would save him."

"But you are not God," Pearl replied. "If you were, and you had the power to keep him from running into the street no matter what, would you not do it?"

"You children gain greater freedom of will as you grow. After all, I do not hold Jane's hand anymore." Mary took a cup of water from Georgie, and he wiped his mouth on his nightshirt.

"We have taken our share of falls and scrapes," Pearl conceded.

"But only small ones. Scrapes teach lessons, they do not kill you," Jane pointed out.

Pearl turned back to Mary. "And you would not have Georgie's first fall happen under a carriage's wheels."

"What I want to know is this," Annie chimed in. "If God sees all, how did Adam and Eve hide from Him in the garden?"

"Why do you not ask Papa?" Georgie suggested. "He is sure to know."

I pulled Annie's blankets up around her. "How many times have your mama or I discovered some mischief and demanded that the culprit show herself—"

"Or *himself*," Annie prompted with a sideways look at her brother.

"—or himself, though we knew full well that she or *he* was ensconced in the wardrobe?"

"You see, Master George?" Nell chimed in as she folded the children's clothes and placed them in the wardrobe. "No need to trouble your papa. Your mum and auntie have the answers, as well."

That night, Mary and I decided that Jane and Pearl were ready to move from the nursery into the empty room next to mine. They would soon be leaving childhood behind to become young ladies. Besides, the complexity of their questions might yet prompt the younger children to pose them to their father, and that would not do.

To her husband, Mary simply explained that the child she was expecting would make the nursery too crowded if we did not move the older girls out. He quite agreed, and we added the task of furnishing the new space to that of creating new clothes for me.

Wright House was not the only province ripe for change. The Rump Parliament had continued to disintegrate. It was simply too fractured to govern effectively, having eliminated all parliamentarians willing to negotiate with Charles I before his death, a purge that had left only a "rump" of the original body. Now Robert bandied about such names as Major Generals John Lambert and Thomas Harrison and Sirs Henry Vane and Thomas Fairfax, and as he relayed them, the conversations between him and his associates had moved beyond military strategy and now erupted into heated debates over government. Should there be another monarchy (with Cromwell as king), some single-ruler design with a council held in check by an elected parliament, or an assembly more closely aligned with biblical models?

One afternoon, as the children attended to their studies, I said to Mary, "If I am to go to state receptions, surely I should be well-versed enough to voice some knowledge, perhaps even views, of the weighty issues of the day."

"You will have very important views," she assured me with a rueful smile. "You are in favor of the army's stand that only pious men may serve in parliament, and you steadfastly believe the higher waistlines now in fashion are indeed much more modest and becoming to an upright woman than the old-fashioned long ones. And no matter what the latest whim in London may be, you still prefer tea to chocolate."

"Are you certain I should risk sparking such dissension?" I asked, brows raised. "And remind me again why it was that I ever left New England."

Twelve

Just before the park erupted into its autumnal finery, Mary proclaimed my clothing satisfactory, and I began to join army officers' wives for tea—exhausting affairs, every one. Failure to look my new acquaintances in the eyes gave me an appearance of shiftiness, whereas direct gazes invariably ended with each woman looking away from me, shame heating her pale cheeks—for trivial sins, really. My dearest wish was that I could grant to others my cursed faculties for a quarter of an hour.

"You see?" I would say to them. "Who among you has not been guilty of resenting your husbands or fathers? Who has not occasionally wished to be free from the demands of motherhood for a few brief hours? Is there one here who has never noticed a man with a fine face or taken a moment's unabashed pride in her work or her beauty? These weigh upon you as sins only because you have been told they were sins! Now that you have seen that these small thoughts do but make you human, kindly silence your consciences, for you are driving me mad!"

Given that this was not possible, I looked briefly into their faces, focusing mainly upon foreheads, then retreated to the periphery and held my tongue.

Pearl, however, held audience whenever she came downstairs with Jane to be presented. She showed off her needlework, always careful to point out some small flaw and explain how she endeavored to improve. In time, I came to suspect that she made these mistakes intentionally, just to provide for herself an opportunity to appear modest. It was purely an affectation. My daughter was well aware of her skill and beauty. Nonetheless, it created about her an air of purity and sweetness that seemed to captivate everyone she met.

Jane was a curious combination of the brigadier general and her mother. She was naturally quiet and reserved, but she had a happy heart. Pearl would not have her dear friend go unnoticed. Of Jane's samplers, she would point out their finest traits, and she spoke enthusiastically of Jane's intelligence and patience. Where Pearl's creativity manifested itself, like mine, through her needle, Jane's blossomed in the kitchen, and because Jane's modesty was genuine, Pearl made it her mission to ensure that every woman present knew just how vital Jane's contributions had been to the extraordinary fare served at Wright House on that particular day. Pearl's loyalty added to her popularity, though more than once I overheard comments about how different the gregarious and agreeable child was from her reticent and disturbing mother.

One October afternoon, with victory in her eyes, Mary waved before me her latest invitation to a state banquet at Whitehall—with my name included upon the summons.

"Mary, I am no one. I am a woman living upon the generosity of you and your husband. I cannot possibly—"

"You are the mother of an heiress of whom several very important families have taken notice. You live in the home of a man who is very important to England and who knows a great many secrets of state. Sooner or later, you knew you must draw some interest. You were *supposed* to draw interest."

"I think I am going to be ill. All those people, all their fears and judgments . . ."

"Enough!" Mary scolded. "Where is my old friend? The one who so loved art and beauty? Wait until you see the ceiling of the banquet hall! You'll hardly notice anything else. Where is Hester Lathrop who smiled and laughed and danced with me in the garden of my old home?"

I smiled. "Somehow, I doubt there is dancing at Whitehall Palace these days."

Mary sighed. "Alas, no, but we can imagine when there was."

We led each other in a country dance we had once loved, stepping merrily around the parlor table and laughing at how easily it all came back to us. The dance came to an abrupt halt when we spun and discovered Robert at the foot of the stairs, a scowl upon his face, his cloak draped over his arm.

Ordinarily, Mary hastened to please him in all things, apologizing for transgressions whether real or imagined. This time, though she stopped, she said nothing more than "Are you going out?"

"I am. You two are rather merry."

"Hester has been invited to Whitehall."

He looked at me. "We do not dance there."

I clasped my hands over my apron. "Of course not."

Mary and I watched him, our faces sober, until he drew on his cloak and left the house. Then we shook our heads, grinned at each other, and finished the dance amid much laughter.

The night of the banquet the mirror presented me with a version of myself not at all unlike that impetuous girl who had boarded a ship to America twelve years before. *That* Hester had gained little sympathy there, though the magistrates would have insisted that they'd shown great mercy in merely marking her a sinner, rather than killing her as the law allowed. Was it not better to keep the reckless Hester locked safely away in dreary, unadorned gray?

Cocking my head dubiously, I said to Mary, "I think the women would like me better in my old gowns."

Mary shook her head. "No woman will fear that you have designs upon her husband. To be utterly honest with you, you are as brazen as a turnip, Hester. Keep your head down, do not stare overmuch at anyone, and all will see only a lovely, reserved widow whose daughter must surely share her charms."

As though anyone could keep her head down at Whitehall Banqueting House. How shall I begin to describe it? The moment our carriage came into view of it, I was struck by the way it rose above the jumble of the old palace surrounding it, as though Zeus himself had lifted the hall from the summit of Olympus and nestled it there as a monument to Greece. Masonry of honey and dun appeared all the richer for the creamy white balustrades crossing it. And the gleaming exterior was but a hint at the grace and elegance that awaited us inside.

Robert, Mary, and I walked through the north doors, and a vast expanse opened up to us. The hall was of double-square proportions, the long walls lined in windows set into deep bays, each bay punctuated by half-columns. Above those stretched a balcony with similar windows and bays. The columns were again white, the walls rich cream, giving the whole space a simultaneously light and opulent feel. The many tables that filled the space glittered with crystal and silver set upon Irish linens—no doubt relics of the first Charles's court.

And what I have yet described was but the paltriest of the hall's beauty. My eyes could do naught but lift to the ceiling, where golden filigree and deeply carved gilded frames girdled a breathtaking array of paintings. Each tableau depicted people in flowing robes and plump, lively cherubim cavorting together. It is the nature of one's chin to remain behind when the rest of the face lifts heavenward, so I stood, mouth agape, and took in the wonder of that ceiling like Pearl when she visited her first London cathedral.

"Robert!" A man's voice attempted to break in on the spell, but I could not pull my gaze away long enough to ascertain its source. "Mistress Wright, and can it be your dear friend Mistress Prynne?"

"John!" Robert returned, his voice warm with camaraderie. "We have not seen you in some weeks."

"I was out of the country" came the reply.

"Hester," Mary prodded, "you remember Sir John Manning."

Reluctantly, for I was captivated by the art, I lowered my eyes to his face. Ah, yes, the man who had struck me at once as a kindred spirit, though I had never been able to define how. So, too, the man who'd had the poor taste to bed Mistress Chapham. He was, nonetheless, quite handsome, and the "Roundhead" cut of his dark hair but emphasized this.

"Sir John. Yes, I remember. Were you not merely Mister Manning at the time?"

He ducked his head in a gesture of modesty as affected as Pearl's. "My efforts in Scotland have gained more appreciation from Lord Cromwell than they merit."

"Congratulations," I replied and lifted my gaze again.

"Beautiful, are they not?" he asked.

"The colors are so vivid," I commented.

"Ah—color is not my forte. The iconography, however, is fascinating," he said.

Mary sighed. "Sir John will not be happy until he has instructed our Hester on the sight overhead. Look, Robert, there is Ambassador de Cardenas." She and her husband drifted away.

"Mistress Wright knows me too well. Have you heard about this ceiling?" he asked, and I shook my head. "These are the work of Peter Paul Rubens. Above us now, you see *Union of the Crowns*, symbolizing the joining of England and Scotland. King James sits upon the throne, an angel overlooking him from behind. Those two robed figures sharing the crown represent the two kingdoms, and the woman between them is Minerva, overseeing the union with wisdom. The narrower paintings on either side are *Hercules as Heroic Virtue Triumphing Over Discord*—you see Hercules with the club standing upon the representation of Discord—and *Minerva as Wisdom Conquering Sedition*."

"In this, both Wisdom and Sedition are represented by females, I see," I commented.

"Such complex ideas could hardly be represented by men. We are best reduced to simpler, brute concepts—one male beating another whose chief interest is in getting men to beat one another."

I tried to study his face to see whether he spoke in jest or earnest, but it was still tilted straight up, and I could not tell. He gestured to the enormous oval in the center of the ceiling. "*Apotheosis of James I*. The late monarch arises to his just reward upon the wings of an eagle, one foot upon a globe. He is led by Justice; she holds in her other hand scales and a thunderbolt, for she is powerful and impartial. The two veiled women are most likely Piety and Religion. You see that Religion holds a rather ponderous book."

"The King James Bible?" I offered, and Sir John nodded.

"Just so."

We moved more deeply into the room, narrowly skirting tables and other attendees as we kept our eyes mainly above us.

"At the far end, where the late King Charles sat before he lost his head over affairs of state just outside, is *Peaceful Reign of James I*."

"Standing to his right," I asserted, "I see Minerva has reappeared."

"Indeed, but now it is Mars she holds at bay."

"And upon whom does Mars tread?"

"A Fury."

"Ah, and there is Mercury, known by his winged cap!" I cried.

"Excellent. And the two embracing women?" he asked.

"I have no idea," I admitted.

"Peace and Abundance. Of all the icons in these paintings, I find they move me most."

I looked at him again; this time he met my gaze, and I saw very clearly what he masked behind his artistic appreciation. "Lecher," I accused, then clapped my hand over my mouth. I really had thought myself much improved, and I was disappointed to have allowed my thoughts to spill so freely. As others were unable to hide themselves with me, I seemed to suffer the same affliction with him.

He stared at me in shock for a moment, then he chuckled softly, and his blue eyes crinkled at the corners. "How come you to call me such a thing? Can a man not be moved by Peace and Abundance?"

"By all means," I answered dryly.

Surrounded by people whose chief interest was to cloak every flaw, every imperfection—in themselves and their state—in the illusion of pure righteousness, it struck me that we were naked, Sir John Manning and I. Naked to each other and utterly untroubled to be so. We were Adam and Eve before the fall, sinners who cared naught for our sins for we did not mark them as such.

"They look as if they might kiss," I observed, lowering my voice to a whisper.

"Do they not?" he replied wistfully, his voice a notch softer than mine. "And right plump and pretty they are."

I started to reassert my original conclusion regarding his character, but Mary rejoined us. "Has Sir John adequately lectured you upon the symbols in each work?" she asked.

"He has," I answered. "Sir John," I asked, "how came you to know all this?"

"I have a number of friends who are artists."

"Have you?" Mary asked. "How lovely. Robert seems to have no time for friendships beyond political allies, and he mentions you often. I would have thought you as embroiled as he, with no time for other companions."

"Quite true, Mistress Wright," Sir John assured her, and I wondered how she could possibly miss the fact that he wanted to devour her. It was a wonder she did not burst into flame from the look in his eyes. Then again, perhaps it was obvious only to me. "I should have said I *had* friends who were artists. They were a part of another life, when I was young. Ah—Sir Henry Vane has arrived. If you ladies will excuse me."

"Of course," Mary murmured.

"Thank you for the lesson," I said, and he smiled and nodded.

As soon as he had retreated beyond hearing, Mary turned to me and said, "You could do worse than John Manning."

"What?" I asked her.

"He is enamored of you. Oh, he is careful not to show it, but I can tell."

"Oh, I do not think—"

"The way he leaned toward you as you looked at the paintings together? And I have never seen him laugh with anyone. He is such a serious and pious man. Think on it, Hester. He is renowned for his upright life and clear-headed thinking. Before he became involved in the reformation of the government, he was studying to become a minister."

God save me from another minister. "Mary, it is Pearl for whom I seek a husband."

"But as Sir John Manning's stepdaughter, she could—"

"I think you misconstrue his attentions."

"Really, Hester, you must let go of the past. Roger is dead. Arthur is dead. And you are far from old."

I was, in fact, thirty, but there were times I felt twice the years.

Much to my dismay, my tablemates included not only the Wrights, but the Chaphams as well. Captain Chapham had spent most of the past year in Scotland and was now Major Chapham. His wife was clearly pleased by his ascension. After an interminable grace, she began her address. To hear her tell the story, her husband had been single-handedly responsible for the alliance between Cromwell and the Marquis of Argyll, and Chapham certainly didn't interfere with her delight in boasting.

As had been the case when we dined together at Wright House, I could not keep my eyes from Major Chapham. If anything, the dark cloud surrounding him had only grown darker, more turbulent. I perceived now a chill in the hall when, before we had been seated, the place had seemed overly warm. For the most part, he tried to avoid looking at or speaking to me, but time and again his eyes met mine, and the muscles in his jaw would flex in tension before he tore his gaze away.

Do not stare! I admonished myself, but to no avail. I could not identify the cause of his gloom, and it pricked my curiosity. I, who would normally have done anything not to know people's secret hearts, was dying to know his.

"Major Chapham," I summoned.

He turned to me with a glower. "Yes?"

"I should like to hear tales of your adventure. How did you find things in Scotland?"

He seemed to measure me for a moment, pressed a fist to his heart as if in pain, then looked away without answering.

It was then that I realized that Robert had been regarding us acutely. Irritated at having my curiosity rebuffed by Chapham, I stared boldly into Robert's eyes, but he had been on his best behavior of late. There was naught inside him that I could use to abash him.

Sir John had been assigned to the far end of our table, and he nodded earnestly at the discourse of a man across from him, though his eyes occasionally flicked down the table, hardly seeming to register me there. I thought of Arthur and how he could look right through me in public. It was necessary, of course, but I died a little every time.

As dinner wound down, Robert excused himself. He worked his way to the head table, leaning over Lord Cromwell's shoulder to whisper in his ear. I had not met the powerful man, in fact had only seen him from a distance. He was, even upon casual observation, a self-possessed man. His coloring was unremarkable, his clothing subdued, and yet there was no doubt who among the throng held the seat of power.

The two men glanced toward our table, though I could not tell precisely whom they were looking at. Lord Cromwell gestured to a servant, spoke to him briefly, then pointed him in our direction. When the fellow arrived at our table, he told both Major Chapham and me that we were to report to the more private chambers below the hall.

I could think of nothing I had done wrong, and yet my heart leaped into my throat. In my experience, being called before any sort of public official did not bode well. What could a summons from Oliver Cromwell portend? I glanced once more at the remarkable ceiling, recalling that it was one of the last things King Charles saw before he was beheaded just outside by some of the very men dining here tonight.

Thirteen

———⋗◦⋖———

We followed the servant outside and down a flight of stairs that led to the undercroft, a grotto-like space constructed of multiple arches and alcoves with vaulted ceilings. Originally designed for the king's more private gatherings, the place left one with the distinct impression that anything might happen here—drunken debauchery, hidden executions. I had no pressing desire to participate in either, and I found myself rubbing damp palms over the skirt of my gown.

What could Oliver Cromwell want of me? Why had he summoned me here with Major Chapham, a man I hardly knew? I glanced at my unlikely companion, who kept his arms crossed tightly over his chest and appeared cold, though I found the temperature quite acceptable.

In the tense silence between Chapham and me, it seemed an hour or more passed. It was then that I remembered the trip across the ocean and Pearl's certainty that somehow I would meet Oliver Cromwell. Irrationally, it seemed to me that this was somehow her doing, that by predicting this meeting, she had brought it to pass. I shook my head and clasped my hands in front of me to keep them from shaking. I was being ridiculous. Surely this had something to do with Robert, our mutual acquaintance, who had recently spoken to Cromwell and looked in our direction.

Despite the fact that time seemed to have slowed to a crawl, I am certain it was only a few minutes before Robert appeared with Lord Cromwell by his side. I found that I could gaze directly upon Cromwell, and while the sight of the powerful man left me awash in cold dread, he did not flinch from me. This was a leader sure of his position, pure in his intentions, devoted to his faith. The warts that marked his face shrank in the light of passion and intelligence shining in his eyes. In all my years of knowing the hypocrisy and weakness that plague my fellow human beings, I have learned to be more apprehensive still in the face of that kind of certainty. A man so certain can destroy or even take a life without the slightest qualm, confident that God is on his side.

I wanted to cry, "Whatever it is that brings you to call me here, it is a mistake! I have done nothing wrong!" But such men are not moved by protestations of innocence.

Then again, few enough would call me innocent.

Robert introduced me, and when I sank into a deep curtsy, Lord Cromwell surprised me with a gentle admonishment. "Arise, Mistress Prynne. I am no king, nor would I be."

He gestured Major Chapham and me into seats side by side at a table in one alcove, waiting until we were settled before sitting across from us, Robert beside him.

"Good to see you, Joseph," Cromwell said to Chapham.

Chapham flashed a nervous smile. "Thank you, my lord. It is good to be back in England."

"Mistress Prynne," Cromwell said, "I am told that you and Major Chapham's wife are friends."

I looked sharply toward Robert, then back at Cromwell. "We have had occasion to converse from time to time, my lord." I wondered if that was a flicker of approval that I saw on his face. Would he have known it to be a lie if I had merely agreed?

"Has she told you how tirelessly her husband has worked for the Commonwealth in Scotland?"

"She has," I replied, working to keep the irritation from my voice. *Ad nauseum,* I added silently.

"Tell me again, Major, about your most recent endeavors there," Cromwell said. I might have felt annoyance at having to hear it all again, but the shroud that enveloped Chapham darkened and roiled ominously, and all I felt was dread.

Chapham kept his attention focused across the table, ignoring me. "As I reported, my lord, I led a small party to—"

"Do include Mistress Prynne in your audience," Robert prompted. "I think it will be of special interest to her."

"Of course." He turned to me and coughed. "I—ahem! Scotland is quite important, as you know. They have been somewhat reluctant to—"

"She lives in my house," Robert reminded him. "She is aware of the situation in Scotland. We were hoping to hear more of *your* last excursion there."

"I—we—that is, Argyll's army and ours required some coordination."

"And you coordinated them?" Robert asked.

"I met with their leaders, and we coordinated exercises."

"Is that all?" Cromwell pushed.

Chapham glanced at me and coughed again, harder this time.

And then I realized why I was there. Robert had experienced firsthand my uncanny perception, and others had been known to comment on their discomfort in my presence. Lord Cromwell somehow doubted Chapham's story, and Robert had offered me to provide proof of its accuracy or falsehood. Hot anger singed me. How *dare* they use me thus?

"My lord—" I began, but Cromwell raised his hand, and I fell silent. His was an extraordinarily compelling air of authority. Involuntarily I recalled in vivid detail that day upon the scaffold, forced to stand mute before the crowd, wanting to shout them all down, but fearful and ashamed. What if Robert or Cromwell had learned how I had come by my intuition? What if my newfound life was about to crumble here as it had in America?

I met Major Chapham's gaze and watched his eyes widen and his face turn red. His throat moved convulsively, his collar twitching. He set his jaw and glared at me in open animosity.

Treason. I had seen the black shadow of his crime but not recognized it, for it was one of the few sins I had never committed myself in deed or thought. Though he looked as if he wanted me dead, I gave no quarter. One of us would be exposed this night, and it was not going to be I. "I did ask at dinner," I reminded him.

He thrust his finger into his collar and cleared his throat several times, looking at Robert. "I spoke with the Marquis of Argyll himself, once or twice."

"Look at Mistress Prynne," Robert repeated. "Did you meet with anyone else of importance in Scotland?"

Chapham glanced over at me and cleared his throat several more times. "No, not really. I . . . I . . . I had my men, a . . . and— What?" he suddenly ejaculated. "Why do you look at me that way?" He stood and addressed Cromwell. "This is of no interest to her. Who is she to the likes of us?"

"She is my wife's friend," Robert replied.

Cromwell remained in his seat, his penetrating stare fixed upon Chapham. "Did you visit with any of the Highland chieftains while you were there, Joseph? Angus MacDonnell, perhaps?"

"No!" he shouted. "No! What business would I have with Royalists like—"

"To Mistress Prynne, if you please," Cromwell said.

"No. I have nothing to say to her."

"My lord," I said, tired of the game, more frightened than I cared to admit, even to myself, "Major Chapham is correct. I have no—"

"Look Mistress Prynne directly in the eyes and tell her that you had no dealings with MacDonnell. Then the matter will be settled, Major," Cromwell assured him, his tone steady and patient.

Chapham slouched, and his tone was sullen. "No."

Cromwell stood, leaning on the table and glaring at Chapham. "Do it!" His voice bounced from ceiling to ceiling, ringing through the archways.

Now, when Chapham looked at me, his eyes were wild, and he struggled visibly to keep his head turned toward me. "I never—I would not—I am a loyal Englishman! My allegiance has always been to . . . to—"

"To whom?" Robert shouted, moving round the table toward Chapham. "To Cromwell or to Charles? Answer the question!"

Instead, Chapham turned and faced the wall. "I may have met MacDonnell somewhere. He is a powerful man, allied with the most influential clans. There were state gatherings. I may have met him at some point, but not intentionally."

"Look at Mistress Prynne," Cromwell said again.

Spinning back to me, Chapham shouted into my face, spraying me with spittle. "It is long since time for us to piss or get off the pot! England needs a king! If the position is not to Cromwell's liking, then it may as well be Charles's!" Next he rounded upon Robert. "This commonwealth will fall, mark my words. We were wrong. There can be no England without a king! Just as the Royalists have lost everything that was once theirs, we in Cromwell's army will pay for choosing the losing side. Well, I will not lose! I will not!" Even as he drew breath to spew more, the irony stuck him. He had already lost. "Bitch!" he seethed, spitting in my face again. "I will see you fall."

I had not seen the guards hiding in the alcoves, but now they stepped forward, four of them, while two more opened the door and more guards poured forth.

"Take him to the Tower," Cromwell commanded as he handed me a square of linen with which to wipe Chapham's saliva from my face.

Chapham appeared to have said all he had to say. He did not protest as they led him away. Dismissed, Robert followed, leaving Cromwell and me alone.

"That was a most intriguing demonstration, Mistress Prynne. Brigadier General Wright has mentioned you and your . . . unsettling . . . demeanor before, but I confess I was skeptical."

"I . . ." I stopped. God help me. How had I come to this?

"You . . . ?"

"I cannot explain it."

"It might be thought some sort of sorcery," he prodded.

I could think of no way to respond, though my thoughts raced. *No, no, no! I cannot be accused of witchcraft! My Pearl! What would become of her?*

But Cromwell resumed in his chair, seemingly disinclined to call any guards against me. "Have you always had this effect upon people?"

I thought back to all those years of shame and degradation, the slow and steady climb that I had made from the depths of ignominy. Well I knew upon what steps had I made that climb. The truth. Every day, everyone I saw knew the worst there was to know of me. They had done the worst that they could do, laying me bare to their judgment, taking my kindness and my charity and throwing it in my face. In time, I had nowhere to go but up. And they? After a while, the letter I wore became a burden upon *their* souls, a constant reminder of *their* darkest secrets.

Indeed, the truth had eventually become my strength, but for Pearl, now it was a weakness, and we had come too far to allow it to catch up to us. In England, adultery was a hanging offense— a sentence thus far carried out only against women. The charge demanded no lower price than witchcraft. Neither indictment left me alive or Pearl protected.

Ever upon the precipice between truth and falsehood I stood, a steep descent to either side. "No, my lord, I have not always been thus. This—effect, as you say—has come to me through my own journey from sin to redemption."

"And you are redeemed, then?" he asked.

I lifted my chin. "I believe that I am."

He rose again, but only to fetch a bottle of wine and two goblets from a nearby cupboard. As he filled one, he said, "It must be a tale worth hearing."

"It was a private matter," I said.

He filled the second goblet and handed it to me. "A sinner's redemption is an instructive thing, as I have just witnessed."

"It is also a deeply personal thing. I paid the price. Whatever instruction may be gained by others must be bestowed as it was tonight."

We stared at each other for a long moment, subtle defiance in me, overt calculation in him. Finally he smiled, but it did nothing to ease my discomfort. "Then I suppose the details are between you and God now. In any case, a woman who exposes truth and leads men back to righteousness"—he nodded toward the closed door, and I wondered whether he meant Chapham only or if Robert had told him about his indiscretions in Ireland—"would seem an unlikely sorceress. If she were to continue to lend her talents to the benefit of this great commonwealth, I would be doubly assured."

A commonwealth that had committed regicide but had yet to effect any stable form of government in exchange. A commonwealth that had taken away Christmas and the theater with no thought of how the people felt about such actions. A commonwealth whose governors had appointed themselves their fellow man's judges on earth. A commonwealth led by a man who could, without a qualm, blackmail a woman whose only wish was to secure her daughter's future. Oh, how *great* a commonwealth indeed.

But its leader had spoken clearly. It was a commonwealth that trusted me only so long as I could be of use to it. To him.

I took a long draft of wine. "I would be honored to serve the commonwealth in whatever capacity I can, my lord."

Fourteen

Dinner churned in my stomach with my emotions all night long, so that by morning I could not tolerate the thought of breakfast. Instead of joining the others downstairs, I went into the nursery where Nell sorted through Pearl's and Jane's belongings to determine which would move with them into the new bedchamber and which would remain behind to be used by Annie.

"Mistress 'ester," Nell greeted me with a glance over her shoulder and a broad grin. She busily folded shifts, and her red hair escaped its cap in curly wisps, tiny ornaments around her plain face. "And 'ow was the gathering last night?"

"Exhausting," I replied.

"What did you do?" she asked.

"We prayed. 'Thank You, God, for the food we eat. Thank You for all our victories. Continue to lead us upon Your glorious path. Deliver us from sin. Punish our enemies. Bless Cromwell. Bless the army.' We ate, and then we prayed some more." I left out the private meeting in between.

Nell clucked her tongue and sighed.

"What?" I asked.

"Nothing," she said, lifting a pair of shoes. "Pearl's, yes?" I nodded, and Nell continued. "Is the banqueting 'all as beautiful as I've 'eard?"

I assured her that it was, describing the paintings and imparting all that Sir John had told me. When she asked what the women had worn, the answer was simple—black. Beautiful shapes, of course, and some lovely lace and embroidery, but little variation in color. She sighed and clucked again.

"Come now," I admonished. "Why such sighs?"

"It's not for me to say, mistress."

"Come, Nell, we have spoken frankly before, you and I, and you have heard many a dubious conversation here in the nursery. You know that you may speak your mind safely."

"Well, it's just a shame that you couldn't 'ave gone way back when the king was there. Lovely masquerades, the older servants say, and women that sparkled like fairies made their gowns. A pure waste, it is." She pulled the last dress from Jane's wardrobe and placed it on top of several others on the bed. Her hand smoothed a few wrinkles from the russet fabric. Jane would be twelve soon, and as her young form was beginning to mature, Mary had started to replace her brighter gowns with less conspicuous colors.

Nell's sentiments did nothing for my upheaval. How much did people miss the old England—the king and the pageantry? Joseph Chapham was so certain of the commonwealth's eventual failure. He had risked much on this postulation.

"Nell," I asked, "you have friends outside Wright House, have you not, and relatives?"

"Certainly, mistress. My folks is country people, but educated, and they write every week, and I 'ave friends 'ere in London. We meet sometimes on our Sundays off—after church, of course."

I picked up Pearl's dresses, still made of pretty blues, pinks, and greens. "And how do they feel about the state of things?"

We both moved from the nursery and mounted the stairs to the higher floor, clothing spilling over our laden arms.

"We aren't political sorts, mistress," Nell said, panting a little. "We gossip a bit about those that couldn't make it that day or tell news from 'ome. Most of us are from the country, come 'ere to find work, maybe avoid a bad marriage, maybe look for one."

Earlier that week, we had moved beds and wardrobes into the girls' chamber, and we laid the gowns on the beds, relieving ourselves of the burdens.

I set to work putting Pearl's gowns in her wardrobe. "But as you point out, London has changed much. Surely you all speak on it from time to time."

Nell gave a guarded, carefully indifferent shrug. It was unfair, I knew, to ask her to walk on such thin ice. After all, her pay came from Robert's purse, not mine. Still, I had been so isolated at Wright House. I dearly wished to hear the sentiments of those beyond our walls.

"I do miss putting on plays and dancing with the children as we did when the brigadier general was away," I said, straightening Pearl's clothes where they hung. "And it is too bad that the younger children will not be able to partake of Pearl and Jane's discussions, but I suppose this is for the best. This will have to become the room in which conversations may happen that the brigadier general will never know of."

Nell had been hanging up Jane's dresses, but she understood my meaning and grinned at me. "All right, mistress, if you must know. We wouldn't mind a bit more finery ourselves, my friends and me, and the kind of dancing and dallying the older girls we'd known were allowed to do. And what with taxes paying for wars all over, no one's employers is paying overmuch, and there's no Christmas gifts to make up for it any. Times could be better."

We were quiet for a while, putting away shoes and books, occasionally conferring to recall which girl actually owned a particular item that was often treated as community property. Meanwhile, I turned Nell's words over and over in my mind. It seemed that Chapham had been paying far closer attention than we at Wright House, better reading the discontent around him.

Regicide was dangerous. When a king ruled by divine right, then changes in sovereigns and social orders were left in the hands of the elite. If an obscure country gentleman could help orchestrate the execution of a king and then seize his power after, what might commoners do when they tired of the new leader?

What if Joseph Chapham was right?

"Ah, here you are," Mary said, stepping into the room. She smiled, but there was tension in her eyes and around her upturned mouth. "My goodness, you two have been busy! I worried that you were ill, Hester, when you did not come down to breakfast."

"I think I ate too much last night," I replied.

"Nell, will you leave Mistress Prynne and me? I brought up Georgie and Annie; they are unattended in the nursery."

"Certainly, madam," Nell answered and left.

"Where are Jane and Pearl?" I asked.

"In the parlor." Mary lowered herself onto Jane's bed and rubbed her hand lightly over her stomach. Her high waists and voluminous skirts usually covered the bulge there, but when she pressed her hand to it, her fecund state became apparent. "Robert told me where you had gone last night between dinner and the closing prayer—something about Lord Cromwell and Major Chapham and your . . . your . . . ability. I was worried. You seemed in a state of shock all the way home, and it was obvious much was amiss between you and Robert, though neither of you spoke much."

I laid Pearl's ribbons in straight, careful rows in a wardrobe drawer. Had Robert bothered to mention that he was the one who had told Cromwell of my "ability"?

"Are you all right?" she asked.

I nodded.

"Come sit with me, Hester. I am sorry that he pulled you into the middle of it all, truly. Please do not be angry with me."

Complying with her request, I sat down and put my arm around her shoulders. "I am not angry with you. I am apprehensive."

"I have made it very clear to Robert that if aught should happen to you because of his—"

"Mary, what if things never fall into place? What if England simply must have a king to survive?"

Mary rose a little awkwardly and went to shut the door. "Leave that to the men, Hester. Just do as they ask. That is our lot—"

"And our daughters'?"

"It is their lot in any case. It does not matter who sits upon the throne or in parliament or anywhere else. A woman's lord is her husband."

"And if her lord has sworn allegiance to the wrong sovereign?"

Mary did not reply. She leaned against the door and stared at some spot above my head.

"Mary, what if the very unions we seek for our daughters set them inadvertently against some future crown?"

Placing her fingers to her temple and shaking her head, she replied, "I cannot see the future. Can you, now? Has your vision moved beyond sin?"

"No. I just—"

"We can only act upon what we know, and all I know is that my husband is in Oliver Cromwell's army. My future, my children's futures depend upon *this* commonwealth."

"No one cares for our futures save *us*!"

"Then you must serve this government," Mary insisted.

"I cannot make it succeed."

"It *will* succeed. It *must*. Hester, you can do something—something important. You can help keep rebellion at bay."

"You do not care for the way of things, now," I reminded her.

"We do not always care for what must be. I do not care for Robert, but he is necessary to me."

"I am getting along very well without my husband."

"Because of mine."

We stared at each other for a long moment; Mary was the first to look away, but also the first to speak. "Remember, you were to be my one friend unsusceptible to politics."

That I might be unable to fulfill that promise was not my choice. I had been dragged by her husband into an arena I had no desire to enter, but since I was already there, it made no sense to trouble her more. I rose and went to her, taking both her hands in mine. "You will always be my dearest friend, Mary."

Tears shimmered in her eyes, and she pulled her hands from mine. "If ever I must choose between you and my husband, Hester, I cannot choose you."

Fifteen

I had imagined myself trapped at Whitehall the very next day, interrogating seditious men and sending them to the gallows, but in actuality I did not visit Whitehall again for some weeks. When Cromwell began to summon me, it was to join various groups for conversation. My instructions were simple. If I detected no more than private faults, like my own, the matter remained between the culprit and God. If, on the other hand, the offense was against the state, I was to unobtrusively drop an embroidered handkerchief on the offender's vacated chair as the guests and I took our leave. I carried five such squares of linen with me each time, but never had use for more than two at once.

It did not take long for rumors to spread. Those invited to meetings at Whitehall with Cromwell, Secretary of State John Thurloe, and me were either drawn more tightly into Cromwell's confidence or they were arrested. After a handful of such meetings, accounts disseminated regarding the evasive behavior of accused traitors whenever they had tried to look at me. Naturally, the first hypotheses regarding this revolved around sorcery and witchcraft, but Cromwell's distinction as a man of ironclad virtue and piety warred with such theories. At last, Cromwell's sentiments prevailed. I had a gift from God that I used for the glory of England—hardly the deed of Satan's emissary.

The notoriety and awe such stories engendered meant that I no longer attended receptions as "the widow living at Wright House." I received invitations upon my own terrible merits, and it became a badge of honor among the upper echelon to be able to hold my gaze in conversation. Many did so at considerable cost. They spoke at length to me, a hundred white lies and momentary shameful thoughts pricking their souls like pins and needles, making my own flesh crawl in empathy. I watched desperation fill their faces, heard dread begin to seize their throats. Rather than forcing people to turn away or allowing them to propel themselves to the brink of public confession, I would contrive some reason to turn away myself. Thus their associates acquitted them of all frailty.

I did it for myself, really. I had no desire to become Mother Confessor to parliament and the whole of the New Model Army. Let them judge one another like rats that bit and clawed their way through the rest of their packs in the trash heaps of London. My chief concern lay in the ultimate consequence of it all. It seemed England could fare no better in the long run than London rats. At least a king of rats, however corrupt, might have a chance of imposing order among the hordes.

Mary was spared it all once she began her lying-in, and she remained at home after little Oliver was born.

The name was Robert's choice, not Mary's, and he was such a plump, cheerful boy—nothing like his fierce, ascetic namesake. I took to calling him Ollie, which Mary agreed fit him much better, and soon the rest of the children and Nell followed suit. The sobriquet annoyed Robert to no end, as it definitely diluted the intended honor to Cromwell, but he was powerless to reverse it.

In April of 1653 Cromwell dissolved the parliament, leaving no one formally at the nation's helm. The so-called Fifth Monarchists hailed the move as a certain sign that Christ's Kingdom was at hand. This group had ascertained that, according to Revelations, Christ would return in 1666, when there would be no need of an earthly government, but I saw no sign of the Savior's imminent approach. To the relief of many in England, a nominated assembly was created and assumed the name of Parliament. At the moment, any form of government, stable or not, would do.

Come July, rumors abounded that William Cunningham, Earl of Glencairn, was plotting a Royalist uprising, even as Katherine

Chidley presented the new parliament with a petition signed by six thousand women calling for the release of political malcontent John Lilburne. These two events brought me to Whitehall two or three times a week to discern for the Council of State the intentions of scores of associates of Lilburne and Glencairn, and subtle symbolism was no longer enough. Rather than merely listening to the conversation and dropping an incriminating scrap of linen on chairs, I was directly involved in interviews.

There was a rather unexpected benefit to all this. As Cromwell compensated me for my services, it meant that I no longer needed to use Pearl's funds to pay for our upkeep, and I began to garner a small savings of my own. Still, it was hardly enough to requite the toll upon my nerves.

Since the two men, Glencairn and Lilburne, and their situations had nothing to do with each other, my intellectual perceptions began to interfere with my intuitive ones. From time to time I would forget whom I was questioning about what; facts became twisted and convoluted.

"I have forgotten," I said to an officer named Jones, "could you tell me again of your business in Bruges last autumn?"

He gave me a look of utter confusion. "I have never been to Bruges."

"*Never?*" I pressed. I could have sworn that he had mentioned such a venture in an earlier discussion of John Lilburne. It seemed a flat lie, and yet he continued to look openly into my face.

"Never. What would I be doing in Bruges?" Jones asked.

Cromwell leaned forward. "We are discussing Major General *Robert* Lilburne in Edinburgh, Mistress Prynne. It was Captain Johnson who spoke of Bruges and *John* Lilburne yesterday."

"Oh." I pressed my fingers to my throbbing temples. I seldom left Whitehall without a headache.

Cromwell's secretary of state and trusted intelligence adviser, John Thurloe, had no compassion. He frowned so deeply that his high forehead seemed to wrinkle all the way to the top of his scalp. "If we called a halt to an investigation every time Mistress Prynne felt some infirmity, we should make no progress at all," he snarled.

At the conclusion of one particularly hot, dank afternoon— the sort where everything that stank in London and the Thames ripened and fermented—Robert Wright and I shared a carriage back to Wright House. My head pounded, my soul was in turmoil, and my and my stomach churned, and at the moment I considered the whole of my complaints to be his fault.

"Does it truly rankle you so to serve your country?" Robert asked.

"I beg your pardon?"

"You clearly feel yourself much put-upon."

Hours of political fencing had depleted what poor store of diplomacy I possessed. "What rankles is the fact that you count my service as some credit to you. You use me to feed your pride, then you call it patriotism."

"Well, well. It has been some time since you unsheathed your claws upon me."

"I am in no mood to fight, Robert, nor am I inclined to mince words for you. Count yourself fortunate that I avoid you whenever possible."

"There is no need, Hester. You hold no power over me anymore."

"Ah, so you cast stones now because you are without sin?" I locked my eyes onto his, and he smiled benignly. *Deeper,* I willed myself, my eyes narrowing, *past that which he admits even to himself.*

His smile faltered. His eyes shifted. Smugness tugged the corners of my mouth upward.

"Witch!" he muttered, looking out the carriage window. "You make me doubt myself when there is no cause for doubt."

"I am but a mirror, Robert. I reflect that which you bring to me, naught else." Then I sat back and relished the silence that lasted the remainder of the ride.

At home in the parlor we found Mary pacing, and she rushed to Robert as soon as we came in. "Have you heard? Major Chapham will not stand trial."

"No?" Robert asked. "I have heard nothing at all, but Hester and I have had weightier matters upon our minds."

Since he did not reach out to Mary in her distress, I did. I embraced her briefly, pressing my damp cheek to hers. "Tell us all."

"Mistress Tobin came today. Her husband told her that, to avoid trial Joseph Chapham has pled guilty to conspiracy, forsworn his allegiance to Charles, resigned his commission, and forfeited all his property. His family shall be destitute."

"He kept his head in exchange," Robert commented.

How did he manage to look so comfortable in the heat? I pulled the cap from my head, and Robert's nostrils flared at the breach of propriety, but he said nothing.

"It could have been worse," I said to Mary.

"It just—it was so sudden. He and his wife were just like us, and now—now they have gone to live with her family. His will have nothing to do with them."

"Sudden?" I asked. "He's been in prison nine months."

She turned to her husband. "What would *we* do, Robert?"

He gave an exasperated sigh. "He is paying for his crimes, Mary. *We* are loyal Englishmen."

Mary cast a stricken look at me, and I knew what was in her thoughts. Loyal so long as Cromwell ruled.

"Have you found all the Glencairn conspirators, Hester?" she asked, her voice strained. "And what of John Lilburne's trial, Robert? What if he still refuses to plead?"

Robert pinched the bridge of his nose and winced slightly. "He will plead or he will die, Mary. Why do you worry? Politics is not a woman's game." I lifted my brows at him. "Generally," he amended through his teeth.

In the end, John Lilburne pled not guilty, and the jury agreed. Parliament honored his acquittal by ordering him locked in the Tower of London, raising cries of "foul play!" all across the city. While I had often wondered how fair were the trials—especially the sentences—extended to those I accused, it now became a constant jab to my conscience. Was there no true justice in England? Who was I to judge others, whatever ability my sight might give me? My own slate was far from clean.

By autumn of 1653 the navy was up in arms, for the treasury was strapped and the seamen were far behind on pay. They marched upon Whitehall and were thwarted by the army, though soldiers, too, were in dire straits. Even the support of the Fifth Monarchists had begun to wane. Robert joined Mary in her pacing, and I seemed to be dropping more and more embellished squares of white linen on chairs at Whitehall Palace. Despite the critical need for a strong leader, Cromwell continued to refuse the crown. In

December, the new parliament forced his hand. They voted to sur-
render their power to Cromwell, then packed up and went home.

On the sixteenth day of that month, Oliver Cromwell took a
title unlike any before in England. In a quiet, modest ceremony,
he was installed as Lord Protector of the Commonwealth. The
Fifth Monarchists decried him as a king by any other name, but it
was deemed cause for much joy by his followers. The happy mood
lasted for days, with celebrations hosted by Robert's colleagues
throughout the week that followed. Perhaps the greatest blessing
was the brief respite in the search for conspirators and the desire
of every officer and his wife to use me to prove his or her integrity. I was allowed merely to *converse*—about children, servants,
recipes—common womanly concerns.

Christmas may have been forbidden, but when it came our turn
to host a fête celebrating England's new order, Wright House
ushered winter in with laughter, gaiety, roast goose, and plum
pudding all the same. Every seat at the table had been taken and
several more added. Since the guest list included the Tobins, I
found conversation that was comfortable and convivial. The children ate at their own table set up in the parlor, their faces alight
at the unaccustomed holiday.

Of course, naught could prevent the men from falling into discussions of politics. It struck me odd how serious Sir John Manning was when surrounded by his associates. In my few dealings
with him, especially during my first visit to Whitehall, I'd thought
him more lighthearted, perhaps even prone to mischief. Tonight,
when Mister Tobin expressed his happiness at having parliament
reconvene so that he might get back to work as one of its clerks,
Sir John engaged him in a rather patronizing lecture on just how
much Mister Tobin might expect parliament and its functions to
change. Later, at a colonel's suggestion that the lord protector's
installation might have been done with greater pomp and ceremony, it was Sir John who chided him for being tempted to back-
slide into the old way of doing things. "Have you forgot why
Charles the First lost his head, man?" he demanded.

The carnal side I had seen briefly at Whitehall might have been
a figment of my imagination had he not clearly acknowledged it at
the time. He spoke politely, if somewhat distantly, to the females

present, and he partook of almost none of the wine. All in all, I found him a disappointment.

The party was a far cry from drunken revelry, but I'd had enough to drink that it seemed prudent to step outside and clear my head in the cold, crisp air, and I slipped through the kitchen and out the back door. The front of the house faced onto the park, the back onto a heavily traveled thoroughfare. *If one must be in London,* I thought as I stood on the rear steps, *it is best to be here in winter, when coal smoke is the prevailing scent in the air. Not pleasant, but neither is it putrid, and that is no small blessing.*

I was surprised when Sir John joined me, closing the door behind him. Once outside, he took a deep breath and exhaled a cloud of steam.

"Well, Mistress Prynne," he said, "do you imagine that the protector will still have need of your rather unique perception?"

"I would prefer to think not," I said.

"You believe the victory sealed then?"

I turned to look at him and was puzzled afresh. His eyes now twinkled much more like those of the Sir John I thought I knew.

"Is any victory ever sealed?" I replied.

"Ah, you are indeed a wise woman, Mistress Prynne. That *is* the question, is it not?"

"And your answer, Sir John?"

"Any system devised by humans will have its flaws and leave us ill-content."

"You prefer a biblical model?"

He waited a long time, studying me in the light that trespassed from the streetlights beyond. At last he said, "What do you see when you look at me, Hester Prynne?"

"I am unsure." I wished that I knew. It was unsettling how easily he changed from one man to another.

"You, unsure? The famous and terrible Mistress Prynne who has passed such certain judgment on so many in the name of the protector?"

There was something about the way he pronounced Cromwell's title that gave me pause—the slightest tinge of insolence.

"I would prefer some other occupation," I told him. "In New England, I was known for my skill with a needle."

"Then why place the point to fellow citizens?"

"When you look at *me,* Sir John, what do *you* see?"

He answered immediately, as though he had already given the matter much thought. "A woman with secrets."

"Not a witch?"

A bark of laughter erupted from him, absorbed by the sounds of the city. "A witch? Yes, I have heard such nonsense, but I confess it did not strike me likely."

"Well, it struck Robert Wright possible, and Cromwell through him."

Sir John crossed his arms against the chill that had begun to cut through my clothes, as well. "Of course. Damn. What is it about you, though? How do you so unerringly find the traitors to the protectorate?"

"There are those who insist that I have made mistakes—accused innocent men."

"Innocence is a matter of perspective. Intention is everything."

I shook my head. This man was an utter enigma—one moment a lighthearted rascal; another a somber supporter of Cromwell; and yet another, a philosopher.

"What *do* I see when I look at you, Sir John Manning?"

"You shall have to tell me someday," he said and went back inside.

Sixteen

———➤•◦•◄———

From the very start, 1654 was a year of conspiracies that seemed to spread like the pox. Perhaps the Royalists were emboldened by the considerable forces raised by Glencairn, enough that Charles II decided the time had come to place Major General John Middleton in charge of them. Perhaps Charles had begun to escalate his position because he had learned that Cromwell was quietly pursuing an alliance with Spain against France—the country that had taken Charles in after his father's death. Whatever the cause, it seemed that the new *Instrument of Government* under which England now functioned was not the panacea England had hoped.

In April, shortly after Pearl's twelfth birthday, rumors came to Whitehall that a group of Anabaptists were plotting Cromwell's murder. Secretary John Thurloe, still Cromwell's chief intelligence counselor, decided it was past time for open conversation. Men whose loyalty had once been considered unimpeachable were to be invited for surreptitious interrogation. The undercroft, he insisted, was the best venue, so that I might hide in a separate alcove and listen.

"Mister Secretary," I explained, "I must be able to look the men in the eyes. I cannot tell anything by their voices."

He paced, stirring the abundant hair that fell backward from his vast forehead. "You said once that you see things—a cloud or a ghostly mantle. We can seat them facing away from your hiding place so that you can look, unseen, upon their backs."

"When I look into their *faces* I may see shapes or colors hovering about the rest of their bodies. Even then, I may not. I have no control over the manner in which this thing manifests itself."

Thurloe turned to Cromwell. "Then she is of no use to us! When anyone is summoned to Whitehall and Mistress Prynne awaits him, he knows exactly why he has been summoned and his guard is up. We can learn nothing if she must be visible."

Cromwell absently stroked the wart on his chin with his thumb. "Then let her remain in the open. Either way we learn where each man's allegiance lies."

"We need more than conspirators, Oliver, we need details. We need to know plans."

Thurloe's latest strategy brought me face-to-face with that which had generally followed, unbeknownst to me, my naming of traitors in the past. At worst, I had assumed each one imprisoned until he confessed his deeds against the state, but I soon learned that I had been mistaken. As before, I sat with men who had raised Thurloe's suspicions, but I no longer dropped a handkerchief as a sign. I simply nodded to Cromwell, and the individual was arrested on the spot. If he was not forthcoming in the details that Thurloe required, the culprit went to the Tower, where he might be *persuaded* to reveal the names of his accomplices and the fine points of their plans.

In deference to my sex, Cromwell saw no need for me to be present while information was wrung from the prisoner, but I found it small comfort. I stood in the protector's receiving room when the first man, one named Cook, was dragged to me directly after questioning, unable to walk under his own power. His face was bruised, his cheeks marked by blistered gashes as though singed by hot iron, as was done to thieves in New England, and his battered lips were pressed tightly together, quivering in spite of his efforts at self-control. Filthy, bloodstained clothing covered whatever the protectorate's most skilled inquisitors had inflicted upon the rest of him.

It was nearly impossible to look into his face. The last time I had seen Mister Cook, he was neatly appareled in a somber coat and pristine collar. He had broken bread with us, holding civilized discourse, and only the slightest shadow of treason had fallen across his brow. I told Thurloe that at the time—some indirect involvement, I had said. Nonetheless, that Mister Cook had been transformed into this broken, despondent creature filled with thoughts of venomous murder and desperate suicide was my burden to bear.

It was a burden I could *not* bear, and I turned and fled into Cromwell's private office. He followed, Thurloe on his heels.

"You must listen to him repeat the information that he has given," Thurloe barked at me. "You must tell us whether it is the truth or whether he has spoken lies designed merely to end the torment."

I ignored Thurloe and turned to Cromwell. "How am I to sort through it all, Protector?" I pleaded, doubling over to fight the roiling nausea that assailed my gut. "I cannot tell whether the darkness I perceive is hatred for the torturer or lies. Goodness knows if the man did not hate you before you arrested him, he does now. My own emotions are so stirred—"

"You pity him?" Thurloe scoffed.

"I look at him and I see only my part in his suffering."

"Suffering he has earned," Thurloe insisted.

"John," Cromwell interrupted, "I think it would be best if Mistress Prynne and I speak alone. See the prisoner back to the Tower, will you?"

"What? She must—"

Cromwell leveled an adamant look at Thurloe, and the man held his tongue and obeyed. Closing the door behind Thurloe, Cromwell drew a chair up for me. "Sit. You are understandably distressed. You are a woman with a woman's sensibilities. We should have taken that into account, better prepared you."

"My lord, nothing could have prepared me for that. He was guilty, yes. I know that. But I do not think that his offense was commensurate with what has been done to him. I saw only some slight involvement."

"And from his slight involvement we may follow the tangled threads that threaten to strangle the protectorate." He eschewed his imposing desk and drew up another chair so that he could sit next to me, softening his voice. "I realize that it is hard to look upon. It is harder still to be the one who must order it done, but it is for the good of all, mistress. For the safety of England and everyone in it—your child, your good friend Mary Wright and her innocent children. What we do to protect ourselves is no sin."

"It feels a sin," I replied. "I am sorry. I cannot master my heart in this."

"You must master it," he argued, though not without sympathy. "These are hard times."

And why are they hard? I wanted to ask. *Your own people so chafe at your constant restrictions and infringements upon their private lives that they welcome any plot to bring you down.*

Only a fool would have said as much to his face, so I said nothing.

The next day I faced Mister Cook again. He seemed somewhat improved. He had been given clean, tattered clothing, and he walked in, however slowly. His head down, he gave me a list of names of Royalists he had seen at coffeehouse meetings. Yes, he admitted, they had spoken of how much better things would be if the rightful king were to return, and rumors and intimations had been made regarding steps being taken toward that goal. Yes, he had given money to a fund, but he was unsure what it would be used for. As God was his witness, he knew nothing more. Then he fell to his knees and wept, begging me to believe him.

"It is the truth," I informed Thurloe, but I knew that he did not fully trust me. Thurloe was a perceptive man. I was no more able to sort through the agonizing mixture of emotions this time than I had been the day before. I only knew that I could not send this man back to face further questioning.

From that point onward, I hesitated to cast suspicion on anyone unless he seemed to me the most dangerous of rebels, and even then it pained me to give him up to Thurloe. Both Thurloe and Cromwell barely concealed their frustration with me. Because of my reticence, it was not until late in May that the full details of the Anabaptists' plotted assassination were discovered and the crime averted.

I found myself constantly plagued by headaches and distress, and the combination took their toll. I could not eat and began to lose weight, my gowns hanging on my thin frame. I had not given much thought to the toll of my frequent absences from life at

Wright House on anyone else until Pearl came to me one night with a tray.

"Aunt Mary says you must eat, even if you will not join us below," Pearl said, setting the tray down on the foot of the bed. It held cold meat, cheese, bread, and wine, but the sight was decidedly unappealing.

"Give her my thanks, but I cannot. Take it away, Pearl."

Pearl set the tray on the floor and sat in its place on the bed. "Samuel Perkins fancies Jane. He follows her everywhere."

"That horrible Perkins boy?" I asked, rather relieved to focus my thoughts upon innocent child's play. "I imagine Jane thinks little of that."

"He's not a boy. He's fifteen."

"Fifteen?" I tried to think of the last time I'd seen him.

"You never go anywhere with us. Aunt Mary takes us everywhere—the park, the market."

"Church!" I blurted. That was the last place I'd seen him. I just hadn't quite connected the young man who sat in the Perkins pew with little Samuel who had goaded the children in the park.

"Yes, you go to church with us, but even when you are with us you are not with us. You seem somewhere far away. And now you do not even come down to dinner."

I thought about that for a moment. It was true. Reaching over, I tucked a tiny wisp of dark hair that had escaped her braid behind her ear. I couldn't recall the last time I'd braided my daughter's hair. "Does Aunt Mary braid your hair?" I asked.

Pearl huffed and fell backward on the mattress. "I braid my own hair, Mother. You know that I have for years."

"I used to do it and weave ribbons in. We should do that again."

She flung one arm across her eyes. "I do not favor so many ribbons in my hair anymore. Now that boys take notice of Jane, Aunt Mary says she mustn't call attention to herself, and since Jane and I do everything together, I thought it a kindness I should do the same. I might have asked your advice, but . . ."

I had noticed how grown up Jane was becoming. At thirteen, her shape was changing, and she moved like a young woman rather than a child. Lying on my bed, arm flung upward, Pearl's form seemed clearer to me than it had in some time. Truth to tell, she was not far behind her friend.

"Does Jane fancy Samuel, then, now that he's growing up?"

"No, but he is not so different from any of the other boys in families her parents want her to marry into."

"Jane is a long way from marriage," I assured her.

Pearl sat up. "She started bleeding yesterday."

"Oh."

"Mother, whom will I marry?"

"I haven't thought about it."

"You haven't thought about anything but Whitehall and whatever it is that you do there. Mother, I do not want to marry anyone like Samuel. I do not think I want to marry at all."

I slid over to her and wrapped my arms around her. "You need not worry on that yet."

"Yesterday, Aunt Mary said that my time might come any day now—that not everyone starts at the same time."

"It may also be a year or more. Be that as it may, bleeding and marriage do not automatically happen at the same time," I told her.

"But it means we can have babies, and for those we marry."

"True, but without marriage there are no babies, so you can wait a good long time."

Pearl chewed on her lower lip. "Mother?"

"Yes."

"Who was my father? Was it the old man?"

I touched her cheek, still a little plump, her face yet a girl's, and wondered whether I might not delay this just a little longer. "It is his name you carry."

"I know that. That is not what I asked. He never lived with us."

"When people ask you, just tell them—"

"*I* am asking." Her eyes, so black, so intelligent, bored into mine. "Mother, what did the scarlet letter mean, and why did the minister keep his hand over his heart?"

I sighed at the pain, like the jab of a needle in my heart. "What do you think?"

"I think the minister was my father, but you were married to the old man. I think that's what the scarlet letter meant."

There was nothing more to say—or rather, I had been spared

saying it and felt no need to press my luck. I leaned past her and
retrieved the goblet of wine from the tray on the floor, taking a
sip even before I fully straightened.

Pearl placed her hand on my arm. "I think I've always known.
I'm sure I knew even when I asked you every day. I suppose I just
wanted to hear you say it."

Not spared after all. Another jab of the needle. "Very well. Arthur Dimmesdale was your father. The letter was my punishment."

"For having me."

"For conceiving you."

"So, like Aunt Mary, you married a man you didn't love—or
were even fond of. And I am to allow the two of you to find a
husband for me?"

I set the goblet back and took her face between my hands. "I
promise you, Pearl, whom you marry will be of no one's choosing
but yours. If I know you at all, you will choose more wisely than
I did."

As though I ever really knew her. Still, her wisdom I did not
doubt.

Seventeen

While we sought scheming Anabaptists, yet another plot to assassinate Cromwell—this one launched by a man named John Gerard—came to light. Gerard was arrested and convicted of treason by such evidence that my services were never called upon in his case. In July, he was beheaded, and Thurloe seemed to decide that he could employ me less often and still ensure the safety of England, for my visits to Whitehall dwindled substantially.

The break did little to assuage the growing sense that inside me was a river, one that was at once fed and dammed by my every circumstance. Once again, I entered the social world of Robert and Mary Wright, which required both revelation and restraint, each in perfect balance with the other. I wanted desperately to break away from the relentless need to analyze, adapt, and accommodate.

In September, my chance came. The Earl of Glencairn surrendered to General Monck at Dumbarton, thus having his uprising squelched, and when Sir John Manning suggested that the Wrights, my daughter, and I join him in a celebratory retreat to his country house in Kent, I jumped to accept. Lord Cromwell granted Robert and me leave, and for the first time since I arrived at Wright House four years past, I took my leave of London. What would I do out there in the countryside? At the time, I thought I might do nothing more than stand in an open meadow, far from everyone, and scream.

From the moment we arrived, Sir John's estate was a balm to everyone's soul, I think. The house was a large, steep-roofed structure of customary whitewashed planks crisscrossed by dark timbers. A few late flowers still bloomed in the gardens, and several bushes offered dark, sweet berries. Inside, the walls were richly paneled, the furnishings worn and comfortable. There were more than enough rooms, so we kept to the same arrangements as at home. Jane and Pearl stayed together; Annie, Georgie, and Ollie shared a room with Nell, who was as excited to be invited as the children; I was on my own, though next to Robert and Mary rather than a floor above.

Poor Annie, now eight, just as Pearl was when we first made our home with the Wrights, tried her best to be placed in Jane and Pearl's room. Since it was not my place to decide, I merely watched from the hall as Annie cornered her nursemaid, who was trying to unpack her charges' belongings.

"But I am too old for the nursery!" she complained to Nell.

"Jane and Pearl stayed there when they were your age," Nell told her.

"You sound just like Mother" came the sullen reply.

"Did you already ask your mother, Miss Annie?" Nell demanded, hands on hips. "You know very well 'er word is law. You're not to come running to me when she says no."

"But she doesn't understand! When Pearl and Jane were my age, there were three girls in the nursery. Neither of them was stranded alone with two dirty, wild little boys!"

"They're neither dirty nor wild, Miss Annie, they are just boys."

Annie tossed her braids over her shoulders. "Bad enough."

Nell sighed and sat on a bed, patting the space next to her, which Annie reluctantly filled. Nell put her arm around the girl and said, "There's things you don't understand yet, Miss Annie. Things 'appening to the other girls that you're not ready for. Now's your chance to lord it over your two brothers. Time enough and they'll be bigger than you and 'ave all the control and the money. Yes, indeedy, boss 'em 'round while you can, love."

Her words were a sharp reminder. Prophetically, Mary had been right, and Pearl had begun her courses on the road to Kent. Now Pearl and Jane seemed to drift on their own in a haze of mystery, sharing secrets Annie was forbidden to hear. No doubt their thoughts were moving toward marriage, the future, all the things Mary and I had whispered about at their age.

At the farthest edge of Sir John's vast and lush lawn, just before the grounds gave way to woods, grew an ancient oak with a trunk so broad that all the children together could not span it with hands touching, no matter how they stretched and strained. This was to be "their tree"—just theirs—the two older girls proclaimed. A few minutes later, Jane joined Sir John and her family inside, where the cook was said to be preparing tea.

I remained outside, under the tree with Pearl, and asked how she and Jane had come to the conclusion that the tree should belong to them alone. She whispered to me, "Because long ago, the oak was the sacred tree of the goddess."

"Pearl!" I grasped her shoulders and gave her a little shake. "Who told you that?"

My vehemence did not startle her in the least. She just gave me a slanted look and said, "Mistress Hibbins did once, when she told me about the Black Man in the woods in New England."

"Mistress Hibbins," I scolded, "was a witch. You mustn't ever repeat anything she said. There is danger in such ideas."

Pearl shrugged and looked away. "I liked the forest. I have forgotten how much I missed it. Now, just now, I feel like being back near deep woods is a kind of homecoming. It is as if this trip were destiny—what has happened to my body and now finding myself here, with this big tree and the cool, dark forest. Do you not feel the mystery here, the sense that something—something *momentous* is going to happen to us?"

The first chill of autumn penetrated the wool of my gown, and I shivered. "If anything of magnitude were going to happen, I should think it would happen in London, not the quiet countryside."

"Oh, no!" Pearl exclaimed. "The most momentous events occur in the quietest, most remote places. That's what I think."

And I, too, recalled the woods of New England—the feel of the cool, mossy ground against my bare back and Arthur's heat above me.

When Sir John came back outside to fetch us, he caught me unaware, while the visceral memory still held me in its thrall. He stopped in his tracks, and once again I felt naked in his presence, though not remotely embarrassed.

"I am intruding," he said, backing away.

"Yes," I said, "I'm afraid you are a foreigner on your own land. I am told that this fine old oak may shelter only young girls in the first blush of womanhood."

It was an impertinent thing to say, but none of us blushed, not even Pearl. She shrugged carelessly and said, "He knows that."

Sir John's eyebrows lifted in surprise, but he said nothing. Instead, he helped me to my feet, and Pearl ran straight to the house while Sir John and I strolled along the forest's edge, choosing the long way back. "That is a remarkable child you have," he said at last.

"Unnerving, at times," I confessed.

"To say the least. My sister and her friends banished me and my chums from that tree's shade when they reached a certain age. They were not much older than Pearl and Jane. How did she know?"

"How does she know anything? We Prynne women are a strange lot."

"You were not born a Prynne," he said, pausing.

I stopped, too, and we stood in the dappled sunlight that trickled through the leaves of branches that trespassed from the forest over the lawn. "No. I was born a Lathrop."

"You and Mary were girls together, I'm told."

"We were."

"And your husband?"

"A friend of my father's. After the wedding, we emigrated to Amsterdam and on to America."

"He was a Puritan?"

"He associated with them. We did not discuss religion between us. And you? Mary says you were studying to be a minister."

He began walking again. "I was, but I was diverted."

I followed. "By politics?"

"Philosophy, actually, then politics. It is a slippery slope from one to the next. What of your fall?"

My heart leaped into my throat. "My what?"

"Your fall—into politics? By what route did you succumb?"

Oh, that. "I care nothing for politics."

His expression was skeptical. "And that is why you spend your days at Whitehall?"

"I did not fall. I was pushed. I do not spend my days at Whitehall by choice."

"But surely your allegiance is to Cromwell."

"My allegiance is to my child. If aught should happen to me, she will be alone in the world. For her protection, I obey Cromwell."

We had come to the far side of the lawn and had to turn again in the direction of the house. Robert nodded toward the door that Pearl had disappeared through. "I wonder to whom she gives her allegiance."

"If she ever tells you, pass it along to me," I replied.

Sir John chuckled. "How is it that every time we speak, we both seem to walk away with more questions about each other than answers?" I shrugged, and he said, "Well, perhaps during your stay we can come to know one another better."

Mary appeared at the kitchen door. "Are you taking tea or not?" she scolded.

A sudden breeze whipped playfully around us and danced off into the woods, rustling leaves in its wake, and I thought that I would rather skip tea and follow that zephyr into the shadows.

Ah, the country! For supper, we had mutton stew and brown bread, currant pudding, and yeasty ale. Through the window poured cool, sweet air. We stayed up late, laughing and telling stories. I felt more myself than I had in . . . years. Many, many years.

Mary and I saw the children off to bed, and by the time we returned to the keeping room, Sir John and Robert were boasting of the protectorate's inevitable triumph over France and the Dutch, just as it had over Glencairn's forces. Scotland would remain a part of the protectorate and Ireland would eventually submit to the yoke. All would be as God had ordained it.

My heart seemed to skip a beat, then resume at twice its original pace. Perhaps I had spoken too freely in the yard. It troubled me that Sir John might think me disloyal and mention it to Robert.

Then Sir John glanced over at me—the briefest glance, barely discernible—and I knew that he was lying through his teeth. The last thing he wanted was victory for the protectorate. For reasons

I could not guess, I had never seen cloud or shadow around John Manning, but in that heartbeat, I saw treason in his eyes.

I dropped my own gaze, peering into the nearly empty tankard of ale I held in both hands. This was not Whitehall, and there was no one here demanding that I give a nod or drop an embroidered linen square. It was a retreat, was it not? Had we not come to forget politics and treachery? I looked back up and raised my cup. My eyes upon Sir John, I said, "To men of good faith."

He did not flinch. Looking right back he lifted his own tankard. "—Who love their country and do right by their countrymen."

"Here! Here!" Robert confirmed, and we drank.

Eighteen

I have said that nighttime magnifies change in environment, making contrasts from one place to another seem almost perverse. I lay in bed listening for street sounds, and finding none, I could not sleep. Wrapping the quilt from my bed around me, I tiptoed downstairs, through the empty kitchen, and out the back door. The cold grass was a cruel shock to my naked toes, so I slipped my feet into Pearl's shoes, left near the door because they were dirty. They were only a little too small.

Silver moonlight illuminated the yard and the very tops of the trees beyond it. The forest itself was black as pitch. Slowly, I wandered over to Pearl and Jane's oak tree, running my fingertips over its rough bark as I walked around it. I stopped and leaned against it, staring into the woods, trying to penetrate the darkness with my mind. A strange fancy betook me that I might find myself out there in the gloom, that another Hester was there, staring back out at me.

"This tree," Sir John's voice broke in, causing me to jump and mutter a bit of blasphemy, "is only for girls in the first blush of womanhood."

"You frightened me," I admonished.

He only laughed softly. "The woods," he continued, taking my hand, "are for dangerous and powerful women."

"Am I a danger to you?" I asked, pulling my hand away.

"Are you?" he replied. "What do you see when you look at me?"

I sighed. "This again? Well, you are man of good intentions, I think. Whatever faults have been revealed to my eyes, I see no darkness in you, John Manning."

"You see sin, do you not? That is what Robert told me."

"I do."

"Is it a sin to realize that you have made a mistake? To know that you have helped to put the wrong man in power, however good his intentions were—are?"

"He is well-intended, Cromwell."

"But too certain of his ability to know the will of God, and because of that, he pays no heed at all to the will of the people. I am for my country, Hester, not for a man. I am no friend to Charles, but right now, I believe that he is what England needs."

"He has never proven himself a leader," I said.

"Leaders we have, though the majority of good ones are in exile, in the Tower, or incognito. What we need is a politician, a diplomat, a man who knows how to appease allies and represent England's interests, yet stay out from under the feet of the true statesmen and let parliament do its job."

"A puppet."

Sir John laughed. "Charles is no puppet. He is a self-serving survivor, but he loves his country."

"So does Cromwell."

He released an exasperated breath. "Cromwell loves his ideals. He does not even know England."

"How do you know Charles is the right man? You admit that you were wrong to have supported Cromwell at first. Have you even met Charles?"

Sir John glanced toward the house. "You are Cromwell's chief informer. What would you have me say?"

"Not true. I only render a verdict upon what is set before me, already known or suspected. I do not gather intelligence."

"And you care nothing for politics, or so you told me."

"I am a woman who, though she wishes otherwise, perceives sin. To men like Cromwell and Thurloe and Robert Wright, that leaves me a close ally to either God or Satan."

"And if you are not allied to Cromwell, you are not allied to God," Sir John concluded.

"Precisely."

"And if I were brought before you?"

I thought about that for a long time, and to his credit, Sir John waited, his face studiously patient. "I see no sin in you," I said at last.

He smiled. "Good. Neither do I."

"After all, sin is a matter of perspective," I reflected.

"Sin is a matter of belief. Some things are there whether you believe in them or not, like this tree." He patted its trunk. "Some things require belief in them to exist, so in truth, they exist not at all."

"Such as sin?" I asked.

"What is sin, Hester? What are its dimensions? How can it be measured? You believe in sin only because you have been told it exists."

"I have seen it with my own eyes."

"And what does it look like?"

"It can look like anything—a shadow, a cloud, a color. At times I hear it instead, like a furtive whisper in the dark."

"What is its shape? Its volume? Its proportions?"

"I do not know. I know only what I sense."

"A man I knew once told me not to believe what my senses tell me. Doubt, he said, is the only path to truth!"

"How can I doubt what I see? Do you deny your own senses?"

He leaned close and whispered in my ear. "Never do I deny my senses."

My reaction was elemental, powerful, shocking in its intensity. For a moment I could think of nothing but the gratification of a man's hand on me, his hips rocking hard against me. Then he straightened up, and the night went cold again. Reason returned.

"There came a time for me when Descartes was not enough," he continued, seemingly unaffected. "Yes, yes, he was right about doubt. Since I studied with him, I have taken nothing at face value. I decide each thing upon its own merits."

"Philosophy after all?" I asked.

"I did not follow you out here for philosophy," he said. "Even less for politics. And I did not follow you to stand upon virgins' ground. I came to take you into the forest."

"And you thought I would go?"

His eyes narrowed, though his lips still smiled. "You are a mystery. From the first moment I saw you, I felt a kinship. I believed you a woman above convention, one who thought for herself, traveled her own path. Was I mistaken?"

I shook my head. "Only in your thought that I had any path. I am a wanderer, Sir John, with no path to follow."

He took my hand again. "Then wander in the woods with me tonight."

For a moment, the dam that checked the river within me came dangerously close to crumbling, and it crossed my mind that this would be a better means of abating the flood than standing in a meadow and screaming.

Where was Arthur now? I wondered. Would he know? When we saw each other again at the end of my life, would he understand that this had meant nothing? Would he forgive me?

Had I forgiven him?

If I were honest, I might admit that I only wanted Sir John so that I could one day look at Arthur and say that I had given myself to a man who felt no shame to be with me. Roger was not relevant here; I had not given to him so much as he had taken from me.

"Hester?" Sir John prompted.

"Not tonight," I said. "I have to think."

"Ah . . ." He rubbed his hand from his chin down his throat in an absent, nervous gesture. "You do realize that I am only proposing a slight tryst, not—"

"Yes, I know. I have to think on it, that is all. One must be cautious before entering the forest. That much I have learned."

"Well, I confess I hope you'll decide to brave the wilderness. However, it is getting too cold to stand out here without sharing warmth, so I believe I'll bid you good night, Hester."

I nodded my agreement. "Good night . . . John."

Nineteen

———⊷◦⊶———

The next day was unseasonably warm, and we took a late breakfast out of doors at a trestle table. The children hurriedly gulped
their food so they could play, and even Jane and Pearl took a step
back from the precipice of womanhood to chase Annie and Georgie playing hide-and-seek at the edge of the forest.

"Stay within hearing of our voices," Robert called to them.

"I thought I heard you up and about late last night," Mary
said to me as she reached in front of her for the butter.

"I always have a difficult time sleeping the first night in a new
place," I replied before taking my next bite of ham. Doubtless I
would fill my gowns out once again with the generous meals John's
cook provided.

"Odd," Robert joined in, leaning back from the table. "I
thought it was you I heard last night, John."

John set his teacup down. "It may have been. I heard Mistress
Prynne and went to see if all was well. She was out here, of all
places. Awfully cold place to be at that hour. We spoke about
philosophy until our teeth chattered."

"Philosophy after midnight?" Robert asked, but he was smiling. There seemed no suspicion in his demeanor.

"Descartes," I answered.

Robert scowled, "Catholic, isn't he?"

Mary gave a soft sigh. "Oh, Robert."

"You know, Robert," John said, "one or two Catholics have been known to do some fairly sound thinking."

"So what sort of thinking kept the two of you outside in the cold?" Mary asked.

"We were speaking of reality," John said. "How do we know what is real and what is not?"

Was that what we were discussing? I thought. *And here I thought we were contemplating sin.*

"I have never understood philosophy," Mary stated. "What can there be to discuss? It is very clear what is real and what is not. I know the difference, and I have hardly given the matter much thought at all."

"It is an intellectual's folly," Robert declared. "Contemplation of such nonsense as whether our lives are real or some . . . dream."

Mary laughed. "That is madness. Sir John, surely a theologian such as yourself has better things to do with his faculties."

"Sooner or later, Mistress Wright, any serious study of theology raises just such questions. A profound examination of faith must sooner or later lead to a questioning of it."

Damn him. He still lusted after Mary. It was as plain as the nose on his face, but neither Mary nor Robert seemed to notice, for they were both in wide-eyed shock at his last pronouncement.

"The last time I checked, John, you Independents were no more atheists than we Puritans," Robert said.

"Not at all. Look at Descartes; he, too, realized that in order to believe earnestly, one must first doubt totally. Let us begin with what you told Mary. How *do* we know that we are not merely a part of someone else's dream?"

"Because we simply aren't," Mary answered, popping the last of her bread in her mouth.

John looked at me and raised his brows, silently offering the question to me. I thought for several seconds and finally said, "I am aware of myself. I do not think the other figures in my dreams can say that. If we were figments of someone else's imagination, we would not know that we exist."

"Precisely!" John cried. "You think, therefore you are. *Cogito ergo sum.*"

Robert nodded sagely. "Of course, and once we have determined that we exist, we know that we must have been created. From this, we take our faith in God."

John gave him a rueful grin. "Not exactly. That is simply our base for all other studies of reality. According to Descartes, once we have divined our own existence, we must determine what else is real."

"That is easy," Mary said, reaching again, this time for an apple, and holding it up. "This is real."

"How do you know that?" he asked.

"I can touch it."

"When you touch it, I cannot feel it."

"Well, you can see it."

"How can we be sure that we are seeing the same thing?"

"What color is it?" Mary challenged.

"Brown," John replied.

"Oh!" Mary exclaimed, exasperated. "You are only being difficult. It is red, as you can plainly see."

"I assure you that what you insist to be red appears brown to me. Then again, I have never seen red as I am told that I should see it."

"What?" Robert asked, his teacup poised at his lips.

"I see the world in varying shades of brown, yellow, and blue."

"What color is the grass?" I asked.

"Yellow."

"What?" Mary cried.

"You are color-blind?" Robert asked. "I never knew that about you."

"You cannot see red at all?" I asked. "In any shade—crimson, scarlet?"

"Not at all."

"Well, that is fascinating," Mary said.

More than you know, I thought.

I took the apple from Mary. "I know what we can agree upon," I said, taking a bite. "It is sweet."

John reached his hand out, holding it open. "Is it?"

I looked down at the fruit in my hand and remembered the night we studied the ceiling of Whitehall together. Adam and Eve again? Reluctantly, I handed him the apple, and he took a bite, chewing slowly.

How had the paintings at Whitehall appeared to him?

At last he swallowed and said, "A little tart, I think, which is more to my liking in any event."

Robert cleared his throat and scowled unhappily. "Then how *are* we to know the apple is real?"

John set it down, and I wondered whether the two bites, once they turned brown in the air, would look the same shade of brown as the rest of the apple to him.

"If I were to bring out a measuring tape," he continued, "and we measured the apple's circumference, would each of us find the same dimensions?"

"Of course we would," Robert said.

"Unless one of us were blind," Mary said, her expression a little cross.

"What if Mistress Prynne were to take out her needle and create a measuring tape that could be felt by its raised threads? Would we not then find the same measurements?"

"We would," I said.

"And if I brought out a scale, would we not all reach the same conclusion about its weight?"

"Of course," Robert said.

"So we can safely assume that if a thing can be measured to all our agreement, it must exist," John explained.

"Fine," I said, recalling his argument the night before. "Tell me, what are God's dimensions?"

"That is a pivotal question," John agreed. "We may also understand the nature of a thing's reality by examining its components. For example, is it likely that I can make a delicious plate of eggs like those we have eaten this morning if all I have available to me are rotten eggs?"

Mary giggled. "I did not know that you could cook at all, Sir John."

We all chuckled, and still grinning, he said, "I can, actually, but I cannot make a decent meal of rancid ingredients. The quality of the product can only be as good as the quality of its components."

"Yes, but where is this going?" Robert asked.

"Mary," John said, "do you love Robert?"

I winced and tried to flash John a warning look. This was thin ice, indeed.

Her face flushed, Mary reached into her lap to retrieve her napkin. "I . . . of course."

John had the grace to look a little abashed at having placed her in an indelicate position. He rushed on. "And yet, as much as you love him, you know that he is not perfect. Even your children, charming and well-mannered as they are, have faults."

"Well . . ." Mary began, casting an anxious look at her husband.

Robert had not looked at her and remained unaware of her discomfiture. "My children and I are as guilty of original sin as anyone else. Only God is perfect."

As though original sin were the only stain upon his soul, I scoffed silently. And there he sat, serene and secure in the certainty of his wife's devotion.

"And if a product cannot be of a higher quality than its components," John continued, "how can a creature as flawed as man conceive of a God who is perfect? There is only one answer. God Himself made us capable of such intelligence. Man is simply too imperfect to have created a perfect God on his own, therefore, God must exist."

Mary smiled, visibly relieved at the endpoint of John's inquiry. "Ah! I see. You must admit, Robert, this Descartes is very intelligent, Catholic or no."

"Then in time," Robert grumbled, "I trust he will see the error of his ways."

"He died several years ago," John replied.

Robert grinned. "Well then, I imagine he is measuring the dimensions of hell just now. Children! Come help clear away the dishes!"

The little band emerged from the forest's edge to do Robert's bidding, while I pondered the conversation. God, perfect? I remembered Pearl's analysis of Exodus when she was only nine or ten, her unwillingness to acquit God of the murder of innocent Egyptian babies. Had Descartes been reading the same Bible we had?

Twenty

———✦———

In the afternoon, while the girls took turns playing draughts on a checkered board and we adults took our leisure, an invitation to supper arrived for the following day. It was from the Blackwell family who lived down the lane. "We passed the road to their house on our way here," John explained to us. "Edward Blackwell and I were chums when we were young. I went off to university, and he stayed home to look after the farm. Now that his parents are gone, it's all his. He married a girl we both knew—Bess. They're good people."

"Have they any children?" Annie asked, looking up from the board.

"Yes. Ah—I am here so seldom, I don't recall how many or how old. Boys and girls—some of each."

So the next day, Nell stayed behind with the baby, and the rest of us walked to the Blackwells. "Some of each" turned out to be Harry, a boy nearly Georgie's age, and Gertrude, a girl nearly Annie's. The two middle Wright children, utterly weary of each other, were shy for all of five minutes and then fast friends with their new playmates. The Blackwells had one other child—a fourteen-year-old by the name of Jack with a handsome face, fair hair, and arms and shoulders already molded by a life of hard work.

Side by side, in perfect synchronization, both Jane and Pearl lifted their hands to their caps to make sure that every strand of hair was in its place.

A well-mannered boy, Jack greeted each child and adult separately. When he came to Pearl, he stammered and his cheeks pinked, a weakness not lost on either her or Jane. Pearl smiled sweetly, cocking her head in that coy manner that comes instinctively to girls. Jane's eyes narrowed. For all that I have never perceived the sins of children, the undertone of the exchange was an obvious one.

Jack addressed all of the children next, asking whether they might not like to go down to the river.

"Oh! Mine cannot swim!" Mary protested. "Is it safe?"

"We'll only play by the water's edge, madam," Jack assured her. "It's perfectly calm there."

"I can keep an eye on them, Mother," Jane offered. "After all, I *am* thirteen."

"*We* can keep an eye on them," Pearl corrected.

Jane cast a wry look toward Jack. "She's twelve."

"I am nearly thirteen!" Pearl protested.

Jane gave her a haughty look such as I had only ever seen her use with her siblings. "Your birthday isn't till March, and I'll be fourteen in June."

"Well, *I* can swim, so if anyone falls in—" Pearl added, but Mary interrupted.

"No one is to step foot in that water!" Mary declared.

By now, Jack seemed fully aware of his role in the tug-of-war between Mary's daughter and mine, and he stood a little taller. Grinning, he said, "No need to worry. It's too cold to go in. Besides, when my cousins are here, I am in charge of as many as a dozen children by the river. I have even saved one or two when we were swimming."

"Have you?" Jane asked, her voice breathless. "You'll have to tell us all about it."

"Watch closely, Jack," Mistress Blackwell chided. She was a lovely, plump woman with hair the color of ripe wheat that escaped her cap in unruly curls, reminding me of Nell. "All your cousins can swim. Besides, the river is running high and fast out in the middle just now—all that rain last week. Even you must stay to the shore."

"Yes, Mother. Come along, everyone." The group headed across the grass and up a small hill, some skipping, some running, the older children walking briskly—too dignified for childish frolicking. "Watch your step there, Pearl," Jack warned, reaching out to steady her when she tripped, and I wondered whether she was clever enough to have done it on purpose.

"Oh dear," Mary murmured.

"One of them is going to be in tears tonight," I observed, and Mary frowned.

I wholeheartedly agreed with John's assessment of his neighbors. They were happy, generous people who delighted in feeding and entertaining friends old and new. My years in London had taught me that the more zealous a man's religion, the more troubled his soul. Judging from the contentment that radiated from Edward and Bess Blackwell, I imagined they were the church-on-Sunday, prayer-before-bed kind of Christians—the ones who spent almost no time in between contemplating hellfire and damnation. I did have an odd sense whenever Bess and John spoke to each other that there was some sort of past between them, but either I was imagining things or they were both well beyond it.

Mary and I chatted awhile with Mistress Blackwell and had moved with her into the kitchen when the screaming began. We bolted outside, where the men had been smoking pipes and talking, to find the still-lit pipes abandoned in the dirt. The three of us ran after them to the river. We did not have to be in sight of children to know which was in trouble.

"Jack! Jack!" the Blackwells' daughter cried.

"No, Pearl, you're not strong enough! Stay here!" That was Jane.

"Jackie! Come back!" The fact that I didn't recognize the voice guaranteed that it was the younger Blackwell boy.

By the time we women arrived, Robert was already in the water, rapidly gaining on Jack, who clung to a rock well downstream, in the middle of the wide and swiftly flowing river, just where it was most treacherous.

"Hang on, son!" Mister Blackwell called as he and John sprinted down the bank to gain a position parallel to rock and boy.

Mistress Blackwell raced down the slope and started pulling the other children back from the water's edge. "Up with you! Up! We've no need of more of you in there."

Mary joined her, pulling Annie and Georgie close, trying to shield them from the possible sight of Jack drowning, while her children fought her to learn of their new friend's fate.

Robert caught up to Jack and stopped, wrapping his arms around the stone, too, and shouting something above the rushing water before he gripped the back of Jack's shirt and headed for shore. Jack made a valiant effort to swim for himself, but his arms moved heavily. Obviously, holding fast to the rock to keep from being swept away had taken its toll. When he and Robert reached Mister Blackwell and John, the two men stepped off the steep bank, up to their thighs in water, and took the violently coughing boy between them. Mister Blackwell pushed Jack from behind, then clambered up himself, and the four sopping males struggled back up the bank.

Before Mistress Blackwell could rush over to them, I tapped her shoulder. "Blankets?"

"Oh, yes, go inside. Take them from wherever you find them."

When I returned from the house, my arms piled so high I could hardly see, I found everyone in a tight group where the men had fallen. The two who had gone all the way in were shivering savagely, and I handed blankets to Mistress Blackwell and Mary. Bess wrapped her son up, and only when he was securely enveloped in the quilt did her calm demeanor slip, her eyes welling up. She pressed his wet head to her bosom, heedless of the cold water that soaked her, too.

Mary blanketed Robert, and John took the last woolen cover to place over Mister Blackwell's shoulders.

Mistress Blackwell wiped her hand under her nose and sniffed, then she stood and began issuing orders like a general. "Don't just stand there, the rest of you," she admonished the children. "Harry, you and Georgie go on and get dry clothes—two sets from your father's things and one from Jack's. And dry hose for Sir John! Lay them out on the beds. Gertrude, you and Annie add a log to the fire. Jane, Pearl, fix these men plates from the kitchen. They'll be eating in front of the hearth. Move!"

Mary and I hustled back to the house to oversee the tasks at hand. She went to check on the boys while I headed toward the kitchen to make sure the servings were generous. Just outside the doorway, I paused and listened.

"It's your fault, you know," Jane upbraided Pearl. "He climbed that tree and went all the way out over the water on that branch to impress *you*, Pearl Prynne." I heard only a sniff from Pearl in reply. "Tears do no good now," Jane continued. "You should have thought before you stood on the bank clapping your hands the farther out he went. *I* was the one trying to coax him to come down. *I* was the one who cared more for Jack's safety than my own pride to have a boy taking such risks over me."

I stepped through the door and Pearl flung herself against me, falling apart into deep sobs. "I am sorry," she wailed against me. "Oh, Mother, I am so, so sorry!"

I held her close and rubbed her back. "He's all right, child. He's just fine. You and Jack both learned hard lessons today."

Pearl rubbed her cheek against my shoulder to wipe away her tears without letting go of me. "Jane's right. We were both being foolish, trying to get his attention, and he climbed the tree to impress us. But she kept trying to get him to come down, and I—I kept encouraging him because then he paid more attention to me. He—he went out on the branch over the fast water, and Jane told him to come down, but I was laughing and clapping and he started to make the branch bounce, and then—and then—"

"It snapped," Jane finished. "He might have *died*."

Pearl resumed sobbing, though softer now. Jane was right, but it irritated me that she only worsened Pearl's distress. It would be best if Pearl felt she was doing something useful, so I disengaged her hands from my waist. "Well, it cannot be undone, and it all came out well enough. Fill the plates. It is the best thing you can do now."

From the keeping room came excited chatter and clomping shoes as the rest of the group returned. I poured ale and listened to the men move to the back of the house to change. Soon we were serving hot food to one foolish boy and three heroes, and everyone was talking at once.

"So Jackie started bouncing on the branch . . ."

"Did you see my father jump into the water? I bet your brother wouldn't have made it if he hadn't . . ."

"I cannot thank you enough, Brigadier General . . ."

"God, John, if I'd lost him . . ."

"But he got up pretty high in that tree . . ."

"I should have listened to you, Miss Jane . . ."

Pearl deferred to Jane, allowing her friend to earn Jack's undivided attention by bringing him food and drink and fussing over him. While Jane ate at the hearth, Pearl sat next to me at the far end of the table and stared at her plate without touching the food.

By the time we had said our good-byes and walked back down the lane, Robert's and John's shoes still emitting soft squishing sounds, Annie and Georgie had grown tired and quietly kept pace with the group. Jane walked with her mother in the lead; Pearl and I brought up the rear. We arrived at John's to find that Ollie was fast asleep. Annie and Georgie perked up enough to regale Nell with the day's adventure, and while they were in the midst of the tale Mary and I went to the girls' room to test the waters. We tucked each of our silent daughters in as we had not in years and kissed them good-night.

Pearl turned her head toward Jane's bed. "I am truly sorry, Jane. Please forgive me."

"I cannot believe I ever called you friend" came the curt reply.

I waited for Mary to admonish her child, but all she said was "We'll see how we all feel in the morning."

We left, closing the door behind us. "Mary—" I ventured.

"I am exhausted," she said. "I shall see you tomorrow."

The house was quiet now, and no light spilled from under the bedchamber doors along the hallway. We had accompanied John here to relax, to get away from all the worries of London, and we had but seemed to replace the old concerns with twice as many new. I wondered whether I would make it all the way outside before I started to scream. Deciding that it would be best to try, I walked through the back door where I found John waiting, a welcome shadow in the night.

Twenty-one

———❖———

"Thought you might like to walk," he said, picking up the nearly closed dark lantern next to him.

I contemplated the offer long enough to calculate the date in my head. My flux should begin in less than a week. Chance was on our side. I took his hand, and he pulled me swiftly along into the shelter of the trees while my heart beat fast in anticipation.

In the darkness we were naught but hands searching, mouths devouring. We were skin, breath, sweat, and pulse. With Roger, I had known forbearance, with Arthur, sacred union. With John, there was only sensation, physical, earthy, satisfying. It meant no more, no less, than any other coupling of beasts in that forest, and I felt wild, unfettered—freer than I had since sailing alone to America. I reveled as much in the feel of my bare skin against the cold ground as in the feel of his warm flesh, and as pleasure ripped through me, I lost any sense of John at all. There was only my body, my senses, my fulfillment.

Then he wrenched himself from me, and I felt the warm, wet pulse of his seed spill harmlessly against my thigh. He, too, had kept his wits about him enough to consider the consequences of this act. I had counted my fall with Arthur forgivable, having been committed in a moment of madness. This was different, calculated, premeditated—rational. I could be true enough to myself, still, to admit that I had known this moment would come.

I knew what John would think of my reflection. *There are no sins, of passion or of reason, if we do not believe in sin.*

"John?"

"Yes? Damn, it is cold." He pulled his shirt over his head.

I picked up my shift and used the hem to wipe away his seed before putting the garment back on. "You never said what *you* thought of Descartes's notion of God."

In a bemused tone, he said, "You've an odd notion of pillow talk, Hester Prynne."

I looked about and shrugged. "We've no pillows."

He stood up, chuckling, and donned his hose. "Fair enough. As for God—the one who bequeathed Moses with Ten Commandments, one of which was 'Thou shalt not kill,' then told him to slay all the Midianites, every male, adult or child, and every female who had known a man? The one whose infallible Word is so unintelligible that his own followers cannot agree on what any of it means so they fight wars and burn each other over it? The deity of the Bible whose acts are as often motivated by petty vanity or vengefulness as compassion?" He gave a short laugh. "God is a human invention if ever I have seen one."

"And so is sin?"

He scratched his head. "Oh, God, Hester, surely you are not—"

"No, no," I said with a smile. "I am not about to denounce us as sinners. I won't ruin the moment with that." I, too, was on my feet, struggling into my clothes. John stepped over to help, and I gratefully accepted. "But what is it then, that I see?"

He gave my laces a firm tug. "Hypocrisy?"

It was so obvious, I felt an imbecile not to have thought of it much sooner. Then again, it was too simple.

"But wait!" I protested. "You lie through your teeth. I should hardly be able to see you for the clouds of hypocrisy that must surround you."

"Perhaps what you see are the emotions of the hypocrite. Perhaps it has more to do with the shame he feels. I have no shame."

That made me think of something else. "Have you known Bess Blackwell?"

"Hester, I have no patience with jealousy—"

"I was only wondering." I examined him and pulled a twig from his hair.

"A bit of youthful exploration when we were children, but we kept it well in check."

I laughed. "*She* kept it in check, you mean. I cannot imagine you using the slightest restraint."

John shook his head. "The pleasure of women is a rather recent discovery, if you can believe it. Sadly, I spent the better part of my youth convinced that celibacy was a virtue." He raked his fingers through his hair and scanned me from head to foot. "If we are fully clothed and divested of all grass and twigs, we should return to the yard at the very least. We both have reputations to protect."

"I might assume you to have been a libertine from birth were it not for that very reputation. How do you maintain such good regard among your discriminating colleagues?"

We walked back through the trees, the little door of the lantern opened only slightly to keep the light from drawing too much attention should anyone be looking outside. Once in the yard, we stood under the giant oak in plain sight, two people with nothing to hide.

"I met Robert and several others at university, where I was quite earnest in my pursuit of a career as a Puritan minister."

I seem to have a penchant for them, I thought.

"Then I met another student who had been reading essays by René Descartes. We traveled to Amsterdam to meet him. It was the beginning of my most valuable education. I met many men with many different ideas about morality, God, and the nature of reality. I learned to be more analytical, to stop accepting what teachers and ministers told me. Unfortunately, as I said, I hit a bit of an impediment when I turned that analysis upon my deity."

"I hit such a barrier myself when I first began to see the fallibility of those in authority," I agreed.

"And how did that come to pass?" he asked.

"Your story first," I insisted. "Mine will come later."

This seemed to satisfy him, and he continued. "I returned to England no longer possessed of the same religious philosophies as my friends, but every bit as much convinced that England was ready to cast off its king and its church and embrace such liberty as the right to choose our own faith."

"So long as we chose the faiths of our leaders," I said.

"It wasn't like that, at first. There were Baptists, Puritans, Quakers, Ranters, Anabaptists, Congregationalists, Independents—"

I shook my head. "But no Catholics or Jews."

"Not so—at first. But as you have seen—"

"The Catholics are routinely ordered from London city limits, the Jews must negotiate carefully, the Ranters' activities are illegal . . ."

"A shame, that," he said of the Ranters—a religious sect that shocked all others by shouting profanity and engaging in licentiousness as the ultimate expression of antinomianism. After all, if they were correct, and religious faith was of greater importance than religious law, why obey all those dreary "thou shalt nots"?

"Hmmm," I murmured. "Their 'free love' notion appealed to you."

"That was not the case at first, either. But as I saw Cromwell's ascendancy being treated like the Second Coming, all while he demurred to take the role of leader, and I watched parliament meet time and again to no avail, I decided that I should familiarize myself with the alternative. It was time to stop merely believing what I was told about Charles."

"And what did you find?" I asked.

John grinned broadly. "Charles is a licentious reprobate. He is also an apt politician who can rally men and money to him with aplomb. It was in his court in France that I decided that it was time to let go of Descartes's admonitions not to trust the senses. I engaged in wholesale discovery"—he perused my body again—"and uncovered a wealth of intelligence."

"Well," I said, "I very much appreciate your sharing it with me tonight, and if everyone else knew how close I was to taking up the Ranters' custom of shouting blasphemies to the high heavens, they would appreciate the extra sleep you afforded them."

"Yes, well, it's rather critical to us both that they never know how grateful they should be. I presume you have some experience at being discreet about such matters."

I might have laughed, but I was suddenly too tired.

Twenty-two

When we woke the next morning, it was raining heavily, the sound of steady thrumming dominating breakfast where conversation seemed in short supply. Nell looked after Ollie, Annie and Georgie seemed subdued by the elements, and as far as I could tell, Jane was not acknowledging Pearl's presence, much less speaking to her. Mary's and my transactions mirrored our daughters'. John and Robert ate much and spoke little, keeping wary eyes on the females present, then retired to the hearth to read.

I tried to speak with Mary after the meal, when the younger children scampered off to the nursery, but she said she had mending to do and brought her basket to the keeping room, where a private conversation between us was impossible. Jane helped her mother while Pearl set to work decorating an apron with delicate, careful stitches—a peace offering, no doubt. I took out a little dress I had been sewing for Ollie and threaded my needle.

With nothing to do but think, I contemplated the fact that I felt no shame or remorse whatsoever for the previous night. Because of this, at breakfast I had been able to speak to John exactly as I had before our tryst, whereas after I had been with Arthur, I was afraid to look at him, certain our crime would be advertised to the world. How could lying with Arthur, a man I loved with all my soul, have left me feeling so sinful while a meaningless tumble felt, well . . .

It had been good. Had I been forced to endure this tense silence on top of yesterday's events at the Blackwells' and all that had happened in London without the release in between, I think I would have gone utterly mad.

And the remorse with Arthur—I hadn't felt that until he looked at me afterward with such regret. It was *his* guilt I had felt all along. After all, just days before he died, it was my idea that we should run away together, someplace where no one knew us. I could have done that and easily left dishonor behind. It was he who could not do it, he who had climbed the scaffold days later and died of shame.

I sighed, and several heads lifted to regard me. I might have left well-enough alone, but I had no patience for the strain among us. Instead I said, "It is a pity that a perfectly lovely rainy day, when we all might be chatting and telling stories, must be wasted in so much anger."

"I am not angry," Robert said.

"That is our cue to leave," John replied. "Dash out to the shed with me, will you? There are dry logs there, and we're running low."

"No one is angry," Mary protested, even as they arose from their seats. "Sit. We've plenty of wood."

"Look me in the eye, Mary, and tell me that you are not angry," I said.

"If we're to keep a fire all day," Robert said, "we'll need more wood, that's sure."

The men beat a hasty retreat, and for a while Mary, the girls, and I listened to the rain pour down the steep roof and rush through the gutters to splash upon the ground. Giggles of delight and boisterous thuds from the upper floor, where Nell and Annie entertained the younger children, only punctuated the tense silence between us.

Ollie began to fuss, his cries carrying down the stairs from the floor above, and Mary stood quickly. "I'll go up, and—"

"Nell will look after him," I interrupted. "Are we to spend the remainder of our holiday seething in silent anger?"

"I had no idea you were seething," Mary said. Then she pricked her finger, muttered "Ouch!" and stuck it in her mouth.

"Well, I am!" Jane exclaimed, rising. "I am so angry that I could just—just spit!"

I smiled. "Good girl, Jane. Let's have it, then."

She walked over to Pearl. "Everyone knows that you are prettier than I am, and more adventurous and worldly. You were born across the ocean and lived in the wilderness, just about, seeing pirates and Indians and Lord knows what all, and you've sailed the ocean and can swim—" She gasped a little before continuing. "You are the sole heiress of a wealthy man, while my parents must dower two girls and send two boys to university, maybe more if Mother has any others."

"I—I—" Pearl stammered, lifting her palms in supplication.

"Well, it's not fair! It's not! Can I not have *one* boy prefer me?"

"Samuel—" Pearl tried again.

"Samuel is a know-it-all peacock! And when he thinks no one is looking, he looks at you, not me. He just can't stand the thought of a girl who will always outshine him, so he tries to make himself believe that I am the one he wants."

"Jane," I said, "you are a beautiful girl."

"I thought you never told lies, Aunt Hester."

"I don't, and you are. Very lovely."

"Lovely as Pearl?"

Suddenly aware that she was mangling the fabric, Mary smoothed her mending out and set it aside. "You have a different kind of beauty—more subtle."

"In other words," Jane snapped, "no."

"This is stupid!" Pearl cried, standing up and throwing her embroidery frame on the floor. "When we came here and found my grandfather had died, whom did my mother turn to? A man? Right after Ollie was born, and Aunt Mary would have crying spells, who understood? The brigadier general? Neither one of us is going to marry Jack or Samuel. Jane, you and I won't marry for years, and even when we are married, we'll need each other, just as our mothers do! Squabbling over boys like dogs over a bone, the lot of us," she finished in disgust.

For several long moments, we were all too stunned to speak, glancing into one another's eyes and then looking away, embarrassed. Finally, Mary sighed and said, "Well, I don't know about the rest of you, but I feel about two inches tall."

Jane toyed with her apron, watching her hands on the fabric and seeming to digest Pearl's outburst.

"I think the two of you should go to your room," I said. "You have things to talk about, and so do Mary and I."

When the girls were gone, I stepped to a window to look toward the shed. "I hope the roof is tight over there," I murmured. "I wonder how long they'll stay."

"I need to ask something of you," Mary said.

"What?"

"Jane is right. Pearl has so many advantages. Once, Jane and I had all the proper connections, so things felt even between us, but now you are in Cromwell's inner sanctum—deeper than Robert even."

"No—"

"As deep, at least. Will you allow me to settle Jane before you seek a match for Pearl?"

"Right now, Mary, Pearl is the least of my worries."

Mary shook her head. "Then you are blind. She is just like you, and if you are not mindful, she will stumble and pay the price."

There are worse things than stumbling, I thought. *Everything has a price.*

Still, I could not fault Mary for doing her best by her child. "I promise, Pearl will not interfere with Jane's future," I said. "Have we a truce, then?"

Mary nodded, but she did not look at me. There was another loud thump from the floor above and Ollie began to wail in earnest, so Mary fled upstairs before any more could be said.

Robert and John returned, smelling of wet wool and carrying armloads of wood. Jane and Pearl eventually came back downstairs with all the younger children, Mary and Nell following. The young ones were a pleasant diversion, but there were subtle changes in the atmosphere. Much had transpired since we had arrived, and none of it could be undone.

The rain slackened but did not stop all night, so a midnight walk was impossible, and visits to rooms not our own were far too perilous, so I lay in bed wishing for another brief moment when intellect and emotion might be suspended by unadulterated physicality. Oh, I could have indulged my needs myself—a woman does not live alone as long as I had without seeking her own hand from time to time—but there was a satisfaction in being skin-to-skin with another human being that I alone could not obtain, and it was that I craved as much as the release, so I went unfulfilled.

We stayed together in the country only a few cloudy days more before word came of suspected treachery among Cromwell's most trusted men, and Robert and I were summoned back to London at once. John thought it best if he joined us on the road but invited Mary and the children to stay through mid-October as we had all originally planned.

Tensions ran high again. I had no wish to return and ventured to say as much to Robert, who promptly questioned my loyalty.

The night before we left, though we knew that sleep would probably come no easier to Robert than to us, John and I slipped out to the woodshed together. There was little time—hose unfastened, skirts up, bodies meeting, seeking, culminating. By the time he lifted me away to reach his own summit outside of me, every knotted sinew in my body had melted, become supple and warm. I should have told him that my menses was due soon so that he could have lost himself as completely as I had, but it was too late. Reluctantly, we parted.

"Hester," John said softly, fastening his hose, "before you go, I have a rather weighty request. If you can tell me which men you will be questioning before they are questioned, I should be much beholden."

"What would you do?" I asked.

"It would depend upon the men."

"You know men close to Cromwell who—"

"The less you know, the better," he said. "Just . . . I shall stop by after you and Cromwell have had a chance to meet—to speak to Robert, of course. I will leave something, my scarf perhaps. You will find it, slip the names into it, and run out to the street to find me before I can leave without it."

It seemed my heartbeat had only begun to slow but it began to race again. I hardly knew what to say.

"It is a great deal to ask," he said, "I know."

"John, if Robert catches us . . ."

"He won't. He has no reason to suspect either of us. Only this one time, Hester. I fear for certain colleagues, and we've no one so close to Cromwell just now. If there were not possibly so much riding on it, I would never ask you to take such a gamble."

"I—I have to think about it."

"I understand. Hester, have you ever seen a man die a traitor's death?" My stomach turned. I had never seen it, but even the thought horrified me. "If you could spare a man that, would you not?"

"And risk it myself?"

"It would never be used against a woman. Besides, merely giving me a name or two is conspiracy at worst, not treason. Your sex would earn you leniency."

"That has not been my experience." The magistrates had counted it leniency when they decided not to hang me for my crime, but the whole town saw to it that I did not escape proper penance. Even Roger could see that, in many ways, the years of isolation and disillusionment I had suffered were worse than death.

John touched my cheek. "Think on it. We should return, in case Robert grows restless and looks to rouse me from my sleep to talk."

John went into the house first, and when I saw a light in his window, I knew that all were securely ensconced in their rooms and that I might safely return myself.

Could I possibly live with having a man hanged, drawn, and quartered upon my conscience? Thus far, I had yet to be an instrument of any conviction more harsh than conspiracy, and the consequences for those men weighed heavily enough upon my soul. But I could hardly risk hanging myself, leaving Pearl the orphaned daughter of a traitor. Somehow being merely physically entangled with this man had suddenly taken on more complications than being emotionally entangled with the other.

Twenty-three

Mary decided that she and the children would not stay in the country the whole time arranged, but she saw no reason to rush. They would be back from Kent by week's end, so I returned to London with only Robert and John. There was much conversation in the carriage, most of it idle, regarding whom we were returning to investigate. There was no way of knowing, as the range of likely candidates had been growing steadily for months. Certainly we all knew of the discontent that bubbled under the surface of even the staunchest of Cromwell's earlier supporters, and for the first time the three of us discussed it openly. England was a nation weary of wars, weary of taxes to pay for them, and craving forbidden frivolity to alleviate the burdens.

That Robert had become a part of Cromwell's London investigations was due primarily to me. Still, when we sent word to Whitehall of our arrival in town, it was Robert who was summoned to Thurloe first—a nod to male ascendance, no doubt. Mustn't let the woman think she is important. John had his place in the protectorate, as well. He held diplomatic ties with the Scottish and the Dutch, both constant thorns in the protectorate's side, and his skills and connections were vital, but he had no part in London intelligence. He was surely anxious to learn the latest object of my upcoming investigation, but it was far more appropriate and therefore

less suspect for him to seek out his own contacts for whatever they
might know than to linger at Wright House. This left me waiting
alone to ponder every possible consequence of fulfilling the conspiratorial lover's promise I had made to him. Somehow I had allowed myself to be drawn into a conflict I would never have
chosen—first by expediency, then by intimacy.

What signified my scarlet letter now? Abdication of responsibility? Association with a cause in which I did not believe? I felt a
pawn on both sides now, and it rankled deeply.

While Robert was at Whitehall, I went to the market and returned to set some lamb in a pot over the hearth to simmer. The
servants had been allowed to visit relatives across the city while
we were away, and since we had returned earlier than scheduled,
Robert and I were on our own for dinner. For propriety's sake, we
sent word to the housekeeper as soon as we arrived, bidding her
to return with all haste. It was a shame to interrupt her holiday.
After all, Robert and I could have easily remained unchaperoned
until morning, but our ever-so-righteous neighbors were unlikely
to consider the fact that either of us would have preferred chewing glass to bedding each other.

He returned, and we sat together in the parlor. He informed
me of all that had transpired that afternoon, including the name
of the man I would question, while I ripped the stitches from my
sewing for a third time.

"You seem greatly agitated, Hester," he commented.

"I am!" I snapped. "I realize that you feel no compunction
whatsoever about what fate befalls this man, but I am not so
immune."

Which was, of course, a blatant lie of omission. It was true that
the treatment of conspirators repelled me, but the greater truth
was that my attention was torn from my needle by my contemplation of what to do when John arrived, expecting the name.

At least it was only one name, and I had decided that I would
not write it down and leave evidence of the crime written in my
own hand.

And yet, I thought, this could be a test. What if Oliver Cromwell had asked John to verify me, my moral fiber, my loyalty?
Would I have seen that in him? It seemed too possible that, in the
heat of desire, I could have missed traces of lies. If his theories re-

garding my perception were correct, I would not detect such deception so long as he deemed his actions moral—or at least, not immoral.

Which was absurd. If he was an upright man testing my moral strength, then he would have to see fornication as a sin, and so I would see his shame from having shared in it with me. Unless . . . he believed that the sin was absolved by its ultimate purpose, the means justified by the end.

No. That was ridiculous. He could not have lied about everything—Descartes, politics, sin—all undetected by me. I had perceived his deceptiveness before; I would perceive it still if deceived me he had.

The tumble of thoughts in my head seemed to hammer inside my skull. *Damn!* I had stitched closed the sleeve upon which I labored. I set the garment aside and went to the kitchen without so much as a nod to Robert. There I added herbs and vegetables to the pot and then sat at the hearth to stew along with supper.

John arrived with tidings of the release from prison of Thomas Harrison, one of Cromwell's many critics of late, but this was hardly privileged information. As a subtle invitation to Robert to speak his news, it was an utter failure. Robert had already told me of the protector's adamant desire that the current object of his scrutiny remain confidential. Instead, we ate dinner, spoke guardedly of how things fared in Ireland, and wondered whether England might find herself at war with Spain in the near future.

It was well before ten o'clock when John declared himself exhausted, thanked me for the meal, and bid Robert and me good night. As planned, when John donned his cloak, his scarf slipped to the floor, and he left without it.

Just the sight of it, lying serpentine on the floor, left me sweating despite the cold that had crept into the room when he'd opened the door. To my own ears, it sounded too pat, too planned when I said, "Oh! Sir John's scarf! He cannot have gone far."

I bolted through the door, anxious that Robert would offer to return the scarf, knowing that it would appear odd for me to protest if he did. There was no proper reason to insist that I be the one to follow him out in the street.

But Robert remained behind. "Sir John!" I called breathlessly, and two houses away, he paused and turned back. "Your scarf."

"I thought my neck a bit cold," he replied.

I caught up and handed it to him, softly muttering, "Major General Robert Overton."

John wrapped the scarf around his neck, frowning. "Overton?"

"Do you know him?"

"I have heard his name, but only in Cromwell's circles, not in any against him. If Overton is a key player in anything, it will come as a surprise to me."

A sigh of relief soughed through my lips. "I pray you are right. I haven't the disposition for all this intrigue."

He smiled and winked. "I think you shall be spared this time."

If only he had been correct. I met the major general in Cromwell's office the next day, and I liked him on sight. He had a pleasant face softened by curly locks of dark hair. The man was utterly outspoken, his voice and face crystal-clear, his manner at ease. He was English but lived in Scotland, only occasionally visiting London, and I wondered if he had yet to learn the significance of my being included in such gatherings with the protector. He did not seem to think it odd, this strange woman sharing his private audience. When we took our places at seats around a small table, he hastened to pull out a chair and offer it to me.

"I thank you for asking me here, my lord," Overton said, sitting down and turning to Cromwell. "Or is it 'Your Highness' now? I'm told it is."

"The manner in which I am addressed seems to have sought its own direction," Cromwell replied.

I had heard many address him so, Robert included, but until now had not done so myself. After all, he was not the king. Apparently I had erred, though thus far Cromwell had forborne saying so to me.

Overton gave him a wry look. "Well then, *Your Highness*, we left things on a rather tense note in our conversations last spring, and it is my fondest hope that you have come to see the wisdom in soliciting broader advice."

"Naturally, I seek wisdom from all corners of the protectorate," Cromwell replied, flicking his hand in a dismissive gesture.

Overton nodded. "A prudent course of action; still, there are those who would pose as advisers who do but hope to gain your favor by flattery, placing you upon a throne in nature if not in name. And not a mere king's throne, mind you, but the very throne of heaven. I imagine it would be heady stuff and hard to resist."

"Major General, surely you do not accuse me of blasphemy?" Cromwell protested. He smiled as in jest, but his eyes held no trace of humor.

Overton smiled, too, no more genuinely. "Not at all, Your Highness, not at all. Others blaspheme in their worship of you. They would intoxicate and befuddle you with power and adulation, when you and I both know that you are, in your heart, an upright, modest man. You must not allow others to cloud your sight, to divert you from your nation's interests."

"And this is how you see things?" Cromwell asked, his face utterly somber now. "I am diverted by flattery?"

A frown creased Overton's brow. "I see a path being built before you, lined in flowery words, a tempting path . . ." Thus far, I saw no hint or shadow of treachery about the man, only deep concern.

"And to what lengths would you go, Major General, to keep me from the path you would prefer that I eschew?"

At this, Overton's eyes widened in disbelief. "Are you accusing me of conspiracy, Your Highness?"

"I accuse you of nothing, I merely ask to what—"

"Do you really think me such a fool?" Overton snapped.

"Fool enough to conspire?"

"Fool enough to speak as plainly as I have if I were conspiring against you. Look to your most ardent flatterers if you are not already too blinded by your own pride to see them for what they are. Sycophants! If you want to be spoken to in all honesty, Your Highness, speak to your detractors."

Cromwell rose. "And you are such a detractor."

Overton stood and faced him. "I am heavily displeased by the *Instrument of Government* as it stands, and I have said as much before parliament. That document leaves rather more latitude to whoever may be lord protector than seems prudent. I have great respect for you, Your Highness, but I need not remind you of the axiom of power, absolute power especially."

Cromwell scoffed at this. "I hardly have absolute power, Major General."

"Perhaps not yet, but you have too much. I am not a man inclined to treason, and I have served your army faithfully. I would never lurk in the shadows and plot your demise, but I will speak plainly in the daylight of my misgivings. Or is it a crime now for a man to have a conscience of his own and speak from it?"

"Certainly not! But at what point does such 'honesty' degenerate into inciting revolution?"

"You need not ask me," Overton said. "You crossed that boundary yourself to get where you are."

"Are you a Royalist now, Overton?"

"I am a Republican and a patriot!" Overton cried. "I have placed myself at risk as much as anyone in this endeavor. I have no wish to see Charles's son on the throne. I've no wish to see anyone on the throne. Not even you!" For the first time he turned to look directly at me, seeming at last to see me as a participant in the discussion rather than mere ornamentation. "What say you, Mistress Oracle? Do I speak the whole truth, or do you spy some darker, more sinister purpose behind my words?"

For a moment I was so surprised I could hardly find my tongue. At last, I said with utter conviction, "You may be the most honest man in all of England, Major General Overton." At Cromwell's dark scowl, I added, "Barring the protector himself. Can you not see that you are both men of honorable intentions who simply disagree?"

Overton shook his head, and it seemed to me that he had some sight of his own, sensing my own duplicity. What had begun as a passionate desire to serve his country had become an insatiable hunger for power in Cromwell. It took no mysterious gift to see this. Cromwell may have refused the crown, but of late he had refused none of the power that it symbolized. He took it all and more. Overton was by far the more honest of the two men; to suggest anything else was a lie, and in his presence I felt accountable.

Then Overton's expression softened, almost to pity, and he looked back at Cromwell. "You should be ashamed of yourself, dragging this poor woman through your rubbish heaps."

"Mistress Prynne is honored to serve the protectorate," Cromwell replied. "Are you not, mistress?"

My voice entirely gone, I nodded.

Overton grunted. "Am I under arrest?"

Cromwell crossed his arms. "You are quite wrong about me, Major General. I am a tolerant man, and I respect the right of men to disagree with me. Since Mistress Prynne is convinced that you have spoken all there was to speak and in all honesty, I see no reason to deter you. I would suggest that you take your own advice. Be wary of those who would cloud *your* sight and divert *you* from what is best for your country."

The men bid each other a hostile farewell, and Robert Wright joined the protector and me after Overton had left.

"Well?" Robert asked.

"Ask her," Cromwell said, nodding to me.

"I meant what I said. He is displeased, as he so plainly told you, but he spoke the truth when he denied being a Royalist."

Cromwell's face lit with that inner flame that could so captivate those who knew him. "That is it! Think how carefully he phrased his answers. He could speak the truth in saying that he was no Royalist, but there are others who would see me fall—Levelers, Fifth Monarchists . . ."

"I would have seen that, Your Highness. Others have tried just such deceptions to no avail. I know a conspirator when I see one, and I tell you, the major general is no such thing!"

Cromwell studied me closely. "You have grown soft of late. You worry overmuch for the welfare of—"

"Is it as he said then? A crime for a man to have a conscience of his own and speak it?" The words were out before I could stop them.

"Hester!" Robert protested.

Cromwell held up his hand to silence Robert and said to me, "It is unwise for a woman to question the most powerful man in England, especially a woman with so much to lose."

For the barest moment I thought of nights long past with Roger. With the cold forbearance I had learned in my husband's bed and perfected on a scaffold in America, I turned to him. "The judgment is yours to make, Your Highness. I can only report the truth of what I see."

Cromwell's expression matched my own. "Good then. I shall send a carriage 'round for you. I trust you'll be fine returning to Wright House on your own. Robert, you, Secretary Thurloe, and I have further business to discuss."

Overton stayed in London a little longer, and though I was not called to interview him again, Robert grumbled at dinner over the man's foolhardiness in meeting with a certain John Wildman. I recalled meeting Wildman during the Lilburne investigations. More recently, he'd been elected to parliament but was prevented from sitting by some scandal. I wondered what business a man like Overton had with one such as Wildman. Still, I thought Overton's situation rather settled.

No one was more surprised than I when in January Major General Overton was arrested in Scotland by General Monck and sent to London to be imprisoned in the Tower.

Twenty-four

In February John took another holiday to his country estate, but when he returned at the beginning of March he looked far from rested. Dark circles shaded the area under his blue eyes, and lines had begun to etch themselves into the skin around his mouth. For the first time I saw a faint stain—a shadow across his furrowed brow. To Robert he presented a man distressed by the many threats to the protectorate, but I saw something else.

During a state dinner at Whitehall we found a moment to speak alone. Nothing drove acquaintances away quite like an art lecture, and soon we were gazing up at the ceiling, just the two of us, an island amid the other attendees.

"How fare you?" I asked softly.

"I am tired," he replied, and the strain in his voice confirmed it.

"I can see that. And you are troubled."

He glanced over at me. "What do you see?"

"You are less certain than you were," I said.

A woman nodded to me from across the room, and I smiled in return, though I found the respectability I had gained of late tiresome. John pointed overhead and assumed his most pedantic tone of voice—"Now, if you will look just there . . ." effectively persuading the woman to look the other way.

"I am not uncertain of my cause, Hester," he said more quietly. "I only find myself in deeper than I had planned."

"Where have you been?" I asked.

"As I have said, in Kent."

"And yet you seem unrestored."

"I was meeting with associates."

"The Earl of Rochester?"

His brows lifted, but his lips went straight. "Quieter," he whispered. "What have you heard?"

"Rumors only."

"We cannot talk here. Can you go to market alone tomorrow?"

"I always go with Mary, or the girls, at the very least."

"I need to speak to you," he insisted.

"I will do what I can. Tomorrow morning? Ten? If the others join me, I shall contrive to separate myself from the rest."

He nodded. "By all means, Mistress Prynne," he said more loudly, "if you have any other questions about the paintings, I shall endeavor to elucidate."

The assignation sounded very dangerous and exhilarating, but surely it would amount to naught. I could scarcely imagine what I possibly knew that would be of any use to John. I confirmed evidence of conspiracy for Cromwell; he did not pass along privileged information to me. So why was it so hard to eat and to lend my full attention to my table partners that evening, and why was it nearly impossible to sleep that night?

At breakfast I told Mary that I needed to go shopping for a particular shade of thread, one to finish a project. When she offered to go with me, I asked that I might take only Pearl as we had a private matter to discuss.

Bundled up in thick cloaks, Pearl and I wandered the shopping district for a while, I scanning the crowded street for John, she smiling shyly at shop boys and grooms. I could not find him, so I stepped into a sundries shop to find the thread and lend credence to my tale. As I perused ribbons, too, John's voice came from behind me.

"Mistress Prynne, how pleasant to encounter you this morning."

"Sir John," I replied, turning. "I should not have expected to find you here."

He smiled tersely. "Even a bachelor such as myself has need of pins and thread upon occasion." He reached toward the spool of ribbon I had just been inspecting, and I felt his other hand slip briefly into my apron pocket. "A lovely shade, that. Perfect for Pearl."

Though I was most anxious to reach into my pocket, it seemed unwise to call undue attention to it, so I waited. "Yes, I was just thinking so myself."

John nodded to my daughter, who watched us both with intense curiosity. "Good day, Miss Pearl."

"Good day, Sir John."

"Have you any sewing yourself to work on?"

"Always," she replied, shooting a puzzled look in my direction.

"How old are you now, young lady? Thirteen, yes?"

"I am, sir."

"Old enough to browse this shop yourself, I'd say. A little taste of independence."

"I—I suppose so."

"Well"—he nodded to us both—"good to see you. I'd best find my necessities and be on my way."

"Mother—" Pearl began, but I hushed her.

While John paid for his needle and thread, I slipped my hand into my pocket and withdrew a slip of paper.

Smythe the butcher, through the shop, out the back door, in the alley.

"Pearl," I said, handing her two coppers, "stay here and buy a few shades of thread to suit your fancy. I will return shortly."

So that I would not appear to be following him, I left the shop ahead of John. I knew where Mister Smythe's shop was, and I walked there as quickly as I could without seeming overly rushed. My heart pounded, and I felt a little giddy, so I again reminded myself that I had no important information to impart. At worst I was agreeing to a clandestine meeting with a man who had been my lover—not a noble thing, but neither of us was married, so it was hardly a hanging error.

Oddly enough, plump Mister Smythe did not so much as look in my direction when I walked through the door. He was busy cutting a slab of pork for a customer, and as I walked toward the rear of the shop he seemed to require a great deal of instruction as to what the woman wanted from him. She held his complete attention as I slipped through the hanging carcasses of slaugh-tered animals toward the door at the back of the shop, holding up my skirts for the brownish-red-stained sawdust on the floor and trying not to breathe in the metallic scent of blood or look too closely at the offal piled beneath his block.

Through the door, the odor thinned in the cold air, though there was an underlying stench of decay. A trio of tattered dogs trotted by, sniffing at the ground. No doubt they knew this place to be a treasure trove at certain times of day. Later, the butcher would toss out the offal piling up inside and they would feast, but now my heart jumped into my throat at the sight of them, for they looked hungry and desperate. I nearly went back the way I had come, but once they seemed satisfied that nothing new had been tossed out since their last patrol, they moved on to other regions. Other than the dogs, the back alley was deserted, and I wondered whether I should have waited a bit to come, but several buildings down I saw John exit another shop and come toward me.

"Is Mister Smythe . . . ?" I asked, unsure whether I wanted the answer.

"I thought you would know," John said with a little grin. "Could you not see it with your uncanny sight?"

"I have only spoken to him once or twice. The cook usually deals with him."

"We mustn't linger. Pearl will think it strange for you to leave her too long. Last night, at Whitehall, you said you knew I'd met with the Earl of Rochester. How? Did you know why? Tell me everything."

"There is nothing to tell. I mean, I know that Rochester and Sir Joseph Wagstaff have been collaborating." I recalled much talk between Robert and his colleagues about those two particular Royalist leaders, constant irritants to Cromwell's army. Then I added, "There was that incident at Morpeth . . ." thinking of the insurgents recently routed in Northumberland.

"Bit of bad luck, that," John said. "We all cursed it at the time."

"Bad luck? John, Secretary Thurloe knew all about it. It was common knowledge. It all is."

He scowled. "What is common knowledge?"

"Why, many of the doings of Charles's supporters, like the

Sealed Knot and the Action Party. Even now Cromwell is sending troops to Rufford Abbey—"

"What?" John nearly shouted. "He knows of that?"

"Of course he knows. Everyone knows, do they not? It is hard to keep an army of two hundred hidden." These were topics openly discussed over supper at Wright House. I had assumed the information quite well known.

"If by everyone you mean everyone in Thurloe's circles, perhaps they do, Hester, but I assure you, there are critical players on the other side who are not under the impression that any of this is common knowledge."

By now my head was swimming. "But I was never told that it was privileged information. I am never given privileged information. All that goes to Robert."

"Who speaks to you."

"Not directly," I said, realization dawning, "but he speaks to his friends in my presence. And I—"

"—A mere woman—" John added, his voice laced with irony.

"Yes, a mere woman—whom might I tell? I fraternize with no one but Thurloe and the Wrights' associates. John, what will you do with this information?"

"I will inform Rochester. What else do you know?"

"I—I am not sure, now. Something about a Royalist plot against Shrewsbury Castle, I think."

"Damn!"

"John—"

Before I could say anything more, he pulled me to him and kissed me, deep and hard, but I was in no mood. Annoyed, I pulled away, and then I saw the reason for his behavior. Two older men had entered the alley and watched us with sharp eyes. Without hesitation, I drew my hand back and slapped him, perhaps harder than I should have in my agitation.

"Sir John!" I said. "I am utterly aghast! Had I known what you intended, I would not have agreed to meet you here."

"Forgive me, mistress," he protested. "I was overcome. Indeed, I intended only to proclaim my suit."

By this time, the men had the decency to look away, but I had no doubt they listened to every word.

"I should have known better than to meet you in the alley, but I trusted you."

"I have been an utter cad," he agreed.

"I must return to my family. I shall appreciate it if you do not press me again."

"As you wish, mistress," he said, and we watched the two men exit at the end of the alley.

"Well played," he told me with a grin. "If ever women do tread the boards . . ."

"Did you know them?" I asked.

His face became somber. "No. I do not think it was their intent to follow us or they would have been stealthier. Think. Is there anything else we should know?"

"We?"

"I. About Thurloe or Cromwell?"

"I do not think so."

John took another look up and down the alley. "Do you know Allhallows Church?"

"Of course."

From his pocket he withdrew a coin—a Dutch guilder—and handed it to me. "Should you learn anything else, anything about uprisings or plans to counter any, go to Allhallows. Outside the church, near the part just rebuilt after the ammunition explosion a few years ago, stands an old beggar man. He is there most days from noon until tea. Drop this into his cup, then return at five o'clock. Go directly to the altar in the undercroft. I cannot promise that it will be I who meets you there, but—"

"John, you ask too much. I have no stake in this—"

"Do you not? Tell me, what was your impression of Robert Overton when you met him?"

I felt the same little tug at my heart I always felt when I thought of that fine man locked in prison. Still, it was not my fault. "I had no part in his arrest," I protested.

"But you did not stop it."

"You fancy me more powerful than I am. I told Lord Cromwell he was an honest man."

"And yet Overton is in prison, and when is he due to stand trial?"

"I have not heard."

A hiss of anger escaped John's teeth. "Nor will you. There is no evidence, so there he will sit, neither convicted nor acquitted. How does the man who has done this keep his hold upon England and the courts? In part, through you. You do not even believe in Cromwell or his cause. You just passively—"

My palm itched to strike him again. "How dare you? All this intrigue and danger, how exciting for you. And if you are caught?"

"A traitor's death."

"Conspiracy, at most. Hanging. And who else will pay?"

He frowned. "What?"

"If you hang, you hang; it was by your own choice. If I hang, I leave an orphaned daughter and cast suspicion upon friends who did naught but shield me."

"Your benefactor dragged you into this 'intrigue and danger,' not I, and what sort of England would you leave to your daughter and her children? Shall she live as you do, used by whomever sees fit?"

"She will have no choice. Husbands, lovers, ministers, kings, lord protectors—it matters not who they are, all men use women as they see fit. Even you."

"Oh, please, Hester. It was all very mutual, as I recall."

"Not that. I mean now. My child waits alone in a shop while you decide to summon me into alleyways and demand that I take your coin and your secrets or else count myself responsible for ills and injustices I had no part in effecting. *You* helped to make this mess when you sided with Cromwell to begin with. The least that you can do is to risk hanging to clean it up again. While you were making your mistakes, I was in New England, making my own and paying dearly for them. You know nothing about me, John. Many, many people have judged me in my life, and not one of them was worthy to do so, least of all you."

I turned and fled the alley, making my way back through the butcher's and out onto the street before I realized that I still held the guilder in my tightly clenched fist. Taking a deep breath, I dropped it into my apron pocket and turned toward the shop where I had left Pearl.

I found her still there, but her face was blotched as if from crying, her eyes wide and frightened. "What happened, child?" I asked, taking her face in my hands.

"I went to look for you, and a man started to follow me. He kept asking my name and where I was going. I wanted to turn around and come back here, but he was right behind me, and I did not wish to walk toward him."

How I wished John Manning were here to see what jeopardy we had placed Pearl in. "What did he look like?" I asked.

"I do not think I have ever seen him, but he could have been anyone we know. He was maybe a little older than the brigadier general and dressed like him or Mister Tobin, but he wasn't kind like Mister Tobin. He frightened me." She slipped her little package of thread into her apron pocket and took my hand in both of hers. "Then a woman who was walking toward me said, 'Good day to you, Mister Rimes,' and I heard his voice, rather surprised, say, 'Mistress Sharp.' I thought if I followed this woman, he would be embarrassed to be chasing a girl in front of someone he knew. It worked. I followed her until I got back here, and I have stayed inside waiting. Where *were* you?"

"I had to stop by the butcher's," I said, but I could not look at her as I said it. I had not lied to my daughter in many, many years.

"I was afraid," she said, her voice full of reproach.

And I might have felt worse for leaving her, but my mind was occupied by the fact that the man she described was no ruffian. He sounded much like the sort of man she would marry, sooner or later, just as I had said to John. I could not protect her forever.

Twenty-five

I tucked the guilder John had given me in the back of a drawer in my wardrobe with the scarlet letter, a further reminder to remain unencumbered by men and their pursuits.

For Cromwell and Robert, those pursuits included marshaling militiamen, a task that occupied most of Robert's time, weakening the link between Cromwell and me for a brief span. Still, Robert and his own associates spoke freely at Wright House, so I knew much of the affairs of state, though the array of names and plots was overwhelming.

Royalist leader Colonel Penruddock had been arrested, along with many of the troops he and his allies had gathered. This stole much wind from the sails of rebellion, and more than one staunch Puritan lapsed enough to lift a tankard or two to the victory. The Earl of Rochester, who had been working with Penruddock, was caught and arrested shortly after, only to escape.

I had not seen John in some weeks, but I heard mention that he had retreated again to the country about that same time, and I doubted the correlation was a coincidence. The ice upon which he skated seemed to be melting fast in the spring sunshine, and I worried for him—for me, as well, should I be faced with having to question him for Cromwell. The new troops were mustered in

London, all five thousand—an impressive display of the protector's power. The Royalist insurrection was considered duly quashed.

However, that sense of confidence was short-lived. Having caught so many insurgents, the courts must now try and hang or behead each as duly sentenced. A group of judges in Yorkshire protested against the proceedings, and Thurloe was dispatched to deal with them. Come May, Penruddock was beheaded, and when next John Manning came to call at Wright House, the lines around his mouth were deeper still and more had gathered between his brows. Solitary strands of silver had begun to snake their way through his dark locks.

"You worry overmuch," Robert chastised him. "All these challenges are but the growing pains of a nation coming into its own. You will see. These executions shall take the fight out of those who would rebel against the new order."

"Of course," John agreed. "Of course you are right." Then for my benefit, no doubt, he asked, "When is Overton to stand trial?"

"The charges have not yet been filed," Robert replied.

"Since Overton was imprisoned, we have charged, tried, and executed many," John said. "What do you suppose holds his case back?"

"We await further evidence," Robert said.

Await any *evidence,* I thought but held my tongue. I refused to grant John the victory.

His eyes met mine more than once that evening, the question there, should I choose to answer: *Shall we meet somewhere, sometime?* And though my body answered *yes,* I only looked away. I had no taste for a liaison to which the specter of Charles II was invited.

June brought me to Whitehall again, and I found myself seated with Cromwell across a table from one Lord Willoughby of Parham. He was a dashing man in his early forties with long hair and neat whiskers that brought to mind a French Cavalier. An unrepentant Royalist, he all but ignored Lord Cromwell and spoke almost exclusively to me.

"I hear that we are of a kind, Mistress Prynne," he said, his eyes a-twinkle.

"We?" I asked. I perceived clouds around him, more cumulus than nimbus, but clouds nonetheless. I could not ascertain the exact nature of them—what sins exactly gathered therein—and I wondered whether, at last, my strange sight might be failing (as though God would be so kind to me). *Of a kind* I wondered; might John know him and have said something of me to him?

Graciously he clarified. "Indeed. Intrepid explorers, we two. I spent some years in the New World myself."

"Oh!" I exclaimed. *Did he know me?* "I did not realize. Were you near Boston?"

"New England?" Willoughby chuckled. "I am not that intrepid. Barbados."

I relaxed immediately. "Ah, you must have been even more adventurous then. I hear that it is a wild place."

"No wilder than Massachusetts, and the weather far gentler."

"Why did you return to England?" I asked.

Willoughby sneered at Cromwell, who thus far had been sitting in silence, arms crossed over his chest, observing our exchange with keen interest. Willoughby finally addressed Cromwell directly. "She poses a relevant question, my lord. Do you care to tell the lady?"

"He is 'His Highness' now," I corrected, and Willoughby snorted in derision.

Cromwell was unfazed. Addressing me without looking away from Willoughby, he said, "Lord Willoughby refused to acknowledge any sovereign in Barbados save Charles Stuart." He lowered his arms and placed his palms on the table, leaning toward Willoughby. "I thought myself rather generous in allowing you to keep your English estates."

"Now there is a word few associate with you, Protector—" Willoughby said with a slight smirk, "—generous. Has he been so with you, Mistress Prynne?"

"What? Generous?" I asked. I glanced at Cromwell, who gazed back rather placidly. "I am paid for my services."

"Paid well?" Willoughby pressed.

"Well enough."

"Well enough to send good men to the gallows?" he asked, his voice strangely pleasant, at odds with his accusatory words.

"I judge no one," I asserted.

"She merely affirms that what men say to me is God's own truth," Cromwell said.

"Have you asked her God's own truth about yourself?" Willoughby rejoined. "Ever asked the lady what she sees when she looks at *you*?"

Cromwell chuckled softly. "I have no need of her there. I know my own truth."

Willoughby's laughter joined his, but there was an edge to the sound. "And your truth is surely the same as God's! Well, I am not so privileged. I am entirely mystified when it comes to your truth, *my lord*. Tell me, mistress, is our protector a loyal Englishman or a tyrant?"

For a moment I felt as though I had swallowed fish bones, throat tightly constricted around sharp points. "T-tyranny," I managed, "is not a sin, Lord Willoughby. A-at least, I do not think that I was ever taught so."

Cromwell leaned back again, his face dour. "I do not think you mean to imply that I am a tyrant, Mistress Prynne," he said.

"Oh, come now, Cromwell," Willoughby said, "you allow her to strip others bare before you. Let the woman speak."

"I did not mean—that is—I do not see that . . ." I took a deep breath. How could I give testimony that condemned others to death for lying and then lie myself? I turned to Cromwell and said, "Surely, Your Highness, you can agree that you are flawed, as are all men from the fall of Adam."

He placed his hands upon the carved arms of the wooden chair, as though he might rise. "Flawed, yes, but a tyrant?"

"I did not say that. If I may speak freely?" I entreated.

Cromwell narrowed his eyes but settled back in his chair and said nothing. I took his silence as assent. To his credit, I had not seen him toss men in prison for petty personal grievances. At most, I decided, he would cease to call on me for these interviews, which would suit me well in any event. I turned back to Willoughby.

"I have had many opportunities to study the protector," I began, "and I will say this: He is true to his wife, in thought and deed. He loves England and believes that he knows what is best for her. He loves power, but it is his genuine purpose to wield it justly. There can be no question that he is a man of rather more pride than the Church encourages, but it is a venial sin."

"Then you should go to church more often, Mistress Prynne,"

Willoughby chided, "for they would instruct you that pride is a *deadly* sin."

"Is that a threat?" Cromwell asked.

"It is Scripture," Willoughby answered.

"Are you conspiring against the protectorate?" Cromwell pushed, but Willoughby was back to ignoring him.

The Royalist turned his piercing eyes back upon me, the effect of which was to further befuddle me, making it even more impossible to divine the nature of the clouds surrounding him. "You say that Cromwell believes that he knows what's best for England, Mistress Prynne, but what of you? Do you believe that he knows this?"

"I do not concern myself with politics, my lord," I said, but my face felt hot, and I was certain that my cheeks had gone quite red.

Willoughby snorted. "Do not concern . . . ? Then what is it that you do here at Whitehall?"

"I report what I see," I said, and I could hear the hollow protestation in my voice.

With a solemn shake of his head, Willoughby replied, "The lady doth protest too much, methinks."

"Do you really think so?" Cromwell said. "I find her refreshingly honest. I suffer no delusions of perfection, and I will concede that I may be overly prideful. I shall take your good instruction to heart, Mistress Prynne, and excuse you from Lord Willoughby's tiresome interrogation. After all, it is he who is answerable to us, not the other way around. He seems unable to comprehend this."

"I am dismissed?" *In what standing?* I wondered. I looked to Cromwell for some hint as to his disposition toward me, but though his face was grimly set, his anger seemed more directed upon Willoughby than me. "Your Highness?" I ventured.

"I have no further need of you today," he said.

"I hope that I have not—"

"We can speak privately later," Cromwell interjected. "I have decided that Secretary Thurloe and I can settle this without your aid. You may leave."

"The protector likes neither my questions nor your answers, mistress," Willoughby said. Though I could not discern the exact nature of his sins, well I could read his face. He was a man whose freedom was about to come to an end, and possibly his life with it.

"I think that I should tell you, Your Highness, that I do not see anything so dark as—" I began, but the expression on Cromwell's face froze the words in my throat. I could only cast a look of contrition to Lord Willoughby before I took my silent leave.

The next day Cromwell granted me a brief audience and assured me that I had not misspoken, but there was no magnanimity in his demeanor.

"I depend upon your honesty, Mistress Prynne," he said, pacing the office with his hands behind his back. "I can hardly chastise you for it, even in regards to myself. Still, I do think that you have come to find it increasingly difficult to perform your duty when the stakes are highest." He stopped and studied me, while I sat, hands folded, in a high-backed chair. "There is a softness in you, even toward the most hardened traitors. God has given you a gift, a burdensome one in many ways, but a gift nonetheless."

He crossed his arms. "Perhaps you should spend some time away from Whitehall to search the depths of your soul. I think that you must find some way to steel yourself so that you may use your gift as God intended. Go to your knees for a time, Mistress Prynne, and have Brigadier General Wright inform me when you are ready to resume your service to England."

It was a shame, I thought, that one simply could not slap a look of smug self-certainty from the face of the most powerful man in all England.

When Lord Willoughby was indeed arrested, I found the fact that it had not been upon my testimony cold comfort.

Twenty-six

───◆◆◆───

Given time by Lord Cromwell for prayer and self-reflection, I spent it well. Mary and I sat together with our needles and found again the old ease that had been lacking between us of late. We took the children to the park and the older girls shopping. Jane and Pearl now sewed their own gowns and basked in our praise of their skill. Pearl's needlework rivaled my own in design and quality. Even from the somber colors prescribed by fashion, she wrought gardens of opulent beauty upon her bodices and sleeves. Dainty blooms and ribbons of silken thread danced delicately across the hems of her aprons.

Whenever John Manning came to call, I retreated to my room and tried to think of something besides my freshly awakened cravings. It was at such times that I came close as ever I might to the kind of introspection Cromwell wished of me. It allowed for a degree of unorthodox absorption that some might have called a sin in itself.

I thought of my time in New England, which seemed to have become more dream than memory. How odd that I had once thought myself constrained in my solitary house by the sea. There my thoughts had taken free reign and wandered into intellectual wilderness as dark and dense as the forest beyond the village, and

I'd had no housemate to call me back, save Pearl and her precocious questions. Had Pearl any future there, it might be tempting to return.

I began to wonder whether I had not been freer there than at any other place or time in my life. In New England, I had answered to no one in any consequential way. In my house on the far edge of town, I traded my services as a needlewoman for most of what Pearl and I needed to subsist; we only went to town when absolutely necessary. During the early years, a minister might have occasionally waylaid me on the street to deliver some impromptu sermon on sin, but I had only to cast my eyes upon those who listened and each was persuaded to keep his distance. After a while, even the ministers tired of me as a subject, for I lived so quietly that I gave their hellfire no further fuel. No one ever asked me to speak or to act. Whatever role I played in their minds required no effort of me.

And Arthur. Why could we not simply have loved? I wondered. Why could I not know with him the uncomplicated pleasure I had known with John? Then, of course, John had insisted upon ruining it. That thought set my teeth on edge. Only men forever insisted upon mixing desire with religion or philosophy or politics. I found myself sorely tempted to march downstairs and say to John Manning, "Be silent; say nothing, ask nothing, and please me."

And then I thought of Oliver Cromwell and what he might think of my soul-searching, and I smiled. I doubted this was what he'd had in mind.

Having been given no frame of time in which to complete my deliberations, I allowed the days and weeks to become eight months. I began to hope that Cromwell might forget me or accept my silence as my resignation from his service. However, in October Robert brought a message bearing the protector's seal. I was to report to Whitehall at the beginning of November.

Ah, but the woman who curtseyed before the lord protector that day was not the intimidated housemate of Brigadier General Wright, bent upon making as few waves as possible. She was the scarlet woman who had once stood before the governor of Massachusetts and the province's most influential ministers and fought to keep her child when some would have taken her away. Hidden between the bodice of my gown and the shift beneath it was a patch of bright cloth embellished in gold thread to remind me that many in my old village had come to interpret the A for "Able," so strong was I with a woman's strength.

Making my obeisance, I glanced around his office. Cromwell's taste for ornamentation seemed to have decreased in direct proportion to the increase in his taste for power. Paintings had been removed, as well as some of the more comfortable, more lavish furnishings. Hard high-backed chairs and a desk, empty of all but a quill and inkstand and a Bible, sat in witness of the protector's asceticism.

"I have heard no tidings of you, save what I have gleaned from your benefactor, Robert Wright," Cromwell chided as I rose.

"I thought I had nothing to offer, Your Highness. I see now that I did but delay the inevitable."

He nodded. "The inevitable. That you must, sooner or later, return to the service of your country."

"That I must acknowledge to your face that I have done my country a disservice upon your behalf," I said.

He crossed his arms tightly over his chest. "Have you?"

Though my heart pounded in my breast, I focused my mind upon the regularity of my breathing and the words I had carefully crafted before the meeting. That my heart beat against the letter gave me courage.

"I have allowed myself to be used to ensnare men of good faith who had committed no greater sins than to disagree with your politics, Your Highness." I had seen men say such things to his face, seen the tight anger, the sneer of contempt, the dark shadow pass over his features indicating an impending arrest. From my lips, the words seemed to leave him dumbstruck. He stared at me, his expression frozen. The warm sphere of courage that had begun as a spot in my heart grew to envelop the pulsing organ. "I cannot, in good conscience, be a party to this any longer," I finished.

Now Cromwell frowned, his thumb flicking absently across the wart on his chin, a gesture that most often meant that he was deep in thought. After a moment he drew a deep breath. "And if I were king, or Charles Stuart perhaps, would you accuse me of using you to retaliate for petty grievances when, in fact, I asked you to reveal the hearts of conspirators against the state?"

"I have made no such accusation," I said. "I told you that I had no clear perception of treason in Lord Willoughby or Major General Overton. They were straightforward men who spoke their minds to you when you asked them to."

"Your observations are not the definitive word, Mistress Prynne. Secretary Thurloe and I have access to evidence that you know nothing of in your limited capacity."

"Then look to that evidence for your convictions," I advised. "Look to me no longer."

He glowered at me in return. "Then we are left to wonder at the purpose of your skill if not for some greater good," Cromwell remarked. "How do you come by it, if not through God to serve your country?"

Having anticipated this, I set my feet a little wider, as if preparing for an altercation as much physical as verbal. "Am I to understand that for disagreeing with you, Your Highness, I am to be accused of witchcraft?"

To his credit, his face colored a bit, and he glanced away, looking a bit embarrassed. "Of course not, but it is a legitimate question."

"I disagree. Of what benefit is my power to me?"

"Blackmail?" he proposed.

"Have you any evidence that I have ever used it in that way? I despise this sight of mine. If ever I would sell myself to Lucifer, it would be to rid myself of it, for the burden is too great! If I could not see your own heart so clearly, Your Highness, I could believe that Major General Overton has been languishing in jail for nearly a year without charges for the sake of England and that Willoughby had been arrested based upon adequate evidence. I have said what I have said, not because I sympathize with Charles Stuart or am in the devil's employ, but because I see your vulnerabilities as clearly as I see everyone else's. Perhaps *that* is why God sent me to you."

This gave him pause, and he fell silent for a long while. This time it was I who stood and he who sat with his hands folded atop his desk, studying them intently. It was several minutes before I realized that his lips moved lightly in prayer.

Finally he lifted his face and gazed into my eyes. "You are an extraordinary woman, Hester Prynne."

I smiled a little. "I assure you, Your Highness, I am quite common."

He shook his head. "No, there is nothing common about you. This is where your prayer has brought you. To an understanding that even a man such as I needs my Lord and Savior to keep me righteous, and in His wisdom, He has sent me you."

Oh my God, I thought, though the phrase was no prayer. "No, no, I only meant—"

"I shall not burden you overmuch. You are right. Secretary Thurloe is an excellent investigator. It is his place to find those who would betray their country. You, Hester, shall no longer interrogate those who have faced the tormenter's tools but rather place the branding iron yourself to my soul."

"Your Highness . . ." I felt somehow sick inside. "I cannot be your judge—"

"No, no," he agreed, "only God can be my judge, but you shall see to it that I am ever honest with Him and myself."

"God knows well enough without me—" I? Lord Protector Oliver Cromwell's conscience?

"A reminder," he said. "A reminder only, that God sees my heart, that fooling myself is futile for it deceives not my Lord."

John was right. There was no God. If there were, the floor would have opened up and swallowed me, and I would have been happily sweating in Arthur's arms while the flames of hell consumed us. Or perhaps *this* was my punishment—my hell on earth.

"I—" I choked on the syllable.

He smiled upon me, a beatific smile such as Christ might have bestowed upon the Roman soldiers as he whispered, "Forgive them, Lord, they know not what they do."

"God bless you, Hester Prynne. I must pray awhile. When shall I send for you again?"

When hell freezes over, I thought. Aloud, I said, "I . . . leave that to you, Your Highness."

"Quite right. Quite right. God will call me to you. For now, I have much to think on. I must determine, in all honesty, whether I act in my own best interests or those of England."

I cannot say what Cromwell's prayers wrought. I know only that Major General Overton remained in jail and that November twenty-first was declared a day of fasting, humiliation, and prayer for the whole nation. The churches were packed with prostrate sinners whose stomachs growled their protests in lieu of their voices.

Thank God no one knew the fault was mine.

Twenty-seven

———✦◇✦———

Weeks later, when next Cromwell called me to Whitehall, he paced the floor of his office, and his desk, which he customarily kept in careful order, appeared to have fallen victim to demons of chaos and rubble. Under a blanket of parchment the Bible that ordinarily commanded a place of honor had been rendered but an insignificant mound. Paper and parchment spilled over the edge of the table like mantles of snow dangling dangerously from a cliff, waiting for the sun to loosen them just enough that they might break away and bury anyone unfortunate enough to walk beneath.

The man himself had not escaped the disorder unscathed. His coat was rumpled, his collar rimmed by a shadow-ring of sweat. Oil-laden hair clung to his scalp. Even the skin around the warts on his face appeared red and irritated, as though he had been ceaselessly thumbing them in consternation.

"Invoices!" he spewed when his secretary admitted me to his chamber and closed the door. Sweeping his hand over the accumulation, he added, "Demands for money that the treasury does not hold! Seamen's and soldiers' salaries, guns and ammunition, repairs to ships, requisitions for horses. Food! Have you any notion how much an army eats?"

"A great deal, I fathom," I replied.

"I dare not levy higher taxes," he grumbled.

"The people are much put-upon," I agreed.

He picked up a large sheet of parchment with curled edges, and the move sent one of the precarious piles on his desk over the edge to splash on the floor. He stared at the mess a moment, then threw the paper he had retrieved onto the floor with the others with a cry of frustration. Raking both hands through his unkempt hair, he turned again to me.

"Spain is well and truly wedded to Charles's cause, and now France is winking at Spain. If they unite, and Charles gains them both . . ." Another frustrated gasp. "We *needed* strife between those two nations! One would think that given their gathering strength—two Papist states allied against every Protestant country—I could bring Sweden alongside with us, but no. What Charles of Sweden calls discretion I call cowardice!"

"It seems the political deck is somewhat stacked," I commiserated, unsure what else to say. This was never my domain.

Cromwell seemed not to have heard, for he carried on, more to himself than to me. "Naval officers I once trusted are resigning their commissions. Did you see the new guard outside? While finances demand that I cut forces in the field, I must increase them here for the plots upon my life—plots right here in London!" His eyes found me again. "How can this be, Mistress Prynne? Look well upon me! Do you not see a man bent upon serving his God and his country? Why can the Lord not give us the slightest advantage in this great battle on His behalf? What have we done wrong?"

I studied him a moment. He was who he was, an arrogant and self-certain man, intolerant and intractable. Far be it from me to call such qualities sins—I had my own share of arrogance—but maybe they were. The question was, would *he* see it that way? He expected a spiritual answer from me, not a rational one. At the moment, all that mattered was that he expected an answer of some kind.

"You strive to serve God," I said slowly, and his face lit with confidence. "That is sure. But it can oft be difficult to know whether our convictions are God's revealed truth or merely our own human will."

As quickly as it had lifted, his face fell. "What do you mean? That a free England is not God's will?"

"Oh, it surely is," I said. "But is England truly free?"

"Of course it is!" he barked. "Is Charles not skulking about the Netherlands even as we speak?"

"I am not privy to Charles's movements," I replied.

"The answer is not political!" he said, his voice quivering. "England has done something to displease the Lord, or He would be with us in all we do. He would sway our allies and set at odds our enemies against each other. You are in attendance at affairs of state. You move among the highest in my circles. What see you there? What sin, what corruption?"

"The parliament, your generals and admirals, your councilors, even you, Your Highness, are all men, all susceptible to pride and self-interest."

"Is that it? Is that it, Hester?" It chilled me when he used my given name, assuming intimacy where I desired it least. "Is God angered to have given us our freedom only to find that we use it to serve our own temporal desires? Yes! Yes!" He took my shoulders in his hands, squeezing hard in his zeal, and I winced, but he did not notice. "In this I have failed!"

My own heart lifted at his words, and I did not care that his hands bit into my skin. Was it possible that Oliver Cromwell could at last see his own frailty? Might there be some chink in his armor of arrogance? "Surely God will be encouraged to hear such humility, Your Highness," I said.

He looked at his hands as if he had become suddenly aware of them, dropping them and pulling away from me. "I knew that I was right; that God sent you to me to clear my vision. I had assumed the battle won. I placed my faith in my colleagues rather than my Lord, but no man is incorruptible."

"Just so, Your Highness," I agreed.

"God wants this country, every man, woman, and child, to reclaim its devotion to Him. I shall proclaim another day of fasting and humiliation!"

Damn! How utterly like him to so miss the mark. "Is it not clearer vision for *yourself* that you seek?" I ventured.

"For all, mistress, for all. This time, I shall declare that every loyal Englishman go to his knees to ask what must be done to heal us. For myself, I shall reconsider the wisdom of my loyalties. No old friend shall go unquestioned in my mind. My trust I will place in God alone—and you, Mistress Prynne, His holy oracle."

Inwardly I groaned. To him, I said, "But will you open your mind to the propositions placed before you after this day of prayer, Your Highness? God may reveal Himself in some unexpected place, some—"

"As you yourself said," he interrupted, "I may have been too quick all along to listen to the wrong advisers."

"I do not recall saying—"

He shook his head. "Not in so many words, of course. Bless you, Hester, you seek always to walk that fine line between respect for the protector and your role as my adviser. It is no easy line for a woman."

"It is no easy line for anyone," I replied.

But he did not react to the irony in my voice. He only smiled and said, "These are difficult times for us all. I am most eager to know your insight after all of England prays together. Bring the Wrights and all your children. You must be at my side in church!"

The following Sunday, Pearl, Jane, Annie, and Georgie were more excited for church than ever I had seen them before. Well they knew what a rare honor it was for citizens as young as they to be invited to attend Saint Giles Church with the protector. (Nell had taken Ollie to our own church so that his childish restlessness would not disrupt what amounted to a state service.) For the first hour, the bright and elegant chapel, the passionate preaching of the minister, and the importance of the people who kneeled with us captivated them. After that, I could see the girls shifting their legs under their skirts, giving each knee a brief respite from resting on the pale polished marble floor. Their heads lifted from their folded hands with increasing frequency as they looked around them—doubtless for some sign that the ordeal would soon be over.

Georgie began to tug on Mary's sleeve and whisper into her ear, but each time he did so Mary shook her head in reply. Two hours into the service, the poor child began to rock from side to side, and finally he said, "Please, Mama," in an audible voice that echoed softly through the Gothic arches of the high ceiling. She took his hand and rose with him, moving to the back of the church. Annie popped up, too, a pleading look in her eyes, and Mary nodded. When Pearl and Jane moved to join them, Robert's dark scowl had them back on their knees, heads dutifully bowed. Of course the trip to the privy was only a minor reprieve, and then Mary and the two youngest were back. All three cast woeful looks at the church floor before resuming their places. When at last we were allowed to rise, I had never been so grateful for a hard, wooden pew in my life, and my prayers of thanksgiving were heartfelt.

Five hours after our arrival, we were released from church. For their patience the children were rewarded with the opportunity to exchange greetings with the lord protector of England. The girls curtsied deeply, wincing a little. Having just made the obeisance myself, I knew how their bruised knees must have protested. Georgie dutifully bowed but scowled as he turned away.

Once home, we found Nell at the table where Ollie sat chewing on day-old bread, a cup of water at his elbow.

"We are fasting this day," Robert said crisply, taking the food away and causing the three-year-old to melt into tears.

"He's a child, Robert," Mary said, reaching an open hand toward him, but he only pulled the contraband closer to his body.

"A little self-denial will not hurt him," he replied.

Ollie cried harder.

Nell rose from her chair beside the distraught child. "Which is why 'e's 'aving but bread and water, Brigadier General. A child 'is age cannot fast."

"Y-you dare—?" Robert spluttered.

"You 'ired me to look after your children, sir," she said. Her chin jutted out, and red stains formed on her freckled cheeks. "I know little ones, and I know that one 'is age *must* eat."

Robert glanced at Mary, who crossed her arms over her chest and gave him a level look. Robert surrendered the food to his wife, who gave it back to Ollie, who was now crying so hard that he could scarcely chew the mouthful he immediately bit off.

"May we be excused to our rooms, Father?" Jane asked.

"Certainly not!" Robert snapped, and I had the distinct feeling that the rest of us would pay for his having lost the battle of the bread to a mere servant. "We will stay in here to pray and read together from the Good Book."

"Perhaps a rest is in order," I suggested. "They have only just returned from listening to God's Word for the better part of the day."

Robert yanked the hat from his head. "I was unaware that the benefits of prayer and godliness expired after a prescribed length of time. This goes beyond us. It is for all England we pray. Do you not think that merits a few hours more?"

"Robert," Mary repeated, the strain of the morning and afternoon in her voice, "they are children."

"Not these two!" he retorted, gesturing to his eldest and Pearl. "They are women fully grown, and it is high time they accepted the duties and responsibilities that go with their ages."

I would not have called fourteen- and fifteen-year-old maids women, but before I could protest, Pearl stepped forward. "Then let Annie and Georgie go upstairs with Ollie. Jane and I will stay." She marched over to the little table by the hearth where the family Bible sat, its gilt-edged pages shining. Taking up the book, she settled herself into a chair at the table and opened it, poring over the pages, clearly looking for something. "Here!" she said at last, laying her finger next to a passage to mark it as she looked around at all of us.

Robert nodded to Nell, who took Annie and her brothers upstairs, Ollie still clutching his bread and sniffling. The rest of us took up empty seats around the table and waited. When all faces had turned toward her, Pearl spoke in a clear voice. "Matthew: Chapter Six: Verse Five: And when thou prayest, thou shalt not be as the hypocrites are: for they love to pray standing in the synagogues and in the corners of the streets, that they may be seen of men. Verily I say unto you, They have their reward. But thou, when thou prayest, enter into thy closet, and when thou hast shut thy door, pray to thy Father which is in secret; and thy Father which seeth in secret shall reward thee openly . . ."

Robert's jaw dropped nearly to the table, and I had to muffle my mirth with a cough. Pearl kept on reading, so within a few lines, just as Robert had gathered his wits together, she had reached: "After this manner therefore pray ye: Our Father which art in heaven . . ."

Jane immediately joined her, hands folded, head bent to hide a grin. "Hallowed be thy name . . ."

Mary and I bowed our heads and added our voices. "Thy kingdom come . . ."

Which left Robert with no choice. "Thy will be done . . ."

So that by the time we had all chorused, ". . . lead us not into

temptation, but deliver us from evil," it would have been sacrile-
gious to start an argument. Clever girl.

"Amen," we finished, and Pearl handed the book to Jane, but
Robert took it from his daughter's hands.

"First Corinthians," he intoned, "Chapter Fourteen: Verse
Thirty-four: Let your women keep silence in the churches: for it is
not permitted unto them to speak; but they are commanded to be
under obedience, as also saith the law. And if they will learn any
thing, let them ask their husbands at home: for it is a shame for
women to speak in the church."

Mary took up the book next. "Who can find a virtuous woman?
For her price is far above rubies . . ."

I must say, in its own way, the afternoon made for one of the
liveliest theological exchanges that had ever taken place in Wright
House with Robert Wright present. At the time, none of us could
have known how that single day of prayer and humiliation would
change all our lives.

Twenty-eight

It was a fair May afternoon some weeks later when Robert arrived from Whitehall and told me that I was being summoned to appear *immediately* before the protector. Throughout those weeks, I had been astonished at the number of arrests made and the quality of those ensnared, and I vainly hoped to be left out of the commotion. The servants, Mary, the children, and I had been in the process of giving the entire house a thorough cleaning, so I wore a plain work gown and apron. When I asked Robert to wait while I changed into more appropriate attire, he said, "There is no time."

He had been in a perpetually foul humor ever since the day of humiliation, so I paid little heed to his brusque attitude, but during the carriage ride he was even more terse than usual. I asked upon what business I had been called, and he said that he did not know, but that he suspected that it had something to do with Sir Henry Vane.

Henry Vane . . . one of Cromwell's men, as I recalled. What now? "Am I to question him?" I asked, almost relieved by the prospect of returning to my old and once deplored position of inquisitor. Of late, I found that I preferred it to my new and even more distressing vocation as spiritual adviser to the most powerful and surely most contumacious man in all England.

"No. Vane has said all he need say. More than he need say."
Even as he spoke, Robert's face paled. "I will leave you with Cromwell. I have asked his permission to return home and attend to
some private affairs. He will send you back in one of his own carriages."

"What affairs, Robert?" When he did not reply, but rather
only set his lips in a grim line, I felt a sickening sense of foreboding-
ing. "What affairs? Oh, God. Tell me that you are not to be arrested? Will Cromwell's mistrust stop nowhere?"

He gave me a look of pure terror. "I? Arrested? Why? What
has Cromwell said to you?"

"To me? Nothing! I have not even spoken to him of late." Fear
churned in my gut, souring there, curds of it mounting and filling
all the space under my ribs. "You are the one being so cryptic!"

"No one is above suspicion, Hester. Not me, not you, no one.
Vane was the tipping point, damned fool!"

"I do not grasp your meaning," I protested. "We are but passing acquaintances of Sir Henry. What has he done, and what has
it to do with us?"

"He published that damned paper, and Cromwell is apoplec-
tic! He's been ranting for the better part of twenty-four hours
about the 'vipers' nest' in his own establishment."

"What paper?" I asked.

Robert lifted a shaky hand to his pallid brow. "Cromwell will
have you read it. He has everyone reading it, demanding to know
whether they are in agreement. 'Was your hand upon this knife in
my back, as well?' he roars, but denial only incenses him further."

For once, I pitied Robert his place at Cromwell's side. "Did he
question you thusly?" I asked softly.

"I knew not what to say," Robert said, his own voice trembling. "He asked Thurloe the same question just before he asked
me. He asked *Secretary of State John Thurloe!*"

"And what did Thurloe say?" I asked.

"He said, 'Now, Oliver, you've known all along that Henry has
been—' And even before Thurloe could finish, Cromwell screamed,
'Do not patronize me, John! I asked you a question!' "

I could not imagine such a scene. "He truly doubted Secretary
Thurloe's loyalty?"

"And then he asked me." Robert drew a deep, shaky breath. "I said, 'I am utterly loyal to the protectorate, Your Highness,' and Cromwell actually threw a copy of Vane's essay in my face. 'You think I do not know what you mean by that?' he yelled. 'Fetch me Hester Prynne! We'll soon know who is who and what is what in this farcical order!' "

During our brief journey, the carriage had filled with the sour scent of Robert's sweat. It dripped from under his tall hat and down his temples, and he wiped the beads away with the backs of his hands.

"Robert, you and I may have our differences," I said, "but surely you know that I will clear you and your family of all suspicion."

"If he believes you," Robert whispered.

"Of course he will believe me," I assured him.

But Robert only shrugged, his hands turned palms-up. "I have never seen the protector in such a state."

Robert did not so much as escort me into the palace. I alighted from the carriage under my own power and followed one of Cromwell's elite guards into the protector's apartments.

The chaos I had witnessed before now seemed but slight disarray by comparison. The floor was littered in paper, and at the foot of one wall an inkwell had been reduced to shards of glass. Above it, a dark stain dripped ominously down the wood paneling. Two high-backed chairs lay on their sides. Cromwell's desk was the only tidy space, its entire contents, Bible included, strewn a good distance from the table, as though swept off with great violence and passion.

Cromwell had been looking out the window as I entered, but he turned on me with madness in his eyes. "What is this?" he cried, as I raised myself from a deep curtsey before him. "What am I to make of this?" He gestured all about him.

I glanced, yet again, all around the room and asked, "Who did this?"

"Sir Henry Vane! A man I trusted!"

"Sir Henry Vane destroyed your office?" I asked, unable to follow his course. Without really thinking about it, I stooped and picked up the Bible that lay facedown and open on the floor, its pages rumpled under it.

"Oh, dear God," Cromwell said, his voice shattered. He reached out and gently took the book from my hands, placing it against his lips and kissing it. "Dear God." Then he hugged it against his chest.

"Well, how . . . how did someone get in here?" I asked. It was an irrelevant question, but it seemed the most easily answered of the many that tumbled about my brain. *When, why, what happened?*

Cromwell looked at me, and he seemed a bit calmer. The maniacal look had faded from his eyes. "Who?"

"Whoever did this. Surely it was not Sir Henry."

Cromwell looked at all the papers that lay strewn about, confusion on his face. "I had them brought in, I think." He set the Bible on his desk, a desert isle amid a churning sea of disorder. Then he leaned over and picked up a pamphlet from the floor. "I wanted them all seized and burned, but it is too late for that." He handed the pamphlet to me.

I read aloud. "*A Healing Question . . .*"

"He should have called it *Why God Despises Oliver Cromwell,*" he said bitterly.

"Oh." I looked at it again and resumed reading: ". . . propounded and resolved, upon Occasion of the late public and seasonable Call to Humiliation, in order to Love and Union among the honest party, and with a Desire to apply Balm to the Wound before it become incurable."

"Apparently *I* am the 'Wound' of which he writes."

"And this is why . . . ?" I gestured to the stained wall and inkwell.

"The condition of the room is irrelevant! It is the condition of the protectorate we contemplate now!" Cromwell shouted, the gleam back in his eyes, and my heart raced from my breast to my throat, trying frantically to beat its way right out of my mouth.

"Of course, Your Highness," I said, righting a chair and sitting down on it. Carefully I read Sir Henry's answer to Cromwell's call for the healing of England. It began innocuously enough, asserting the cause and those who fought it to be just. I thought perhaps the protector's mistrust had reached new depths, but at last I found the passages that had so incensed him.

Apparently Vane felt that God had, indeed, ordained the death of the late king for good cause, but since that time, some "great interruption" had "risen up to accommodate the private and self-ish interests of a part" rather than the common good. He likened the current government to the Norman Conquest, asserting that "if these breaches be not healed," they would work to the advantage, not "of public interest, but the private lust and will of the conqueror." That he was paralleling Oliver Cromwell to William the Bastard was undeniable.

In ill-concealed terms, he referred to Cromwell as an anti-Christian tyrant and laid open the notion that parliament, not the lord protector, ought to lead the army. This would ensure that "all just cause of difference, fear, animosity, emulation, jealousy, and the like" would be "wholly abolished and removed."

Toward the end, he delivered a stinging admonition. Cromwell himself had resisted the crown because he had once believed the people capable of governing themselves. Now, Vane chided, "if the bringing of true freedom into exercise among men, yea, so refined a party of men, be impossible, why hath this been concealed all this while? and why was it not thought on before so much blood was spilt, and treasure spent? Surely such a thing as this was judged real and practicable, not imaginary and notional."

God had not abandoned England, Vane concluded in rather oblique terms, its leader had.

"What am I to do, Hester?" Cromwell entreated as I stood and set the essay on the desk next to the Bible.

"What shall I say, Your Highness? He does not call for your murder or overthrow. He does but ask that you reconsider the part you have come to play in the state that men such as you and he once envisioned."

Cromwell's knowing eyes narrowed, the left one ticking dangerously. "If ever I thought that I must doubt the side you have chosen, Hester Prynne, then I would know that the corruption of this world could be cleansed by nothing short of a river of fire and blood. Naught could prevent innocents from being swept away in the deluge."

Innocents like Pearl, Mary, Jane, Annie, Georgie, and even little Ollie? I need not ask. It was all in his menacing gaze.

"Then you have your answer, Your Highness, and have no need of me."

"Where does your heart lie, Hester?" he asked.

"Wherever it must, Your Highness. I am no politician. I am a mother and a bosom friend. I do not know Henry Vane and can attest to nothing in his affairs. You must do as you will with the knowledge that even those you have trusted so long and so well question your wisdom now. I can say with utter certainty that Robert Wright is unshakable in his loyalty to you, and where he goes, his wife follows. Whether or not you still trust my word is for you to decide."

"Then you do think me an anti-Christian tyrant who would hurt your friends for my 'private and selfish interests.'"

"I believe that you may have faith in everyone at Wright House."

But the air in the office crackled with skepticism. Neither of us had spoken fully what was in our hearts, and neither of us was deceived by that which the other held back.

Twenty-nine

The palace had been in an uproar, gossip and general panic jamming the cogs of the protectorate's machine. The simple act of ordering a carriage had been a major undertaking, so I did not gain Wright House until nearly supper. From the street below, I could see the silhouettes of Mary and Robert in deep conversation in the window of their room on the second floor. For the life of me, I hoped the children and Nell were fully themselves. I had had quite enough of distraught people for one day.

For just a moment, when I walked through the front door and saw a visitor at the table, lifting a cup to his mouth, I was tempted to turn around and walk back out, but I had nowhere to go.

With a sigh I removed my cloak, dropped it onto a chair, and said, "Good evening to you, Major Chapham." Perhaps it was unfair, but just at the moment he seemed the one to blame for the whole mess. He was, after all, the first man Cromwell had asked me to help interrogate. His presence brought back that night in the grotto of Whitehall with crystal clarity.

He gave me a strange quirk of a smile, and the ever-present cloud that hung about him roiled darkly. "It is just 'mister,' now, Mistress Prynne. You may recall that I was forced to resign my commission."

"Yes, I seem to remember something about that. Do you mind terribly if we dispense with games? I find I have walked on all the eggshells I can for one day."

"Cromwell being disagreeable, is he?"

"Cromwell is . . . irate. No. That word is too mild." I pressed my fingers to my forehead. "I am at a loss to describe his current disposition. What are you doing here?"

"Well, we are dispensing with even the most rudimentary civility, aren't we?" he commented, rising.

"Hmmm," I replied. If I were truly of a mind to dispense with all civility, I would have fetched a broom from the kitchen and beaten him with it all the way down the street. I was not of a disposition to converse with the likes of him. Still, I kept my voice even as I said, "Apparently you are aware of the state of things in the protectorate; therefore you must know that your presence in this house is a danger to everyone living here. The last thing Robert needs to make its way to Whitehall is news that a known traitor spent an evening at Wright House."

"You wound me," Chapham said, his tone oily, his lips tweaked at one corner. "I have no grudge against Robert. I am only here to help him, as he is even now explaining to his wife upstairs."

"Help him? How?" I demanded.

"You of all people, Mistress Prynne, know that I will do whatever I must to survive. As it happens, I have made amends through Cromwell's son, Richard. More accurately, through a friend of Richard's. In any case, I have managed to find a back door into the protectorate's good graces."

"And yet I do not see a clean conscience in you."

He snorted in derision. "I was reduced to living with my wife's family. Let me assure you, my conscience has been the least of my worries."

"Well, Robert still comes and goes through the front door, Mister Chapham, so I hardly see how you are in a position to help him right now."

"In times like these," Robert interrupted, and I turned to see him paused at the hallway entrance, "more than one door in is called for."

"Robert," I warned, "you cannot trust—"

"Hester?" Mary called from behind her husband. "You're home?" She sniffed, and her voice sounded thick, as though she had been sleeping or crying.

"Yes, Mary. I was hard-pressed to find a carriage. Are you all right?"

Robert remained in the center of the doorway, blocking passage between the hall and the parlor. He raised his hand and pointed at me, his face floating, drawn and haggard, above the appendage. "If you do anything to talk her out of this or to ruin this arrangement, then you may find other accommodations for your daughter and yourself." And then he dropped his hand and stepped aside.

When Mary did not immediately make an appearance, I swept past him and found her at the foot of the stairs, her face swollen and red, the left side more than the right, her eyes still wet with tears. "Oh, God, Hester," she lamented, "how am I to tell Janie? What am I to say?"

I rushed to her and took both of her hands in mine. "What? What is it, Mary?"

"Not here," she protested.

"Come, then, we'll go to my chamber," I replied.

She shook her head vehemently. "Theirs is right next to yours."

Still holding one of her hands, I led her up the stairs anyway, pushed her into my room, and shut the door behind her. Then I went to the girls' room. They sat together on Pearl's bed, holding hands, looking guilty and heartsick.

"Mother!" Pearl cried, releasing her friend and hurrying over to me. "What is going on? Aunt Mary and the brigadier general have been in a row, and we know it has something to do with Jane, but every time their voices became loud enough to really hear, they lowered them again. We're afraid she's getting married. Is she, Mother? Is she?"

I glanced over at Jane, who suddenly looked much younger than her fifteen years. She had drawn her knees up to her chest and wrapped her arms about them, resting her chin there, her face pinched and wan. "Is that it, Aunt Hester?" she asked in a near whisper.

I shook my head, but my heart had become a piece of lead that dropped heavily into my belly. "I have heard nothing about it," I said, which was the truth. "Still, there is obviously something afoot and you two are clearly not above eavesdropping. I need you to go down to the nursery and help Nell and Annie with the boys."

Jane's lips trembled, and her eyes welled up as she looked around at the walls of her room. "Annie will at last get her wish. She'll have my place here with Pearl."

"We do not know that," I admonished, but the sick feeling in my gut said otherwise.

I stood in the hall, watching the girls descend the stairs, and did not return to Mary until I heard the nursery door open and Nell greet the girls. When I opened my own door I saw that Mary had lit a lamp, but now she lay on the bed, one arm flung over her eyes, the other over her belly as she wept. I poured a bit of water into the basin on my dressing table, dipped a piece of cloth in, and wrung it out before I went to her and gently pulled her arm from her face. Tenderly I used the cool wet cloth to wipe her tear-stained features.

"Who is he?" I asked, quite certain of the girls' conclusion.

"Edward Mudd of Surrey, a friend of Joseph Chapham and a distant relative to Richard Cromwell on his mother's side."

"Have you met him?"

This made her cry harder. "N-no. Robert hasn't even met him. All we know is that Joseph insists that he would marry his own Elizabeth to him if she were not already wed."

"Mary, you cannot allow this!" I cried.

She sat upright. "What choice have I? Robert is set on it! I have spent the better part of the afternoon begging him to arrange a meeting between them first, before we have done anything irrevocable."

"But that only makes sense. Why would he not agree to so reasonable a request?"

She buried her face in her hands a moment, then wrapped her arms across her chest, fighting to control her emotions. Finally she said, "Robert is right. If Jane saw him, she would never . . . but she must know sooner or later!" Now she took my hands and squeezed so hard I thought my fingers would break. "This is wrong, Hester! This is terribly, terribly wrong, but Robert will not be moved!"

"What is it? Is the man deformed? Is he an idiot?"

Mary swallowed hard. "He is fifty-three years old."

A sigh slipped through my lips. "The same age as Roger when I married him."

"Oh, God," she moaned, releasing my hands at last. "Exactly?"

I nodded. "Has he any children?" I asked.

"All grown."

Seeking a silver lining, I said, "Well, at least she won't have to go right to raising any."

"Small comfort! Oh, what am I to tell her?" Mary asked again.

"Why is Robert so set upon this?"

"He feels that it will prove to Cromwell our loyalty. We will become family by marriage."

"Why would Joseph Chapham be willing to help you out in this way? After all, it was Robert who suggested to Cromwell that I be used in interrogating Chapham, leading to his downfall."

And now her voice hardened. "Honestly, I think Joseph knows that it's all falling apart. He believes in his heart that Charles will be king, and when that happens, he wants us stranded on the wrong side of the fence."

"Did you say as much to your husband?"

Her swollen eyes narrowed, and she turned the more ravaged side of her face to me.

I gasped. "He *struck* you?"

"He is terrified. There is no reasoning with him," she said. Then she added, "How long do you think it will take them to find an equally advantageous match for Pearl?"

I shook my head. "We can live on my savings and Pearl's inheritance. We will leave England if we must."

Mary sniffed again. "Jane and I have no such advantage."

We fell silent, and I thought long and hard. "Then we shall plan a wedding fit for a union so important. It will take months, absolutely months!"

"Long enough for the protectorate to crumble?" Mary asked, cynicism a razor's edge in her voice.

"How much longer can it last?" I asked. "What does Chapham know that we do not?"

"I do know something," Mary said. "Robert told me when we were arguing."

"What?"

"Joseph Chapham is a spy for Cromwell. He has been in meetings in the Tower with John Wildman."

"Wildman? The man arrested last year for his part in Penruddock's Uprising? The very rebellion for which Penruddock himself lost his head? What—?"

"Chapham told Robert that Wildman has agreed to return to the Royalists as a spy for Cromwell, and Joseph Chapham himself is to join him."

"Perhaps we are not powerless, after all," I said. I rose from Mary's side and went to my wardrobe, pulling out a drawer and reaching behind the scarlet letter. In the farthest corner rested a guilder, and my fingers closed around it. I pulled it out and set it next to the basin on the dressing table. "Tomorrow afternoon, I am going to Allhallows Church. This is a matter requiring much prayer, and I may be late in returning."

"May prayer do you more good than ever it has done me," she grumbled.

"Prayer and a bit of action may do us a world of good," I said.

"When shall I tell Janie?"

"She already suspects," I told her. "But you can't go to her with your face looking like that."

A tear spilled over her cheek. "I cannot tell her without crying."

With another of countless sighs heaved that day, I went down to the nursery and called Jane upstairs with me. Alone in her room with her, I decided that the direct approach would lead to fewer hysterics. If I was too kind, the girl might sense how abominable it all truly was.

"Where is my mother?" Jane asked from her perch at the edge of her bed. She was still pale, but she was trying her best to behave like a young woman old enough to wed, her hands folded in her lap, her back straight.

"She is calming down. This hasn't gone as she had envisioned, and she is emotional."

Her breath caught in her throat. "Is it that bad?"

"It is not what she had hoped." What I hoped was that I sounded brisk, businesslike, not rushed, like a liar.

"Well?" Jane prompted.

"His name is Edward Mudd."

She stared at me a moment. "You're joking."

"No."

"I am to be Jane Mudd?" she cried. "Jane *Mudd*? No wonder my mother is hysterical. All my life I have thought to be nothing but a virtuous woman, and yet my name shall be Mudd!" And then she started to laugh. And laugh. And laugh, though the merriment was tinged with something else—a touch of hysteria. "A-and when you come to v-visit and cross our lands, the horses shall d-drag you through the Mudds'!" She laughed so hard that she held her sides and gasped. She stopped long enough to suck in several deep breaths, then started again until tears poured down her cheeks.

In the horror of it all, I hadn't even stopped to think of what a silly surname the man had. Relieved to have cause for some mirth, I allowed myself to join her, chuckling over the unfortunate appellation. After all, I might yet spare her the fate, though I dared not raise her hopes by saying so.

Finally she gathered her wits about her. "Well," she sighed, "so long as he is not over rough when he tosses our baby sons in the air, for I'll not tolerate any slinging of Mudds . . ." and giggled again. "What else?"

"He's fifty-three years old."

Which wiped the smile right off her lips.

"No," she said. It wasn't an expression of disbelief or dismay. It was a statement.

"Jane—" I moved to sit next to her, but she stood abruptly.

"No! No! Why would they do this to me? Why? Is it not bad enough that I have never even met him? Am I to have no say at all?" she shouted.

Good girl, I thought. *Get mad. Yell. Stomp your feet, but do not cry. Learn to hold a part of yourself back so that if ever you must lie under an old man who strains and groans against your young body, you can endure.*

"Times are perilous, Jane. Your parents seek to secure your future."

"With an old man? When there are plenty of young ones among my father's friends?"

"Well, blood is thicker than water, and this one has the thickest of all," I explained.

"What does that mean? We're not Royalists. Blood means nothing!"

"Unless it is shared with Lord Cromwell. Mister Mudd, it appears, is a distant cousin by marriage."

She headed toward the door. "Well, I shall go downstairs and thank my father for choosing a man of such thick blood, but I prefer to wait for someone in whom the humor flows a bit thinner. Fifteen years I have lived to please him, and *this* is how I am to be rewarded?"

"Marriage is not a reward," I told her sternly. "It is a necessity. And for all you know he is a good man who will so value a young wife that he will make your life all you would ask otherwise. Besides, the older he is, the sooner he dies. There are worse things to be than a widow."

She looked at me again as she had just before she'd burst into laughter when she learned his name, but this time no merriment followed. "Forgive me, Aunt Hester, but you have never struck me a happy woman."

Thus I realized that I was not talking to a girl after all, but as her father had said, a woman fully grown. I reached out and brushed my fingers over her face, so like Mary's at her age. "You have the right of it. I am hardly the best adviser to you here. But ask yourself this: To what lengths are you prepared to go to prevent it? You heard your parents. Your mother spent the entire afternoon trying to dissuade your father and was struck in the face for her efforts."

Jane gasped. "What? Father . . . ?"

I led her back to the bed and pulled her down next to me. "You have the misfortune of having been born into a political family during tumultuous times."

"And if the scale tips?" she asked.

"You are a very smart young lady," I commended her.

"Pearl and I have ears, you know. We hear the conversations in this house."

"I know."

There was another long pause, and Jane ran her fingers over

the flowers Pearl had embroidered onto the apron she wore. "You would not do this to Pearl."

"If I thought it was the only way to save her, I would."

"But you would not do it to save yourself," she returned.

She was right. I would not. But Jane was not my child.

Thirty

Many weeks had passed since John had given me instructions for how to reach him, but when I rounded the corner to the rebuilt wall of Allhallows Church, there indeed leaned an old beggar man. Upon closer inspection, he was undeniably quite old; no actor's tricks aged his face. He smelled of beggar, too, unwashed flesh and filthy clothing slept in on streets covered in refuse. I hesitated, unsure whether he was the man of whom John had spoken or simply an old man begging for alms. Despite the condition of his clothes and the deep wrinkles in his face, there was a keen intellect in his dark eyes. What did I risk—a guilder?

I dropped the Dutch coin into his tin cup.

"Thank ye, mistress," he mumbled.

I waited a moment, my eyes drawn heavenward by the fortress-like, dark brick tower of the church that loomed over the lighter stone wall where we stood. I wished he would say something, anything, to indicate that he understood the significance of the coin, but he stood silently until a younger man passed. Then the old man rattled his cup and whimpered, "Alms? Alms for an old man?" The younger man's response was unfit for the venue.

Since it seemed unlikely that I would get anything else from the old man, I entered the church. It was not our place of worship, and I had never been in it before. With my head bowed prayerfully, I was able to study the brass plates that studded the floor in various places. It had once been a Catholic church, but some of the more zealous Protestants who had taken it over had obliterated the engraving in places. There were lovely carvings, an altar tomb, chapel screens, the pulpit with its curved staircase. Still, there was a gloomy, oppressive feel to the place, perhaps because of the clouds outside. The brick and wood were dark and the light through the opaque windows diffused and weak.

I had not wanted to wait long for John, so I left Wright House just before tea. Now, with an hour or so to linger, I wished that I had eaten before I left. There was nothing for it now, though, so I sat in a wooden pew and bowed my head.

It was then that I realized how very long it had been since I'd prayed. Obviously I had knelt and assumed a position of humility in church, but really it was the minister who prayed. My mind might or might not have followed the words, depending upon the Sunday and what had passed the previous week. Many times I might think to myself, "Please God, let there be no one to interrogate for Cromwell this week," or "Please let him see the error of his ways," but I did not believe that such thought counted as actual prayer, as I never truly expected an answer or any particular favors from the Almighty.

It had seemed to me, ever since I had stood on the scaffold with Pearl, that God had merely wound up the universe and then gone to sleep, letting the minutes, hours, days, and years of human existence tick by unnoticed.

If God was watching, he would have seen Arthur suffering under the weight of sin and guilt and done something about it. A just and watchful god would have relieved some of the burden so that it would not crush Arthur, as it eventually had. Arthur would have died of some nobler fate than mere shame and weakness.

At the very least, God would have etched symbols of sin into chests other than his. A strange thing, that. Many swore that when Arthur confessed and tore open his shirt on the scaffold that day, they saw a letter much like mine seared upon his breast as though by a red-hot iron. I, holding him in my arms, saw nothing. I saw only the frail form of a man too weak to bear my love. The only hot iron I thought of was the one burning inside my bosom as my Arthur fled to the ultimate sanctuary. He had chosen hell over my bed, and I wanted to scream to heaven above at the betrayal, the injustice. But there was nary a sympathetic face in that crowd, not for me—Hester Prynne, scarlet woman. Only for Arthur—poor, ill-fated, yet ever-holy man of God. I could not give it to them, my pain. They had taken nearly all anyway—my dignity, my joy—and so I swallowed my pain and did not cling to him when they took his body from me.

But I had more or less stopped speaking to God even before all that. Why had I done that? I dared not pray for my enemies, for I feared such prayers might twist themselves into curses. In the deepest part of my heart I cursed every Puritan hypocrite. I prayed for myself and Pearl, but again with no real belief that anyone was listening. In truth, I think the last time I prayed to a God I thought heard me, it was to thank Him for Arthur Dimmesdale.

Here, in the quiet of Allhallows, I could face the possibility that my last real prayer was what had ended prayer altogether for me. Arthur had been a mixed blessing in the end. I opened my eyes and looked at one of the softly lit windows. Would I thank Him still? After all the pain and all the humiliation that Arthur had allowed me to bear alone? After the scarlet letter and the cursed sight it brought?

I closed my lids against even that poor light. Yes! I would still thank Him. Arthur had been weak, I could admit that, but in his weakness he had given others strength. When people needed someone to give them hope that salvation might lie beyond their wretched lives, Arthur, burdened with his own guilty heart, reassured them with a perfect understanding of human frailty. He understood my frailty when all others pretended it was beyond their ken. He might have been forced to hide his feelings, but I never once doubted his love. All others could look at me in enmity, but Arthur's secret love sustained me. Though John Manning could sate my body, it was Arthur my heart still craved.

John Manning! My reason for having come. I found I quite literally had to catch my breath at the thought of actually committing treason against my country. Not against my country! Against Oliver Cromwell and the insane fear he bred. What I had come to do was out of loyalty to Mary and her daughter, and my daughter, too, for I would not see Pearl wed as poorly as Jane, just to stay securely in a country where she was a rightful citizen.

God could judge my allegiance, whether just or vile, if He was awake, but I would not pray and ask His leave. I rose and went down a set of ancient stone steps to the old Saxon chapel in the undercroft.

It was strange to go from the wide-open cavern of the church above to the small, confined grotto below. The atmosphere there was colder and smelled musty from centuries sealed away from fresh air. Candlelight flickered across the stone walls. Just as I wondered what I should do there, a man in a dark hooded cloak joined me. Between the darkness of the grotto and the shadow cast over his face, I could not make out his features, but his voice was not that of John Manning.

"I thought old Harry had lost his mind when he told me that Hester Prynne had dropped a guilder in his cup," the man said. His voice was quiet, a soft tenor that made him sound rather young.

"Do I know you, sir?" I asked.

"Not well. You may have seen me, but we have never spoken."

"Will you remove your hood?"

He laughed softly. "And end up a guest in the Tower? No, thank you."

"But I am here, and I dropped the guilder into the cup."

The hood of his cloak moved from side to side with the slow shake of his head. "I know not why."

"I wish to speak to John Manning," I said.

"Sir John is otherwise employed," he said.

I could be as stubborn and oblique as anyone, so I replied, "I will speak to no other."

After a pause, the man said, "What is your business?"

"Information. I have given him intelligence before. He will know that I can be trusted."

"And I am with the same organization for which he works." The words floated from the shadowed mouth inside the hood. "So you know that I can be trusted."

"I know no such thing."

We stood in silence in the close confines for what felt like several minutes. At last the hooded man said, "There is a coffeehouse in East Smithfield—Will's, it is called. In the back are stairs to an apartment. Knock six times on the door at the top of the stairs, then retreat to the alcove at the foot of them. If Sir John is at liberty to receive you, he will be there, but he may be engaged with someone else. Wait as long as you see fit, but if some minutes pass with no acknowledgment, best you be on your way, for he is either absent or embroiled in some transaction too important to interrupt."

"And if he is absent?" I asked.

"I will tell him you seek him," the stranger replied.

"Thank you," I said and left ahead of him into the still-light spring evening.

East Smithfield was an easy walk, but it took me some time to find the coffeehouse. It was small, wedged tightly between a tavern and a chandlery, and its sign was modest and easily missed. Though this street was some distance from the Smithfield slaughter yards, the stench of rotting carcasses permeated all, and I wondered that anyone could consume coffee here, though there would be tallow aplenty for the chandlery. The alleyways of London toward dark were no place for a woman alone, but I drew my hood over my head and braved the one behind the coffeehouse. Sure enough, steep wooden steps led to an unremarkable door in the second story. At the base of the stairs was an alcove between the two establishments. The passage was utterly deserted.

I mounted the stairs and paused at the door, my hand lifted, when I realized that I heard a woman's voice within. She laughed and said, "Watch out where you toss those. We'll never find them again!" The voice plucked lightly at some string in my memory, and my hand lingered as I tried to identify the note.

"They'll be on the floor somewhere." John's breathless voice carried clearly through the wooden planks. "We'll never make it to the bed."

"Ah," the woman cried, "to hell with my garters!" Then frustration tinged her urgent tones. "Your breeches lace is tangled."

Mistress Chapham! I sucked in my breath and gave the door six slow, deliberate raps, smiling when I heard her cry, "God's blood! What if it's Joseph?"

"Skittish woman, how would he know to look for you here?"

"What if he followed us?"

"Here are your garters. Hurry. Whoever it is will not wait long, and it may be important."

"And I am . . . ?"

"Delightful, but I cannot be selfish just now. Much rides on the few who know of this place."

"Well, I know of it and got little enough of a ride," she grumbled.

At that, I padded quickly and quietly down the stairs and slipped into the alcove, a space blacker even than the alley. Moments later, Mistress Chapham, her hair and face covered by a hood like mine, seemed fairly thrust out the door, which closed quickly behind her. Her head swiveled quickly back and forth as she perused the alley, then she ran lightly down the stairs. She paused to glance into the alcove, her hand pulling the hood over the lower portion of her face, and I drew back to the darkest part of the recess.

A soft, feminine laugh drifted from behind her hand. "Trust me, my dear, I've left nothing for you. Drained him dry, I'll wager."

Knowing her gibe for the lie it was, I let the remark pass, but thought to myself that, even had I arrived later, if she was as poor with a prick as she was with a needle, there would be plenty left for another.

I let her walk down the alley and round the corner, and even waited a few beats more before I ascended the stairs again. This time, my knock was answered at once.

"Hester!" John cried, clearly surprised to see me. He raked a hand through his mussed hair and reached for his coat, which hung on a hook near the door.

"Leave it," I said. "I have seen you in less."

He left the garment where it hung and gestured for me to enter, which I did.

"How did you find me?" he asked.

I looked around the tiny room. There was a narrow bed, still neatly made. A chair in front of a small writing desk had been overturned. John gave it a regretful look and righted it, then turned to me with a speculative smile. I left his question unanswered and said, "Joseph Chapham's wife? Have you no taste, no discretion?" I hated the pettiness in my own voice, but truly—Charlotte Chapham?

John frowned. "I have no time for petty jealousy, Hester. Besides, it is not as though you are here on my invitation. Someone must have sent you."

I pulled the cloak from my shoulders and hung it on another

hook next to his coat. "I do not know the name of the man who sent me. I met him in the undercroft of Allhallows Church upon your instructions."

Now his dark brows lifted and interest lit the shining orbs beneath. "What brought you to Allhallows?"

"Information that I hope comes not too late, given your last visitor." He scowled again, and I said, "Do not flatter yourself. You can do with her as you please. I have come to tell you that her husband is a spy in Cromwell's employ."

John merely nodded. "As is Charlotte in ours."

At the use of her given name I winced. Would I feel differently if it were Mary or Mistress Tobin who had fled the apartment when I arrived? I paused for a moment to think, concluding that surely I would feel differently. I was not in love with John, had no wish to possess him, I simply loathed the thought that he might be as pleased by the likes of Mistress Chapham as he was with me.

I gave voice to none of this. "Are you certain she is on your side? Neither Chapham is trustworthy. Her husband will twist in whichever direction political winds may blow."

"She knows that Cromwell has broken a loyal member of our order, though she was recalcitrant regarding his name. A rough tumble generally loosens her tongue. If you hadn't interrupted, I'd have had it from her before she left."

I shook my head at him. "I can give you the name, and you've no need to put yourself out for it."

He grinned and said, "I'll gladly put myself in, though."

I shuddered a bit. "Even in a slattern like Charlotte Chapham, and I defy your notion that I am jealous. It is pure pride that I prefer not to share a needle with a woman of such poor craftsmanship or dexterity. The name she would give you is John Wildman."

"Impossible!" he scoffed. "Wildman would never—"

"I gained his name through Robert Wright."

John dropped his tall frame onto the bed and scratched his head. "Wildman has been a most passionate Royalist."

"Perhaps it takes more than passion to make a comfortable abode of the Tower," I replied.

"Why come to me now? I thought this battle not to your taste."

"Robert Wright has betrothed his daughter to a fifty-three-year-old distant cousin of Oliver Cromwell," I blurted, surprised by the urgency in my tone. I had not realized how much I needed to talk to someone of common sentiments regarding the present situation, and I was pleased by the appalled expression on John's face.

"Whatever for?" John asked. "Surely Cromwell still trusts him."

"Have you read Henry Vane's essay?"

He nodded. "Before it was published. But what has it to do with Robert?"

"What has it to do with anyone save Vane? But Cromwell sees it differently. To him, it is a full-scale assault by every Englishman in London."

"So Robert would exchange his daughter for Cromwell's confidence?"

"At Joseph Chapham's suggestion," I explained.

"The bastard," John muttered, and I liked him all the better for it. "Chapham knows as well as anyone that Cromwell's days are numbered."

"And he seeks to bind the Wrights to the wrong side," I agreed. "Mary told Robert as much and he struck her."

"Sweet Jesus. It's madness."

"What I seek from you," I said, "is some guess how many days Cromwell may have. Mary and I hope to delay the wedding . . ."

John looked up to where I stood, pity in his eyes. "For your purposes, it is not just Oliver Cromwell you must outlast, but the protectorate itself. Even if an assassin manages to reach Cromwell, his son will be right on his heels."

"Then why waste your efforts to kill him?" I cried, frustrated beyond measure.

"Because Richard is weak. Install him as lord protector and the rest of England will usher Charlie to the throne on a path strewn with roses." He reached up and took my hand. "Which will still take time."

"Too much time," I said and felt a weight drag upon my shoulders.

John pulled me down upon the bed, now with both my hands in his. "But Cromwell has virtually canonized you. Pearl is safe."

"No one is safe."

"Then will you continue to help us?" he asked.

His hand had crept up my arm and over my shoulder to the nape of my neck. Oh, the uncomplicated intercourse between a

man and a woman. No politics, just lust, straightforward and easily satisfied. I did nothing to stop his hand in its course. I simply
closed my eyes and said, "I do not know what else I may learn."

He leaned toward me, and the weight that had ridden on my
shoulders of late pressed me forward to feel his breath on my lips
as he spoke. "But if you do learn anything of importance, you
know where I may be found. Then again, you need not bring intelligence in order to meet me here."

Truer words were never spoken. Intelligence had naught to do
with what followed, only a need stronger than my aversion to
Charlotte Chapham or my worry for Jane and Mary. I did not
think again at all until the shudders of pleasure had subsided and
John had collapsed atop me, his head next to mine, his breath a
gentle tickle on my neck.

"I should return," I murmured, slowly untangling my limbs
from his and pushing at him. "It is dark. Mary will be frantic."

He rested his head on his bent elbow, a sleepy look in his eyes.
"I will take you home."

I shook my head. "It would be improper."

"We'll pick up Mistress Tobin and say she accompanied us."

"Mistress Tobin, too?" I asked.

He shook his head with a grin. "I like her husband far too
much to trespass, and she loves him too much."

"She'd have naught to do with you?" I asked.

"Came close," he replied with a shrug, "but had second thoughts
and sent me packing. Anyway, she and her husband have been
working with the Royalists for some months now. She will provide
us with an alibi."

Having learned of unknown allies all about us and with my
body utterly at ease, my wits had left me altogether. I descended
the steps with John, my hood down my back and nary a glance
into the dark alcove in the alleyway.

Thirty-one

—————◦—————

Mary and I did everything we could to delay Jane's wedding all through the summer, making much ado of the guest list to ensure that all the most important people would be on hand to attend. Of course, many of them were associated with the army or served in the diplomatic ranks, so it was nearly impossible to set a date that suited all. Pearl insisted upon plenty of time to embroider a veil worthy of her dearest friend, and Jane required Flanders linen for her wedding gown, which took forever to obtain.

Robert was no fool. He fumed and stomped and growled, knowing full well our strategy, but he was no more able to thwart our course than we were to foil his entirely.

Cromwell, pleased to welcome the Wrights into his family, made no demands upon my time so that I might better assist in the preparations. Besides, Robert informed us, Cromwell's health had been suffering, and he was convalescing. This left me with no information to impart to John Manning, though twice I mounted the stairs to his secret apartment above the coffeehouse to lie naked beneath him, no pretexts, no manipulations, nothing more than skin between us.

After the second meeting there, we had only just left and gained the alleyway when we heard boots echoing in the street and rounding the buildings toward us. John pulled me into the alcove a scant second before four soldiers raced past, feet thundering as they climbed the stairs we had vacated. They broke into his apartment, and from our alcove we listened a moment to the sound of furniture being tossed about and glass broken. Then we slipped out and stole through the chandlery before we could be discovered. It was best, we decided on the street, that we not meet again unless I had vital information to impart. If such an occasion arose, we would meet elsewhere, as the apartment was no longer safe for John to use at all.

In the meantime Mary, Jane, and I might well have delayed the wedding a year but for the arrest of Henry Vane in September. Nerves newly frayed, Robert invited Mister Mudd to London from Surrey to meet his intended. He then informed us that a date prior to the year's end must be set and that Jane would wear her clothes in whatever stage of preparation they had reached by that time.

The thirteenth of December 1656: the date was set with the sort of grim resolve usually reserved for an execution. In November, good Mister Mudd arrived in London, having left his estates in the care of his eldest son and daughter-in-law, who lived there with him. At Wright House the succulent scents of roast goose and plum pudding wafted into every corner of the house to welcome our auspicious guest the moment he arrived.

Jane wore a lovely blue gown that set off her eyes, and most of her hair was covered in a pretty new cap trimmed in lace, though a hint of her blond tresses was allowed to peep out around the edges, framing her face charmingly. Pearl had opted for gray (a color which suited her no better than it did me) and a plain cap that covered every strand of her dark hair. Today was Jane's day to shine. If only her face had not the greenish cast she had awoken with. She insisted the violent illness that had afflicted her all morning must have been due to something she had eaten the night before, but it was far more likely that nerves were the culprit.

It seemed that even a seasoned soldier like Robert could be rattled by three glaring pairs of feminine eyes. Mary, Pearl, and I made no attempt to conceal our hostility, and though we had no particular design to, we seemed finally to drive him into his bedchamber to read. Oddly, only Jane appeared to have forgiven him for what he was doing to her.

"These are dangerous and uncertain times," she had told Pearl several days before, in a conversation Pearl relayed to me later. "This is not merely my marriage. It is the security of my brothers and sister as well."

This had been in response to Pearl's offer to use her own money to spirit her friend out of England before Edward Mudd arrived. "Her father has won her over completely," Pearl bemoaned. "She is going to go through with this."

Easier said than done. Too distraught to sew, too nauseous for even a cup of tea, Jane now sat at the table alternately bunching and smoothing her skirts. The street was a quiet one, but a handful of carriages rumbled past while we waited, and Jane looked as though she might be ill again each time we heard wheels on the cobblestones. At last a set paused just outside, and Robert's feet drummed rapidly down the stairs. He burst through the hall door with "He's arrived!"

Robert passed swiftly through the parlor and then the front door, while Pearl reached for Jane's hand. Jane, however, was too fast. She stood just as Pearl's hand would have clasped hers and went to her mother, who embraced her and then gave her cap a slight tug to straighten it, though it was not askew.

"Nothing permanent happens today," Mary reminded her daughter. "You will only meet him. If you find that you cannot—"

Before she could finish, Robert opened the door again, speaking over his shoulder as he came back inside. "Yes, have your man return well after supper. We have a feast over the fire!"

He stepped to the side, beckoning in a man beyond our sight, and for several moments none of us breathed.

Looking back, I cannot say what I expected. I only recall that Edward Mudd, in the flesh, was not it. He was no Roger, misshapen and dry, nor was he some aging version of Cromwell (related merely by marriage, I reminded myself when I saw him). He was a portly man, no more than an inch taller than Jane, with a lion's mane of silver hair and merry blue eyes that crinkled deeply at the edges when he favored us all with a wide smile. Though I resisted with all my heart and soul, I liked him immediately.

Robert made introductions, and Mister Mudd's eyes widened when they fell upon his future wife, then filled with more than a hint of uncertainty. His cheeks turned pink when he took her smooth, young hand in his aging spotted one and bowed.

"M-miss Wright," he stuttered, his voice trembling. "I had no— that is—Joseph Chapham did not say how—how—how beautiful you were. Are. You are—" He blinked, his round face bemused.

Jane curtsied, her own features serene, her smile sweet and warm. "Mister Mudd, you are too kind."

Ah, poor soul. Translucent threads of lust and shame snaked their way from the floor at his feet to spin a gossamer web around him from ankle to crown. He had been unprepared for Jane's youth, knew himself unsuited to it, and yet now that he had set eyes upon her, knowing her to be within his grasp, he wanted her badly. The guilt and desire she inspired tightened their knots, entangling him beyond extrication.

I sensed nothing from Jane—no compulsion to break commandments of obedience to parents, no wrath. Whether this was due to her youth or her pure intentions I did not know. She gazed at him as if she were not entirely sure what she saw. A future husband? Perhaps a kindlier father than the one she'd been born to. What could such a man possibly be to her?

"Please," Mary said, her voice breaking the silence that had fallen, "do sit down."

We all took our places around the table, and Mister Mudd recounted the journey from Surrey while a kitchen maid entered with tea. I noted with approval that he did not complain of the cold or inconvenience of traveling to London in winter. He preferred to speak of the good company he had found at inns along the way. His already merry face lit all the brighter when Nell brought Annie and the boys downstairs to be introduced, and the conversation then turned to his family. Bursting with pride, he told us that his son's wife was expecting his first grandchild, then he colored deeply, and his eyes slid to Jane. The woman who carried the child he spoke of was most likely older than the prospective bride to whom he had given the news.

"I do love babies," Jane said, her face still carefully neutral, but her voice, at last, betrayed a hint of doubt.

Mary cleared her throat. "It would be nice to have another new mother around when . . . if . . ." She sighed.

The thought of planting children in Jane's womb sent one more filament of lust shooting through Mister Mudd's cocoon. It twisted itself around another made of shame, and the resulting cord wound around his throat and strangled whatever he might have added to the conversation. I had felt no less troubled in the presence of a torture victim than I did watching Mister Mudd's soul thrash about helplessly in the net of his warring emotions.

Somehow we made it through dinner, primarily by avoiding any and all discussion of babies, weddings, husbands, wives, or anything else an engaged couple might naturally discuss. Instead, we spoke of the virtues of country food over city and whether walks in cold air were a bane or a boon to the health. Apparently Mister Mudd enjoyed such bracing exercise, while his son felt his father took his life in his hands every time he set out on a long trek. Jane glanced at Pearl as if to ask, "Do you suppose I'll be expected to go?" She cast a forlorn look out the window at the cold November night and shivered slightly.

"You needn't worry, Miss Wright," Mister Mudd assured her, as though he'd read her mind. "You may come or go as you please. You might well prefer to stay by the fire with my daughter-in-law. I've no doubt you'll get on famously."

Being of an age, I thought silently.

"The women have spent all day preparing for your visit," Robert told Mister Mudd well after the meal had been cleared away. "I imagine they are exhausted. Besides, wedding preparations are their domain, betrothal agreements ours."

Subtle fellow. We all told Mister Mudd how very pleased we were to make his acquaintance, and he took Jane's hand one last time before she curtsied and bid him good night. It was an odd thing indeed, a stairway crowded with four women and not a word among them. We passed the floor where the nursery was dark and silent and climbed to the next.

The girls were far beyond being tucked in, but Jane sat docilely at the dressing table while her mother pulled the cap and pins from her pale hair and set to brushing it. Pearl and I sat on her bed, Pearl's head resting on my shoulder.

Finally Jane sighed. "He would be a perfect favorite uncle, would he not?"

"He is kindly," Pearl offered.

"And amusing," I added.

"And about to become a grandfather," Mary grumbled.

"Mary!" I protested.

"This is absurd," she continued, looking at Jane. "You are not marrying him."

Jane took the brush from her mother and set it on the table. Then she stood and went to the window, staring at the lantern lights that moved along the busier street behind the house. We watched in silence as she drew the drapes and turned back toward us. "He is not so bad. He is not bald or ugly or humorless. Would I rather wed a Samuel Perkins, or if Mister Chapham is to find my match, a prig like his horrible son Christopher? Have you thought of how many pompous, self-righteous, small-minded men of two-score-and-some my father knows? Mister Mudd may be old, but at least he came of age when men still knew how to smile and laugh. And Sir John once said that many country folk still celebrate Christmas."

She walked over to Pearl and took her hands in her own. "Can you imagine Christmas, Pearl? Has your mother ever told you of it?" She looked at me and said, "Do you think we might? Celebrate Christmas in the country? And dance?"

Mary shot me a warning look, but I ignored her. "I think that he would give you anything you asked for. If you ask for Christmas, you will have a feast that shames tonight's, a house bedecked in evergreen and holly, singing and dancing long into the long night."

"And what else into the long night?" Mary spat.

I paused a moment, letting the thought in my mind develop more fully before I gave it voice. "Jane is right. Edward Mudd is a man who remembers fun. He is nothing like Roger—or even your father—but that does not require you to accept him. What say you, Jane? Can you marry Mister Mudd, or shall Pearl and I spirit you away? You have only to ask, and we will do it."

"*They* can find a place in the country, Janie," Mary beseeched. "Somewhere in Cornwall or Norfolk, far from London."

"Never to see you or Annie or the boys again?" Jane asked.

"Just for a while," Mary replied. "Until London settles down. If you marry him, you'll be all the way in Surrey—"

"Which is much closer than Cornwall!" Jane protested. "I have thought long and hard. Mister Mudd will do."

Pearl, who had been uncharacteristically silent through the entire conversation, rose and placed her arms around her friend. She looked at me over Jane's shoulder, then her gaze drifted to the door. I told Mary that we needed to let the girls get some sleep. We closed the door as we left, and I held Mary as Pearl had Jane, while Mary wept for her daughter's future. In time she drew away and descended to her chamber, and I turned toward mine, though I took a moment to stand outside the girls' door.

"It's all right," I heard Pearl over Jane's muffled sobs. "Nothing is truly unchangeable. You've a month to decide. Why, even if you go through with it, and then you hate it, my money will still be there, and my mother will take us anywhere you want to go."

"If . . . if I hate it," Jane echoed, her voice thick.

"Maybe you won't," Pearl assured her. "Maybe it will be just fine. But if it's not—"

"Would you leave your mother, if it were you?" Jane asked.

Without the slightest hesitation Pearl replied, "I would," and I sucked my breath in at the certainty in her voice. "If I had to leave Mother to find happiness, I would. She would have it no other way."

I had never considered such a thing. My Pearl, abandon me? But she was right. If ever she had to leave me to find her happiness, I would kiss her cheeks and send her on her way. Loneliness and I were, after all, old friends.

Thirty-two

For a week I watched good Mister Mudd strive to resolve the clash
between his conscience and his cock. It was an epic battle indeed,
but at last it was his integrity that emerged victorious. With a sigh
of regret and a wistful expression, he suggested to Robert that it
might be more appropriate to introduce Jane to his youngest son,
a bookish lad of twenty-three years who had gone to university
and was a lawyer in a town not far from his father's estates.

Jane was ecstatic, as were Pearl and Mary. I was so pleased
with Mister Mudd's good sense that, had I any inclination to wed
ever again, I might have offered myself in Jane's place. Cromwell
was perfectly content to pass Robert's daughter along to a different member of his family, and it was agreed that Mister Mudd
should return to London with his son, Harry, after the new year.

With the time gained by the delay and the joy of a more suitable
match, the girls set to embellishing Jane's Flanders linen gown. I
might have joined in, but Cromwell decided to use my spare time
to assuage his conscience over a recent concern of his.

James Naylor, a Quaker preacher, had ridden into Bristol while
his followers strewed the street with their garments as Christ's followers had done when he entered Jerusalem. It was an act that
Naylor insisted had been meant to demonstrate the spirit of Christ
that was within him. Parliament saw it as an act of blasphemy and

sentenced him to be flogged, his tongue bored through with a hot iron, and his forehead branded.

On what would have been the day after Christmas, had anyone recognized the old holiday, Cromwell summoned me to Whitehall. His office was once again the tidy retreat it usually was, though a slight stain still marred the wall from the inkwell he had heaved against it months before. Cromwell himself looked as neat and self-possessed as ever he had. Though he appeared calmer, a half dozen guards remained in the chamber with us, despite our usual custom of talking alone. These had been selected from the hundred or more others outside the chamber, so it seemed to me that he had grown no less suspicious than when he had felt so utterly betrayed by Vane.

Also present was Secretary Thurloe, who rose from his seat at Cromwell's nearly empty desk at my arrival, nodding a greeting in my direction. He appeared stern, as always, in his black garments and stiff pristine collar. His pale hair fell neatly from his high brow to his shoulders.

"Ah, Hester," Cromwell greeted me. He moved slowly, and I recalled news that he was troubled by gout. Though he had felt free to use my given name, I curtsied low and replied, "Your Highness."

His brow furrowed slightly, and he brushed his thumb lightly over the wart on his chin. "I have written a letter to parliament," he explained, "advising clemency in the Naylor affair. I am offended by the man's actions, of course . . ." He paused, looking at me with an air of expectancy.

"We are *all* offended, of course," Thurloe prompted, rubbing his fingers impatiently over his vast forehead.

"Of course," I agreed. *Where was this going?*

Cromwell nodded his satisfaction. "Deeply offended, but I informed the members of parliament that I felt the flogging carried out some days ago was sufficient punishment. After all, I'm told that the concept of the spirit of Christ within is in keeping with Quaker theology."

"Many Quakers deny Naylor as one of them these days, Your Highness," I said.

"So I hear. That is of no consequence, either way." He waved a dismissive hand and began to pace, then winced and stopped. "For all that we hear these days of my assuming powers to which I am neither legally nor morally entitled, I have received word from parliament that no clemency will be granted. The remainder of the sentence shall be carried out as planned." He sighed heavily and leaned on his desk, head bowed, yet I sensed no true weight of remorse. This was no man troubled by his inability to wield his power on behalf of another.

Suddenly it occurred to me that this was why some guards had been stationed within the chamber, despite a lack of any plausible threat—not to shield the protector from the possibly bloodthirsty Hester Prynne, but to spread the news that he had been quite willing to bow to the will of parliament, and any rumor to the contrary was patently unwarranted.

"You must be heartsick, Your Highness," I said. "To be able to retain command of the army for yourself alone and yet be thwarted in your earnest attempt to seek justice for Naylor . . . it must be maddening."

He shot me an irritated glare. "I assure you, it is."

"Can you not see the protector is sorely troubled?" Thurloe demanded. "He seeks your good counsel in the matter."

"Of what use am I? It seems the matter of his conscience is quite clear," I replied. Turning to Cromwell, I added, "You have written a letter. What more could the lord protector of all England possibly be expected to do to help this poor man?"

He was trapped, and I confess I enjoyed watching him squirm. Though I was not entirely certain what role I had been expected to play in this charade for the benefit of his chosen witnesses, I was clearly failing, and yet the presence of those very witnesses forced him to play out his hand. "I wondered if that be not the problem."

"A number of MPs have resumed discussion of offering Lord Cromwell the crown," Thurloe said.

"Indeed?" I studied Cromwell, who looked suitably troubled by the weighty decision to be made, though I sensed no genuine indecision. Whatever choice he would make had already been made. Power. This man desired power as some men desired women, as some desired vengeance, as some desired gold. Naught had changed in that regard. "You will refuse it, of course," I said at last.

"Do you think I ought?" he asked. "I wondered. They have a point, those who have brought it up. It would settle the constitution, remove all doubt about what powers are justly mine. The role of a king is well defined by historical precedent; the powers of a lord protector are, as yet, not as clearly defined. And yet, I have to know that whatever decision I make is made in England's best interests and not my own. You are right, of course; I must turn down the crown. Not to do so would be an affront to all for which my comrades have fought and died. We must simply trust in our Lord to guide us in creating the role of our new leader."

"Not to mention that turning down the crown would settle the constitution," I echoed. "Remove all doubt about what powers are justly yours."

The guards exchanged glances, apprehensive, uncertain. Cromwell and Thurloe did the same, but with an air of grim dissatisfaction. I had proved disappointingly uncooperative.

"Have you forgot the new purpose you have given me, Your Highness?" I asked. "I am to give you my honest assessments, to speak from that which God shows to me."

"What God—?" Cromwell ejaculated, his face darkening.

Thurloe gestured a dismissal to the guards, who nearly tripped over one another on their way out the door.

"I could be king of England!" Cromwell spewed, hardly noticing their exit. "The offer has been made time and again, and time and again, I have turned it down! What other man would deny himself such privilege?" Cromwell shouted.

"A man who deems it not privilege enough!" I challenged.

"Now see here!" Thurloe interrupted.

"And when did *he* become privy to the counsel between us?" I demanded, indicating Thurloe: "The secretary and your personal guards are now invited to witness your confessions?"

"You are *not* my confessor. You are my *adviser*."

"Well, one thing I am surely not—your pawn!"

"I asked you here in good faith—"

"Good faith? Your mind was made up before I ever walked through that door. Before you thought to send for me, I'd wager."

Cromwell stared at me a moment, then seemed to deflate. "Nothing can be hidden from you, can it, Mistress Prynne?" he said, his voice suddenly softer.

"Your Highness," Thurloe said, but Cromwell stopped him.

"Leave us, John."

"Oliver—"

"Go."

Thurloe looked at me. "I do not know who you think you are—" he began.

"It is a queer thing," I told him. "I cannot fathom how a man who does such dark things as you keeps so clear a conscience."

"I have done nothing wrong," Thurloe snapped.

"Torture," I supplied. "Incrimination of men who do but act upon their own good consciences. Silencing all dissent, including that which might truly serve to inform the protector's rule. All with the best intentions . . ."

"The best," he said, his head high. "I do what must be done to ferret out traitors, especially those who would do the protectorate harm."

"You are the worst thing for it," I answered softly.

Thurloe stepped toward Cromwell. "Oliver—"

"Enough," Cromwell said. "Let me speak to her."

Though Thurloe made no sound, I heard a growl somewhere in his soul as he stalked out and slammed the door in his wake.

Cromwell walked gingerly to the window and, hands behind his back, studied the city beyond, king of all he surveyed, though he wore no crown to show for it. "You overstep your place."

"Then I misunderstand my place. I thought I was to speak the truth to you."

He turned back and stared hard at me. "The truth. What is the truth, Hester Prynne?"

"You know it yourself," I said. "Look in your heart. You know very well why you do not wish the title of king."

He did not speak at first. He took slow, deliberate steps in my direction, and what had begun as the flame of ambition cooled to a smoldering desire to retaliate. "And what is *your* truth? You have never said."

The hair rose on the back of my neck. "Mine? As I recall, you proclaimed it between God and me."

Undeterred, he said, "We have a mutual acquaintance."

"We have many." My flesh prickled with alarm. Something ill was afoot.

He smiled, and the room felt colder. "Robert Wright, of course. And Sir John Manning."

My heart skipped a beat. "And any number of diplomats and statesmen . . ."

"Any number," Cromwell agreed, "but while Manning is a passing acquaintance to me, I think you are on rather friendlier terms."

"He takes a meal at Wright House from time to time." My heart increased its rhythm threefold.

"Is that all he has taken?" Cromwell asked, his brows lifted.

I have learned much about Puritan men in my life. They deal all too well in rumor and innuendo, but nothing makes them retreat like cold, frank acknowledgment of the body. Oh, salacious and sanctimonious allusion can be indulged in, provided it is cloaked in the proper indignation and delicacy, but the sort of discussion that forces such men to acknowledge that, no matter how piously they may pray in church, they, too, sweat and groan like heathens in bed is quite another matter. Furthermore, the worst we could expect, Manning and I, was a forced marriage where we would quietly agree to forgo a number of conventions, such as obedience and fidelity.

Both these facts gave me the courage to look Cromwell squarely in the eye and say, "Are you asking me whether I have fornicated with John Manning?"

"Another mutual acquaintance has implied—"

"I did not ask you what anyone else has implied," I insisted. "I want to know whether you are asking me if I have committed the sin of fornication with John Manning. If that is what you wish to know, then ask. If you are going to cast aspersions upon my good name, question my integrity, then you will take the responsibility upon yourself, Your Highness, and lay it at no one else's door. Ask me then. Say, 'Mistress Prynne, tell me true, have you fornicated with Sir John Manning under the roof of your dearest friends, for I believe you to be made of just such stuff.' Only then will I answer."

With each repetition of the word "fornicated," Cromwell stiffened. "Would you present yourself as stainless, Mistress Prynne?"

"Certainly not. Long ago I told you, it was by sin that I came by my sight. Neither would I present myself as a harlot. True, I have fallen, but I paid dearly, in America and beyond, and learned much. What have you learned, Your Highness?"

"Do you think that I have fallen, Mistress Prynne?"

His head was lifted at a stubborn angle, but though he stared down his nose imperiously, there was vulnerability in the gaze that met mine. He wanted to believe, wanted so desperately to believe that he was on a righteous path, and yet, in the back of his mind a voice niggled and prodded and whispered softly enough that he could almost—almost—pretend not to hear it, yet clearly enough not to be ignored: *You do it for the power, Oliver; you do it for the place it will earn you in history. Heaven is not enough. It is eternal glory on this earth you crave as much as the glory of God.*

And I could almost pity him, the most powerful man in England.

"Perhaps your soul remains lofty, Your Highness," I conceded, "but your mind walks a narrow precipice. You do not need me or my sight to tell you this. You know it yourself."

He crossed his arms tightly over his chest and sighed. "What am I to do? Take the crown? Refuse it? Abandon my position altogether? Say to parliament and every man who risked all he has and is to place me here, 'Take this cup from me'?"

What *would* I have him do? He was right; to take the crown would limit his power, and yet betray the principles for which he and his comrades had fought so hard and risked so much. To refuse the crown and stay in his office was to live with constant temptation, the promise of all the power he could grab. His determination not to abuse it would be no match. A mere constitution would prove no barrier to Cromwell's lust for supremacy.

Invite Charles back to England and install him upon the throne? It was the best of all solutions, and the direction England seemed to be turning, but to suggest it would place me on a gibbet inside of a week.

"It is not my place to advise your actions, Your Highness, only to remind you to hearken to the still small voice within."

He looked somewhere over my head. "I am no Elijah. No David nor Solomon, either. I am no king."

"For better or for worse, you are a leader."

His eyes snapped back to mine, and he was fully present again, fully confident of his rectitude. "For better or for worse?" he challenged.

He was not the only one who walked a narrow precipice.

"Whatever decision you make, Your Highness, will have its benefits and its drawbacks, and you alone will bear the burden of responsibility for it. The cup is before you, like it or not."

A tiny muscle ticked under his left eye as he regarded me in silence. I stared straight back.

At last he turned away. "So it is, Hester, so it is. You may go now."

"As you wish, Your Highness." I curtsied and turned to leave.

"One more thing, mistress. Pass along my regards when next you see Sir John, will you?"

We were not entirely acquitted then. I gave the protector a small smile. "It may be some time. He does not come to Wright House so often."

Cromwell's smile matched my own. "Doubtless you'll have occasion to see him before I do."

Thirty-three

Outside Allhallows Church, I dropped a florin into the beggar's cup—a sign agreed to earlier that all communication with me must be stopped, an admission that somehow Cromwell had discovered me. I could only hope that, from this, John might ascertain that he was under suspicion, too. There was no way to know, for he quickly cooled his relationship with Robert as well, and I did not speak with him again for many months.

The remainder of Naylor's sentence was carried out, despite Cromwell's valiant letter writing on his behalf. A few months later, Cromwell saw no need to consult me when a man named Miles Sindercombe tried to set Whitehall on fire and was sentenced to a traitor's death. It was, after all, a clear-cut case of treason, one worthy of hanging, drawing, and quartering. Thank God, it was not to be. The man somehow obtained poison the night before his execution was to take place, and fled this earth on his own terms. Like dragon's teeth, each malcontent or assassin eliminated was replaced by myriad others, so pleased was England with its kingless freedom.

A document called *The Humble Petition and Remonstrance* was submitted before parliament. As predicted, it offered Cromwell the crown—and all the legal limitations that went with it. At first it seemed Cromwell might accept, and though he did not call upon me again, I wondered whether I might have persuaded him, whether he had listened to that voice and accepted the need for checks upon his supremacy. In the end, he refused, saying, "I will not build Jericho again." In place of the original document, a new one was drafted, *The Humble Petition and Advice.* Far more to his liking, it made Cromwell lord protector for life and granted him the power to choose his successor, sure to be his son Richard. I was glad not to have been a part of the deliberations. The allure of power was stronger than my strange sight, and would have won in any event. This way, none of it was upon my conscience.

All these events washed over Pearl, Jane, Mary, and me in waves of curt, tense conversations among Robert and his colleagues at our table and over mugs of ale in the parlor. We, meanwhile, immersed ourselves in women's work. Harry Mudd, it turned out, was a young version of his father, on his way to becoming plump and with a full head of thick, nut-colored curls. His eyes were as yet unlined, but he smiled often, and one could see just where the wrinkles would form one day, tiny permanent testimonials to his joviality. In short, Jane declared him perfect, he declared Jane perfect, and a wedding date at the end of May was set. None of us was willing to dampen the first happy time any of us could remember since the holiday at Sir John's country house.

The once-dreaded subject of a wedding became, I suspect, the topic of Jane and Pearl's furtive, giggling, blushing conversations. Eagerly we all plied our needles long into the night, working on gowns and aprons suited to our vision of the wife of a country lawyer. The only thing that weighed upon us was the notion of Jane's moving all the way to Surrey.

"Have no fear," Jane proclaimed with a sunny smile. "I shall find someone perfect for Pearl, preferably someone right next door, though down the street will do."

To me, in private, Pearl sighed. "I am truly glad for Jane. There will be a place in my heart for Edward Mudd all my life for letting her go and giving her to Harry, but I could not do it."

"Do what?" I asked. We were in my room, and I put away laundered clothes while she examined the latest project trapped in my embroidery frame. It was a sampler for Jane's new home: *House and riches are the inheritance of fathers: and a prudent wife is from the Lord.*

"Live in a tiny town in Surrey."

"It will not be so much smaller than our village in New England was."

Pearl frowned. "This French knot is loose. So is this one. Do you not recall how suffocating it was in America? How close the sky, how tiny the houses?"

I walked over and squinted at my handiwork. It was getting harder to see up close, and I suspected that I might need spectacles. "I liked it. There was such predictability. The knots are fine. This is not to be worn. In a frame on a wall, the knots will hold."

Shaking her head in disapproval, she turned away from the frame. "Utterly predictable. Day in and out, the children taunted me and their mamas frowned at you and tut-tutted when you walked past, as though they were carved from soap themselves, so much cleaner and purer."

"Did it seem so to you?" I asked. She was right, of course. I had just imagined that she had forgotten. She had changed so much that I sometimes wondered how much she remembered of the days of the scarlet letter.

"Did it . . . ?" she echoed, stopping short of finishing my foolish question. "Did you think I had forgotten how the other children threw mud at me?"

"I recall you throwing mud at them."

Her face contorted into a scowl I had not seen in many, many years. "I hated them."

"Hate is a strong word," I admonished.

"Strong enough," she replied. "I hated every one of them and their mamas. I hated their fathers who called me witch-baby and gave you wayward looks when they thought their wives weren't looking. I loathed those pompous officials who stopped you in the street to prattle about the wages of sin. And you, with your letter, looking downcast as though you deserved it."

"Didn't I?" I asked. Somewhere long ago, I had given up that notion, but I had often wondered what Pearl thought.

"No more than any of them," she answered. "Why should you have worn the letter and not they?"

"There was a time that you would have naught to do with me without the letter. You refused to acknowledge me when I appeared without it." I didn't expect her to remember that time, three days before Arthur's death, when we met in the darkness of the forest. While Pearl played at the brook's edge, Arthur and I spoke at length, and there, with him, I had felt free to cast aside my letter. Then I asked her to come and greet my friend. Not only had she refused to do so, she threw a temper tantrum and calmed only when I took the letter up again and set it back upon my breast.

Now she lay back against my pillows and stared up at the ceiling. "Would there have been room for me if you had married the minister?"

"What do you mean? Of course there would have been. You were of us both."

"I felt there wouldn't. I cannot explain it," she said, and her voice was so soft I had to sit beside her and lean toward her. She would not look at me. "That day in the woods. Do you remember, Mother?"

"There were many days in the woods," I said, a sharp pain in my breast.

Pearl smiled a little. "I loved the woods. They were big, and no one there disapproved of us. Not even the minister that day, though anywhere else, any other time, I think he would have preferred we disappear."

"Pearl!"

"You were blind, Mother. He stared at me with such horror."

"He only worried that some aspect of you might reveal him."

She snorted. "God forbid!" Then her face softened, looked profoundly sad. "You were not yourself that day. Your hair was down and your cheeks were pink, and you looked so young—too young to be my mama—and the way you looked at him, even as you beckoned to me. There seemed no space for me between you."

Without thinking, I raised my hand to my hair, loose now as it had been that day, only now it was laced with strands of silver, I knew. Fifteen years had come and gone, and I was nearly thirty-five years old. "He wanted to be a father to you, Pearl. He kissed you, though you washed it off in the brook. Do you not remember that?"

"He wanted to be a husband to you. And he wanted his fame. He did not want me. Even he thought I was the devil's child."

I laughed. "He of all men knew whose child—"

Pearl bolted upright. "You knew nothing of him and me! Oh, I was a good enough daughter in the shadow of the woods or the dark of night on the scaffold. I remember that other time, when we were coming home from the governor's deathbed late at night, and the minister was standing, looking so miserable and alone, on the scaffold. He called me up to him then, too, but he went white as snow when a meteor lit the sky and he saw the old man standing there, watching us."

So she remembered much more of her younger years than I had ever thought—the night we had discovered Arthur weeping on the scaffold alone and the day in the woods, when we planned an escape together that never happened.

"He claimed you, at last," I chided softly.

She nodded. "That was so strange. Even when I climbed up to him on the scaffold before the whole town, I knew that he would at last acknowledge me. Suddenly, I didn't hate him anymore. I didn't hate anyone. He kissed me and . . ."

"What?" I prompted.

"It is insane."

"What?"

"Somehow . . . somehow, it felt like my whole life had been a dream up until that point, a nightmare I couldn't make sense of, but neither could I wake. And then, I just did—wake up. Nothing really changed. There you were, with your letter and the minister in your arms, but both—the letter and the minister—were so much smaller than I had ever noticed. I . . ."

"You . . . ?"

"I realized then, for the first time, no matter how crazy it sounds, that I loved you." Tears formed in her dark eyes but did not spill over. "My own mother. I think I always loved you, but I didn't really know it until then. I couldn't really feel it. Couldn't feel anything but confusion and hate."

We were silent for a long time, and she lay back down.

"I'm sorry," I said at last. "I should have taken you away from there long before."

Pearl shrugged. "We had things to do there, I suppose. Where would he be now, if we had left? Still pale with his hand ever over his heart?"

I tapped her hip, and she scooted over so I could lie beside her and look up. A faint crack that I had not noticed before traveled the ceiling, and the paint was beginning to yellow with age.

Where *would* Arthur be now if Pearl and I had not been there, daily reminders of his sin? Would it have consumed him all the same? Perhaps we would be happily together right now if I had met him in the woods sooner, proclaimed our love no sin, and insisted that he accompany us out into the wider world.

"You are right, Pearl, there were many aspects of our village life that suffocated."

"I like London. I like the hustle and bustle and the people who come and go at Wright House. I like boys"—she giggled—"the way they move when they're lifting something heavy and the way their cloaks swirl about them in their Sunday finest at church."

"Well, there are plenty of boys to admire in London," I agreed. "But when you are a wife, you are not supposed to notice how any man looks lifting something heavy, save your husband."

"As though it were a candle you could just blow out," Pearl said.

"If it were," I agreed, "I suppose you would not be here."

"Have you ever been sorry I was?" she asked.

"I was overwhelmed at first. The weight of the shame was a heavy burden to bear." I turned my head toward her and saw she was watching me closely. My breath caught in my throat, for it was like looking into a mirror just a few years before she was born. She had a solemn side, just as I'd had. "I regret nothing, Pearl Prynne—my Pearl of great price, my only treasure, purchased with all I had. You have been worth every bit of it."

I took her in my arms, and she nestled comfortably there, as she had not when she was an infant.

"So you would have me seek you a husband in London?" I asked.

"I am in no hurry," she replied.

Neither was I.

Thirty-four

The wedding was every bit the joyous event we had planned it to be, attended by over a hundred of the most important people in London. However distant the relationship, the groom was family to Cromwell, and the lord protector and his wife insisted the celebratory banquet be held at Whitehall after the religious rites. John Manning attended, of course, but at his questioning gaze I gave him an almost imperceptible shake of the head. Naturally he would be curious about why I had cut off communication so abruptly, but the specter of Sindercombe's suicide and the hideous death he had escaped by it still loomed in my mind, and I dared not speak to John here.

The Chaphams told everyone within hearing of their role in introducing the groom's family to the bride's, though they left out their initial choice for the match. Edward Mudd had endeavored to let go entirely of his infatuation with Jane, only a few complicated tangles of covetousness entwined about him. After a number of cups lifted to the health of the newlyweds, he seemed to decide that I was a perfectly acceptable object of affection, and he asked three or four times whether I might not enjoy the life of a country squire's wife. Such was his nature that it was easy to laugh with him and keep the conversation from ever seeming at all serious.

Jane glowed, looking fresh-faced and fetching in her gown of cerulean Flanders linen, bedecked from knee to hem in all the flora and fauna Pearl's needle could create—roses, lilies, birds, and even a rabbit subtly sewn in for fertility. The old witch Mistress Hibbins would have approved of the surreptitious pagan symbol at the Puritan ceremony. Harry's round face beamed atop his snowy collar. Even Robert was in good spirits and overlooked those guests who overimbibed a bit.

For a moment we could almost forget that in response to the latest changes in government a new pamphlet littered the streets of London, a dark and dangerous work that proclaimed it no murder to kill the lord protector, but rather an act of supreme moral righteousness. In deference to the occasion, the large armed contingency of 150 men that accompanied the protector at all times had been stationed outside the banqueting hall rather than in it, but they were there, ever diligent, not partaking in the merriment.

A few days later we bid a tearful good-bye to Jane. Pearl held up well, allowing Annie and Ollie the public weeping. Georgie, a strapping lad of ten, had stayed in the house rather than risk tears before witnesses, but he watched through the window, running a sleeve under his nose from time to time.

Pearl and Jane had done most of their crying privately before the wedding, and so their eyes only misted as they embraced. Jane pulled away and said, "I fear I shall never see you again."

"Silly goose," Pearl replied. "I'll come and see you, and you will visit your parents, surely."

Jane ran her fingers lightly over the stitches adorning Pearl's collar. "You are destined for greater things, Pearl, grand adventures."

Pearl did not deny it. She only hugged her friend close again and said, "You will always be my dearest, truest friend."

"Take care of Annie," Jane beseeched. "Do not leave her at the mercy of the boys."

"Never," Pearl promised.

Jane turned to Annie. "At last you are free of the nursery."

Annie nodded, but a sob bubbled up from inside her. At twelve, she hovered between childhood and the first blush of womanhood, and though she had often wished to leave the nursery, it obviously hurt her heart to lose her sister in the process. She looked at Pearl a little uncertainly.

"Time to tell you all the secrets Jane and I have shared in that room," Pearl said.

"Not all!" Jane said with a laugh.

Nell clucked her tongue. "Losing two of you at once, I am. Janie off to Surrey and my Annie to the upstairs room."

Mary embraced her daughter as if she were moving to America rather than Surrey. "Write every week!"

"I will, Mama."

"And let me know the very moment you know you are with child. Send word with a servant. Do not rely upon the post."

I had to laugh. "How indelicate," I teased Mary, who broke the embrace to scowl at me.

Harry walked up and put his hand on Jane's back, causing her to blush. Any sort of physical intimacy with a man was still new to her, and a great source of pleasure, from the smile that lit her tear-stained face.

"God willing, we'll send word soon, Mother Wright," he said with his own happy grin.

"I've a cousin looking for nursemaid work," Nell piped in. "Say the word, and she's on 'er way!"

Jane smiled at me, and we kissed each other's cheeks. "You'll come visit, too, won't you, Aunt Hester?"

"Of course," I assured her.

Robert took Jane's hands loosely in his own and touched her brow with a brief kiss. "Keep a good house, child."

Ever the warm and loving father, I thought.

"I will, Father," she said.

"You shall be welcome at all times, Brigadier General," Harry assured him.

And then the couple was settled into the carriage with Edward, and the carriage rattled away down the cobblestones. Annie's sobs increased in volume, but before Nell could reach for her, Pearl had dropped her arm over Annie's shoulders. "There's work to be done on your stitchery, Miss Annie," she admonished softly. "Shall I show you the secret of daisies?"

Nell turned and beckoned to Georgie at the window. He came out reluctantly, his eyes red-rimmed, but he capitulated to a game of keep-away in the park with his brother and nurse. Robert went inside to pore over some set of documents, while Mary and I stood arm in arm and watched the boys and Nell, Mary sniffling occasionally.

We settled into our new life at Wright House. Pearl took Annie under her wing, patiently teaching her to sew and embroider, adding little embellishments to the girl's aprons and collars. With no one her own age about, it seemed to me that Pearl grew suddenly older, more womanly, overnight. She was fifteen, a magic age, when the whole world lies open to a pretty girl.

Robin Durham, the boy who had once stolen Pearl's ribbon and proclaimed her too beautiful to be a witch, was now seventeen and an apprentice to a bank clerk. His mother, a woman who had wanted nothing to do with me when I first began my foray into London society, approached me after church one Sunday and told me that Robin was interested in courting Pearl when he finished his apprenticeship. I explained to her that Pearl was too young yet for me to make any commitments on her behalf, but that I would consider Robin's suit. He must have said something to Pearl, for each Sunday after, he and she found an excuse to exchange a few words and shy smiles—occasionally even an afternoon stroll home ahead of their parents.

Oliver Cromwell was reinstalled as lord protector, this time for life, under the new *Humble Petition*. This ceremony was every bit as lavish as his first installation at the beginning of the protectorate was Spartan. The affair at Westminster Hall had all the markings of a royal coronation. That summer John Lilburne, whose political machinations had been among the first to bring to me to Whitehall for Cromwell, died of a fever in Kent. Foolishly, John Manning attended the funeral, and Robert chastised him when he returned, warning him that Cromwell's informants had cast some aspersions upon his loyalty to the protectorate.

John was growing reckless, and I worried for him, though I dared not make contact. Cromwell and I had exchanged only a handful of words at Jane's wedding and then at his installation, but I saw suspicion in his eyes when he looked at me, and the fact that he had not called upon me for some time spoke volumes.

In February of 1658, I had no choice but to break the silence between John Manning and me. No longer in Cromwell's employ, as far as I could tell, I again accepted jobs requiring a needle and had been commissioned by Saint Giles Church to embellish a new altar cloth for the Lenten Season. Upon delivering the item, I was led through a maze of administrative offices to bestow it upon one of the ministers and receive payment. I had no need of the money, but the work kept me occupied.

I had expected the errand to take longer and told the driver of the hired carriage not to return until quite a bit later. The day was bitter cold and wet, and I had no desire to wait outside, but neither did I wish to stay in the church. I had been to Saint Giles more than once, so I knew the area. Less than a half mile away was a shop where Mary often purchased more exotic spices, and I knew her to be nearly out of Jamaican allspice. Since I was so close, I decided to spend the extra time and some of the money I had just been paid buying her a quantity of the seasoning.

The walked chilled me clear through, and the rain dampened my woolen cloak. To my delight the shopkeeper must have lit a fire in the stove, for the warmth embraced me the moment I walked in, and I paused just to absorb the heat and breathe the richly scented air, for he sold tobacco in addition to spices and the blend was intensely pungent. At first the place appeared empty, the apothecary-style cabinets and jars unattended. Then, in the quiet, I heard a man's muted voice drift from behind a wooden case at the back of the store.

"Not sure I believe everything Willys says. How can anyone really be sure he's given up his Sealed Knot loyalties?"

"His information has been unimpeachable for the last two years. We dare not fail to act upon this," a second man replied. "Thurloe is convinced the Marquis of Ormond is here, in England, and up to no good."

I stood, feeling suddenly suffocated by the thick air. The second voice was Robert Wright's. I had not thought of it, but he often ventured here for tobacco.

"Ormond would be another fine feather in Thurloe's cap," the first man conceded. "Especially if he's here on Charles's command."

The Marquis of Ormond? In London? He was one of Charles's closest friends and a trusted adviser—this was commonly known, and John had spoken of the man as well. I could not fathom why such a man would have chanced the shores of England, as naught but danger awaited him here, so it must have been important indeed.

A third man stepped through a curtain behind the front counter carrying a glass jar filled with rich brown tobacco leaf. "Found a little more right here," he called out, then spied me. "Good day to you, mistress," he greeted, and I nodded, not daring to speak. "Be right with you."

By the time Robert and his cohort moved from the cabinet that stood between them and me, I had pulled my hood over my head. There was a chance Robert would recognize my cloak, but it was black wool, and one of my few unadorned items of clothing, so I hoped it would be unremarkable and he would not spare me a glance.

While the men concluded their transaction, I slipped silently out the door and back onto the street where the light drizzle suddenly struck my face like the tips of a thousand needles. One way or another, I had to get word to John.

I waved down another carriage, only momentarily regretting the loss of the extra coins I had paid the first to return for me, and told him to take me to Allhallows. To my dismay, no beggar lingered in the usual place there, whether because of the rain or because the system had been exposed I did not know. Next I went to the coffeehouse where John had kept his meeting place, but no amount of coin or cajoling convinced the owner to reveal any knowledge of a Sir John Manning. Finally, I asked the driver to take me to Smythe's butcher shop, the place I had walked through to get to the alley where John had given me that guilder so long ago.

The stout butcher was closing the shop. The door was locked, but through the window I could see his murky form sweeping—doubtless the sawdust that had been laid upon the floor to absorb whatever blood was shed during the day. In the rippled surface of the glass my own face stared back at me pale and distraught.

At my insistent knocking, the butcher opened the door with a smile that revealed several missing teeth. "Have a crisis with the dinner, do we, mistress?" he asked, stepping to the side to let me pass.

Once in the shop, I pushed the door closed. "Please, Mister Smythe, please, I must find John Manning. I *must*."

"Manning?" he said, scratching his head as if confused.

"Please, Mister Smythe. Three years ago, John had me use your shop to get to the alley to give him important information."

"My shop?" He shook his balding head.

"I walked right past you."

"I am sure I never saw you. I've no wish—"

"Mister Smythe, the Marquis of Ormond is in *grave* danger!"

His mouth stretched into a thin line. "Tell me what you know."

"I need to see John."

"If you can trust him, you can trust me. You're asking me to trust you," he replied.

It was true. "I only know that Thurloe knows Ormond is here."

"Who told him?"

"The man said Willys."

"Impossible! Sir Richard is one of us," Smythe argued.

"He's a spy! He's been one for at least two years, from the conversation I heard."

"Whose conversation?"

I hesitated. "I dare not—"

"You had better dare. How am I to know your information is credible?"

"Because I am Hester Prynne."

"Who cut off contact with the party a year ago." Smythe's broad face remained resolute.

"But who now has information—"

"From who?"

I sighed. "Brigadier General Wright, though he is unaware of his role as informer."

The corner of Smythe's mouth lifted. "There now, that wasn't so hard."

"Can you find John?"

"I can get this into the right hands." He turned and stepped behind his counter to pull out a side of bacon. "Take this. You cannot walk out of here empty-handed. Never know who's watching."

I paid him for the meat, thanked him for his help, and walked out onto the nearly dark street. The driver of the carriage had waited for me, and I climbed wearily in. The protectorate had to fall. Sooner or later, it had to, such was the upheaval in London of late. How I would have preferred to be one of any of the women who had surely visited at the butcher shop that day with no greater worry than dinner, but I had my Pearl to consider. In two months she would be sixteen, and I would prefer to have a world of options open before her. I had no desire to make for my child a political match.

Thankfully, Robert said nothing of seeing me in the shop all evening, so I was sure he had not recognized me. If he had, I was set to tell him that I had gone there to buy allspice but saw none in stock and left. Sir John arrived just after dinner, ostensibly to discuss with Robert some work he had been doing in Sweden, but I could see by his face that he had come to see me. I was helpless to communicate with him. I had given Smythe all the knowledge I had, in any event. John left late, dropping his scarf before he left, surely so that I could retrieve it and take it to him for a moment alone. This time, Robert spotted the strip of wool and handed it to John before he could make it through the front door.

I searched my mind frantically for another excuse. "Watch that frog, Sir John," I said, gesturing to the closure on his cloak. "It needs mending."

He nodded. "My thanks, mistress."

The next morning Robert rode to Whitehall, and Nell took the boys to the house of a family with boys their age and a nurse she counted a friend, while Mary and the girls went a-visiting to the Tobins'. Susan was recently engaged, and both Pearl and Annie were to take part in the nuptials, so there were plans to be made. I pleaded a headache, but as soon as Wright House was empty I bundled up and headed through the streets to the same sundries shop where John had found me with Pearl and slipped the note in my pocket.

He entered very nearly upon my heels. "Took your time," he muttered, reaching past me for a spool of black thread.

"Should I have announced my intentions to all so that I might have come sooner?" I asked.

"Are you sure about what you told Smythe?"

"Positive. Is Ormond in England? If he is, does that not verify my—"

John pressed a finger to his lips. "Not here," he whispered.

"The Wrights have all gone for the day," I murmured.

He nodded curtly and walked away to pay for his thread.

I bought a bit of lace to trim a collar and returned home to pace the floor along the parlor table, annoyed when the cook entered to inform me, "There's a deliveryman at the kitchen door begs a word with you, Mistress Prynne."

I almost snapped at her for not having the good sense to know that Mary was the one to deal with merchants coming through the kitchen when it occurred to me that *Mary* dealt with merchants coming through the kitchen, and none would think to ask for me. "Send him in here," I told her.

Pulling a tattered slouch hat from his head, John entered through the rear hall. Even his clothes were covered by an oversized cloak that added considerable bulk to his frame.

"Cromwell ought to hire the Wrights' cook to guard Whitehall," he grumbled. "Thought I was going to have to cut her throat to get in here to see you."

"You wouldn't!" I scolded, and he shook his head, chuckling. "John, you know I've no taste for this intrigue."

"And yet you sought me out when you came by this news."

"It seemed important."

"It was," he confirmed. "As we speak, plans are underway to get Ormond out of England."

"How much longer, John? How much longer can Cromwell hold on?"

"If you had not abandoned the cause—"

"Abandoned it? Cromwell suspected us, John, you and me."

He frowned. "What?"

"I dared not speak to you, but at the very least he knew we were sleeping together."

John sighed. "Is that all?"

"How do you think he knew?" I asked. "Of what interest should a simple affair between us be to him, unless he saw that relationship as some kind of threat? Charlotte Chapham—"

"Please, Hester, your dislike of the woman—"

"Is beside the point. I know women. She would be no happier to share you with me than I was sharing you with her. If anyone betrayed us, it was she."

"Neither of you owns me."

"I have no desire to," I assured him, "but the Chaphams are a petty pair, the both of them. I would not put rash actions for personal vendettas past either of them."

"Can you draw Robert into conversation? Find out whether he knows anything about—"

"Have you heard nothing I've said? Cromwell *suspects* us. This is far too dangerous—"

"So this is to be the extent of your help to Charles's cause?" he asked, his lips pursed sourly. "We can expect no more? You have access to Cromwell's most secret thoughts!"

"I have angered Cromwell. He does not call on me for advice these days, and even Robert is more guarded around me. I am telling you, John, somehow I have aroused suspicions."

"But you heard this bit about Ormond."

"Because I had gone to Robert's favorite shop. He did not know that I was there."

John lifted his hand and scratched the back of his head. Then he reached in a pocket and handed me a small vellum scrap with an address. "My newest retreat. If I am not in residence, slide a message under the door. Make it look like a bill for mending or what you please, just in case it's found. My last two apartments were ransacked in my absence, but a bill will incriminate no one. I'll assume the first number I see to indicate an hour of meeting, the second number a date. So long as I find the message, I'll be there to meet you, but meetings are of greater risk than ever, so I make no promises."

"They are of great risk indeed," Robert said, and both John and I turned to the hallway door, I with a gasp, he with an expletive.

Thirty-five

"I—I thought you had gone to Whitehall," I stammered.

"As I wished you to think." Robert walked farther into the room, and John stepped warily aside to let him pass. "Last year, when Lord Cromwell told me the two of you were involved in some kind of conspiracy together, I told him it was preposterous. He had been unwell. I thought illness had left him overly nervous. Of you, Hester, I said that your loyalty to my wife would prevent you from placing her at such grave risk. I obviously overestimated your loyalty. Then again, a woman who would betray her country would surely not blink to betray a friend." Shifting his gaze to John, he said, "I have known you since we were at university together. I knew you to be a pious, God-fearing man . . . or so I thought. Tell me, is it true the two of you are lovers?"

John and I exchanged glances, and Robert barked, "Ha! I always fancied myself a good judge of character, but I see now I was mistaken. I thought you a sexless sort of woman, Hester. Is that how you come by your sight? It takes a sinner to know a sinner, and there is no sin you have not committed?"

"So what now?" John asked, ignoring the insults, ever the pragmatic one.

"Now I tell Lord Cromwell that I have proof positive of your betrayal and depravity."

John gave him an ironic grin. "And are we to accompany you to Whitehall for the grand revelation? Shall we all just climb into your carriage together and have a pleasant ride?"

Robert smiled, too, a hard smirk. "Would you do that for me? For the sake of friendship past?"

"Have you brought a guard with you?" I asked, craning to look in the hallway beyond, almost expecting to see at least one or two of Cromwell's best soldiers.

"I wasn't that certain I would get my proof," Robert replied. "I tell you truly, last night, when I suspected that John had dropped his scarf so that you could have some excuse to return it, and then you said what you did about his cloak, I hoped that I was being overly suspicious, irrational. But I knew that you had been in the tobacco shop, knew that you had fled and mentioned nothing of it at dinner. Then John showed up—it all seemed to fall into place, and I realized that Lord Cromwell might well be correct."

"You saw me," I muttered. "It is so ridiculous. I only went there to buy allspice for Mary."

"And yet you came back so late yesterday evening. And today, you and John knew just where to find each other from a mere, casual reference to a cloak that needed mending. I think you two have met there before."

"As you have ascertained, my friend," John said, still smiling pleasantly, "Hester and I have a . . . deep friendship." He laced the words with meaning.

"It goes deeper than that," Robert said, his own smile having long since vanished. "Hester asked you how much longer the protectorate could last, and you said she had abandoned the cause."

"There you have it!" John argued. "Hester has not been involved in a year or more."

"Because the protector had become suspicious," Robert rejoined.

John sighed and pinched the bridge of his nose, wincing as if a pain had sprung between his eyes. "Do you mind if I take off this cloak? It is hot in here." Pulling the garment from his shoulders, he gestured to the table, and Robert braced himself, as if to do battle. "No one's going anywhere just now, Robert. We might as well be comfortable."

"*You* are going nowhere," Robert said. "I am going to Whitehall to report this conversation."

"Fine," John said. "By the time you get back here, Hester and I will be gone, and mark my words on this, you will not find us."

"You will never be able to return to England," Robert replied.

"Which is why we need to talk," John said. "Hester has been a conspiratorial bitch for, what"—he looked to me—"three years now?" To dissemble was pointless; I nodded, and he continued. "And I have been a traitorous bastard far longer. A few more hours here or there will mean nothing."

"Well," I said, floundering for what to do next, "we may as well be civilized about all this." I stepped into the hallway long enough to call into the kitchen, asking the cook to bring out a pot of tea, and returned.

"There is nothing to discuss," Robert insisted. "You have nothing to say in which I have any interest."

"Think of it this way, you're gathering more evidence," John said, and I cringed. Did he truly need to condemn us so thoroughly?

I needed to get Pearl from the Tobins'. We could go to Amsterdam. Having once lived there with Roger, I knew parts of the city quite well. Surely John knew people here in England who could retrieve Pearl's money. My accounts would be seized in the name of the protectorate, but legally, I was quite sure Cromwell and his colleagues could not confiscate Pearl's. Tie it up a while, yes, but I had made a living by my needle before. I could keep us afloat until we could get her money, and then I would find some good and prosperous Dutchman's son or an English ex-patriot, or the protectorate might have fallen by then and we could return . . .

John had sat down at the table, and Robert reluctantly joined him. I was the last, warily sitting at the far end and scrutinizing Robert for any weakness to exploit, but he seemed utterly certain of his righteousness.

"Robert," John said, "you are a reasonable, if absurdly rigid, man. And you have two good eyes. Surely you are not blind to what is happening. The protectorate is crumbling, held together only by Oliver Cromwell's iron will."

"And the will of God!" Robert cried.

"The will of God?" John shouted back, showing his own emotions for the first time. I raised my hand to silence them, but John was a step ahead of me. With a worried glance toward the hallway that led to the kitchen, where servants might hear the commotion, he lowered his voice. "Is it the will of God that the whole country should be spoiling for the death of its leader? Is Lord Protector Cromwell the same Oliver you fought with back in 1642? If he had been then who he has become, would you have fought so hard to place him at the helm of this country?"

"This is to no avail, John. I am Cromwell's man."

"Then you will sink with him by the time he is finished running this country onto the rocks."

Robert stood. "We will not sink! We will ferret out every traitor—"

I rose with him. "Then you will have to arrest the better part of London, Robert! It is inevitable; do you not see that? Even you are so afraid of Cromwell that you were willing to offer your fifteen-year-old daughter to an old man to buffer your family against his zealous insanity!"

"It worked out fine. Jane is happy and—"

"No thanks to you! It was Edward Mudd's good sense saved Jane from a lifetime of misery."

A poisonous vine of uncertainty shot from Robert's chest, black, thorned, and serpentine, wrapping itself around his torso, binding him and constricting the depth with which he drew breath. He gave a shallow gasp. "All the more evidence that Edward Mudd was a good man despite his age. I'd not have married Janie to some miscreant."

"You knew nothing of his character when you consented to that betrothal," I said. Ah, and now a haze took shape, the pallid, indistinct mist of cowardice that he tried to keep hidden, even from himself, and he saw it in my eyes, for he turned from me in horror.

"You've no right to judge me, Hester Prynne!"

"I do not judge you, Robert. I only see you for what you are."

John looked on, fascinated. "What do you see, Hester? What is it that you see?"

But I could not speak, the ache in my own chest was so strong. It was like looking upon Arthur all over. Robert wanted so to appear strong, inviolate, and immanently respectable—he craved recognition and admiration. But inside . . . inside was a man who knew that he had deeply wronged the only people who really mattered. He was a father who would have turned his back on his child rather than risk his good name. In the end, it was another man who had taken fatherly good care of Jane.

He turned to John, a pleading look in his eyes as he made one last attempt to justify all that he had done. "Have you never wanted to believe in something, John? Hester?"

"We have," John answered. "But we do not cling to blind faith. Sooner or later, Robert, everything you and I helped to build will crumble to dust because it was never what we'd hoped for. Pretending otherwise changes nothing."

"Cromwell has chosen Richard . . ." Robert began, rather weakly.

"Richard lacks his father's will and sheer magnetism. A government cannot be built upon a single man, Robert. The king's powers have been clearly defined over centuries of dealing with incompetent or merely immoral rulers. There were good reasons for the limits placed upon them."

"But you yourself believed it was time to eradicate the monarchy!" Robert protested.

John shrugged. "I was wrong."

I said to them both, "It is no sin to be wrong."

To his credit, John did not crack the slightest smile when he said, "She would know."

Robert sat once again, his face resigned. "I want you out of my house, Hester. You and Pearl. I am going to Whitehall and reading reports until tea, and then I am coming home, and there is to be no sign that you or your daughter were ever here or I send word to Cromwell and he will have you in the Tower by nightfall. You will leave not the slightest shadow of your activities upon me or my family."

"You cannot erase me," I said. "I have stitched Pearl and me into the hearts of every member of your family."

"If I am right, and the protectorate stands, then we will carry on without you." He sighed, glancing at John, then back to me. "If you two are right, then kindly remember that my family once welcomed you, Hester, and gave you refuge in trying times."

I turned to John, but again he had anticipated my concern.

"I shall stop by the Tobins' and send your child home," he said.

Home? Where was that now?

I wasted no time. I did not even wait for Robert to leave before

I raced to the attic and dragged two trunks from there to the girls' room, where I began madly to pack. It was much easier to tell Annie's things from Pearl's than it had been to separate what was Jane's when we had packed her up, but I realized how truly I had spoken to Robert below. Nearly every gown, shift, and apron Annie owned bore the distinctive art of either my needle or Pearl's.

I do not know how John got word to Pearl or what he told her, but less than an hour after Robert's departure Mary and Pearl rushed up the stairs of the parlor house, having left Annie behind at the Tobins', and in grim, efficient silence, they packed with me.

"Mary," I began, when we were packing my things and Pearl had gone to fetch an extra trunk from the attic, "I just—"

"On the way here from the Tobins'," she interrupted, "I kept asking myself why. Why would you do this to us? To me. And then I decided it didn't matter. There is nothing you can say that will make me understand."

"I do love you, Mary. You, and Jane, and Annie, and Georgie, and little Ollie, I do."

She stopped trying to cram gowns into a trunk and looked at me. "I know that."

Tears that I had not indulged all morning welled up and spilled over. "Thank God. Thank God you know that." And we embraced so tightly that neither could breathe. Pearl dragged in the extra trunk, but Mary and I did not let go of each other, so my daughter simply left the trunk at the door and moved over to the one I'd been packing. She took a few things out and transferred them to the new trunk so that the first now shut easily.

With nothing more to be said, the three of us finished cleaning out the wardrobe and cupboards in my room and hauled our leather-bound trunks down the steep stairs with loud, heavy thumps. Pearl and I bid terse, teary good-byes to Mary and dragged our things into the street. To my surprise, we had no need to seek a carriage. One awaited us, and though John was nowhere to be seen, the driver seemed to know where we were going.

I wished I did, too.

Thirty-six

———◆———

I never learned what had become of John that day. So much happened afterward that I never thought to ask him later. The carriage sent for us took Pearl and me to a safe house outside London, where we were fed stale bread, cold stew, and sour beer and told by strangers to rest, for the next day's journey would be long. We woke early, ate another cold meal, and resumed our expedition on little-traveled roads by horse and cart. A taciturn guide rode astride his own mount several paces ahead of us. He was perhaps fifty or so years old, but there was no softness of age to him. Deep crags etched his face, his lank hair was iron-gray, and his body was hard and lean. We made very few stops, even for food, and the wind was bitter, the air heavy, but our guide seemed untroubled by such trifles as rough roads, hunger, and cold.

The expedition might have been all the more miserable had Pearl been like most girls her age, whiney and self-involved, but she was utterly captivated by the adventure of it. In many ways, she became again the child who voyaged with me from America.

"Do you think that anyone is in pursuit of us?" she asked, but did not wait for an answer. "What would they have done with you, Mother, if the brigadier general had not let you go? What would have become of me? Dear God, would I have been the brigadier general's ward? Would he have chosen a husband for me? Well, if that were so, I'd drink a hundred barrels of sour ale and eat a thousand bowls of nasty, cold porridge to escape."

I had to laugh at that, patting her leg pressed against mine where we huddled together on the cart seat under a lap blanket. "Enough sour beer and you'd marry a goat and never know any better."

"I'd marry a goat cold sober before I'd marry a man Robert Wright chose," she proclaimed with a snort. "What do you suppose Jane will think of us?"

"You know her better than I."

Pearl sniffed loudly. The damp, cold air had turned her nose quite red, and I handed her an embroidered handkerchief. I had grabbed it from a trunk in haste, and did not until that moment notice that it was one of the old ones that I had once dropped upon the chairs of traitors as a signal to Cromwell.

Pearl wiped her nose on it and carelessly stuffed it up her sleeve. "She'll envy us, though she'd never have had the nerve to leave England if it were her."

I sighed. "I am sorry that my folly has forced you to flee."

Pearl turned to me. Several wild strands of dark hair had worked themselves free of her hood, and the wind sent them dancing around her face and over the dark wool that could not confine them. Her black eyes sparkled, and her cheeks bloomed like bright roses. Her lips, red and a little chapped, broke into a wide smile. "Oh, Mother, it is the best thing we have done in years!" She paused and looked thoughtfully at the rolling hills, then up at the leaden sky bending so close above us. "Robin will be very sorry, though."

"Ah, yes, Robin. Did he tell you that he'd had his mother ask for you?"

She did not look at me. "Yes."

"Would you have had me accept?"

Her head shook emphatically back and forth within her hood. "I had no wish to marry him. He will stay in London, but he would be content to live a quiet life there, never partaking in the excitement to be had."

"What excitement?" I asked, wondering what had enthralled her there. After all, the Wright children did not attend affairs of state.

Now she drew back a bit to look at me, and I was struck anew at the keenness of her gaze. "You and Sir John will win. The lord protector will be assassinated." At this, our guide turned his head sharply to look at her, but he said nothing. He was, after all, on our side. "And the king will be restored. When that happens, there will be parties and theatrical performances, and musicians in the street."

"All that overnight?" I asked, wondering if she knew something more than I.

"Oh, yes! Nell said so, anyway. Well, maybe not overnight, but it would happen."

I chuckled. "Nell said that? I had no idea she spoke to you of such things."

"Oh, she would never spy, as you did." She giggled. "You! A spy! And here I thought you were so dreary and dull. Tell me, did you and Sir John ever . . . ?" She let the question hang, full of meaning.

Our guide's back straightened, but he did not turn around this time.

"Pearl, that is in an impertinent question!"

"It is not. It's perfectly pertinent."

"Not remotely."

The girl gave me a slanted look from under her hood. "Well, if you hadn't, you would have said so just now."

To my dismay, I actually felt myself blush.

"You did at the country house, didn't you?" she pressed. "No use denying it! I wondered at the time, but then I decided you wouldn't dare. If only I had known."

"Pearl!"

"I let Robin Durham kiss me," she blurted, then added more sedately, "more than once."

I sighed. At least we had moved off the topic of my affair. "Did you? When you knew full well you had no intention of marrying him? Naughty baggage." I wasn't truly angry, but I could hardly express approval. God forbid my daughter fall into the same trap as I.

Finally she had the grace to lean toward me and lower her voice. "When he said he wanted to use his tongue, I thought it would be completely revolting, but actually, it was quite nice."

"Oh, Jesus!" I exclaimed, and the guide turned to frown at me. It made me wonder whether he was some religious zealot disillusioned by the commonwealth. "Pearl Prynne, I shall never again let you out of my sight."

She simply looked at me again with my own dark eyes and laughed.

The ride ended after dark at a squalid inn where Pearl and I forsook the louse-ridden bed for the cold, hard floor. Before we slept, though, we eagerly wolfed down more cold food and flat beer. Our travels continued thus to a secret port north of Dover, and from there we left by ship to Belgium. The voyage, made in the dark of night, hardly gave Pearl and me time to enjoy the lovely feeling of being on a boat again, though to cross the Channel is not the same as an ocean crossing in any event. On board the ship we received the most exciting news of all. We were for Bruges, where the king was holding court until he could return to England.

Before we disembarked in the city of Sluis on the Belgian coast, the ship's captain handed me a substantial purse, which he said had been entrusted to him in the name of one Sir John Manning. As soon as possible, the captain expounded, Sir John would retrieve money from Pearl's savings and mine and send that along to keep us. From that, he would take back the money he was advancing to us now. To that end, the captain said, I must sign several papers giving Sir John the right to access our accounts. Well, John had entrusted us with his own moneys for now; it seemed I had little choice but to reciprocate, though it caused me no little trepidation. Conspiracy and a few trysts with a man were one thing, my daughter's fortune altogether another. I signed the papers with a lump in my throat.

The sun should have been high when we ended the last leg of our journey by canal in a shallow boat, but clouds of steely gray hovered over Bruges. The city reminded me much of Amsterdam, with its canals lined by charming, steep-gabled row houses. Beautiful, ancient churches stretched skyward, and an old belfort, relic of the Middle Ages, dominated a market square where shops sold the fine cloth and exquisite lace for which the Flemish were famed.

An emissary from Charles's court greeted us at the landing. The young man was only a little older than Pearl, perhaps eighteen, and there was a lean, hungry look about him that troubled me.

Pearl appeared to deem him unimportant and beneath her no-tice—a blessing, I decided. I had enough on my hands without her flirtations. The young man introduced himself as Henry, one of the king's couriers, and led us to a boardinghouse for unmarried women.

We had seen little enough of the city, but it was obvious none-theless that there were many more luxurious accommodations than these. I was more than a little disappointed until I learned that our living expenses were to be borne by me, with no help from the man who would be king of England. Then I was grateful for the economy of the place. Besides, it was clean and offered us stable refuge. For that reason alone, it was as welcome as a pal-ace.

Once we had met the landlady, Henry hauled our trunks up three steep flights of stairs to our room, then asked whether we might have coin to spare for his supper.

"Surely there is a feast every night at court," Pearl replied. "There will be food aplenty when you return to . . . where *is* ev-eryone else staying?" She surveyed the parlor with eyes ablaze. "Why have we been sent here? Does the king not know that my mother saved the Marquis of Ormond's life? We should be given a place with the rest of his court."

The boy gave us both a queer look. "There's not enough for those of us already here. The king hasn't quarters or fare for more."

"But—" Pearl began, and I placed a firm hand on her shoulder.

From the purse I'd been given on board the ship, I gave the young man enough for a hearty meal, and he smiled gratefully. "If I was you," he said just before he left, "I'd not let anyone else know you've got money. Especially not the king."

Pearl and I looked at each other, but neither of us had any an-swer for the questions in the other's eyes.

"Do you think we'll see Henry again?" Pearl asked when we had gone upstairs to unpack. "Does the king even know we've arrived?"

"I hope so. I have no idea what we're to do next. We have some money, and both of us are skilled with a needle, so we will not starve, but I would prefer to have some contact with other En-glishmen and -women. How else are we to know the state of things at home and when we may return?"

The room we were to share was small and dark, with narrow beds pressed against opposite walls. Henry had stacked our trunks between those beds, obscuring the lower portion of a window that struggled to allow in some of the gray light beyond it. A single modest wardrobe stood next to the door.

"There is not nearly enough room for all our things," Pearl said.

I sat down on the bed and dumped the contents of the purse from John onto it.

"How much?" Pearl inquired.

"Guilders," I said, surveying the coins. "God bless John Manning. I'm not sure how much is here, at least not in terms of what it will buy and how long it will last, and I'm too tired now to think on it. Tomorrow, I will worry about money."

Pearl surveyed the trunks piled high between the beds and the inadequate wardrobe. "What are we to do with all this?"

Before I could answer, the owner of the boardinghouse tapped on the door. I dusted off the trifling Dutch tucked into a corner of my brain, where I had left it when I'd left Amsterdam years before. Even if I had remembered none, the word *"diner"* was recognizable and very welcome. *"Dank u, mevrouw,"* I replied, and we followed her down to the dining room for hot roast beef and potatoes covered in rich gravy—the first decent meal we'd eaten since our last breakfast at Wright House. Perhaps it wasn't peacock tongues and roasted swan, as we might have expected in a king's court, but to us it was every bit as delicious.

Thirty-seven

Oh, to be Pearl's age and feel perfectly free to air my resentment at being left to languish nearly a month in a boardinghouse while King Charles attended to the inconsequential business of regaining his throne.

"Would it cost him his crown to spare a quarter of an hour and receive us?" Pearl railed to me after stubbing her toe on a trunk in the confines of our room. We had not been able to unpack, so we continued to trip over our cases. "Would the whole world fall at Cromwell's feet if King Charles made some small effort to obtain decent lodgings for a heroine of England and her wealthy and very eligible daughter? Has he no notion what a fine prize I might be for some handsome, worthy Royalist whose loyalty must be rewarded?"

"You seek a match from the king, do you?" I asked dryly as I finished sewing a button back on to one of Pearl's gowns.

"Introductions," my daughter replied in a tart voice. "An invitation to a royal ball or two. Some taste of what it is to be a member of a king's court. To be anything other than stuck in this tiny, airless—"

"If you move the top trunk you can open the window."

"This is ghastly," Pearl declared.

Pearl was absolutely right; our lodgings were entirely unsuitable. Another week there would be more than even our close relationship could bear. The city, however, was pure heaven, every aspect seeming to have been designed to delight the eye. Unable to endure the confines of the apartment, Pearl and I had spent many days wandering the streets. We strolled the marketplace, and standing in childlike wonder, gaped up at the tower that stretched heavenward from the Church of Our Lady, dwarfing even the ancient belfort. Later, we walked through the cavernous sanctuary, listening to the echo of our footsteps and gazing upon the *Madonna and Child* sculpted by Michelangelo. Resuming our excursion, we went to admire the gilded effigies of Charles the Bold and his daughter. The weather was warming, and gardens and window boxes had begun to bloom with tulips and daffodils, which Pearl and I studied so that we might reproduce them in silken threads.

In the course of our small expeditions, I had spied a quaint town house for rent, but until I knew whether we could afford it, I refrained from mentioning it to Pearl. "Our gowns should be ready for the last fittings," I suggested instead, and this seemed to brighten her up.

At least the delay in an audience with His Highness had allowed us time to receive generous funds from John's agents and to procure credit in a number of stores. This meant that Pearl and I could see to it that we would be suitably attired for the grand event when we were finally summoned to an audience.

I indulged in only one gown of dusty lavender silk. Pearl, however, had been trapped far too long in somber tones for a girl of her nature. She ordered silk gowns of rose and amethyst, embellished in rich Belgian lace and awaiting blossoms from her own needle. My gown was quickly fitted, but given that Pearl had two and that she insisted each be as snug as possible, revealing as much shoulder and bosom as a maiden dared to show, her alterations took much longer. I left her at the shop and set out upon my clandestine errand to meet with the owner of the town house.

He was a shrewd man, not given to smiles or idle chitchat, but the house itself more than accommodated for his demeanor. It was part of a long row of residences and very narrow, but it had four charmingly furnished floors. There were comfortably upholstered chairs, pretty tables, and papered walls hung with pleasing landscapes and portraits. The lower floor was not unlike Wright House, with a parlor and kitchen. Upstairs, each floor had a bedchamber that offered a large bed and—praise God—a generous wardrobe. The attic held servants' quarters and a small storage room, and there were servants' stairs at the rear of the house. The rent was within our means, provided we truly needed the house for the three months he demanded in advance.

At this point, it seemed unlikely that we would be invited to take up residence with Charles's court, and not having been able to communicate with John or anyone else who might know, I had no idea what to expect on any front. He sent money, but no news. All I knew with any certainty was that if either Pearl or I stubbed a toe on our trunks one more time, heaven knew what mayhem would result.

Every corner of the residence was well worth a surly landlord, even one whose English was terribly awkward throughout nego-tiations but became quite fluent when the time came to collect the advance. I doled out the agreed-upon sum and told him we would move in within the week. When he assured me that he could find a cook and a maid with good references, I decided that he was actually quite charming in my book, sullen manner and all.

Pearl was thrilled when I retrieved her and shared the news. "Do you think the king was only giving us time to settle ourselves suitably?" she asked, forgetting that, up until that moment, she had considered our settlement his responsibility. "Now we will look the part of court ladies, and our home will be an appropriate place to receive our new acquaintances. Which gown shall I wear for our first meeting with His Majesty? Do you suppose I'll have any time at all to work on it myself? I would like the members of the court to know my skill."

"Pride is a sin," I admonished her.

"Pah!" she replied.

Though she was nearing adulthood, my Pearl appeared to my eyes as John did. I knew her to be guilty of a host of sins, but none showed in her—no threads of shame or wisps of guilt. I thought of John's postulation about my sight—that it was hypocrisy I saw, rather than sin. Well, my Pearl was genuine, however flawed. It seemed a good explanation for the purity of her, despite her awakening into the frailties of womanhood—kisses shared with a

boy she would never marry, desire for worldly wealth and pleasure.

We moved into the town house and accepted delivery of our
new clothes. Behind the door of the very first bedchamber that
Pearl had ever slept in alone, I heard her practicing for social
events we'd yet to hear any hint of an invitation to.

"Well, yes, Your Grace," she said, "it was a bit of a harrowing
journey from England. We rode for days, then crossed the Channel at night, you see, and the winds had whipped up crashing
waves," (I had no recollection of these) "but my mother and I are
made of sterner stuff than these silken gowns might lead you to
believe." She giggled. "Really? Or so fair a face as mine, you say?
You are too kind, sir." A little gasp of mock surprise. "Oh? Your
eldest son is in need of so valiant a wife? But I am only the granddaughter of a baron, Your Grace. Well, yes, I suppose that exceptions are made . . ."

We had worked up the arrival of the summons so grandly in
our minds that the moment it actually came was rather disap-
pointing. There was no royal scroll unfurled and read to us in
ringing tones by a handsome herald. Instead a young page appeared on our doorstep in rather shabby finery—velvet worn
bare in patches and embroidered in tarnished gold. He handed us
a folded vellum sheet that had obviously been torn from some
other document, as there was writing on the back—incomplete
sentences about something entirely unrelated to the news that
King Charles wished to meet us two days hence.

Pearl stayed up that entire night finishing the yellow and red
tulips that adorned her pink gown. I went shopping the next day
and purchased for her a necklace from which a single pearl hung
to adorn the bit of pale bosom her new gown displayed. It seemed
a fitting token for an event the likes of which I would never have
predicted in the prison cell where I gave her life and named her.

The day of our audience we ate lightly so that we would be
able to sample and enjoy all the dishes we anticipated at court.
After breakfast we carefully braided each other's hair and twisted
the plaits into ornate coils. It had been a long time since I'd studied my own reflection closely, but as I sat with Pearl gazing at hers
over my shoulder, I realized that the face I'd once worn was now
hers. Mine was the one with lines between the brows and around

the mouth, framed by dark hair shot through with a goodly share of silver.

A carriage had been sent to collect us, but no royal crest adorned the sides, and I suspected it was a common hired vehicle. The hard, worn benches within confirmed this. Like the coach, the king's residence was also disillusioning. It was large enough, but shockingly Spartan inside. The pious lord protector of England had taken on a life of greater luxury than the heir to the crown. I wondered where the magnificent objets d'art were. The silver? The tapestries? Even the king, it turned out, was sitting at a table in the library on an ordinary chair that hadn't the slightest trace of thronelike aspirations. Two other men sat with him, though they rose when a servant wearing finery as tattered as any we had seen announced Pearl and me. We curtsied low before the man who endeavored to wrest England from the iron grip of the the lord protector.

"Arise, Hester Prynne," he said to me, "you and your lovely daughter."

Pearl's eyes sparkled and her cheeks glowed.

He was as unlike Cromwell as anyone could imagine. Where Cromwell wore his hair simply to his collar, Charles wore his in thick curls that fell well past his shoulders. His clothes were cut well, so they had no doubt been costly, but they had also been stitched some time ago. The two other men, both better dressed, waited silently while the king received us. Among the trio were subtle currents of hostility, and I wondered whether it were better to have remained unacknowledged after all.

"Your Majesty is too kind to take the time to meet with two such unimportant women," I demurred, though he was not rightly "Your Majesty" yet to me. Scotland acknowledged him; England did not. Nodding to his companions, I added, "I know that you have much pressing business, so I hope that we do not intrude."

Charles shook his head and smiled. "We would not have missed a chance to meet the mystical Mistress Prynne. More than one good friend of ours has passed a night or two in the Tower upon your word, and now you are here, having served our cause, we are led to understand."

"Your Majesty," I began, "I was living with friends whose safety depended upon Oliver Cromwell . . ."

He waved his hand in dismissal. "So we have been told. As it happened, your work earned you a place with Cromwell that permitted you to be of use to us. We appreciate your service. Perhaps you might consent to apply your talents on our behalf." My heart sank into my stomach, but before I could reply, Charles laughed, a rich, genuine sound such as I had never heard from Cromwell. "I have no need to see souls laid bare before me. I'd never trust a man who did not have a bit of sin in his heart." His eyes found Pearl again. "This is a lovely child you have brought to adorn our hall."

Pearl curtsied again nervously. "It is a great honor to be in your presence, Your Majesty."

All three men regarded Pearl with warm appreciation in their eyes, though none was enshrouded in so deep an emotion as lust. She was a beautiful girl, but these were men of honor, and there were more pressing matters at hand.

"Mistress Prynne," Charles said, drawing my attention back to him. "May I present the Marquis of Caracena?" I seemed to recall Robert Wright mentioning the Spanish general once or twice. The man appeared a bit older than me. He had a high forehead and nearly black hair, along with the broad mustache and pointed beard favored by Spaniards.

I curtsied again, though not as deeply. "How do you do?"

"And Don Juan of Austria," Charles continued.

Don Juan's hair was thick and dark. He was much younger than Caracena, but like the other Spaniard, he wore a mustache and beard, small ones that accented his swarthy good looks. I had heard of him, too, a military man of some accomplishment and the natural son of the king of Spain. The silk of my new gown pooled around me as I made another obeisance, and I was pleased, after all, to have dressed for the company I found myself in.

We spent perhaps a half hour in the library, seated around the table with Charles and his companions, and while the men obviously endeavored to keep the conversation bright, tension remained.

"We cannot begin to tell you, Mistress Prynne," Charles said, "how we have missed our beloved country. A generous burgomaster here in Bruges has taken great pains for our comfort, but this is not where we would be. If only *Spain*," he uttered the word with a slight hiss and glanced momentarily to Don Juan, "felt our urgency."

A fire blazed briefly in Don Juan's dark eyes. "If the rightful *king* of England"—the barest trace of scorn laced his use of the title—"could raise funds . . ."

"Your King Philip could ensure our victory," Charles snapped.

"He is not made of gold, nor of men," Don Juan replied.

"I have no doubt that talk of money and armies is of no interest to the ladies," Caracena interjected in a smooth voice. "There will be time enough to discuss these matters later." He turned back to Pearl and me. "I trust you have found adequate accommodations."

"We have," I replied.

"Good. Good. A comfortable abode should make your stay in Belgium more enjoyable."

Pearl had kept an attentive look on her face when the adults spoke of politics and war, but when it became clear that we were not about to be invited to join the court, she blurted, "But shall we see you again, Your Majesty? After today?"

"Pearl!" I chided, and Charles scowled at her horrid breach of etiquette.

Don Juan, on the other hand, laughed. "Do not hold it against the maiden, Charles. Can you imagine coming all this way, and having a pretty new gown made, if I do not miss my mark, only to discover that the man who would be your king lacks the requisite fairy-tale court?"

"Oh, I didn't expect a large court," Pearl protested. "I know this is only temporary. I just—"

I could hardly clap my hand over the girl's mouth, so I stepped between her and Charles. "She is clearly out of her element."

Charles smiled ruefully. "She is not far off the mark. Ordinarily I would have a full entourage, but my treasure is entirely committed to the battle at hand."

"Naturally, you must allocate funds wisely," I agreed. The increasingly obvious fact that Charles was in dire straits was too awkward to discuss. With a feeble laugh, I added, "Besides, I doubt His Majesty has ever imagined having a pretty dress made for any occasion."

There were a few obligatory chuckles, but Pearl plowed on.

"Well then, you must all come to supper at our house. It would be an honor, would it not, Mother?"

"Pearl, these men are too important—"

"Supper?" Charles interrupted.

"His Majesty must speak for himself," Don Juan said, "but I would happily accept your hospitality."

"Miss Prynne might well cheer young Emil up," Caracena supplied.

"Emil?" Pearl asked.

"Emil Jäger von Althannburg," Don Juan supplied. "The son of a family friend of my queen. Emil's father is Count von Althannburg of Austria."

"Ah, yes, Spain's queen is Austrian by birth, is she not?" I asked.

"She is, and as I said, the count is a favored acquaintance of hers. He has permitted Emil a bit of travel, and the queen thought the boy might learn a thing or two from us here, so Emil accompanied me just after I returned from Valenciennes. Alas, thus far in Bruges, we seem to have done little more than plan campaigns that come to naught, and there are no young ladies at court, certainly none of similar station to Emil's, a fact he has pointed out to me on numerous occasions."

Pearl's smile was dazzling. "My grandfather was a baron!"

"Was he?" Don Juan asked, and I knew that Pearl did not hear the patronizing tone in his voice. There was an ocean of difference between a dead English baron's granddaughter and a very much living Austrian count's son.

Still, I could hardly rescind Pearl's invitation. "If it please Your Majesty," I said to Charles, "it would be an honor indeed. Our house is modest, but we would endeavor to do you and your friends justice."

"We shall consult with our secretary," Charles said, "and send word when we may be at leisure to be received."

Once we had been dismissed and found ourselves back in the carriage that had brought us, I glowered at my daughter. "What were you thinking? The impudence! To invite King Charles to supper as though he were Mister Tobin or Sir John!"

"Well, he accepted, didn't he?" Pearl challenged. "And Don Juan is bringing the son of an Austrian count! Is that not exciting? Is that not exactly why we came here?"

"It is not!" I snapped. "We came here fleeing from Oliver Cromwell."

"Who was pursuing you because you were spying for the king."

"I wasn't spying."

"What were you doing then?"

The child's questions had been a thorn in my side for as long as she'd been able to talk.

What *had* I been doing? "I was passing along information," I explained—which was not the same thing. Was it? I wasn't *looking* for information, searching out secrets, abusing Cromwell's trust.

Liar. Perhaps I had not sought Cromwell's trust, but I had chosen to abuse it, and I could not abdicate responsibility for that now.

"Anyway," I said, my voice ringing testily in my own ears, "I did not do it so that you could meet the sons of foreign noblemen."

"You did it so that I would not have to marry some horrible Roundhead."

"The daughter of a 'horrible Roundhead' has been your best friend for eight years," I chided. "And now, by marriage, she is related to Cromwell himself."

Pearl lifted her chin. "And still she would swoon at the chance to be courted by a noble foreigner."

"That is quite a leap," I said, "from supping to courting. Do not fool yourself, child. That boy will marry an Austrian girl of higher rank than a baron's granddaughter. This is not a fantasy behind your bedchamber door. We shall receive the king and his coterie, but you will behave yourself and keep your feet firmly on the ground."

I might have given such a command to a storm cloud with equal success.

Thirty-eight

The lure of a meal brought the king to our house less than a week later in a gathering that included Don Juan and Caracena, along with a fair-haired, portly gentleman by the name of Sir Edward Hyde, and an older gentleman with graying hair and a beard after the Dutch fashion. His name was Sir Edward Nicholas. Both Edwards, it seemed, were among the king's most trusted advisers, and as such invited to share in a night's diversion. I had been informed, of course, that they were coming, and the cook had brought her daughter-in-law and niece to help prepare a feast that would satisfy twice as many guests.

As promised, the young Emil Jäger von Althannburg also accompanied them, and I will admit that neither Pearl nor I could have dreamed of a more beautiful boy. Well, perhaps "boy" did not do him justice. He was a young man, newly turned twenty, with fair coloring and a handsome face. Golden hair fell past his shoulders, and his soulful, poetic blue eyes were the key objects of Pearl's attention all night. I realized I would have to speak with her about the manner in which most males interpreted such a prolonged gaze from a woman. I sensed no outright lust, but I wondered whether it was merely the veil of his youth that protected him from my probing sight.

The collection included one more surprise. Our guests had just been served libations in the parlor when someone else knocked at the door. The maid let the visitor in, and I cried out "John!" in a most unseemly manner before I caught myself and said, "*Sir* John." Though I had not been inclined toward spontaneous displays of sentiment since my youth, it was all I could do not to throw my arms about him, so relieved was I to see a familiar ally among these new, terribly important and potentially dangerous associates.

We spoke of the weather and of all we English missed about our homeland. In time, we gathered closely around the table, though it had been extended with leaves as far as possible. While the cook and her helpers served hearty beef and vegetables swimming in gravy, we ate and drank and laughed more than I had since I could remember.

"Oh yes," the king chuckled at one point, "you may mock me all you wish for that time I found myself stuck up a tree at Boscobel House, but 'twas naught compared to the night I spent on a balcony outside a certain lady's bedchamber when her husband came home unexpectedly. At least I was clothed in the oak tree!"

We were indeed many miles from Cromwell's England. Here was an echo of the merry land of my youth, where a bit of ribaldry was seldom thought to hurt anyone.

Pearl's eyes sparkled and she blushed at being included in such unseemly conversation with such important men (though I did sometimes wonder whether she forced the color to her face, knowing that others found it fetching). One look at Emil proved that my daughter was not the only young one so captivated by the wickedness of the topics. True, he was young, but not so young that I could not detect a subtle change when he looked again at Pearl. The talk settled a bit as we moved to the subject of military tactics, at which point Emil turned his attention from Pearl and joined in.

"My father's first preference," Emil told me, his English heavily accented, "was that I serve in the Austrian army fighting the Turks. I will, of course. It is my duty. But he consented to allow me to travel some, and he felt I might learn much about strategy under the tutelage of such men as Don Juan and Condé."

"Condé?" I asked. I had heard the name before. Robert had mentioned the French general on several occasions. In fact, he greatly admired the man's military prowess, but he had never spoken of him in conjunction with Charles. "Are the French not on Cromwell's side of late?"

"Marshal Turenne and the Prince of Condé were once colleagues, but after a messy bit of intrigue in France, Condé has consented to assist our cause. There is some intelligence regarding the Vicomte de Turenne and a possible attack on Dunkirk," John explained. The other men present shot him looks of warning that swept over Pearl and me, then back to him. He shook his head at their alarm. "Hester has been privy to military conversation for years." With a wink at Emil, he added, "Pearl as well. A bright girl, that one."

"Conversations Mistress Prynne did not hold in confidence," Sir Edward Nicholas noted, tugging at his pointed beard. I studied him a moment. Like Cromwell, pride was his great transgression.

"My indiscretion was for my country," I said in my own defense.

"So it was," agreed plump Sir Edward Hyde. Who knew how many opportunities to stumble had presented themselves to a man of his political involvement? But he was an upright man as far as I could tell—no shades of dishonor or whispers of shame were imparted by his presence. I liked him. During the course of the evening, he brought to mind Jane's father-in-law, Mister Mudd.

Pearl leaned forward over her empty plate. "Then Turenne will fight with Cromwell?"

I caught her eye and motioned for her to straighten. She would have to learn to move differently in gowns with lower necklines. Even after she sat up again, Emil's eyes lingered low, and a faint shadow fell over him.

"Cromwell is allied with the French in all matters regarding Flanders," Don Juan answered. "After all, a piece of the Spanish Netherlands is a fair deal indeed for a relatively small commitment of English troops to France's cause."

I took a sip of wine and kept my eyes on Emil until he seemed to sense it. He looked at me and blushed a bit when he realized that I had observed the direction of his gaze. With the boy back in his place, I said to Don Juan, "Surely they know Spain will not tolerate such a venture. King Philip is determined to keep his supremacy in

Flanders. He would never stand by and allow England and France to gobble it up bite by bite."

"Then the Royalists will ally with Spain?" Pearl asked.

"Of course," Charles replied. "Cromwell must not be permitted to gain another inch of land. Such an advance would have deeper implications than mere boundaries."

"Have you a real interest then?" Emil asked Pearl. "My mother and sisters find politics dull."

"Oh, not I," Pearl assured him. "Why, had I known my mother was a spy, I would have helped her. Who would have suspected a mere girl such as I?" She gazed wide-eyed at the men around her, who humored her, laughing and agreeing that no one would have suspected such a thing.

Sir Edward Nicholas did not join in the levity. "It is not a common activity for the fairer sex. It is most unusual for a *woman* to find herself in any sovereign's innermost circles."

"I do not think that to be true, good sir," Pearl protested. "I imagine kings' mistresses to have known countless military and political secrets through the ages."

Nicholas and Hyde, Caracena, Don Juan, and I looked at her with eyebrows raised, but Emil grinned and coughed into his napkin, while Charles and John laughed outright.

"You were quite right, Sir John," Charles said, "Miss Prynne is an extraordinary young woman. Can you imagine, Miss Prynne, what would become of our bid for our rightful crown if the beauteous Catherine Pegge were to turn spy for Oliver Cromwell?" he asked, referring to his current paramour. "Perhaps we should take greater measures to ensure her loyalty."

John held the last of his wine up in salute. "If the satisfied smile upon her lips when she is in your company is any measure, Your Majesty, Catherine is firmly in your favor." Then he drained the glass.

"Very much in my favor," Charles agreed. "Refill your glass, Sir John. It has been too long since we've enjoyed such a good vintage in my court."

"Too long indeed," Nicholas joined in. "And too long since we supped in such fair company, for the conversation has turned to subjects most unsuitable."

John reached for the bottle and poured. "You forget, Sir Edward, Mistress Prynne knows the darkest secrets of every man she meets. She is not easily shocked."

I could have knocked him over the head with the bottle. It was difficult enough to make people comfortable in my presence without reminding them of my sight. "I do not invite myself into their hearts, as you know, Sir John."

"But *Miss* Prynne has no such sight," Emil commented, nervous uncertainty in his voice. It was more question than observation.

"Not I," said Pearl. "I have not my mother's experience in life. Yet."

Thus far, Emil had admired Pearl's beauty, perhaps contemplated stealing a kiss or two, but at the girl's deliberately provocative statement, the shadow about him darkened. I shook my head at her, but she did not notice. Far too pleased was she with the color she had brought to his fair countenance.

"There is a question," Charles said. "Whereby do you come to this remarkable sight of yours?"

"I am merely more perceptive than most, Your Majesty. It came, I suppose, of living nearly ten years among the many hypocrites that inhabit Massachusetts."

"Surrounded by those pompous Puritans nearly your whole life. No wonder you risked so much to help our cause," Charles concluded.

"Now, what of Dunkirk?" I asked, turning the conversation back to safer territory.

The night actually ended early the next morning, but I was not too tired to leave the rear door to the servants' stairs unlocked so that one of that company might return unobserved. Oh, the sheer luxury of those hours until dawn with John—no fear of discovery. At breakfast, I went to the kitchen to retrieve a tray for two. The cook did not bat an eye, probably assuming the second meal to be for Pearl, who would surely sleep until noon. John slipped out after breakfast, and I slept again until well after my daughter had arisen.

As the weeks passed, Charles and his associates met two or three times each week at our house, and from the amount they ate it was clear that our simple but hearty fare was more sumptuous than any found in the king's court.

Tensions in Flanders were heating. Spain and the Royalists were in the midst of preparations to take a stand in the north of France, and Condé, the famed French strategist who had turned on his own country to fight for Spain, often joined our gatherings. The discussions became so adamant that we adults hardly noticed that Emil and Pearl had begun to slip away to the parlor, where they sought corner seats away from lamps and talked in hushed tones. I might have insisted that they remain with the rest of us, but I sensed little beyond innocent flirtation and unfulfilled desire between them. It all seemed tame enough, though still I wondered whether Emil was simply too young to be fully revealed to my scrutiny.

For the first three or four weeks of meeting with the king, John left with the others only to return by the back stairs until morning. Then he took to leaving right after the meal, not to be seen again until the next gathering. He was a restless man, that I had always known, but I felt isolated without him. He was the only adult in Bruges I might have truly counted a friend. I suppose it should not have come as a shock to me the afternoon that I saw him strolling through the market with a lovely young woman, but somehow, it did. They paused to purchase knots of *krakelingen* from a cart, and as they ate the sweet pastries, John took the lady's hand to his lips and licked a bit of the sweetness from her fingers. She scolded him with a coy smile, but did not pull away.

She was young, her face unlined, her hair a soft ginger with no trace of the silver that so liberally streaked my own of late. I imagined how firm her young breasts felt to his hand compared to mine, which had nursed a babe and endured the effects of time. It was difficult, looking upon this girl, not to think about the fact that my years of lovers and stolen passion were waning, and while I cared for John as deeply as I had cared for any friend in my life, it seemed that true love would never be mine again. I felt cheated to have known that sweetness so briefly.

If Arthur had lived, surely I would have thought nothing of the toll the years had taken. Our visages would have weathered the years together, growing more dear with every wrinkle. I would have run my fingers through his soft curls as they grayed, or perhaps they would have thinned and disappeared altogether, and I would still have thought him angelic in his looks. But Arthur was a memory, a ghost frozen forever in the fourth decade of his life, incapable of ever dismaying or being dismayed by me.

I felt lonely standing there in the marketplace of Bruges, and it seemed to me that the crowd there cut a wider berth around me than anyone else, just as it had whenever I visited the market in New England. I was Hester Prynne, still the fallen woman, still the image of sin committed and yet unredeemed.

Even my constant companion of those early days, my little Pearl, was becoming a woman in her own right. Today she was at home, having pleaded a headache when I told her that I was going to market, but soon she would have her own home, and I would venture out alone as a matter of course.

What nonsense, I thought, the notion that those around me here shied away. No one even noticed me until John looked up and waved. What had he to hide? He had never led me to believe that I held a singular place in his bed. In truth, that wasn't what I wanted. I think I wanted only not to be forgotten. John had certainly left me free to seek another if it pleased me, but he also knew that I was not like him in that regard. I might not have required complete devotion from a lover, but neither was I blithely inclined to take any number of men to my bed. He knew that he was singular to me. Surely he knew that I felt his recent absence from my life.

I took a deep breath, forcefully exhaling my self-pity. Then I waved back, made myself smile, and turned to seek out fresh flowers for the house, refusing to watch him leave with his lady. When I returned home with my purchase, the maid told me that Pearl had gone out as well, presumably to look for me, but the market had been crowded, and I could have easily missed her. It would not take her long to give up and return, I decided, and in the meantime I arranged my blossoms in a vase that would decorate the table when the king came to dine that night.

Looking back, I do not recall thinking it odd that Pearl did not pause to speak with me when she returned an hour later. She mumbled something about dressing for supper; I realized that I needed to, as well, and we went to our respective chambers to change our clothes. So it was that I received my second shock of the day when our esteemed guests arrived. Pearl greeted Emil, and

I saw instantly the gilt thread that bound them, one not as sinister as the one that had united Arthur and me, for neither was married to another, but their transgression was close enough.

I looked among the men who had come, seeking John's face, in need of a friend, but he had not accompanied them. Throughout the meal I found my mind crowded with images, first of John and the woman in the market, then of Pearl and Emil, and they left me with no appetite or even patience for conversation. I thought of Arthur for the second time that day, remembering how, when my heart was filled with turmoil and dissatisfaction, his lyrical voice would wash over me, soothing my spirit, calming my soul.

"Dear God, Arthur," I said to him, my voice silent, the words expressed only in my heart, though I hoped he might hear them wherever he was, "what has our child done?" It was yet another burden we should have shared that I bore alone. I wondered if he knew—if he was somewhere regretting that he had left me to raise our child without him. Perhaps that was his hell.

I almost hoped so.

"Mistress Prynne?" Hyde prompted me.

"I beg your pardon?" I said, regretting the harshness of my thoughts. "Forgive me. I have had a dreadful headache all day."

"A shame," he said. "I did not realize you were unwell."

"I did not know myself," Pearl said, concern in her voice. "You said nothing about it."

I looked at her. "We did not speak much after you returned from . . . the market."

She blushed and looked away, while Emil kept his own expression carefully bland and studied an unremarkable painting on the wall to his left.

When talk turned, as it always did, to politics, Emil announced that he was going to Dunkirk to fight with Don Juan and Condé. "I may not return," he announced solemnly, "but I will have served a noble cause. We must restore King Charles to the throne and make an example of the regicides of England."

I stared at him a moment. So that was it. He had convinced my daughter that he was going off to war, perhaps never to return. I could almost hear his sincere voice as Pearl would have heard it: "If not now, we may never have another chance, and I love you so, Pearl."

My gaze shifted to the girl, who suddenly seemed to find the design on her plate fascinating. "It is very brave of him, you must admit," she said softly, peeking over at me.

"Oh, I will admit, child," I said tightly, "the boy has nerve."

"Oh dear," Charles muttered as his eyes followed mine, and Don Juan cleared his throat.

"Turenne and Castelnau have already marshaled their troops," Condé commented, breaking the uncomfortable silence that had fallen. "We can delay no longer."

"If this impudent boy returns in one piece," Don Juan assured me, "I will bring him here and we will settle matters satisfactorily."

Ah, yes, with some addition to her dowry to compensate a future husband for a ruined bride, I thought. "He might hope not to return," I rejoined, unable to mask my ire.

Pearl let out a tiny gasp, and Emil shot to his feet. "I love her!" he proclaimed.

"Well then," Don Juan snapped, "you might have thought of her well-being. Sit down. You are about to go into battle, risking your life and leaving her behind."

"I shall marry her when I come back," Emil insisted without resuming his seat.

"A man as imprudent as you most likely will not come back."

"You cannot say that just because—" Emil protested.

"I said *sit down!*" Don Juan barked, and at last Emil did. "As for marriage . . ." He gave me an apologetic look.

"The count would be less than amenable," I deduced.

"He has a match in mind," Don Juan explained.

Emil looked frantically back and forth between us. "I know the girl Father would have me wed. She is a gem of paste compared to Pearl."

"This is neither the time nor the place for this discussion," Don Juan said.

"Yet I don't suppose we can leave this good woman here with her errant daughter and the matter unsettled," the king supplied.

Hyde spoke with good sense. "Well, we are far from England and have kept our gatherings small. Provided there are no *complications*"—he raised his brows—"Miss Prynne may return to England with no one the wiser."

"But—" Pearl began, and I shushed her sharply.

I sighed. "It may be a moot point in any case. We can do naught right now but wait and see what Dunkirk brings."

"It will bring victory," the king proclaimed, "and send us home in good time."

Raising my glass, I said, "God go with you all to Dunkirk. I would have Charles on the throne and my daughter safely back in England."

"To Dunkirk! To victory!" the rest chimed, and we drank.

Thirty-nine

The battle lasted but two hours before the Spanish and Royalists surrendered to the French and English armies. The loss was such a blow to Charles that we saw him only once when he returned, and our meal was a solemn one indeed. Don Juan, who bore the blame for that loss, had fallen entirely from favor. Neither he nor his young companion was invited to accompany the king, which meant that Pearl was dreadful company, sulking over her untouched plate.

The morning after that last royal visit, Pearl and I breakfasted lightly from a tray in the parlor. I tried to offer her what comfort I could in the form of good sense, though I ought to have known better. "He could not marry you anyway, you know," I said. "Fortunate you are that he did not leave you with child."

"I love him," she snapped. "You of all people—"

I stopped her before she could finish, "—know the consequences of such impetuousness."

"Of what use is money, Mother, if I am to be like any other girl, given no choice in her life?"

"Your wealth does give you a choice, petulant child! You have far more choice than I had. More choice than Jane. You shall be able to say aye or nay to any appropriate match."

"I want Emil."

"He is beyond your bounds."

"I disagree."

"There are realities," I argued.

Pearl rose from her upholstered chair. "Indeed there are. The reality is that I have funds enough to make my way in the world, and Emil stands to inherit his own."

"He has a bloodline to maintain."

"Then let him find a wife to maintain it if he must. She need not be me."

It took a moment to find my voice. "Then it has come to this? For my one sin, I bear a child who has no greater aspiration than to be some man's harlot?"

"You are a fine one to cast stones, Mother," she seethed. "I aspire to have the man I love and to be loved in return. Emil is no Reverend Mister Dimmesdale to cower from love and feel ashamed of it—ashamed of *me*. I will hear from him soon. Wait and see."

Her words sent that old familiar ache through me, and I recalled Arthur marching in the Election Day parade toward his last triumphant sermon, passing me with nary a glance in my direction. His illicit lover had no place in his mission that day, but I was able to bear it because we'd already made our plan to escape New England together. True, Roger had learned of the plan, and I was worried about that, but Arthur had finally intended to be with me. In light of that I was convinced that we would triumph in the end.

At least I'd thought Arthur's intention was to be with me. I had no inkling as he passed by that ere two hours passed he would unburden his conscience on the scaffold and abandon me in death. How could Pearl any more truly ascertain Emil's ultimate intention than I could Arthur's? Even if Emil was a stronger, truer man than Arthur, such heartbreak could certainly come to Pearl one day as well. I would spare her that, if I could. Settling an arm about her shoulders, I asked, "And if you bear him a child?"

She spoke with such confidence. "He would acknowledge our child, even if he could not make him his heir. Our son would lack for nothing—an education, connections. There are worse things to be than the bastard of a nobleman."

"And a daughter?"

"I have made my way just fine."

"Ah, Pearl, you are sixteen. You have yet to make your own way anywhere."

However well-intended, this served only to anger her. She pushed me away and stomped off to her room. A fortnight later she received a note by messenger and slipped out the servants' door after dinner, not returning until dawn. I waited for her in the parlor, but when she let herself in she only glared at me a moment in the gray light, her chin at a mutinous angle, then shut the front door and crossed to the stairs to seek her room.

I left her to herself and retired to my own chamber, where I took the scarlet letter from its hiding place and laid it over the back of a chair, where Arthur would have sat had I the power to summon him there.

"What should I have said?" I demanded, imagining him at the mercy of my ire. "Who am I to advise her? Damn you, Arthur Dimmesdale! Did you really think Roger's torment agonizing enough to atone for what you left me to? Could you truly have believed yourself redeemed by your shame? You knew what an incomprehensible child she was, how unbiddable, and yet you left her entirely to me, with no one to turn to when her nature brought her inevitably to trouble."

I sat heavily on the edge of my bed, still staring at the letter, but conjuring Arthur's face in its place. "You loved me! You know you did. How could you have been ashamed of that? I never was." A strange laugh bubbled in my throat, mingling with smothered sobs. "How foolish we were. For seven years I tried to feel shame for loving you. Oh, I could feel shame for my sin, for losing control, but for loving you? Never! And you? You shuffled about the village with your hand over your heart and never once considered that perhaps, just perhaps, your love for me was your redemption all along. Was I not worthy of some love in life?"

At last the tears I had refused to shed the day Arthur died poured forth. "You ever press your penance on me. 'Let Hester bear our sin in public. Let our little child's ill behavior reflect upon Hester's poor mothering. Let Hester raise that child to womanhood, and if the girl should prove her mother's daughter—well, that is just the point; she is her *mother's* daughter. No one will lay the blame upon me, moldering in my grave!' Damn you, Arthur!"

I imagined the look on his angelic face—the shock that his devoted Hester could hurl such invectives at him. "Hester," he might protest, "I laid claim to Pearl and all that was amiss in her nature."

Not here, he hadn't. Not in England. But to all those we had met since leaving America, she was Roger's child. To everyone but Mary, I had denied even the existence of Arthur Dimmesdale. Once again, I was left with the question *Who am I to judge?*

Besides, in all fairness, he had asked my help, and I had refused. The day that I stood upon the scaffold with our baby in my arms, he all but begged me to reveal her father. In front of everyone, he admonished me, "Be not silent from any mistaken pity and tenderness for him; for, believe me, Hester, though he were to step down from a high place, and stand there beside thee, on thy pedestal of shame, yet better were it so, than to hide a guilty heart through life."

He had known, even then, how my silence would destroy him, but I had not listened. Now the words came back to me, their weight so much more fully understood with the perspective of time, now that I knew how events would unfold.

"Take heed how thou deniest to him," he chided, "who, perchance, hath not the courage to grasp it for himself—the bitter, but wholesome, cup that is now presented to thy lips!"

And what was my reply? "My child must seek a heavenly Father; she shall never know an earthly one!" That choice had been no one's but my own.

In his own way, Arthur had been true. He told me the day we created Pearl that he was not a strong man. He repeated it to me when I stood on the scaffold without him. He admitted his weakness yet again the day we met in the woods with Pearl. "Be strong for me," he pleaded, and I thought I could be strong enough for us both.

I stood and took the letter up again, clasping it tenderly to the spot it had once occupied. "It was never for your strength I loved you, Arthur," I confessed. "It was for the beauty of your face and your voice. It was for the fragility of your heart, because it forgave me any weakness in my own. You knew me, and you loved me. It was enough."

Exhausted, I lay the letter on my pillow and rested my cheek against it, just as I would have liked to rest upon Arthur's chest, and in my mind we bore my worry for Pearl together. When I awoke much later, the letter had left a faint impression on my face that took some minutes to fade.

Pearl finally left her room for dinner. "I supposed I had to face you sooner or later," she said as she seated herself at the table. For all her bravado that morning, she spoke softly now.

"How can I judge you," I asked, "sinner that I am?"

She shook her head. "Your only sin, Mother, was in believing that you had sinned. I love Emil, and he loves me. The sin is that anyone else deems it his place to say us nay."

"His father will deem it his place."

"We do not need his approval," Pearl replied. "Nor the church's, either. Our love is sacred in itself."

I caught my breath, suddenly assailed by memories of Arthur in the woods. "What we do," he had said the day we lay together, "has a consecration of its own." I recalled those words years later, when I urged him to flee with me. "We felt it so," I reminded him, "we said so to each other!" That was the day that Pearl would have naught to do with me, for I had taken off the letter.

Toying with my food, I said to her, "Still, I would prefer that you never endure what I endured in New England."

Pearl sighed. "Let people say what they will, do what they will. Besides, New England is a world unto itself." She took a bite and chewed carefully before she swallowed and added, "There is one person's blessing that we should very much like to have, though I know I ask much of her."

I looked up into her pleading eyes and said, "I want you to be happy. I will love you no matter what you do."

Her voice grew softer still. "That is not a blessing."

I sighed. "It is a blessing . . . of a kind. I have sins enough to account for, I would not add that of deeming it my place to say you nay."

"Can you love Emil?"

I reached across the table and took her hand. "I will try—if he makes you happy and does you no harm save that which you have already consented to."

I would have gladly given him a traitor's death when he wrote Pearl again a few days later to say that he was being called home abruptly and unexpectedly. Oh, he wrote effusively of his intention to return to her, of his undying love, and my Pearl believed every pretty flourish of ink upon the page. My cynicism was powerless against the strength of her faith. Time would teach my Pearl about pain, I thought. I could not shield her from it.

Summer's end brought us sadly good news. Cromwell's daughter, Elizabeth, had been taken ill and died. I would never rejoice in the ill fortune of his family, but the incident seemed to send the the lord protector's health into decline.

On the third of September, 1658, that which so many had sought, risked their own lives for, and even died excruciating deaths to bring about happened of its own accord.

I learned of it several days later, when the maid let John Manning into the foyer, his face gray and strained. He doffed his hat and ran a hand through the dark hair that had begun to grow out since he'd arrived in Bruges. "I have news."

"Is it Mary?" I asked, my throat tight. "One of the children?"

He shook his head. "It is Oliver Cromwell. He is dead."

How shall I explain my emotions? It was not entirely unlike being told that Satan himself had died—not smote by the hand of God in an epic battle, but in his bed, from a simple fever. Such news would be welcome, indeed, but so, too, would it unravel the very fabric of the universe as most believed in it. How could such a force simply die like anyone else? It wasn't that I thought Cromwell to be Satan; he had just been to me a creature of indomitable power. I could not imagine him lying cold and still.

I do not know how long I stood just inside the door, staring at John in wonder. I think I muttered, "My God," and then John followed me into the parlor where I sat down to absorb the event.

Without being told, the maid brought enough tea and cake for us both, and John pulled up another chair to face mine. The mantel clock ticked off a minute or more before he said, "I would have thought you gladdened by this news."

"Are you?" I asked. Steadied by the thought of something to do, I poured milk into the bottoms of our cups. "If you are, you cover it most admirably."

He leaned upon his hands and sighed. "Oliver was my friend for many years. It is hard not to think of that time now. Hard not to mourn the man I liked. Still, I rejoice for England. But you never liked him, did you?"

Adding tea and stirring, I replied, "Neither did I hate him. I pitied him and resented him, but never hated. He wanted to be a good man."

John accepted the cup I offered and nodded his understanding. "I did not wish him dead. I knew that he must die, and I wished dearly for the change it would bring, but . . ." He shrugged.

"What now?" I asked him. "Can we go home?"

"Probably," he answered. "Richard is the lord protector now and seems in a conciliatory mood."

"He is softer than his father was."

"And for that reason, he will not last."

"Is he to be killed?" It made me sad to think he might. I did not know Richard well, but he had struck me a decent man, however weak. A father like Oliver Cromwell was bound to raise weak men or strong, nothing between. Henry, Cromwell's only other living son, held Ireland in an iron grip for the commonwealth. He was of the latter breed, but as the younger son he had not been named his father's successor.

"How matter-of-factly you speak of the filth of politics these days, Hester."

I thought on that a moment, staring down into my cup. "I thought myself so worldly when I left New England, but I was only arrogant. There are many more layers to innocence than one might ever imagine, and we are ever unaware of them until each barrier is breached."

"Deepening our sins with each violation?" he asked, a skeptical expression stamped upon his too-quickly aging face.

"Yes," I answered, surprised at my own certainty.

"Then lay the fault with God for bringing us into a world where none can survive but by sin."

"Has that not been man's own choice?" I asked.

He scoffed at that. "'In Adam's fall we sinned all'?"

"It is not in our nature to remain innocent," I replied, and he nodded.

"On that we agree. In any case, I leave for England tomorrow, and if it is safe, I will send word, should you wish to return."

I smiled. "Thank you."

This had been such a long-awaited turn for us both, yet it was not enough, I felt. I desired a deeper solidarity with him now. "Will you stay to supper—perchance longer?"

There was something in his demeanor—the way his eyes shifted toward the clock on the mantel, the manner in which his body straightened, the breath he drew to speak and the words that did not immediately come. At that moment, I knew I would never again share the bed of John Manning.

At last he cleared his throat and said, "I should be pleased to stay, but I've another appointment."

How could he have sought any other at this moment? I wondered, unable to help the hurt I felt. "She cannot have shared so much of this epoch with you," I said. Then I winced. "Oh, please, do not tell me that Charlotte Chapham is in Bruges."

He grimaced and shook his head. "I am nearly as relieved to be quit of her as I am Cromwell. As for this epoch, it has reached its conclusion. These are new times, Hester."

"Someone younger?" I asked, not really wanting to hear the answer. Perhaps I should have been just as glad to leave the foibles of youth behind, to leave foolish mistakes and passions to Pearl and her friends.

"Someone different." He set his cup and saucer on a nearby table. "I am a restless man, Hester, but an honest one. I never pretended to be anything other than a libertine. Still, I should miss you very much if we ceased to be friends."

Next to Mary, he was my dearest friend. In many ways, my affection for him was nearly equal to my love for her. He would never again be my lover, and well I sensed that naught could alter that. Our bedding had been merely physical—satisfying but not essential. It was his friendship that I held dear, and I would not imperil it over a misplaced sense of possession.

We stood, and I took his hands in mine—the gesture a poor substitute for what I had sought but a bond nonetheless. "I would miss you, as well, John. Shall I see you in England, then, dear friend?"

He grinned. "In England. At last."

Even as I look back upon that day, I cannot fully articulate how utterly it seemed to me that everything had changed. I had no defined concept of what was to come. It was as if I had been caught up in a windstorm, when in an instant, the gale ceased and an eerie stillness engulfed the land, leaving me to wonder when and in which direction it would resume, for resume it must. Where would these new winds blow the course of my life?

Forty

When word of Cromwell's demise had first arrived, many an Englishman assumed that Charles II would be packing for England, leaving poverty and exile a distant memory, but Richard's ascension to lord protector complicated things. Acting upon Sir Edward Hyde's advice, Charles bided his time in Flanders, though not without taking effective steps toward regaining his throne. The first of those steps was to distance himself from Spain, an alliance that could not possibly endear him to his would-be subjects. This meant that Bruges, with its undeniable Spanish alliance, was no longer an advantageous place to hold his exiled court. I was not invited to a farewell audience when the king's court packed up and moved to Clèves, but a page did come to our house with a letter thanking me for all I had done to relieve the king of his burdens here. His sentiments were very like John's, and he wrote that he looked forward to a reunion in the land of our birth.

"We cannot leave, too!" Pearl wailed. "How shall Emil find us?"

"Stop acting like a child," I scolded, at my wit's end. "We will linger here yet a while longer. I would prefer to let things settle a bit in England ere we venture home again. If Emil truly wishes to find you, he will, but you would do well to set your sights elsewhere."

To his credit, and much to my surprise, he did write to her. The letter was dated in early August, not long after he had arrived in

Austria, but did not arrive until November. His mother's father had died, and there had been some contention regarding his title, since the man had died without any living male heirs. Apparently the hope was that Emil could claim that title, as well. For himself, he said, he would gladly pass it to a likely cousin, but his mother was making much ado about it.

He loved Pearl, of course, et cetera, et cetera. Pearl brandished the missive as proof of his unfailing devotion, denouncing me for a cynic, then wrote her own letter, presumably to tell him that we were returning to London.

My correspondence with Mary was of a more practical nature than Pearl's and Emil's sentimental missives. I wrote to Mary, and she penned back assurances that Pearl and I were ever welcome at Wright House. Robert, she claimed, bore me no ill will. Doubtless this had much to do with the fact that with each passing month Richard Cromwell's grasp upon the reins of the commonwealth grew steadily weaker. Also in my favor was Richard's lack of interest in pursuing *all* his father's old enemies; I was no longer in a position to harm the commonwealth, and it was a daunting-enough task for him just keeping up with those who were. All of England was becoming restless, not for a new lord protector, but for a king. The Wrights stood to gain much from my having befriended one.

Even so, the news that traversed the Channel heralded much strife in parliament. Some still hoped to define the role of the lord protector more clearly, allowing that Richard should be recognized as such, whereas others insisted that if one man was to rule England, it should be a king, and Charles II would do as well as any other. Until parliament could resolve this, I was in no hurry to leave Bruges. Pearl and I could do well enough either way, but I had no desire to find myself in the thick of such dealings again.

Another six months passed ere I finally concluded that perhaps England was regaining her sanity. Major General Robert Overton, a man whom I had proclaimed three years earlier to be the most honest man in England and who had been imprisoned ever since with no charges leveled and therefore no conviction, was at last released from the Tower. Three years of illegal imprisonment had not tarnished his good character, and he at once set about trying to unify the factions threatening to tear his beloved country apart.

If he could again step into the fray, who was I to cower in Flanders?

Pearl had heard nothing more from Emil, a fact that she attributed to his being uncertain where to find her. Now she was eager to leave, since he would be more likely to seek her out in England at this point. I rather imagined we had heard our last from him. There were doubtless many lovely and distracting influences in his homeland. Still, I decided that it was pointless to contradict her and chose to be grateful not to have to fight her on the move.

We made a few more excursions to lace shops, making sure we'd have enough to share with the Wright women, and set out across the Channel once again, this time in the light of day and without fear.

It had been a scant thirteen months since Pearl and I had fled London at Robert Wright's insistence, and yet that year and a month had ravaged the man we'd left behind. He was terribly thin, his cheeks and eyes sunken, and as he stood on the steps of his house he watched my daughter and me alight from our carriage with grim resignation. Though the spring sun shone brightly on the street, he stood in deep shadows with Mary at his side.

Mary looked very much her old self. There was no change that I could see in her face or body, but there was something in the way she stood—a little straighter, perhaps, a little stronger, yet with visible effort—as if the heaviest of burdens rested on her shoulders but she refused to yield to it. She seemed determined to prove how gracefully she could bear its weight.

Annie, Georgie, and Ollie had been waiting at the street's edge, where the sun lit their lovely faces. Pearl had no sooner placed both feet on the road than a breathless Annie raced to embrace her, her own words of greeting interspersed with the welcome her sister had bidden her to pass along. At last a bit of lavender silk peeping out from Pearl's cloak caught her eye, and she insisted that Pearl toss the outer garment back so that she could admire the Flemish gown underneath, cooing at the lovely color and lace embellishments. At thirteen, Annie was starting to transform into the woman she would become, her features as fine as Mary's and Jane's, her coloring as pale.

Georgie, though two years younger, was the same height as his sister. Like his father, he wore his darker hair close-cropped, and he had his sire's serious demeanor, at least at the moment. He bowed politely to me, but I would have none of it and ruffled his short hair. Then he broke into a smile and withstood the crush of my arms good-naturedly. Ollie, now six and bearing a headful of curls, stayed at his mother's side until he had determined that we were indeed the Hester and Pearl he remembered. Then he seemed to decide that we were nothing worth lingering for and begged his siblings and Pearl to accompany him to the park, which they did.

Through it all, Robert and Mary remained on the steps, and when I moved toward them, Robert nodded in my direction but went inside. With his absence, the shade of the house seemed less dark, somehow more like an ordinary shadow. Mary came down the steps, opening her arms to me.

"It is good to have you home," she said.

"It is good to be here. Are you sure about Robert?" I asked, gesturing toward the door.

"Likely as not he does not want to face you," she answered. "Well, he should have thought of that earlier." Then she sighed. "Let's not talk about him just now. We had a letter from Jane yesterday. She was so hoping to come so that she could welcome Pearl home, but she's been feeling out of sorts lately."

"Out of sorts?" I asked, eyebrows raised.

Mary smiled a little. "She did not say anything outright."

I laughed. "Oh, wouldn't that be wonderful?"

"Well, now that Pearl is back, we shall have to work very hard to introduce her to some suitable young men. Perhaps Robin Durham? She seemed to fancy him before."

I had written to Mary, of course, of my worries for Pearl and her infatuation with Emil, but it was good to be able to talk again. We stayed in the shade of the house, somewhat sheltered from inquisitive neighbors, for I was not yet ready to renew those acquaintances. Arm in arm, we watched the children in the park across the street.

Georgie's earlier somberness departed entirely, and he chased his younger brother in an indulgent game of tag, allowing Ollie to catch him from time to time, just as his sisters and Pearl had once done for him. Soon a handful of other neighbor children answered the call of spring and the shouts of friends, and the game was truly afoot.

At first Pearl demurred when it came to racing through the grass in silk. She and Annie stood under an oak chatting together, pausing to shout occasional encouragement to the younger children or to heckle the older. At last, Pearl's lively nature got the best of her, and she lifted her skirts to join in the fun, pulling Annie along by the hand.

"Pearl!" I called, wondering which of the other women who watched from doorsteps or the edge of the park would censure the girls. "You are not a child!"

"Let them go," Mary said. "She will be fine."

I glanced around. Two housewives turned to each other in quick conversation, but I was too far away to hear them or even see their expressions clearly. If they disapproved, so be it. Several others seemed just as pleased to have the older girls there looking after the group, and they went inside to attend to other things.

"Where is Nell?" I asked Mary.

"She returned to the country last month. Her mother took ill and seems unlikely to recover. Nell is the last daughter unmarried, so she is staying to help her father. Annie and George are of an age to help with Ollie; we manage fine on our own."

"It will be strange without her. I'd come to think of her as one of your family," I said. I would miss Nell for her honesty and cheery temperament, but I of all people knew how circumstances could change, moving us from one place to another upon the whims of fate.

Supper that night was strained. Robert was mainly silent, and he ate sparingly. His children spoke in hushed tones, as though they knew their father to be unwell in some way and in need of gentle tones and faultless good manners. Mary alone chatted cordially, encouraging Pearl and me to tell all our stories of Bruges. I wondered whether I should speak of the king in Robert's presence and decided it would be safe to speak of his dire straits. Surely that would please Robert. Instead, he seemed to retreat all the farther, leaving the table to stand and stare into the fire.

I cast an anxious glance at Mary, who only looked after him with thinly veiled frustration.

We stayed up late that night. All the parlor lamps were lit, and Annie showed Pearl her latest project, a lovely gown of indigo wool. Though the dress was unfinished, Pearl began at once to see the perfect place for a primrose here and a spray of embroidered lavender there, and she promised Annie a length of Belgian lace as soon as she'd unpacked it. Ollie and Georgie—no, George, he had gently but firmly told me—played at draughts. Ollie was really rather good at it and was the more likely of the two to jump several of his brother's disks, capturing all, and landing at the back row to crow, "King me!"

George took it all in stride, but under his careless smile was genuine vexation. "You're having good luck tonight," he conceded to his brother, "but such luck cannot last forever."

"He's a strategist, too," Mary said in defense of the younger child's skill.

"Forgive me," Robert muttered, rising. "It is late." They were the first words he'd spoken since supper and his last for the night as he went immediately abovestairs.

Mary stood, too, and announced to the children that their father was right and that it was time for bed. Hugs and kisses were exchanged. Then Annie took over, ordering Ollie to wash well before he went to sleep and telling George to see to it.

"Do I look like Nell to you?" George retorted.

"Yes!" Ollie shouted, then took off running up the stairs, just beyond his brother's retaliatory reach.

Annie rolled her eyes and shook her head. "They are such children," she complained sagely to Pearl as they climbed after the boys.

There was a good bit of general thumping and bumping on the wooden floors above, but eventually the children settled in for the night. Mary got up from her chair to stir the embers of the dying fire and extinguished all but two lamps on the long table in the parlor.

"I missed this," I said to her, "you and I talking here in the gloom, the house all quiet."

"So have I," she replied. "Oh, Hester, if you had any idea how many times I could have used a friend this past year."

"Has it been that bad?"

"Richard is weak," Mary said, dropping heavily into the chair next to mine and resting her chin in her hands. "Everything Robert fought for, everything he has built our lives upon is crumbling around us. You have seen him."

I nodded but said nothing. There was more for her to tell, and I was in no rush. The fire snapped, and I remembered the day I first met Robert. I had seen about him the mantle of adultery. He had walked up to us draped in its ignominy as if it were a cloak of ermine on a prince's shoulders. That was before he knew his wife had a friend who could see it, who would reveal his crime to the one he'd committed it against. Now he wore his sin heavily, like a cloak of sodden wool.

"There was another woman again?" I finally asked.

Mary sighed. "Charlotte Chapham."

"Dear God," I grumbled. "Wherever I turn, that dreadful woman rears her venomous head."

Mary nodded. "It was she revealed you and Sir John, you know."

Of course. "I did not, but it makes perfect sense. She was there the first time I called upon him. It should have dawned upon me that she would watch him, glean and use whatever information suited her purposes at any given moment."

Mary cocked her head at me and frowned. "She was with Sir John?"

"She was playing both ends against the middle between the Royalists and Roundheads," I explained.

"But when you left, Robert told me that *you* and John were lovers."

"We were, but . . ." It all seemed relatively straightforward, perfectly reasonable whenever I was with John. Somehow I doubted Mary would understand the way things were between us. "It was complicated."

Straightening up, Mary exclaimed, "Charlotte Chapham! Really, Hester. Can you imagine either Robert or Sir John turning to *her*? How can men be such fools?"

"How stand things now between you and Robert?"

"How should they? He faulted me, naturally. Charlotte was so much more understanding of the weight he'd borne with Cromwell's death, he claimed. I, of course, he believed to be utterly protected from it all, happily raising children and keeping house, knowing nothing of the peril England faced. As though anyone in this city could be so unaware! As though the security of my children and this house were not of paramount importance to me."

"How like Robert to see things that way."

"That is what I give him then—a happy wife who is finished listening to his political woes. He chose his side, not I. Let him bear the weight of disaster alone. Let whomever he wishes bear his weight, for I am quite done with it. After all these years . . . well, I do not know what other women find in his bed. Whatever it is, it has never much moved me.

"Oh, God, Hester, I just wish this whole political farce were over. It is the uncertainty that wears at everyone so. If parliament would just hand the crown to King Charles's son, Robert and I would know where we stand. Then maybe he would rise above his self-pity, and we could all get on with our lives."

It was a step in the right direction when a few weeks later Richard Cromwell resigned from the office his father had left to him. Shortly after, his brother resigned as lord deputy of Ireland. In August a small group of insurgents held the city of Chester in the name of Charles II, but the victory was short-lived. The leader of that small army, Sir George Booth, was arrested as he attempted to flee in women's clothing. Sir Henry Vane, the man who had so infuriated Cromwell with his heartfelt pamphlet, was back at the forefront in matters of government. This time he found himself at odds with the Council of State, a group of men appointed by parliament to rule in place of the protector. Vane strove relentlessly to save the place of the army in the commonwealth, but parliament was wary of such an arrangement. They had entrusted too much power to the army before.

All this we learned from good Mister Tobin, for Robert had utterly distanced himself from the turmoil at parliament. It was just as well. From one week to the next it seemed impossible to know whether England was ruled by the Rump Parliament, the Council of State, the Committee of Safety, or some other hastily gathered oligarchy. John Thurloe was dismissed as secretary of state; then he was reinstated. Henry Vane fell in and out of favor with surprising alacrity. Mister Tobin wrote fast and furious all day, then reported to the Wrights and others close to him about heated debates and reports of conspiracies that were sure to bring the full weight of the Royalist army to the shores of England any day now.

I certainly hoped that Charles was able to raise the funds he needed. Rule by committee, or, in our case, one committee after another, was tearing England to pieces.

December twenty-fifth came and went at Wright House with nary a mention of Christmas, but bits of holly and evergreen decorated any number of London doorways, and the army had its hands entirely too full with rebellions from inside and out to do anything about it.

The arrival of the year 1660 was heralded by riots that trapped us inside Wright House and a passionate desire across the land for one ruler, however flawed. Those members of parliament who had opposed the regicide of Charles I eleven years earlier (and were cast out of parliament for their loyalty) reconvened, and finally their wisdom prevailed. A new election placed into power one last group: the Convention Parliament, whose chief duty consisted of but one task: to offer the crown and title of king of England to Charles II. After a brief flurry of negotiations, on May eighth, Charles accepted.

Robert took to his room with a bottle of strong spirits and drank himself sick. Mary and I taught the children to dance.

Forty-one

Charles landed in Dover on the twenty-fifth of May. In London, preparations for his return were carried out with great excitement. Butcher shops and bakeries could scarce keep up with the demands for feasts to come, not to mention their own needs, for many had hired new street hawkers to sell food to the crowds that would throng London streets when the king returned to the city at last.

From Dover the royal entourage made its way to Canterbury, and in the days' delay, a much-awaited letter arrived at Wright House bearing an Austrian seal. Pearl snatched it from Mary's hand and raced to her room, leaving me to provide food and a cup of ale to the fellow who had brought it with great haste from Dover. Having taken care of the carrier, I resolved that I was entitled to some knowledge of what the letter contained, and I sent Annie upstairs to spy.

Annie's eyes danced when she came back downstairs. "Pearl read me the whole letter. Oh, Emil is so romantic, so sweet, so perfect," she sighed.

"Yes, yes," Mary said. "So Pearl has told us. What did the letter say?"

Annie sat down across from Mary and me, crossing her arms

on the table and leaning forward. "Much of it I cannot say, for I am sworn to secrecy."

Her flushed cheeks spoke volumes, and I had no doubt that Annie had been given some idea of the intimacy of Pearl and Emil's affair. I could only hope Pearl had better sense than to tell all.

"This I *can* tell: Emil and his parents are with the king. As soon as it became clear that the king was to be restored, Emperor Leopold wished to send some emissary to wish him well. Emil wrote something about a common interest regarding Spain." Now she straightened and looked a bit bewildered "Actually, that part of the letter was rather dull. The important thing is that Emil begged to be that emissary, but the emperor said he was too young. When Emil threatened to travel to England anyway, his father agreed to be the emissary."

"To prevent his son from doing anything foolish," I supposed, "like wedding a fairly unimportant Englishwoman."

Annie shook her head with confidence doubtless imbued by Pearl. "They shall be together, no matter what his parents may say."

I looked at Mary and said, "It is the 'no matter what' that worries me. You'll note she did not say they would *marry*, no matter what."

"Of course that is what they shall do. How else could they be together?" Annie asked.

It was some small blessing that Pearl had apparently stopped short of telling Annie that she and Emil had already consecrated their love. Mary thanked Annie for her information, then offered to go upstairs with her daughter and send mine down so we could speak privately.

There are times when it is futile from the start to attempt to speak sense to a child. Ah, that is unfair. How could I call her a child? I married Roger at her age.

I began there. "When I married Roger," I said to her as she walked through the door from the hallway, "I thought only of the adventure of it all. We were going to Amsterdam, far from my dull little village. He had money, and I would not have to mend the same sad gowns time and again. It seemed a very good match, an excellent decision."

Pearl sat down at the far end of the table. "You married a man more than three times your age." There was something about her rigid back, the set of her lips. She was intending to hold her own against any advice I might give.

Still, I had to try. "Looking back, it seems an obvious poor choice."

"There is no comparing our two situations," she said.

I rose and moved toward her, stopping at the chair next to hers and resting my hands on its tall wooden back. "There is a lack of looking forward. There is a failure to understand the workings of men and women. You assume such feelings as you and Emil share to last forever."

"We have been apart well over a year, and yet the first opportunity that arose, he came back to me. And look at you. Have you ever stopped loving the minister?"

"I think—" I had to pause a moment and ruminate upon the words before I spoke them. "I think it has been easy to love Arthur because we were apart so long. He was—still is—whatever I would have him be, and never at all what he really was."

"You were not apart. You lived scarcely two miles from him the whole time we were in New England."

Of their own accord, my hands tightened on the wood beneath them. "In many ways there was an ocean between us. What wrote Emil of the match his father wanted? The girl of whom Don Juan spoke?"

"It does not matter," she protested.

Now I pulled the chair away and sat beside her, capturing her hands in mine and keeping them despite her resistance. "It will, Pearl. I have never known a man who was true—not Roger, who loved his books more than me, not Arthur, who chose his public stature above all, not Robert to Mary—no man."

Pearl's dark eyes looked too deeply into mine. "And especially not Sir John? That is what this is really about. He cast you aside—"

"He did not cast me aside," I snapped. "We had an agreement, and it was never exclusive nor forever."

This time Pearl tugged her hands away with such force that they slipped from mine, and she stood to pace. "Then you may choose to love as you will, but I may not? Of all people I would expect such hypocrisy from, Mother, you were the last."

"Can you not see what misery my sins have brought me, Pearl? A man's bed offers such brief pleasure. The one thing, child, the only thing that has brought me any lasting joy is you. I only want to keep you from the woe I have known."

Pearl stopped and took my hands this time, pulling me to stand with her. "And by what means did you gain me?"

"Pearl—"

"What shall I do, Mother? I have found a man who will travel the continent for me. I love him. Shall I send him away and marry some better match? Shall I seek a union like Aunt Mary's, some more lasting joy such as hers?"

I sighed, having no answer.

"I think we can love each other forever," she said softly. "Truly, I think you and my father could have, too. Sometimes, such loves are worth all battles, all costs."

"Can you know that Emil will bear the cost with you? I was such a fool once."

Pearl drew me to her, and we embraced tightly. "I am not your judge, Mother. I am only your Pearl, and my decisions must be my own."

She was right, of course. There was naught that I could do.

On the twenty-ninth of May, we participated in a celebration the likes of which I had never seen. The Wrights, Pearl, and I took to the streets with the rest of London. Robert came, lest his willingness to abandon the old cause fall into question. It was an uneasy time for those men who had cast their lot with Cromwell, for who knew how Charles II would deal with them? Robert stood to stiff, wretched attention while those around him danced and cheered.

Swaths of bright cloth that had doubtless been stored away in a thousand attics were aired at last in the forms of new aprons, caps, and scarves. Cheery ribbons woven in maidens' hair waved in a breeze that carried a mélange of scents: the musky smell of humans and horses, the dank odor of the Thames, and the sweet essence of the flower petals strewn in the path of the procession and crushed underfoot. Shouts of joy and raucous laughter rang in my ears, and to every cry of "God save the king!" that came my way, I could not help but reply joyously in kind.

As the parade approached, there was a sudden crush of bodies, everyone hoping to lay eyes upon the man whom parliament had only just declared retroactively to be king throughout the years of his exile. Pearl grabbed my hand and pushed her way through the throng, using her elbow to dig and fingers to pinch without compunction. We reached the front of the crowd shortly before the king passed by, and we joined thousands sinking to their knees like the trough of a wave racing across the sea.

My head was properly bowed, but I peered upward to see that Charles rode, looking resplendent. His long dark locks flowed from under a high-crowned hat adorned by bright plumage. Foot soldiers in scarlet coats surrounded His Majesty, their plumed helmets shining, ceremonial spears tipped skyward. Behind him rode General Monck, the man who had once arrested Robert Overton for Oliver Cromwell. Monck was no man's fool, and even as he'd served the commonwealth in the past few months, he had also been negotiating with the king in the Netherlands, thus ensuring himself a powerful place in either regime. A little after them came Sir Edward Hyde, his smile, pleasant under any circumstances, so bright as to cast an arc of light all around him. Even somber Sir Edward Nicholas looked immeasurably glad and waved to the multitude (of people who doubtless had no idea who he was). Others marched by in their finest clothes, attire of rich colors and sumptuous embellishment such as England had not seen in many years.

One might have thought Robert to be the only soul in England less than delighted by the turn of events, but I knew that such was not the case. Men such as Robert Overton, while they had not been pleased by the course of the commonwealth under Cromwell, were no happier to see it end with the restoration of Charles II. Then, too, there were those who had orchestrated the death of Charles I. Today's happy occasion tolled their death knells. No such royal declarations to that effect had yet been made, but none could question the imminence and severity of the judgment that awaited the regicides.

The thought of their fate was enough to cast a moment of gloom over the festivities for me, but then Pearl sang out, "Emil! Emil, here I am!" and I confess, I forgot those poor men at once.

Emil had been marching at the rear of the procession with the less important participants, and now his head swiveled and his eyes scanned the crowd.

"Here!" Pearl raised her hand over her head and waved jubilantly.

"Pearl!" I chastised. "He must finish the parade. He cannot—"

"Pearl!" Emil shouted. With a happy laugh he broke away from the man and woman he had been walking with and trotted over to where we stood, despite the protestations of his companions. In Bruges he had adopted the styles of Charles and his advisers. On this day, he wore the clothes of his countrymen—a long embroidered coat and low-crowned hat. When he pulled Pearl to him and kissed her full on the mouth, the crowd roared and clapped their approval of so lusty a display after so many years of staunch public propriety, and the two were showered in rose petals.

Perhaps it is my own wild fancy or perhaps it was real, but every time I think back upon that moment, I recall that the petals floating about them were exactly the same shade as those on a rose bush that grows by the prison door in New England.

Forty-two

———⟫•◦•⟪———

The three months after Charles's triumphant return were tense ones at Wright House. Due to my late father's title and my services to Charles, I found a welcome at court among the lower-ranking nobles. Though I offered to introduce Mary and Robert there, they were understandably apprehensive about their place in the new order. Neither was eager to risk discovering their family and friends permanently out of favor. Today, it was anticipated that Charles would present to parliament the formal disposition of those who had served in Cromwell's army, and Robert had gone to hear the news.

As some testament to Pearl's good sense, she used her wealth and her needle to befriend the right young women and had gained broad acceptance among her peers at the king's court. From her place there, she simply sought every opportunity possible to be alone with her Emil. When she was at home, she hummed or worked on her sewing with Annie. She helped George with his studies and taught Ollie simple battle strategies with lead soldiers and encouraged him when he trounced her at draughts. In fact, she had just been sitting at the end of the table with the boy, about to "king" his piece in front of her as ordered, when Robert returned. His face was gray, his mouth a grim line, and Pearl needed no instructions to lift the board carefully and suggest to Ollie that they move the game upstairs.

I stood, about to offer to leave as well, so Robert and Mary could talk privately, when Robert dropped into the chair his son had vacated. "We are fully pardoned," he announced.

Mary was on her feet in an instant, smiling. "But that is good news, Robert. Very good indeed. Is everyone pardoned then? Did Hester not assure us that the king was a reasonable man who would understand that you and the others had but done the only thing you could under the circumstances?"

Robert had been rubbing his hands over his gaunt, tired visage. Now he stopped and glowered up at her. "I did what was right! I fought for God and country. I had choices all along, Mary, and I would make them all again."

"It is over, Robert. You should be counting your blessings, praising God and celebrating because you have been spared by a kind and forgiving sovereign—"

"Kind? There were exceptions to the pardon, of course."

"Exceptions?" I asked.

"John Coke, Andrew Broughton, Edward Dendy—"

"Regicides!" Mary protested. "You were not of their ilk."

"We served the same cause, Mary."

"So what? So what if you did? You did not kill the king!"

It was an unaccustomed emotion for me, pity toward Robert Wright, but I felt it for him now and was compelled to speak. "What would you do?" I asked him. "Share their fate?"

He paused, fought to control his face, swallowed hard, started to speak, then swallowed again. "They will be tried, of course."

"Of course," I agreed, softly adding, "and executed. There is no other possible conclusion."

He rubbed his hands over his face again. "Hanged, drawn, and quartered. Men I admired."

I reached out to touch his hand. "I am so sorry."

He jerked his hand back as though burned. His eyes found Mary's, but the moment his began to mist, he lurched from the chair and walked out the door onto the street.

"Robert!" Mary called after him.

"Let him walk," I said.

"What am I to do with him?" she asked. "He can swear his

loyalty to Charles, pick up the pieces of his life—our lives—as though none of this had ever happened."

"He cannot," I explained, remembering another in a similar plight. "He must confess his part in it, whatever part that may be, and pay whatever price must be paid."

"He was not on that scaffold, Hester!"

"I know that, and so does Charles. Besides, Robert is distraught, not stupid. All that I am saying is that you cannot shield him, and it is better that you do not try."

In the middle of October, when the trees were shedding their leaves and readying themselves for the snow to come, Robert insisted upon attending the executions of five of the regicides. After that, he was a ghost of the self-certain man in the portrait that still hung on the parlor wall. The other painting I had noticed my first time in Wright House, the one with Oliver Cromwell, had been taken down. An innocuous depiction of fruit hung in its place, and I realized that I had no idea what had become of the former.

Robert had taken to wandering the streets late at night, a hazardous occupation for a man of sound mind and body, much less one in Robert's state. Whenever Mary woke to find him gone, she would rise and build a fire in the parlor to wait for him. I found her there one night and asked, "Have you come to love him that you worry for him so?"

"Love?" She frowned. "I would not have him beaten to death on the street. I would not wish that on a dog."

"Go to sleep then. I'll wait up."

Mary sighed. "I am his wife."

"And I am your friend. You need your sleep."

"What of you?"

"I am not overseeing a house and three children."

"Annie can hardly be counted as a child."

"Let me talk to Robert," I said.

Mary returned to bed, and Robert returned just before dawn.

"You are alive, I see," I said to him.

He paused and stared at me as though I might be a phantom, his eyes so deeply shadowed and his face so thin he might have been a skeleton himself. "Hester," he muttered in greeting. "You ought to be abed."

"So ought you."

"I do not expect you to understand."

"There is a certain self-indulgence to shame, is there not?" I asked, and when he would have stepped past me to go upstairs, I moved into this path. "The weight of it makes for fine stones with which to build a wall."

"What can you know of my shame, Hester Prynne?" he growled. "What have you ever known of shame? You are incapable of it."

"We are not here to speak of me. So you have fallen, Robert. You were not the first, and you shall not be the last."

"I did not fall!" he protested.

"You did, and more than once, in more ways than one."

"Judge not, Hester, lest ye—" He stopped and heaved a weary sigh. "I need to sleep."

"Sleep at night, then, and stop wandering the streets hoping some ruffian ends your misery for you. You've a wife and children to think of. Shame is a waste of time, Robert, and it serves no one but you."

"Me? How?"

"You have somehow convinced yourself that you belong on that scaffold with those other men, and now you think that you can atone by slow self-destruction. Well, you cannot. What you have done you cannot undo."

"I would not undo—"

"I do not mean your allegiance to Cromwell. I mean accepting the king's pardon. I mean watching those men's guts ripped from their living bodies before your eyes and not dying with them."

"Stop," Robert whispered.

"You are alive, Robert. Your wife is alive, your sons and daughters are alive." I placed my hands upon his shoulders, pained by the feel of his bones even under the thick coat he had not yet removed. "Do not waste those gifts. Live while you may. What you owe you owe not to Cromwell or those men or even the king. You owe it to those who tied their fates to yours and wait for you here every night that you go seeking a murderer. Do not be an idiot, Robert."

He looked as if he might say something but thought better of it. Still wearing his coat, he went upstairs. I took up the lamp and followed after, passing him on the landing on the way up to my room.

"Hester," he called softly, "you truly love my family—my wife and my children."

"I do."

"I—I'm glad of that. They have needed you."

"They need you," I answered, and in the shadows cast by my light I saw his head nod. Then I bid him good night and resumed my climb.

It seemed as if my head had only touched the pillow when I woke again. Some time must have passed, though, for I could smell breakfast cooking downstairs. It was not that, however, that had awakened me. Annie stood next to my bed, dressed but with her pale hair down her back.

"Aunt Hester," she said, "Pearl begged me not to tell you, but I think something's wrong."

I raised myself on one arm, wiping my bleary eyes with the back of my free hand. "What is it?" I mumbled.

"This is the third morning that she has been violently ill."

Falling back against my pillow, I groaned in despair.

"Is it serious?" Annie whispered.

"No, darling," I said, then thought better of it. "Or rather, yes. Maybe. One thing's sure; it was inevitable."

Pearl was still looking a bit green about the gills when I went to her room. I stood in the doorway, arms across my breast, and she gave me a look that clearly conveyed the fact that she had no intention of discussing the matter before rolling over and giving me her back. Rather than argue with the girl over whether or not she was a woman, fully grown and capable of running her own life, and whether or not it was necessary that I speak with Emil's parents, I mentioned nothing of my intentions before I left for Whitehall.

Emil's parents occupied a status above mine at court, given that they actually lived at Whitehall. I had been invited to do this as well, but having seen the shabby conditions of the chambers in which the king did not reside, I preferred Wright House.

Regardless of my residence, I often visited the palace. While Robert had been willing to look past my involvement in the Royalist cause, he had not been so generous with John. Whitehall was the only place John and I could talk when he had the time. As he had for Cromwell, he worked in a largely diplomatic capacity, so he spent much time entertaining emissaries who had come for Charles's restoration and lingered through the months after. Now that he could dispense with his role of pious Roundhead, it was the wives of emissaries whom he most amused. Despite his exploits, neither guilt nor shame ever cast a shadow across his face, and he remained a man with whom I could enjoy wholly honest conversation.

My association with him made me a common guest at court— the word meaning both "customary" and "a commoner." Therefore, the Austrian emissaries occupied a sphere for which I was unqualified, and they never sought me out. It would be awkward, I supposed, for them to face the mother of their son's mistress, a woman renowned for her ability to perceive sin; it would have made it impossible to pretend that we did not understand the nature of our connection. None of this was their fault, so I had respected their desire to remain strangers. Annie's visit to my room changed all that.

It took the better part of the morning, but I found the Count and Countess von Althannburg playing cards in one of the salons with their son and several other nobles. Emil saw me first, and he cringed slightly at the sight of me. Then he spoke to his parents, who glanced my way and turned in their cards to their game mates. They were a handsome couple, both looking serene and unperturbed by my appearance. Emil's father looked much like Emil, but he lacked his son's dreamy quality. His were the eyes of a pragmatist rather than a poet, and his face was more angular. The countess had a sharp nose, but it was softened by a full mouth and the honey-colored hair that framed her face. Both wore courtiers' clothes—a long coat for him, lavishly full skirt for her, bedecked in ribbons and lace. I still lived among Puritans, so my gown of black silk trimmed with only a modicum of white lace and subtle needlework about the collar and cuffs must have seemed quite severe to them.

Emil made introductions, and we attempted to make conversation. I discovered the countess spoke English quite well within certain limits, but her husband merely greeted me, then fell silent. I did not know whether he was reticent or did not speak the language.

Our business was best discussed in private, so we left the salon to make our way through the halls while I wondered whether the countess's lexis was broad enough for the task at hand.

Those sections of the palace in use by the king were opulent indeed, the walls hung in silk with large gilt mirrors and comfortable furnishings. They were also the most in demand by the members of court, so we sought instead the rooms whose wooden floors were marred by the dampness that seeped into the palace from the Thames and whose upholstery smelled musty and looked dull.

The countess maintained polite conversation, expressing dismay at the disrepair of so much of the palace, conveying hopes that all would soon be restored to its former richness. It was difficult to ascertain how much of the conversation the count followed, for he seldom looked at us and said very little. Even with his wife, there were enough gaps in the conversation that I felt some anxiety in broaching the subject of our children.

In the end it was the countess who introduced the true purpose of our meeting. She paused outside a small, dark library that was currently unoccupied and gestured inside. "This room is rather cold and the chairs are hard, but it is kept reasonably clean. The books are dull—mostly religious and very old—so I find that I can be left alone in here."

We followed her inside, and she turned, saying, "Your daughter has told you that we are returning to our own country?"

This halted my steps in the middle of the chamber. Now I regretted my decision not to speak at length with Pearl that morning, as she had told me of no such plans. Rather than admit this, I simply said, "Soon?"

"By the end of the month," Emil answered. "Winter will be here soon, and the weather will not be conducive to travel."

"And Pearl?" I asked.

"She will travel with us," Emil replied.

The countess smiled, the sympathetic smile of a woman who knew what it was to worry about a child. "My husband and I have grown quite fond of Pearl," she said slowly, searching for the words as she spoke. "We are not . . . so . . ." She turned to her son and said something.

Emil thought for a moment. "Unyielding," he said.

"Unyielding," the countess repeated. "We are not so unyielding as your Protestant countrymen. Your daughter will be well cared for."

"You could come with us, if you like," Emil suggested. "Pearl will have her own house."

"She is with child," I told him.

He nodded sheepishly. His mother did not seem at all surprised by the announcement. She merely said something to his father, and they conversed briefly.

"It doesn't sound German," I said to Emil.

"Hungarian," he said. "It is just as well you do not understand. Father can be rather . . . tactless, I am afraid."

I crossed my arms, as much in reaction to the chill as to his unpromising declaration. "Then I presume that he does not see this as anything he need concern himself with."

"No—that is not it, not at all," Emil said. "But if I leave it to Father to explain, it will sound . . . cold." He gave a frustrated sigh. "I love Pearl, Mistress Prynne. I truly do."

"Emil," his mother said at last. "I think that you and your father should return to the salon."

"But what if you need help translating?" the young man protested.

The countess patted his arm. "We will find a way to understand each other." She nodded toward the door. "Go."

Reluctantly Emil spoke to the count, and the two men left, their footfalls fading down the hall.

The countess shrugged. "Young love. We remember this, yes?"

"It can be fleeting," I said.

"Fleeting?" The countess frowned.

"Short."

"Ah, you fear that Emil will . . . what is the word?"

"I fear that Emil will lose interest altogether."

"Have you seen them together?" she asked.

"Not as often as you, it would seem," I replied.

"She comes to court often."

"I thought she came to . . . I thought she and Emil were . . . alone mostly." I could not recall the last time I had blushed, but I felt my face go warm, and I turned to study the leather spines of the books on the shelves.

"Come," the countess said. "Sit." She spread her sumptuous

skirts and lowered herself gracefully into one of the chairs. I followed suit and found that she had spoken the truth about the hardness of the furnishings. "You thought she spent all her time in Emil's bed?"

It was foolish to be embarrassed. Life had certainly taught me that it was best to deal with things head-on. I met her eyes and said, "Quite frankly, yes. She has not spoken much of you."

The countess sighed. "Your Pearl, she would rather marry Emil than be his mistress."

"I would certainly prefer that."

"But you know that is impossible," she said, and I heard regret in her voice.

Ignoring my own uncomfortable role in our affiliation, I began to study her intently. Surely there was some weakness in this woman, something I could exploit to Pearl's advantage. She had a serenity much like John's, but not the same element of defiance. She seemed sinless, and yet, somehow, not entirely pure. The Countess von Althannburg baffled me.

"Why is it impossible?" I asked.

"There is another family," she explained. "Contracts have been signed, a dowry arranged."

"Pearl is no pauper," I said.

"So Emil has told us, but she has no . . . connections . . . to titles, property, certainly none in Austria."

"Are you so in need of such a daughter-in-law? Is that why you pursued the other title in your family last year?"

The countess's gaze grew frosty. "That was . . . a family matter. It had nothing to do with money, nothing to do with your child." She took a deep breath and smiled again. "And that is what we are speaking of? Yes? I promise you, Pearl's child will be cared for. If it is a boy, he will go into the army. We will buy him a good commission. If it is a girl, we will see to her dowry. She will marry a . . . I cannot think how to say it . . . not a nobleman, but a rich man. Yes?"

"And if Emil's heart changes?"

"Your Pearl will be the mother of our son's child. We will take care of her and any children she bears Emil for as long as she lives in Austria."

"And if she should wish to leave?"

"That would make things difficult. We would wish to see that our money was spent on a proper home for Emil's children."

"In other words, while Emil may wander at will, Pearl must live as a pathetic cast-off if she is to keep your support for Emil's children. Well," I said, rising, "I certainly see how 'fond' you have grown of my daughter."

The countess stood as well, holding her hand out to me, though I did not take it. She turned her palm up in supplication. "I do like your daughter very much. If it were up to me . . ."

"What?" I asked, and when she did not answer, I repeated it. "If it were up to you, what?"

"It is not up to me. It is not up to either of us. Love is a game we women play. Marriage is a man's game; they make the rules."

At this, it occurred to me that I had become rather skilled at men's games; more often than not, it was simply a matter of being on the right side.

Forty-three

"Rise, Mistress Prynne," King Charles commanded, and I straightened to smile up at him before I glanced around the rest of the room.

The last time I had been in the undercroft of the banqueting house, it had been to question Joseph Chapham, an event that had set the course of my life for the next ten years. It was strange to be here with the king, Edward Hyde, and a handful of other royal advisers; some were gaming, all were drinking ale and conversing comfortably.

The king gestured that I should join them, then sat next to me. "You requested that we not hold this audience in our usual chambers. We trust this will suit your purpose." He gestured about the grotto.

"It will, indeed, Your Majesty. You were too kind to see me so quickly after I sent my request."

I had told Pearl about my conversation with the countess less than a week ago, but there was much unsettled between us. For one thing, Pearl had pressed me to answer whether I would join her in Austria. The answer to that hinged largely upon this meeting with King Charles, though I held back from Pearl that I had requested an audience.

"Dear Mistress Prynne, you offered us sustenance—quite literally—when we were in sore need. We do not forget our friends."

"I was counting on that, Your Majesty. You see, if it is not too much to ask, I am in sore need myself just now."

I was surprised at how readily the king granted my request. To my good fortune, it so happened that he had recently settled a similar matter between his own brother, James, and the daughter of his dear friend (and now lord chancellor) Edward Hyde. In truth, my business took but five or ten minutes, though I stayed several hours drinking wine and supping. There was still much disorder to set aright, the king and the lord chancellor complained. Estates were all topsy-turvy. Naturally, lands taken from Royalists by the commonwealth had to be restored, but Charles was loath to take those lands back from good men who had but sought to serve their country under the other government. The evening was much like those in Bruges and brought home sharply how much I would miss my friends in England.

For the first time I could see the past ten years, not as years that had somehow spun out of control, but as the grand adventure they had been. I had moved in powerful circles, helped shape the whole world, in my own small way. Oh, I knew that in a hundred years—less, actually—the name Hester Prynne would be swallowed by time, never spoken or read of like the names of the company I kept that night would one day, but I had been a part of it all, just the same.

I came home well after midnight to find Robert sitting up, reading by lamplight.

"So, now it is you who wanders the streets with the cutthroats and thieves," he said by way of greeting.

"I came by royal coach," I explained, "quite safely. Still up these late nights, are you?"

He nodded. "I am. Sleep does not come easy to me, but I have taken your advice about staying indoors."

"Well, that's something," I said.

"Will you sit?" he asked, and I took the chair he motioned to. We sat in silence, though the quiet lacked the strain so often present between us. After a while he said, "I have always wondered, Hester, though I never dared ask. How came you by your sight?"

"I sinned," I replied. "I sinned and never repented."

"So have I," he said. "So have I and a thousand others, nay, tens of thousands. What was your sin? Was it so grievous?"

"My sins are many," I answered.

"May no one ever know the sins of the woman who sees the sins of us all?"

"How can I hide them? My sins. Let us begin with absence—from my husband's life, even from his heart, though looking back, I think he opened it to me as much as a man such as he ever could. Abandonment—for I left the one dearest to me to wander alone in a moral wilderness when I might have been his guide, for better or for worse. Admission—only to the least of my sins, the one that was no sin at all. Arrogance—for I believed myself truer than anyone I knew, when really, I still concealed much. Abdication—of responsibility for the direction of my life and the effects of my decisions." I smiled. "Of that, I have just this night repented. I do hereby take full responsibility."

"Another fault we share," Robert conceded. "I might have abdicated responsibility as well, had someone not reminded me of those who count upon me. Your sins seem no greater than anyone else's."

"I have not finished," I explained. "Absorption—in myself and my own mind, with little thought of the misery of others. Association without genuine affinity—pretense for the sake of expediency. List 'appeasement' with that last sin."

"Then God save all England," Robert said, and I nodded my agreement.

"Let me see . . . Ambition? No, that is no sin, not even for a woman, though some would say otherwise."

"Arraignment of your fellow sinners?" Robert suggested.

"Ah, well, that goes without saying, doesn't it?" I replied.

"It was I tempted you to that fall," he said with a rueful grin.

I nodded. "Right in front of your wife, wretch."

"Wretch indeed," he agreed, and he relaxed a bit, leaning his head against the back of his chair.

I thought a long time. "Ambivalence—even now; I think I just might like you after all these years of thinking you a hypocritical lout."

He sighed. "I am a hypocritical lout."

"Would you like my advice?" I asked. Not waiting for him to

answer, I said, "Tell that to everyone you know. Every time your actions betray your words, say to your fellows, 'But then again, I am a hypocritical lout; you can hardly trust a word out of my mouth.' It makes life much simpler."

"How will you proclaim your list of sins to all your fellows, Hester?"

"I shall just have to find a single symbol that will cover them all."

I went to bed feeling lighter of heart than I had in many, many years. I slept hard, and I suppose because I had been out so late, no one woke me for breakfast.

Mary came in with a tray after the family had eaten dinner. "Are you well?" she asked.

"Quite," I said with a grin and a stretch. I peeked into the bowl on the tray. "Lamb?"

She held the tray out of reach and taunted me. "I thought you were ill. Now that I know you were just being self-indulgent, perhaps you should wait until supper to eat."

"I was up late," I said.

She settled the tray on my lap. "I know, and I do not know what you said to Robert, but he has actually strung as many as a score of words together into complete sentences several times today. For that, you may eat your dinner in bed." She lowered her voice to a whisper. "But you were out late, as well. Are you and Sir John . . . ?"

"No," I whispered back. "I was with the king."

Mary stared at me, clearly struggling to determine whether I was in earnest. It was not that she was ordinarily gullible so much as it was entirely unlike me to say such a thing in jest.

Still, some devilment in me pushed me on. "*And* the lord chancellor."

"W-what—to what purpose?" she asked, taking up my napkin and shaking it out.

The mischief left me, and I picked up my fork. "I had a favor to ask of the king. The lord chancellor just happened to be there, and we had a lovely night renewing our acquaintance."

"To think you once came here seeking *our* connections for Pearl."

"Pearl. Now that is the matter at hand. Is she here?"

"She went to Whitehall. Are you really going to allow the child to go with that boy and ruin her life? Jane wrote, and she said she and Henry would be happy to take the infant. Pearl could take a trip to the country and return with no one the wiser, and she would know the infant was well loved."

"It would not ruin her life, I think. It would not be ideal, I grant you that, but do you not admire the courage of a girl who demands happiness from life and lets none deny her?"

"Look at Jane," Mary said. We had been through this before. Mary would concede that Jane's good fortune had been extraordinary. The couple were still very happy and expecting their first child very soon. Mary was utterly convinced that Pearl would be every bit as lucky if we could only find a suitable match.

I had been unwilling to leave it up to luck. Mary and I were better examples of that strategy.

It was nearly suppertime, and I had joined the rest of the family in the parlor when Pearl stepped through the door, holding it open for Emil and the count and countess. "Lord and Lady von Althannburg, may I present Brigadier General and Mistress Wright and their children?" she asked.

Mary and Robert came to their feet in stunned silence, and Annie gasped, staring slack-jawed at Emil. I rather imagine that having him walk through her door was like meeting a fairy-tale prince in the flesh; Pearl had spun such fanciful stories about him to her. George bowed and said, "How do you do?" while Ollie examined Emil and his parents a little suspiciously. I stood a moment after the rest and wondered what Mary's little boy was thinking.

Count von Althannburg looked around at the assembly without so much as a smile. Then he turned to me. "You have a library?"

"No," Mary said, coming forward. By most standards, hers was the home of a prosperous family, but it was clear that the count did not deem it so. "But my husband and I will take the children abovestairs and allow you some privacy."

"My wife will take the children," Robert corrected. "I have been the closest thing to a father the child has had since she was eight years old. I will stay."

Nine, really, I thought, but I understood. What Robert had not done for Jane, he would do for Pearl. While he suggested that Emil's family take seats at the table, Mary gathered her brood and urged them up the stairs.

I was already well aware that, by now, the king had spoken to the count. Charles would have explained that he was most dismayed to have discovered that the son of Emperor Leopold's agent had disgraced the daughter of one of his favorite subjects. At this point, the king of England had already conceded to Emil's father that Austria and England did not have a strong alliance, or even much need of one just now, but that in Austria's ongoing struggles with Spain and with the Turks, it was best to have as many friends as possible. He would hate to see this incident tarnish what might become an important alliance for the emperor. Besides, it was not such a poor bargain for young Emil. The girl was beautiful, bright, wealthy, and the granddaughter of a baron.

Oh yes, without a doubt the count had already begun to see things as Charles would have him. Given that, it was easy enough to allow Robert to negotiate the match. He saw to it that Pearl's dowry was well protected in the agreement, and when the count insisted that the marriage must wait until they had returned to Austria so that it could be done in a Catholic church, Robert sharply replied that there was free worship in England and more than one Catholic church to choose from. Under no circumstances was anyone leaving the island until the knot was tightly tied.

Through it all, Emil and Pearl beamed joyfully. I had never seen my daughter look so breathtakingly lovely, and once or twice I saw her future father-in-law's face soften when he looked at the happy couple. He may not have been ecstatic about the match, but neither was he entirely put out. The countess barely concealed a satisfied smile. Though she had said little, she was obviously pleased.

Negotiations concluded, Mary invited the von Althannburgs to supper, though I am sure she dreaded an acceptance. The meal was already prepared, and she had not been expecting company. Perhaps they sensed this, or perhaps they thought the fare would be poor. Either way, they expressed their regrets and insisted that they must return to the palace.

We all spilled onto the front steps, but the countess took my arm and held me back a moment. "Is your daughter as indomitable as you, Mistress Prynne?" she asked.

"She plays by her own rules," I said.

"Well, no doubt she learned the game from an accomplished player. You will join us on our estates?"

"Let us get these two married before we make any further arrangements," I said. "I shall bring her to Whitehall in the morning."

That night Pearl came to my room in her shift and chatted cheerfully about wedding plans and marriage while I brushed out her hair. It was thick and dark and fell nearly to her waist in glossy waves, and after I had brushed away every tangle, I let the silken strands run through my fingers. I had been able to delay thinking much about parting, occupying my mind with the necessity of getting Pearl married, her future secure. Now the scent of her, the feel of her hair shook my resolve.

Pearl sighed and closed her eyes. As if reading my thoughts, she said, "Well, now that we're to be Emil's family, there is no longer any doubt that you shall come to live with us. You'll have to start packing, for we shall have to leave right after the wedding. Emil says it gets much colder much faster, and snows far more in his country."

I plaited her hair for bed, my fingers performing the task without any assistance from my brain. A new country, a new language, new people who must grow accustomed to my oddness, if ever they could . . .

There was a part of me, some corner of my mind that had been worrying over it all these years, the oddity that so repelled acquaintances, and of late I had arrived at a conclusion: I believed that I could yet rid myself of my terrible sight. It was my penalty, not for loving Arthur, but for all the other sins I had spoken of to Robert. The scarlet letter had failed to punish me. It had left me arrogant, self-righteous. In truth, I had yet to pay my debt, and that could only be done at the scene of my crimes, in the presence of those against whom I had committed them.

The dearest cost of all sat at the dressing table before me now, staring into my face reflected in the mirror. "You are not going," she said.

A strand of her hair had escaped my ministry, and I began to undo the braid so that I could capture it, but Pearl stood, pulling her hair from my hand.

"You are not going," she said again, and the wounded look on her face was nearly my undoing.

I almost said, "Do not be silly, child, where else would I go?"

Unable to say that, and yet unwilling to give voice to my design, I turned away from her, my vision a blur, my eyes hot just before the tears spilled over.

"Say something, Mother! Speak to me! You went to all this trouble to see to it that Emil and I could wed only to—" She inhaled in a little gasp behind me. "This is why you went to the king. You didn't want to go with us, but you could not leave me to so uncertain a future. The only way you could be free of me was to see me married!"

Still, I could not look at her. The hurt and betrayal in her voice was like acid. I could not bear her face. I cried, "No! Oh, how much easier it would have been to have some pretext to go with you, some good, pure justification like the call of a mother to her child." At last, shame for my cowardice forced me to face her, meeting her dark eyes swimming with tears. "I could go with you then, see my grandchildren . . ."

"Then come, Mother," she pleaded, grasping my hand and placing it upon her still-flat belly. "Come and be at my side when this baby arrives."

"We could not travel the same path forever, Pearl."

"Yes, we could," she argued, lifting my hand away and squeezing it tightly. "That is the way of mothers and daughters; they travel the path together, for the way is never easy for women."

"That may be the way of most mothers and daughters," I conceded, "but when were we ever like most?"

"Closer than most. Closer than Jane and Aunt Mary. We say everything to each other, no matter how shocking or unconventional. We speak not only our hearts to each other, but our minds, as well. Who else shall ever know my mind as you have? Not even Emil!"

My hand had begun to ache, so I wrested it from hers, though I was loath to break the connection. "You have a mind like few others," I granted.

"Like yours," she replied. "Everything that is peculiar about me came from you. I need you."

I shook my head. "Everything that is unique about you Emil

shall come to know and cherish. You need to make a life of your own, unhindered by my strangeness."

She glared at me. "Do not think to make this sound selfless, Mother. Do not insist that you do it for me."

"Fine, then. I do it for me. Never shall I regret giving you life. Never shall I regret the things I have done to bring you to woman-hood. But the time has come for me to resume my own journey, begun many years ago, before you were born."

"You're going to America, aren't you?" She blinked, and the tears she had stubbornly refused to give in to escaped at last. "So in the end, he wins. I was right all along, even as a child; there was never room for us both in your heart. *He is dead, Mother, and I am alive.* How can you do this? How can you?"

"Pearl—"

"I shall never forgive you. Do you hear me? Never!" She spun and stormed from the room, slamming the door behind her.

I stood there feeling as though all the air had been sucked from the room. It was scarcely worth trying to inhale, because I knew there would be nothing there to breathe. Just as my lungs defied my heart and took a deep gasp, Mary opened the door without knocking. She took one look at me and rushed over to enfold me in her arms. I sank to the floor, taking her with me, and there I cried in great heaving sobs while my friend rocked me like a child.

Pearl did not speak to me again until the morning she stood at the altar wearing a gown of rose-colored silk and creamy Flanders lace. Just before the ceremony she had officially converted to Ca-tholicism, which was a matter of expedience. She had never pro-claimed a faith in her own mind, so the one she owned in public mattered naught to her. She was happy, laughing gaily and chatting effusively, but when she spoke to me, there were no smiles, no warmth in her voice.

The king insisted the couple spend their first night in one of the more sumptuous chambers at Whitehall. This was at once an offer of luxury and of protection. While I doubted the count would at-tempt anything as dishonorable as tampering with the union, a wedding consummated under the king's roof would be unbreak-ably sealed, even as far away as Austria. The emperor's honor was entwined in it now.

I stayed at the palace, too, so I could rise early and see the entourage off. The Wrights eschewed the king's residence, ill at ease in the place they had frequented under a different government. It was John who joined me in saying good-bye to Pearl, lending me strength with his quiet presence.

At first Pearl turned away my offered embrace. Then she changed her mind and clung to me like a little girl. "Please come, Mother," she whispered against my ear. "Please. I do forgive you, and I can't stay angry. I love you so much."

"I cannot," I murmured back to her, forcing the words past the painful lump in my throat.

"I don't understand," she said. "I cannot fathom . . ." Tears cut her words off.

"I hope you never do," I replied. I pulled back and touched her cheek. "Seek your own happiness, little Pearl. Follow your heart; wear it upon your sleeve. Be true. Be true. Be true."

She nodded. "I will. Always."

And I knew that it would be so.

I felt John's hand on the small of my back as the carriage pulled away and I waved to Pearl. Far sooner than I would have wished, the traffic on the street swallowed my child up, giving me only the briefest moment to capture the last glimpse I would see of her ever in my life. Hot tears coursed down my face.

"Shall we to my quarters?" John asked. "I'll take your mind from your sadness." There was no selfish lust in his voice; it was a genuine gift he offered.

Nonetheless, I shook my head. He had been right in Bruges; we had been all we could be to each other. I had done all I could for Pearl. These epochs were over. Now, it was my time.

Forty-four

When I disembarked in Boston Harbor, I wore the hood of my gray cloak low over my face, unready to be known just yet. It seemed wrong, somehow, to walk among these people as if I were one of them, but soon enough I would resume my old place. There was no need to hurry.

One of the men on the dock, a familiar fellow of perhaps a score and some years, accepted my coin readily enough when I asked him to help me transport my things to the village. But when I told him my exact destination his face paled, and he peered closely within my hood. I looked out at him, at his troubled heart, at his hatred for a father who had beaten him daily, at his loathing of himself for doing the same to his own sons more than once. I started to reach toward him, but when he recoiled I remembered who I was and dropped my hand to my side.

I rode in silence at his side, a wide space between us on the seat of the wagon, each of us hugging our own side of the board, careful not to let the rough terrain toss us into proximity. It was springtime, and the earth was greening. Trees stretched their branches over the road, touching their delicate fingertips above us like lovers parting.

The narrow path from the road to the cottage was long, and the man who had brought me lagged behind carrying my trunk.

When I arrived at my old doorstep, I spied a half dozen boys play-ing on the seaside, tossing rocks into the waves and frolicking as Puritan children do when there are no adults about. One of the bigger boys in the troop stopped and stared at me, and one by one his playmates followed suit, watching as I took out my key and turned it in the rusted lock. I paid them no heed and stepped in-side.

Spiders, creatures of thread and industry, kindred souls, had done much work over the past eleven years. Dust had fallen over their handiwork, rendering the interior of the cottage a study in grays. Underneath, I knew, were a floor and furnishings of oak and maple that would glow warmly once they were cleaned. The curtains drawn over the windows were sorely moth-eaten and let the bright spring sunshine trickle into the single chamber.

I took off my cloak, draping it across my arm. Already I was thinking of the work that must be done if I was to sleep here to-night, though it seemed cruel to sweep away the labors of the cur-rent occupants. Hearing the labored breathing of my hired helper, I rushed to tell him to leave the trunk outside so that I could clean without having it in the way. The children, I noticed, had crept closer, and I turned to regard them.

"It is her!" the older one shouted. "I told you!"

They all froze, eyes upon the bosom of my gray gown, where the letter glistened in its old accustomed place. "She's a ghost!" another cried, and they all ran, shouting after one another, "Look out! She's coming!"

I was doing no such thing. I asked my helper to leave my trunk where it was and I set my cloak atop it. He, too, stared at the let-ter, his face grim.

"About your boys—" I said.

"Those were none of mine," he replied, looking after the group that had just fled.

"No, I mean . . ." I touched the letter. "About your boys, and your father . . . well, he did his best, just like you. It is a hard life here."

His sad eyes met mine, but he did not speak.

What words might I offer to a man such as he? How should I suggest that he was rather like me—an imperfect human being who knew what it was to be measured and found wanting.

"Perhaps if you were more forgiving," I said.

"I recall your child," he said, looking away. "I'll thank you not to tell me how to discipline mine."

"I do not wish to tell you how to rear your children, nor would I judge you, for I am unworthy. I only meant that you should forgive *yourself*, Jonathan." He started when I said his name, obviously surprised that I had recognized him. How old had he been when I last saw him? Fourteen? Fifteen? I continued. "They're just like you, you know, and take their father's displeasure harder than his blows. Let your heavenly father judge you and your sons, and leave your earthly one in his grave. He was an angry man, and that had naught to do with you."

His gaze dropped again to the letter, briefly, then he turned and strode quickly back whence he'd come, his steps barely restrained. I suspected that he wanted to run like the children.

It was long past nightfall when I finally brought in the mattress I'd beaten and left outside to air after Jonathan's departure. I started to leave the one that had belonged to Pearl outside, but decided it would be best not to let it collect dew. By the time I extinguished the lamp, the cottage was home again. The only thing missing was the sound of Pearl's breathing. The only thing that I had added was the beautiful beverage service she had sent me from Austria, along with a letter expressing her hope that her gift would find me before I left England and assuring me that she was well and happy. The service held a place of honor on the sideboard, upon a round of beautifully embellished linen, something Pearl had wrought while we were in Bruges. I kept them where I could admire them daily, though I doubted I would ever have occasion to use the fine china pot and cups.

Ah! I almost forgot. Above my bed hung a sampler begun in this very room many years ago. In stitches far finer than a child's hand should have wrought, it said, "And be not conformed to this world: but be ye transformed by the renewing of your mind."

That first Sabbath, I wondered if word had traveled so quickly, or if no one had sat in my place at church in over a decade. Either way, my spot upon the pew stood empty, a span wide enough for three people. I sat in the middle of the space and looked up at the pulpit, almost expecting to see Arthur, surprised at the sharp pain in my breast when another stood in his place.

If the new minister had planned on commenting upon my return, he thought better of it when he looked into my face. He could not have known what had transpired in my life, but I think he sensed that I had taken on men mightier than he and won. In the end, he looked away and did not meet my eyes again. It mattered not. I had not come for the likes of him.

I missed Pearl, of course, and Mary and her children, and even Robert, having made my peace with him. At night, from time to time, I missed John. But for the most part, I was content. I enjoyed my solitude, taking in sewing to earn my keep. (I had left most of my funds in England as a dowry to ensure Annie Wright her choice of husbands.) Once again, the poor of my village were kept warm against the cold by the craft of my needle. At night, in the firelight, I set free my fancy upon gowns for Pearl's children, first a daughter, then a son, then another. Every so often, a knock sounded upon my door in the dark, and I woke to attend a deathbed or a difficult childbirth. In time, there was no need for the cover of dark. If a child broke his brow on a sunny afternoon, my neighbors called upon me, even above the local physician, to sew the gash.

Women who had once taken my charity with scorn began to creep shyly to my door on Sundays after church with offerings of coarse bread or meager vegetables. "Mistress Prynne—" they would begin, then look away in shame.

I would invite them in and say, "Speak your heart, sister. I wear the letter and cannot judge you."

And they would tell me of doubts and fears that could not be shaken, of hopes and dreams abandoned but never forgotten. Women whose clothes and hands were rough and whose bodies were thin imbibed from china cups and felt, if only for a moment, dignified and valuable. When the first of the village matrons arrived with her crock of cream and loaf of white bread, the village derelict's wife rose to leave, but I would have none of it. In the cottage of Hester Prynne, there was neither rich nor poor, sinner nor saint. There were only sisters.

Many years ago, we had all been comforted by a man of God, a man who could speak to our troubled hearts with sympathy beyond mere intellectual understanding of human frailty. He was a man whose voice captured all of the passion, all the love and hate, pride and shame, desire and loathing a human heart could ever possibly hold, and when his voice poured forth from the pulpit, it had washed away our burdens.

I had been greedy. I had taken him for myself, and in the process destroyed him. Surely I might have realized when I clasped Arthur's hand to my breast and begged him to know me that the rest was inevitable. What had Roger said to me once? "By your first step awry, you did plant the germ of evil; but since that moment, it has all been a dark necessity."

Now I could do naught but try to give back to Arthur's flock what I had taken. I listened when they poured forth their doubts and sorrows. They counted themselves the deepest sinners, when in fact they were merely human. Merely women. Merely wanting more than lives of hard toil and submission. This, perhaps, I understood better than even Arthur did.

"Tell us true, Hester Prynne," begged the mother of eight children, "can a woman whose pride makes her crave some recognition from her family for her labor ever hope for grace? Would a virtuous and loving woman not find contentment in service to them?"

"Sister Hester," asked the farmer's wife, "how can a woman forbear her anger when her man casts off her wisdom as trifling? Can he truly think I have worked by his side all these years and learned nothing of the land myself?"

"Mistress Prynne," queried a maiden, cheeks aflame, "how shall a man demand chastity in a bride yet tempt her so before the vows are made?"

They gazed at me with expectant eyes, and I spoke of what I'd learned.

"I know a woman," I told them, "who knows how to love. I know a woman who understands her own mind and who will take nothing less in life than all that she wants. I know a woman who gives herself wholly, mind, heart, body, and soul, and she is wiser than to tarnish her gifts with shame. Sisters, ours is not the generation to embrace her insight, for we have been taught too long and too well the lie that the gift of ourselves is poor and unworthy. We have come to believe it, and this lie taints every honest feeling, every true thing we would do."

"Our daughters, then?" the mother asked.

"Some, perhaps," I said. "Those who inherited from us only

our passion and none of our shame. But we must not entangle them in the snare with us."

"But we must," the farmer's wife protested. She was older than I and had known me for many years. "Do you not remember that day? The day you stood upon the scaffold? Would you have us set our daughters up to such a punishment?"

"That day?" I scoffed. "That day was no punishment. That was the day I was set free. Oh, if only I had had the wisdom to know it! I might have called Arthur down from the balcony above the scaffold to stand with me. I might have saved him."

"You mean if you had shared with him your penitence?" the maiden pressed.

I sighed and looked down at my letter, my heart heavy. How could I teach them what I had learned from Pearl and all our friends and adventures across the ocean? Though I had been fully redeemed in these women's eyes, it was because they thought the letter had transformed me. They did not know that it and all my years away had only made me more of what I was—myself.

Epilogue

In the end, neither my sisters nor their daughters grasped what I had hoped to offer. They were too corrupted by the common: the common good, common knowledge, common sense. This was why I had transplanted my Pearl; the ground here was too sterile for the extraordinary to blossom.

How I miss my wild Pearl with her sparkling eyes. How eagerly I devour her every letter, filled with details of her children's lives unfolding. They have children of their own, now, who travel widely, speak many tongues, devour everything life has to offer, and I smile to know that Arthur and I had some part in their making.

Mary writes to me, too. It was she who wrote of John's death in 1675. She included in the missive a clipping from one of London's more salacious papers. It repeated a bit of conversation overheard at his funeral:

"There lies Sir John Manning," proclaimed Lady G—— "an impenitent sinner and the only man who never lied to a single woman. Not so much as 'I shall see thee in the morning.'"

"He may never have lied to one," avowed Lord H——, "but God knows, he lay with more than his share. Can't hate him for it, though. Many an Englishman benefited by way of a more skillful wife."

Now that, I thought as I read it, was a eulogy John would have appreciated.

Mary also writes of King Charles's exploits, slipping in bits of scandal and politics, and I find I do not miss the intrigue.

I like the quiet of my cottage. I do not mind the loneliness I have chosen. On those few occasions when it seems burdensome, I wait until dark, when my journey is private, and walk to the churchyard. Off by itself is an old grave, and I lower myself to the ground, though I know I will pay hell trying to stand back up, as old as these joints have become. If I am assured that all are abed, I take off my accustomed cap and let down my long, white hair.

"I am coming, Arthur," I tell him. And just as I lead my neighbors safely past the gates of hell, I know that one day I will pass through those portals myself to bring him back to me.

Acknowledgments

I owe a debt of gratitude to so many people who helped *Hester* come into being. First I must acknowledge my wonderful editor, Nichole Argyres, whose shared passion for *The Scarlet Letter* and enthusiasm for this book made the experience of writing and publishing *Hester* such a joy. I also want to thank my agent, Kristin Nelson, for all the faith and hard work. She is at once an utterly honest critic and an optimistic cheerleader (not to mention she throws a great party). Kristin, you've been an invaluable guide on this journey.

I am truly grateful to the members of my critique group: John Orlando, Jennie MacDonald Lewis, and Stephen R. Kramer. Thank you for hours of thoughtful feedback over coffee and tea at Stella's and for humoring me when I sent you chunks of forty-plus pages, despite our thirty-page guideline. Jennie, your insights from your time in England were invaluable. All of you have been so supportive of this project from beginning to end, and you made it much better than I could ever have alone.

From the very beginning, I knew that Hester would have a third man in her life, but I also had to honor Hawthorne's intent that Arthur Dimmesdale be Hester's only true love. In searching for the right character, I discovered inspiration in the blogosphere. While I have never met William Smith, the self-professed libertine, and the character of John Manning is not based on him person-ally, his writings under the blog "Confessions of a Libertine" were instrumental in fleshing out John's character. Will also read through the rough draft of *Hester* and provided his own thoughts. Many thanks, Will.

The support of my family has been crucial and my relation-ships with them inspirational. From my husband, I have learned what it is to have one true love, and that is reflected in Hester's emotional fidelity. Words cannot express my gratitude to him for his faith in my writing. I thank my son who, at the age of eight, looked at me after watching *The Prince of Egypt* and asked, "Mom, did God really kill all those babies in Egypt?" Ah—the questions of children. It was only fitting that Pearl should wonder the same thing. My daughter inspired me, too. Like Pearl to Hes-ter, she often looks at me with my own dark eyes, but when she speaks, it is clear that she is becoming very much her own young woman—one we can both be proud of.

I cannot fail to thank all my colleagues in the English depart-ment at Columbine High School over the years, for countless con-versations about *The Scarlet Letter* and for never making fun of me when I presumed to build upon such lofty ground. Oh—except for Lisa, who makes ample fun of me in all cases. Her I thank for keeping my head on straight. Frank DeAngelis, thanks for bringing the Puritans to life for me and my students. I thought of you in your black robe preaching "Sinners in the Hands of an Angry God" to my sophomores while the Wright children and Pearl were on their knees in St. Giles Church.

Finally, a thousand thanks to the Debs. It would have been so easy to give up without all of you.

Reading
Group
Gold

HESTER
by Paula Reed

About the Author
- A Conversation with Paula Reed

Behind the Novel
- *Hester* and *The Scarlet Letter*

Keep on Reading
- Recommended Reading
- Reading Group Questions

For more reading group suggestions,
visit www.readinggroupgold.com

 ST. MARTIN'S GRIFFIN

A Conversation with Paula Reed

What inspired you to write a companion novel to *The Scarlet Letter?*

I think it goes back further than even I might have suspected when I started this project. It surely began with my odd fixation with all things Puritan. I was a Pilgrim for Halloween when I was in elementary school, which was not exactly a common costume. Thanksgiving has always been my favorite holiday. By the time I reached my senior year in high school, I had read about the Puritans so extensively that I was able to write a major term paper about them off the top of my head, using extensive facts in support of my thesis, but faking my bibliography because I didn't want to dig through books to get page numbers. (I still occasionally have nightmares that my high school diploma is revoked when my former English teacher discovers my perfidy. I am then forced to simultaneously teach and retake Composition for the College Bound.) In college, I showed up at the annual Halloween Mall Crawl in Boulder, Colorado, attired as the world's toughest English major, wearing street gang attire. The back of my jacket proclaimed me a member of "The Scarlet Letters." Nobody got it.

Hands—down, my favorite class to teach is American Literature. My favorite unit? The Puritans. My favorite lecture? Calvinism. (How pathetic is that? I have a favorite lecture. And it's on Calvinism.) My favorite book? Well, it's not a part of the Puritan unit; it's in the Romantics, but can you guess it? That's right. I hand out copies of Nathaniel Hawthorne's classic work and tell the kids that they must do their best to love it as much as I do. Barring that, they must pretend to. Recently, I had a student come up and tell me that I had taught her mother twenty years ago. She said that her mother would forever associate me with *The Scarlet Letter*, which had become one of her favorite books. A colleague once told me that whenever she thought of Hester, she pictured me, and my dark-haired,

dark-eyed daughter as the mischievous Pearl. (For the record, my daughter was always much better behaved.)

My first published novel, *Into His Arms,* is a romance novel. The heroine, Faith, is a Puritan, and she falls in love with an atheist. An atheist pirate, actually. Hey, it's a romance novel.

But why another novel about *Hester?* Wasn't *The Scarlet Letter* enough?

No, no, no. You see, as wonderful as the original work is, with its effusive, rich, and vivid prose, its compelling characters (specifically Hester and Roger), and its time-less moral (you should have been in my class the year I taught this and the Monica Lewinsky scandal hit), it is marked by Hawthorne's great affliction. That is to say, it is a romance with a strong and vibrant heroine and a dud as a hero. (If you doubt that this is a pervasive Hawthornean flaw, read "The Minister's Black Veil," "The Birthmark," and "Rappaccini's Daughter.")

For pity's sake. What did Hester Prynne ever see in Arthur Dimmesdale? After all, Roger is no peach, but he is a serious scholar who dabbles in black magic. That, at least, is interesting, but Arthur is a dishonest man who cares more for his image than his character, though he doesn't have the strength to just accept that about himself. He isn't even intellectually rigorous, Hawthorne tells us. His only virtues are his gifts for empathy and public speaking—not usually the sexiest traits, but don't tell high school speech kids that. This is a relationship that needs further explanation if the reader is to believe that Hester has a modicum of self–respect.

There is also that big gap in the novel, those years between when Hester and Pearl depart from New England and when Hester returns alone. For a reader who has invested her heart in Hester, it is a gap that begs filling. She is such a magnificent creation, and she gets such a raw deal. Enter my affinity for a happy ending. Now, I would never dream of changing the destiny Hawthorne had given Hester. She is, after all, his creation, but it seemed to me that it was not exactly blasphemous to tweak the way that ending feels. And what about Pearl? After an entire novel in which this child is nothing but a symbol, Hawthorne breaks the spell and sets her free to be a real human being, then tells us nothing of her life. What sort of woman would Hester Prynne raise? How would Pearl look back on her one-dimensional, symbol-of-sin years? So many questions left unanswered . . .

Will you be writing other novels based on classic literary works?

Who knows? In a day and age when authors are counseled to stick with a formula that works for them, I have the problem of getting bored doing the same thing. Besides, offhand I can't think of another work that I feel compelled to expand upon, and I have learned that if I do not feel a driving need to write something, it doesn't work out well for me.

Have you left behind romance as a genre?

I can't answer that either. I love a love story, and I am still very fond of happily-ever-after. At the same time, the stories I feel compelled to write don't fit easily into the romance market. I like to take on issues of politics, religion, and sex. Actually, as you can see, I have all kinds of fun mixing those things together. (I'm not at all fit for polite conversation.) Unfortunately, the concoction seldom produces a conventional romance novel. Then again, maybe the time just isn't right. The unconventional may yet become fashionable, and then I'll dive back in.

**Okay, so you love *The Scarlet Letter*. What other
books are on your "favorite shelf"?**

I have a passion for American writers. I love
The Great Gatsby. When people ask me whether I
dream of writing the great American novel, I explain
that I can't, because Fitzgerald already did. It is the
essence of America. *The Catcher in the Rye* feels like
an old friend every time I open its cover. Kate Chopin's
The Awakening always moves me. Hemingway sucks
me in, pisses me off, makes me think, no matter what
the work. Twain makes me laugh and often nod my
head in emphatic agreement, but I'm not terribly fond
of *The Adventures of Huckleberry Finn*. So sue me.
A Pen Warmed-Up in Hell rocks.

My tastes are not limited to classic American writers.
My second favorite book of all time is by South Africa's
Bryce Courtenay: *The Power of One*. There is a stalwart
optimism trapped in those pages that speaks straight to
my soul. England has produced many of my favorites,
as well. The Bard goes without saying, but I include
George Bernard Shaw and Terry Pratchett in my list
of smart authors who always make me laugh. My heart
broke when I heard of Pratchett's Alzheimer's. For long
road trips with family, I recommend Douglas Adams's
audio books.

Obviously, I do not turn up my nose at commercial
fiction. I like John Grisham (even his sports books,
though I hate sports) and John Krakauer, and I have
a ball reading Bill Bryson. I think everyone should
read *A Short History of Nearly Everything*.

It's beginning to dawn on me that it is easier to say
what I don't like. I don't like mystery novels. I don't
know why. They just aren't my cup of tea. I don't read
horror. I think Stephen King is an excellent writer; I just
can't read his stuff and sleep at night. For the life of me,
I just can't get into fantasy. Not even Tolkien. When
it comes to science fiction, I am picky. Orson Scott

Card is my contemporary favorite, and I remain fond of Asimov, Bradbury, and Heinlein. Other than those authors, I'm not inclined to partake. I loathe self-help books but certainly don't begrudge the genre to others.

What is your writing routine?

While I was on leave of absence, I wrote six hours a day, four days a week. One day, I would love to do that again. Now, my priorities are roughly: family, work, spiritual life, exercise, and writing. This means that I write when I can. I may go weeks without writing a word. On vacation, if my kids are busy and my husband is at work, I can still put in hours and hours and hours. I try to write at least thirty pages a month, minimum. My critique group keeps me motivated to do that much. I had a student teacher part of the time I worked on *Hester,* and I put in a lot of work over a summer, so my wonderful group often accepted upwards of forty pages at a time.

I seldom listen to music. For one thing, music with lyrics I know is highly distracting. I am compelled to sing, and then I can't possibly write a completely different set of words. Instrumental music fades from my awareness so quickly that it's not worth bothering with. If my kids are playing Guitar Hero (which means songs that I know the words to are playing very loudly), I pop in my iPod and listen to Gregorian chants or classical.

If I'm on a roll, I eat meals and write at the same time, but I don't tend to snack while writing. I do, however, consume copious amounts of tea, hot in winter, iced in summer. Black tea. None of the fruity or flowery stuff. I drink Darjeeling at writer's group.

I do much of my writing in the family room amid my family members. When I'm in the zone, very little distracts me, but I like being with people. If that room has been overrun with noisy teenagers, I take my

laptop to the living room. I have a desk in the bedroom that I never use. I need more light and space than that affords. Every single thing I need, my notes, my research, everything is in my laptop (with the exception of my teacup).

Are you working on anything now?

People ask me this all the time. The answer is always yes. I went five years between contracts, so people assumed I wasn't writing. Actually, I just wasn't selling. I have no idea whether what I'm currently working on has a market. I only know that I wanted to write it, so I am. At any rate, the answer is always yes; I am always working on something.

Hester and The Scarlet Letter

Some excerpts from *The Scarlet Letter* and their coordinating passages in *Hester*

For many readers, their last encounter with *The Scarlet Letter* was in high school, and they remember it well enough to nod at some places in *Hester* and say, "Oh, yeah, I remember that." But for those times when you find yourself thinking, *I know my English teacher said something about this, but for the life of me, I don't remember what,* here are a few refreshers:

The first glimpse in *Hester* of her ability to see the sins of others:

No one ever knew; it was not the shame of the scarlet letter that punished me daily. It was the knowledge it imparted—the ability to look into a man's eyes and see what was in his heart.

Hawthorne's introduction to her ability:

Walking to and fro, with those lonely footsteps, in the little world with which she was outwardly connected, it now and then appeared to Hester,—if altogether fancy, it was nevertheless too potent to be resisted—she felt or fancied, then, that the scarlet letter had endowed her with a new sense. She shuddered to believe, yet could not help believing, that it gave her a sympathetic knowledge of the hidden sin in other hearts. She was terror-stricken by the revelations that were thus made. What were they? Could they be other than the insidious whispers of the bad angel, who would fain have persuaded the struggling woman, as yet only half his victim, that the outward guise of purity was but a lie, and that, if truth were everywhere to be shown, a scarlet letter would blaze forth on many a bosom besides Hester Prynne's?

In *Hester,* a scenario involving Mistress Hibbins is referenced as follows:

I remained outside, under the tree with Pearl, and asked how she and Jane had come to the conclusion that the tree should belong to them alone. She whispered to me, "Because long ago, the oak was the sacred tree of the goddess."

"Pearl!" I grasped her shoulders and gave her a little shake. "Who told you that?"

My vehemence did not startle her in the least. She just gave me a slanted look and said, "Mistress Hibbins did once, when she told me about the Black Man in the woods in New England."

"Mistress Hibbins," I scolded, "was a witch. You mustn't ever repeat anything she said. There is danger in such ideas."

Here's how it originated in *The Scarlet Letter:*

"Fie, woman—fie!" cried the old lady, shaking her finger at Hester. "Dost thou think I have been to the forest so many times, and have yet no skill to judge who else has been there? Yea; though no leaf of the wild garlands, which they wore while they danced be left in their hair! I know thee, Hester; for I behold the token. We may all see it in the sunshine; and it glows like a red flame in the dark. Thou wearest it openly; so there need be no question about that. But this minister! Let me tell thee in thine ear! When the Black Man sees one of his own servants, signed and sealed, so shy of owning to the bond as is the Reverend Mr. Dimmesdale, he hath a way of ordering matters so that the mark shall be disclosed in open daylight, to the eyes of all the world! What is it that the minister seeks to hide, with his hand always over his heart? Ha, Hester Prynne!"

"What is it, good Mistress Hibbins?" eagerly asked little Pearl. "Hast thou seen it?"

"No matter, darling!" responded Mistress Hibbins, making Pearl a profound reverence. "Thou thyself wilt see it, one time or another. They say, child, thou art of the lineage of the Prince of Air! Wilt thou ride with me, some fine night, to see thy father? Then thou shalt know wherefore the minister keeps his hand over his heart!"

Laughing so shrilly that all the market-place could hear her, the weird old gentlewoman took her departure.

The rosebush, in *Hester:*

When he pulled Pearl to him and kissed her full on the mouth, the crowd roared and clapped their approval of so lusty a display after so many years of staunch public propriety, and the two were showered in rose petals.

Perhaps it is my own wild fancy or perhaps it was real, but every time I think back upon that moment, I recall that the petals floating about them were exactly the same shade as those on a rosebush that grows by the prison door in New England.

The rosebush, as Hawthorne described it:

This rose-bush, by a strange chance, has been kept alive in history; but whether it had merely survived out of the stern old wilderness, so long after the fall of the gigantic pines and oaks that originally overshadowed it,— or whether, as there is fair authority for believing, it had sprung up under the footsteps of the sainted Ann Hutchinson, as she entered the prison-door, we shall not take upon us to determine. Finding it so directly on the threshold of our narrative, which is now about to issue from that inauspicious portal, we could hardly do otherwise than pluck one of its flowers, and present it to the reader. It may serve, let us hope, to symbolize some sweet moral blossom that may be found along the

track, or relieve the darkening close of a tale of human frailty and sorrow.

In *Hester,* these are Hester's parting words to Pearl:

"Seek your own happiness, little Pearl. Follow your heart; wear it upon your sleeve. Be true. Be true. Be true."

She nodded. "I will. Always."

And I knew that it would be so.

In *The Scarlet Letter,* this is Hester's advice to Robert:

"Would you like my advice?" I asked. Not waiting for him to answer, I said, "Tell that to everyone you know. Every time your actions betray your words, say to your fellows, 'But then again, I am a hypocritical lout; you can hardly trust a word out of my mouth.' It makes life much simpler."

"How will you proclaim your list of sins to all your fellows, Hester?"

"I shall just have to find a single symbol that will represent them all."

And Hawthorne summarizes *The Scarlet Letter* with his own moral for the reader: "Be true! Be true! Be true! Show freely to the world, if not your worst, yet some trait whereby the worst may be inferred!"

![book icon] Recommended Reading

Nathaniel Hawthorne

First of all, for those interested in reading more Hawthorne but not feeling committed enough to tackle *The House of the Seven Gables* or *The Blithedale Romance,* Hawthorne was often at his best when he wrote short. I think of "The Minister's Black Veil" as the *Reader's Digest* version of *The Scarlet Letter;* it's much shorter, but the themes are ultimately the same. "Young Goodman Brown" is another great example of Hawthorne's writings about Puritans and also the devastation we feel when we face the potential for darkness in those we love. Actually, I'd recommend almost any of his short stories—they're always food for thought.

Angel and Apostle by Deborah Noyes

Like *Hester, Angel and Apostle* provides another take on *The Scarlet Letter.* This book focuses on Pearl as the main character. It is darker, and Noyes takes quite a few major liberties with the original story, but it provides a completely different reimagining of what might have become of Hester Prynne's eldritch daughter.

Roger's Version by John Updike

Updike gives a decidedly modern twist to *The Scarlet Letter.* Roger is a theology professor married to Esther and vexed by Dale, a grad student determined to prove the existence of God with a computer. It's an intense read in terms of both sex and theology (two of my favorite topics), so prepare to hunker down and put on your thinking cap.

The Awakening by Kate Chopin

As a historical fiction writer, I always find it frustrating when people assume that women of certain eras always happily filled the roles men gave them. "A woman of that time would never..." they say in reference to thoughts, feelings, and actions they deem "too modern."

Obviously Hawthorne was aware that women chafed under Victorian restraints, but Kate Chopin wrote of this theme in a woman's voice in 1899. *The Awakening* was seen as shocking and even indecent in its time, but I have no doubt that Hester Prynne would recognize Chopin's protagonist's longing for personal fulfillment and passion.

The Crucible by Arthur Miller

If you've only seen the play or the movie, you still haven't fully experienced this fictionalized account of the Salem witch trials. Although some scenes are taken directly from court documents of the real trials, the play was actually written as a response to McCarthyism and the House Un-American Activities Committee. Miller includes commentary in the first act that dissects our tendency as human beings to polarize ourselves politically and theologically. Tragically this play written in the mid twentieth century about events in the late seventeenth century remains relevant to America today, plus it blends sex, politics, and religion with a mastery I envy.

And, if you enjoyed *Hester,* you could read my first novel, *Into His Arms,* which also features a Puritan heroine. She meets a man not entirely unlike John Manning. But this novel is a romance—so if you were hoping Hester and John's relationship would end happily-ever-after but were disappointed, *Into His Arms* might fit the bill.

Reading Group Questions

1. Do Mary and Hester have a fairly equal relationship, or does one woman give more than the other?

2. Neither Hester nor Mary have had happy marriages. Hester implies that their daughters will have better luck. What do you think Pearl and Jane's marriages will be like as time passes?

3. Hester's chief motivation in the decisions she makes is to protect her daughter from elements in their society that are unkind to women. If you could shield the younger women you know from parts of our society, what elements would you protect them from?

4. Few people in today's world would be shocked by the relationship between John and Hester. However, the fact that they would not be shocked does not necessarily mean they would approve. What do you think of it?

5. Did you like John, or were you put off by his unrepentant libertinism? Did you feel that Hester had found a positive relationship or had merely fallen into sin again?

6. Against her will, Hester is caught up in a great deal of political intrigue. How did you find yourself reacting to the affairs of state in Oliver Cromwell's Commonwealth? What benefits and drawbacks did you see in England's brief break from the monarchy?

7. How would you feel about having Hester's ability to sense the sins of other people? She obviously sees it as a curse, but might there be some advantages? What if it forced you to see the deepest faults of those you love most?

8. In *The Scarlet Letter,* Hawthorne tells the reader that the moral is: "Be true!" Hester Prynne must wear the letter A to signify that she is an adulteress, and it makes her stronger than Roger or Arthur, who both conceal their sins. In *Hester,* Hester gives Robert a different list of sins for the letter to symbolize. Now for the moment of truth: If you were to show freely to the world some trait by which your worst might be inferred, what symbol would you wear?

*Keep on
Reading*